VLAD MORANSKI:
A PIECE of WORK

Willowbrook Press
www.kensamanski@gmail.com

Cover art by Luc Samanski
Computer design and layout by Luc Samanski
Print and bound in Canada

Library and Archives Canada Cataloguing in Publication
Samanski, Ken, 1958-
Vlad Moranski: A Piece of Work / Ken Samanski
ISBN 978-0-9880095-3-0

Monday, June 25th

BJ Williams bookstore was buzzing with Brits and frantic with Frenchies, a perfect cover for an unpublished writer to sneak in and check the status of eight white books with a hot-looking woman adorning the cover. Assuming my books were still on display in the back corner, I had no choice but to pass within a metre of the cashiers. I covered the left side of my head with my hand as I zipped by the same cashier I had sweet-talked two days before. Why the paranoia? Even if they'd spotted me and my illegal books, I wouldn't have been sent to a Parisian slammer. Nevertheless, I wanted to avoid a potentially embarrassing situation over which I would have little control.

I reached Morgan Davis's life-size portrait. And not far from his derrière—more importantly—my books were still there. But something was different—a green circle the circumference of a pop can had attached itself to the cover. Stuck below the woman's head, it read "Pam's pick of the week." My eyes popped out my head. I wanted to touch the book but something wouldn't let me. My feet froze. I took a long look to my right, then to my left, the walls sprouting Prince Charles-size ears, listening to my thoughts, and big French Sarkozy noses snooping about my location. One more cursory look and I picked up *my* book. The green circle set my brain into imagination topspin. I held it a few centimetres from my eyes, using my calligraphic powers to study those five handwritten words.

"Her" letters were impenetrable. Damn—who was this Pam? Assuming she was a store employee, did she put the sticker on the book or did someone else put her name on it for a joke? Or did *she* do it for a joke? My eyes made a rapid sweep of the store, looking for a Pam. The search halted abruptly when a red-haired, sloppily dressed male store clerk by the name of Bret brushed by me. His evil grin, matched by a sinister stare at the sticker, had me convinced that he was the master forger. A thin woman in her sixties approached, grey hair hanging over her shoulders but conveniently stopped above her name tag. Betty smirked as she wedged her slight body between me and a *real* customer to rearrange some livres. I prayed her nimble fingers would leave the other seven alone. After all, my pages were quiet, minding their own business, and never once spreading out and invading Morgan Davis's sacred territory.

I breathed a sigh of relief when Betty moved on to another aisle. A nervous smile returned to my face as I flipped to the back cover of my book. Rereading the faux testimonials, more out of pride than anything else, I noticed a hair sticking out of the book. I pulled out the world's thinnest bookmark and held the foot-long blond strand in my hand, imagining that it belonged to Pam and that she was trying to tell me something. And, of course, that she was gorgeous.

I closed my eyes and prayed that Charlize Theron's first name was originally Pam. A finger tapped my shoulder. It felt more like a jackhammer than skin wrapped around tiny bones. I jumped. And had there been an Olympic event for the standing high jump, my gold medal would have been a lock. After a safe landing, I slowly turned my head, the book still gripped in my hand. And no one on God's green earth would have confused Charlize Theron with the tapper, her name tag clearly visible. Pam had a lot of booty to shake.

"Do you have a minute, Mr. Moranski?" asked Pam. Trying to smile, she revealed a set of crooked teeth so tightly wired her mouth resembled an over-protective bowling pin machine refusing to release its pins.

Without warning, an awkward feeling rushed through my body—a sensation best described as a craving for fifteen minutes of smorgasbord fame crammed into fifteen seconds of purée in a blender. My sixth sense told me that the jig was up and I was in a spot of trouble. Although fleeing and yelling, "You'll never take me alive" might have garnered a YouTube moment of levity in the store, I just stood there like a dusty, first-edition book for which a second edition would never come. An awkward half minute passed in silence. It was so quiet you could hear a book drop.

"Yes, I have a minute," I said, my mouth unable to decide if it wanted to quiver or smile, "but I'm curious why you would want to speak to me." We found a quiet corner.

Pam pointed an accusatory finger at me. "I watched you put all of your books on the shelf two days ago!"

My eyes dive-bombed to the ground. "That wasn't me! That was my brother Carson." The lie continued. "He just told me today what he had done. I decided to come in and pick up my books because I know what he did wasn't ethical."

"Ethical shmethical," she said, hands now on her hips. Floating above her brown eyes were bushy eyebrows that would have looked cuter had they been less "uni."

"Shmethical? What does that mean?" I said, feigning interest.

—

4

"I make up words. That's what I do," she said, huffing. "Anyway, that wasn't your brother. I read your book and I can tell your brother would never sneak books into a bookshop. No, that would take a diabolical mind or a *diabomind*, as I call it. And that diabomind was you!"

"Do you mind if I use some of your words in my next book?" I asked, flattering the woman. I spent a second to take her in. She was draped in a gigantic white sweater, a blue scarf hanging like a dead man in a noose from her right shoulder and a matching red one from her left. A worthy replacement for the French national wrecking ball? She wanted to speak, but I continued talking. "Wow, I can't believe you read my book in just two days. That's amazing. You must be a vivacious—" I paused at my intentional faux pas. "Sorry, I mean *voracious* reader."

"I've been known to stay up all night to read a book. My nickname in the store is 'The Night Reader' or just 'NiR, That's me, NiR, got it! NiR! That's capital 'N,' small 'i,' capital 'R.' I've asked several times to have my name tag changed, but the bastards here will not change it. And I even have to put 'Pam' on my 'Pick of the week.' I'm thinking of going to the union."

I had to admit, she did have shiny, beautiful skin that hung off her jowl, reminiscent of a favourite winter sweater tied around one's waist.

"That's a real shame," I said, freezing heaven and earth on my face to avoid rolling my eyes. "Though I wouldn't suggest that you go to the union on *that* one."

"Anyway, I don't give a rat's ass or a 'rass' about your opinion. Oh, and did you know that I still hold the store record of reading *War and Peace* in twenty-three hours?"

"And that was in Russian, I heard."

"Bugger off! You're just trying to sweet talk—or 'swalk'—me."

I interrupted, "'Swelk me' sounds better, no?"

"Don't you dare make fun of me! This is what's going to happen." She paused and grabbed my wrist. I felt a crack in my elbow. "I'm going to leave your book on the shelf but *you* are going to sleep with *me*."

I burst out laughing. She was not laughing. I stopped laughing.

"Listen, Pam, I think your vocabulary is super funky, but I'm not going to sleep with you."

"I haven't had it in a while and you're it, baby." She put her hands over her head and shook her hips. "I only go after the good-lookers. And I don't even mind that you're in your late forties. Right? Hell, I'm only

—

5

thirty years old." She briefly looked at herself. "I'm a pretty good catch, don't you think?"

"Pam, please."

She gazed at my ass. "Let me guess: you're about 180 pounds, still some muscle on you?"

"That's enough; just be reasonable."

With a smile on her face that looked more demented than alluring, she put her lips next to my ear and whispered, "NiR always gets what NiR wants."

I jerked my head back and nearly bumped it against a wall.

"Helen!" Pam said in an impatient voice. She briefly looked in another direction.

I grabbed her hot sweaty arm and shushed her. "What are you doing?" I whispered.

"Oh, just calling the senior manager to tell her we have a thief in the store."

"Please don't say anything to anyone in here. Let's just talk about this. When do you go on your break?"

"In an hour."

"Good," I said. "Why don't we meet outside the store for a coffee and discuss this?"

As she walked away, my ego forced a sentence out of my mouth. "Just out of curiosity, what did you think about the book?"

"It was a good read. The protagonist Carson Moranski is funny, real and a doting father. I would call him a 'further.'"

I walked over to my books and thought about removing the sticker to remove any undue notoriety, but then it hit me like a Webster's Dictionary across the face: leave the sticker on and hope it attracts attention. And though my book wasn't on BJ Williams's inventory list, I'm sure they could've used the ISBN as a way of coding it.

Unsure if I could kill an hour wandering, I hid my face in the section specializing in fictional stories about Paris. Depression set in after I stopped counting at twenty, sadly realizing for the first time that my book was one of many lightweights. Even some of the titles: *I was a Franco Phony* or *My Frenchie was Oh-la-la and Then Some* or *I Don't Pick up my French Tarts at the Patisserie* were more interesting than mine. But I had the only book with a hot French chick on the cover. Booyah!

I browsed through the first page or two of a couple of them, mentally mocking their litany of tired clichés. "Is that a baguette in your pocket or are you just happy to see me?" and "His Eiffel Tower was erect more than once that evening" were just a few pitiful examples.

Outside, while I stared at the window display waiting for Pam, four police cars, throttled engines and bad trumpet–sounding sirens blaring, jigsawed their way up the busy street.

A patch of clouds rolled in, an unhealthy mixture of black, purple and blue steel wool.

"Hello, where are we going to go for coffee?"

Pam sidled up undetected under the Vlad women radar system. "Hi . . . um. How about you pick the place? I'm not that familiar with the area."

"There's a Starbucks not too far away. I'm dying to try their new Bibanno."

"What's that?" I said in a voice coated with boredom.

Her cheeks jiggled in excitement. "It's their latest drink—a mixture of strawberry, banana, whey protein, fibre powder, and milk. You should try one."

"Save that overpriced milkshake for Arnold Schwarzenegger. I'll stick to an espresso, thanks. They *do* have them?"

"Of course. But espressos are boring. I call them 'borpressos.'"

"You certainly have a way with words. Maybe you should write your own dictionary. You can even buy a Klingon-speak dictionary."

"Have you forgotten where I work?" she said in a scolding teacher tone. "We sell an incredible variety of dictionaries and of course we have the Star Trek dictionary. The occasional total loser comes in here looking for that lame-ass book."

"Great. Maybe I'll buy two of them," I said, my sarcasm ringing through loud and clear.

"As long as you buy my Bibanno and make love to me I don't care how many you buy."

My sandals screeched to a halt. She attempted to brake as well, but simple laws of momentum relating to mass propelled her two steps further. Nervous laughter gushed from my lungs. She countered with heavy, disgusting breaths. Quick to notice that she was as serious about the sex as she was about her Bibanno, I stopped laughing and stared into a pair of eyes that were dark, deep and unflinching.

"That's enough, Pam. At first I was excited that you put the sticker on my book and even that you find me attractive, but it appears you want a sexual favour for your efforts."

"Gee, you're smarter than you look, there, pretty boy writer. I call them 'pretbows,' by the way."

"I don't care what you call them . . . or us. There is no possible way that you and I are going to jump in the sack."

"That's fine. I'll go straight to the senior manager with *your* books and they'll be thrown in the garbage." I wanted to speak, but she continued, "Do you realize that BJ Williams is the most popular bookstore in the world? We even have a store in Zimbabwe."

"Good. Maybe you could get a transfer there. Because you're evil."

"Hey, I didn't make the rules; I just play by them."

"What do you mean? You *are* making the rules."

"No kidding! Anyway, I've read that line in so many books I just wanted to say it myself."

"I admit, Pam, you do have a sense of humour and you got the goofy word thing going, but you and I are not compatible."

"Hey, honey, I can be as *pretty* as an angel, but I ain't one."

Vlad, this woman's crazy. Talk about something else. "You have an accent from somewhere in the States."

"Midwest. I bounced around a lot."

"Wow, my favourite baseball team is the Cincinnati Reds. Are you from there?"

"No, and I don't give a shit about baseball. Baseball players make too much money. Just a bunch of fags running around in pyjamas. And I know you're trying to change the subject. I call people that do that 'chanjects.'"

"I have to ask, how did someone from the Midwest with such a funny vocabulary end up in Paris?"

"And I'll say it again—when are we going to get it on?"

Christ! Again! Vlad, be calm. "Come on, it's not going to happen."

"Why's that?" she asked, her manner suggesting it wasn't a rhetorical question.

"Pam, don't make me say it."

"Because I'm robust?"

"No, because you're obnoxious and you're holding me hostage."

She raised her hand and pretended she was shooing a fly. "You're free to go. I'm not keeping you here."

"Yes, but you'll take the sticker off."

"And I'll tell you-know-who, too! Just in case you were unaware, I have power in that store. For five years, I've been suggesting books to

—

customers so fuckin' stupid they don't even know the difference between the *New York Times Magazine* and the *New Yorker*."

"The people you run into when you don't have a gun, eh?"

"I'm being serious. It amazes me how dumb shits can walk in off the street and have no clue about what they want to read. They come up to me and say, 'I've heard that Leonard Elmore writes great dialogue but I can't find any of his books.' 'That's because there's no such person, fuck-nuts,' is the reply on the tip of my tongue, but instead I have to force a cutesy smile and say, 'Oh, I get his name mixed up too. It's Elmore Leonard. Tee-hee.'"

"Do they ever ask for *Nimoy* Leonard?"

"That's *really* fuckin' hilarious." She added to her sarcasm. "Does someone write for you?"

"You've seen my writing. What do you think?"

"I said enough about your book already. And I'd work on your lame-ass stand-up routine; it's obvious that your brother in the book is the true comedic genius."

"Fine! I'll sleep with you as long as you never say that again!" *Did I just say what I think I said? Am I still that competitive with my brother? Am I insane?*

"Oh goody," she said, and returned to her growing wickedness. "I sure touched a nerve there."

The constant din of traffic was forming a death lullaby in my ears. Thoughts of my brother occupying my mind, I was unaware I was walking directly into traffic. A Renault Twingo beeped its little metal-ass horn. Without warning, a force greater than that of the car hooked my arm and yanked me away. The next thing I noticed was a bead of sweat running down Pam's forehead—a horrible, dripping reminder of the woman who had just saved my life.

"Vlad," said Pam, her facial expression reeking of potential arrangement sex, "you're not getting out of my life that easily!" From then until we reached Starbucks, she walked closest to the busy street.

Our Bibanno and espresso ordered and paid for by yours truly, we waited at the other end of the counter—the "Barista bar"—to pick up our drinks.

A barista, eyes fixed on the waiting customers, said, "Strawberry-banana Bibanno."

"That's mine!" Pam grabbed the drink and sucked a third of its reddish, sweet, icy glop, enjoying it like a vacuum cleaner making love to

—

9

a carpet. I watched in amazement. Perhaps she could die of brain freeze initiated by excessive Bibanno inhalation. I would call it 'binge Bibannoing.'

"Solo espresso," said another employee with an Italian accent.

"*Grazie*," I said.

"*Prego*," she replied.

Pam unhooked her lips from the emaciated straw and interrupted. "Wow you *speak* Italian!" I sensed her sarcasm. Disappointed by her will to breathe, I had no wry retort, no quick quip from the lips, no crotchety comeback.

We found an empty table. "Well, loverboy?" said Pam, trying to sound sexy.

No words came out of my mouth, because I wanted to puke. I did catch a lucky break when she pluged her bouche again with her exhausted straw. Twenty seconds of excruciatingly, irritating slurping passed by. Soon Popeye's famous quote, "I can't stands it no more," muscled its way into my brain.

"Pam," I said, "the way you're going after that Bibanno, I feel sorry for your straw. I think I heard it say, 'please . . . please, kill me!'"

"That's hilarious, *loverboy*."

"That's enough," I whispered. My eyes bounced around the store, praying that the other latte sippers understood this woman could never be my love kitten. I studied the sparse arrangement of coffee grounds in the bottom of my cup. There was no discernible message.

"Look," I said, "nothing is going to happen between you and I."

"Actually, *Mister* writer, it's you and *me*."

"Whatever! Anyway, get that thought out of your head about the two of uh—"

She smacked her empty Bibanno cup on the table, its noise and my embarrassment resonating throughout the café.

"Fine! The sticker comes off AND I spill the beans to the senior manager." She waited a second and then pointed a chunky finger in my face. "And your *career*? Over! I call it a 'carrover.'"

"Doesn't 'cadaver' sound more apropos?"

"You're such a smartass. Don't you care about your career?"

"To be honest, I've never had a career as a writer. I just put my books in the store to say that the biggest bookstore chain in the world has my book."

"Whatever. Listen, honey, I've got a double reinforced metal bed. It

---

even has steel girders on the sides and titanium bolts used for hip replacements for elephants. Do you read me? I'm ready to go tonight. Let's get it on!"

"Pam, I'm trying to be nice but, well . . . here goes. I don't care if you sleep on a slate pool table or in a dump truck or on an eight-lane highway. I'm not doing it with you AND you can take the stickers off my books and even chuck them in the garbage. I don't care. I'll prostitute my words, but I'm not going to prostitute myself."

Pam abruptly stood up. "I gotta go and make a living. Oh and, by the way, I'm taking the stickers off and I'm telling Helen . . . the SENIOR MANAGER."

"Fine, that's about the ninetieth time you've told me that. Do whatever you're going to do. You're on a one-way ticket to hell."

"Fuck you, ya hack!" She jammed her chair back under the table, making sure it rang out, and marched toward the door. I let her comment pass, but I was curious how the senior manager would treat my books once my cover was blown.

I hid behind an arch directly in front of the bookstore, making my move inside when I noticed Pam approaching a cash register with a handful of my books. She held them with arms extended as far out as possible, as though she were carrying a dead skunk. She stopped at a cash register. I ran in and positioned myself about three metres away, her billboard-sized back facing me. A high shelf provided a perfect cover between me and my book usurper.

"Helen! Miss senior manager! If you have a minute could you come over here please. I have something very important to show you." Pam the *hall monitor* was anxious to report her delinquent discoveries to *principal* Helen. Helen walked over to the cash register where Pam was holding court. The neighbouring cashier stopped her business and looked toward Pam. I shifted a handful of cookbooks to enhance my view.

Pam handed my books to Helen. "I'm thrilled to report I caught someone sneaking his books—*these* books!—into the store." Helen took the books and politely steered her away from the gawking customers. And it probably wasn't the first time she'd had to have a "business" chat with the sticker queen.

The ladies were standing directly on the other side of the bookshelf from me; had I removed about ten more books, I'd be able to count the angry freckles on Pam's face.

Helen held five copies of *French Like Me* up to Pam as if she were showing a child a picture book. "I have to find the writer of this bo—"

"His name is Vlad Moranski, and I can see him through the shelf!" She pointed directly at me. I nearly shat my pants.

"Wow, you're kidding!" said the senior manager. She stuck her head through the opening I had created. We almost bumped noses.

My face approaching a never-before-seen deep shade of red, I said, "Ya got me." Judging by her iridescent smile, I was in no immediate trouble. And if my sixth sense was working properly, I had just become a minor celebrity. We simultaneously walked to the end of the shelf, Pam following closely behind. About to shake hands with Helen, I said, "*Enchantez*. I'm the author of those books in your ha—"

"You see, boss? There he is! The thief!"

"Slow down, Pam," replied Helen with an expression on her face that I interpreted as, "Shut up, Pam, or I'll put a bridle in your mouth." Helen pointed my books toward me to accentuate my presence. "Our store just sold three of *this* author's books. *And*—if that's not enough—one of the customers who bought one was none other than Simon de Nadeau."

Still not fully comprehending what had just happened, I stayed cool. "Excuse my ignorance, but I don't know who Simone de Beauvoir is." I paused, waiting for a laugh. Helen laughed. I laughed. Pam was without laughter. "I mean, of course, Simon de Nadeau!"

"Funny stuff," replied Helen. "Simon de Nadeau is . . . sorry, Vlad. If I can call you that?"

"You can call me Tuesday, if it makes you happy."

"Vlad will do."

Helen turned to Pam, who by this time had built up enough rage to knock over all the shelves with one mighty swing of her arm. "Pam, you can go back to the reference section and help Sylvain stock the shelves. A shipment of the *Doctor Who: Character Encyclopedia* just came in." Helen looked at me. "Even the French love it."

I told her it was a great book. I had never even heard of it. I readied a joke about Roger Daltrey ever being a character in the show, but Helen directed her attention back to Pam. "Please handle them with care. Some dictionaries have come in as well."

"Fine," said Pam. Then she whispered in my ear, "I'm not finished with you yet, you 'litbas'" and lumbered away.

"Vlad," Helen said, touching my shoulder, "Simon de Nadeau is

———

12

one of the most famous literary critics in Paris. He often even critiques English books."

"You're kidding!"

"Why don't you come into my office and we'll discuss this further."

"Show me the way." *Total bonus, she sold three books so she owes me about eighteen euros.* I moved a stack of books off a chair that looked the least busy in Helen's office and sat down. She entered soon with a frothy thing in a BJ Williams mug and an espresso.

"Hope you don't mind a cappuccino, Vlad? I'm not sure when the tradition started, but I always give one to the writers *I* discover." Helen hung on to the "I" a little too long, but, lost in the moment, I let it pass. We chinned cups. "Vlad, here's to a promising career."

"Yes, Helen, here's to a promising career." I took a sip and looked at her. "Whose career are we talking about?"

She laughed. "You have a great sense of humour. I can't wait to read your book."

I wasn't kidding about the "whose career" question. Helen moved a stack of books off her chair to the corner of her desk and sat down.

"My humour transcends pretty easily in the book, but it's truly about a man's love for a city. Call it 'Mancity lit' or 'cit lit' maybe. Do critics have a classification for books about men that love cities?" I laughed at myself, thinking NiR would've had an amalgamated word ready in a second.

Helen snickered. "Not to the best of my knowledge, but maybe Simon de Nadeau will think of something." She took out a pad of paper and scribbled something.

"Tell me more about this character, de Nadeau."

She scribbled another line. "He comes into our store every other month—dressed to the nines, wearing the latest cologne and a two-day stubble." She paused and put her hand over her mouth, and then leaned closer to me. "Although some of the ladies argue that it's only a *one*-day growth. And his cheekbones?! Good lord, they must have been carved by a relative of Michelangelo. Oh and don't get me started about that radiant smile of his."

"Helen, I have to ask: What's in your espresso?"

"What do you mean?"

"Your descriptions are positively hilarious. You are definitely quite a storyteller. Do you mind if I use some of your clever words in my next book?"

"I would be delighted. What's your next book about?"

I wondered if my brother Carson had written anything lately. "That's a great question. I'm tossing around an idea about a mother and her three sons contemplating doing away with an overbearing husband-slash-father.

"Uww, that sounds interesting. Are we talking about a dark psychological piece of literary fiction?"

"On the contrary, I think it will be a light humorous piece of literary conniption."

"That sounds terrific. Where do you get your ideas?"

"Oh." My eyes wandered for a second. "I just steal them."

"That's funny."

"Not really," I said under my breath, wondering at the same time why my conscience had made a vocal appearance. "So what do you have in store for me in your um *store*?"

She picked up her cellphone and tapped. "Okay, I've got you down for a book reading in three weeks or maybe even earlier."

"I'm clueless about this business, but if I'm going to read, don't you need lots of books available?"

"Of course. You're self-published right?"

"Yes."

"Is your book connected to Createspace? Lulu? Any of those companies?"

"No. I just paid a printing company in Canada to make fifty books."

"And it's extremely doubtful you have an agent?"

"Secret?"

"Ha-ha! I'll ask again. Do you have a book agent? Someone who gets you a deal with a publisher? A person who gets you an advance if your work is good enough? I could go on forever, here."

That was my cue to stop her. "Helen, I come from a seriously different line of work, so no to all of that."

She paused and looked up at the ceiling. I'm sure the wheels were turning behind that furrowed brow of hers, but I could only guess at her next sentence. I took a sip of my cappuccino and let her brow furrow. My thoughts turned to Natasha. I had arranged to see her later in the evening and would have a hell of a story to tell.

Helen refocused on me. "Don't worry about the extra books. I'll take care of that detail later."

"Sure. I'll leave it up to you."

"I even have an agent that might be able to help you."

"Well, if you think I need one." She looked amused. Did she think I was a country bumpkin when it came to this business? I was. Lost in the excitement and desperate for cash, I forgot to ask Helen about signing a similar contract to the one I'd signed at the other Parisian bookstores. I had to trust her, and trust had never been one of my strong suits—I had my father to thank for that. My mind wandered to a time when he was still in our home.

"I've got it, Vlad. Vlad, you're not listening."

"Sorry, Helen. I was just thinking about someone from my past."

"Think about her later."

"It was a him."

"As I was saying." She paused to be dramatic. "If Simon is keen on your book, you're going to become very popular."

"How do you know he'll even review it?"

"I'm not 100% sure, but trust me, I run this city when it comes to English books."

Okay, her ego was the size of her store and she was impatient, but the odds on what had just happened to me were about a million to one. I lifted my cappuccino and gave her a toast. "I'm all yours."

"Vlad, I know a *lot* about books." She scribbled something else on her notepad and then tapped her cellphone. "And, Vlad—it doesn't hurt that you're an attractive guy."

Oh, no—is she interested in me? "Thanks, Helen. I'm sure you're a bit of a cougar yourself." *Great*, I'm flirting with a woman a generation my senior.

"Thanks, Vlad, but I'm happily married."

She scribbled something down. Cellphone untouched. Detail was important in my old job.

"One day, I'll take some pictures of you. And about a week before your reading, I'll put a few up in the front window. Though you write 'cit lit,' as you say, we have to get the ladies in here to see those cheekbones and that square jaw of yours."

Helen you're sending mixed messages again! "Um, thanks, Helen."

"And for the record women read fiction far more than men so I assume in your book you have a complicated relationship between a man and a woman?"

"Of course."

"Excellent. I can't wait to read it."

"Helen, I have to ask. How did my sticker got on the cover?"

"I assume it had something to do with Pam."

"Yes, she put it on and then extorted me for sex. Well, she tried."

Helen smiled. "That's a great idea for a plot."

"I'm surprised at your flippancy."

"It's not the first time she's said some . . . *strange things* to authors. The poor girl—I feel sorry for her, although I never outwardly show it. I have an awful feeling that if I was nicer to her, she would just use me."

"So you wouldn't fire her for the game she was playing?"

"Not at all. She's good at her job and her antics kind of spice up the place. Without her and Simon, this place would be boring." Silently placing her cup back on the desk, she stared at me with bedroom eyes. "Anyway, we have you to package and promote." She wrote something down again. "So, Vlad, are you free to come over for dinner one evening? I notice you have a tiny biography in the book. I have to find out more about you. One can only glean so much about an author by reading his work."

"I'm busy with my girlfriend tonight, but I could meet you some other time this week."

She scanned her cellphone. "Tomorrow is my only free night. Okay, you're coming tomorrow and I won't take no for answer."

"Of course, I'll be there. Where's your place?"

"My apartment is in the 8th *arrondissement*. Is there anything in particular you'd prefer to eat?"

"No, I eat anything that doesn't move. Well, if I'm incredibly hungry I don't care if it moves."

"I'll make sure it doesn't move."

"It's your dinner." I stared at her, wondering if that last joke made her think I had more than a few rough edges. And would she figure out how sharp those edges were? *Christ, Vlad, snap out of it—she's a businesswoman. And she's friendly. She doesn't have time to go deep into your head.*

"Here's my card." She wrote 8 p.m. on the top right corner and scribbled directions on the back. "In the meantime, I'll dig into your book ASAP. Be prepared to answer a lot of questions. And you'll get a chance to meet my husband and my daughter, but please come alone, as we'll need to talk business."

"That would be great. Should I bring anything?"

"Just wear a dinner jacket."

16

"Your wish is my command."

We shook hands. Helen remained seated and scribbled madly. I heard the paper squealing in pain.

I stopped by the door. "Helen, how much did you charge for my book?" *I was getting a huge break, but my wallet was fucking empty. Come on, Helen. Offer me something.*

She lifted her head but continued writing. "I thought ten euros was an appropriate price."

"Yes, that's what Byron is charging at the Albany Bookshop. And Shakespeare and Company is selling them for the same price as well."

Her look turned serious. "Vlad! Some other time about bonehead Byron. Because you're self-published, I have to pull some serious strings to set up a TVA account for you. It's your publisher that pays you an advance, but between you and me, I can send some cash your way. It wouldn't be the first time."

I decided to hide my financial desperation. "I spoke with a woman here two days ago; I think her name was Veronica. She said something about TVA." *Shit, Vlad, why are you bringing her up?*

"I'm not only the senior manager, but I'm also the OWNER of this store, so don't worry about Veronica. What I say goes!"

"Wow, senior manager and owner, you can't get any more hands-on than that."

Beaming, she returned her gaze to her paper and her pen went back into overdrive.

On the main floor, I noticed a stack of *New York Times*, Sunday edition, which included the sacred book review section. It was priced at sixteen euros (twenty-four Canadian dollars), and, old habits dying a slow death, I grabbed the top one, my body language suggesting I might buy it.

I walked around the nearest corner and out of sight of the cashiers and pieced through each section. No book review. Someone else had ripped a page out of my playbook. I placed the paper back on the stack and took another. This time, I found one with my prize inside, the cover review written by Dave Eggers. I had to have it. I placed the book review on a stack of books, ironically hoping no one would steal it while I returned the newspaper.

I was tempted to rip the sixteen-euro price sticker off the front page as well and stuff it in my pocket as a souvenir, but maybe it contained some kind of microchip (hidden from the naked eye and detected only by the front alarm system . . . or by bats). An expert with alarm systems, I walked by the front door and waved the book review section through the two portals while I pretended I was looking at a stack of books on the sidewall. No alarm went off. I walked over to the other side of the alarm and grabbed a *FUSAC*—the free anglophone magazine on how to survive Paris provided a perfect baguette; the *New York Times* book review, the filler. My magazine sandwich wrapped tightly in hand, I waited for someone to walk out at the same time, ready to blame him or her if the alarm went off. One foot between the portals, the alarm was quiet, but I heard a voice.

"Hey, *litbas*." I turned around. Pam was stacking some books and getting my attention. Shit, did she see me sneak the review into the magazine?

Keeping a few metres away, I calmly said, "That's the second time you've said that. What does *litbas* mean?" *Vlad, you have to get out of here.*

Her face turned red. She wanted to yell, but there were customers walking between us. "You don't know dick-on-a-stick, do you?" She had me speechless. "You don't know your ass from a hole in the ground. I'll let you figure it out."

"Pam I gotta go. This situation already got weird once today," I said, eyeing the front door.

"It's NiR and fuck you," she said under her breath.

"Don't you mean 'fuyu'?"

"Get out of here before I scream rape."

"*Charming.*" I paused a second and added. "Anyway, I have a feeling I'll be back here, so I guess I'll see you around."

And with a pair of eyes double-barrelled with vengeance, she said, "It'll be sooner than you think, ya bastard."

Early in the evening, I stepped into Natasha's bookstore. She winked at me while she attended to a customer. To pass the time, I picked up Chandler's *The Lady in the Lake*, opened the cover by its bent right corner and scoffed out loud at the price.

The customer said nothing as he exited the store. Natasha looked out the front window, I assume making sure the last customer of the day had disappeared down the street.

"Well, sir, if you make mad passionate love to me, I'll consider reducing the price by a euro or two."

"Gee," I said, scratching my head after I placed the book back on the shelf. "I wonder where I've heard that before."

Natasha laughed as she turned over the "open" sign on the front window. The blinds down and one light still shining from the back room, we kissed.

"Natasha, with that light shining on us, do you think we've struck a romantic silhouette for the passersby?"

"That's so amorous, Vlad." We sloppily smacked lips and she threw in her tongue for free.

"I finished your book," she said with a smile, "and I'm dying to tell you what I think about it." I reciprocated her wandering tongue and put my hands on her chest but she skipped behind the cash register. "Hold those hands for a second. I have to empty the till and put the money in a little vault in the back room." I kept my hands up, pantomiming that I was playing with a couple of huge dials on a sixties shortwave radio. She walked back, laughing. "What are you doing?"

"Walk a little closer and you'll find out." She jokingly positioned her tight-sweatered abundant chest into the double-D cups formed by my hands. I continued adjusting her hooters. Natasha gushed out a laugh causing her body to jiggle. "Natasha! Please stay still! I've got Tokyo on the shortwave."

She teasingly pulled away from me but grabbed my chin with her slender index finger and a playful thumb. Each fingernail was manicured and sealed in a coat of mauve, matching the faint makeup around her eyes.

It took three glasses of wine, a ripe tomato and a garlic-coated baguette, as well as two-thirds of a chorizo sausage before I finished unravelling my event-filled day at BJ Williams.

Natasha sipped on her second glass. "Vlad, soon you won't be able to get your head in the door."

I placed my hand on her thigh. "Don't worry, I'll never change . . . dear."

"I hope not."

"Anyway, what's for dessert besides you?"

"Très drôle. How about we amble toward the Seine and grab an ice cream cone. There's a little place that has even better gelato than the last place we visited."

We walked hand in hand along Boulevard St-Germain, the clouds tailgating across the sky. Natasha commented several times about the noisy traffic, yet all I heard was the sweet sounds strung together by the charms knocking on her bracelet.

We finished our cones as we walked toward Notre Dame. She spied a cozy spot on a bridge recently vacated by, I assumed, another couple of lovebirds. We ran. Out of breath, we simultaneously commented on the oncoming *bateau mouche*. Soon it would pass underneath us, its lights bouncing off the walls bordering the Seine, causing party-goers along the quay to wave at the boaters as if they were rock stars.

Natasha yelled something that got lost in the crowd. I was happy just being with her and being lost in the crowd. She put her arms around my neck. "You spoke so much about your afternoon adventure I didn't get a chance to tell you my thoughts about your book."

I placed my hands around her waist. "I'm all ears."

She brushed the hair away from my left ear. "Hey there, pretty boy. You might want to keep those big ears covered."

I winced, thinking that Pam had called me the same thing. And, thank God, I had left out the sex-to-keep-the book-on-the-shelf-with-an-insane-woman part when I'd explained my day's events to Natasha. I jokingly pulled her searching hands away. "Enough about my ears. My book, remember?"

"I'm trying to think of the best place to start. I th—"

"Wow, this sounds serious." I darted my head over her shoulders as if I was looking for someone. "I'm wondering if Simon de Nadeau is listening to this conversation."

"Can you handle a backhanded compliment?" She grabbed both of my hands as if she felt a need to prepare me for a heavy blow, a blow that I was ill-equipped to handle. Her electricity was still passing through me. "Have you ever considered writing for Letterman or O'Brien? Because I think your abundance of one-liners is hilarious!"

"Sounds good so far. And the backhanded part? Don't worry; you can say whatever you want. I'm thick-skinned and don't bite, a crocodile without teeth." I was lying.

"Well, writing novels may not be your forte. Short stories, maybe?" She placed a hand on the back of my neck. And there it was: a warm, backhanded compliment disguised as a romantic attempt to deflect any hurt I felt. The electricity short-circuited, and I looked away for a second. She put her hand on the side of my face hidden from her view and gently nudged my dejected mug until our eyes met.

"Natasha, you surprised me with that last comment."

20

She kissed me on the cheek, sending a bolt through my body. Good, the tingles came back; the power failure was over.

"I'm sorry, but I assume you want my honest opinion."

I kissed her to show that my skin was at least semi-tough and my lips were at least semi-soft. "Don't worry; I can handle it," I said, sluggishly working the corners of my lips into a smile. "But I am curious. What did you think was lacking in the novel?"

"The most important thing, in my opinion—and remember it's only my opinion—is that your book needs a hook in the first paragraph. I guess I'm looking at it from a sales viewpoint."

"I did hear that before from the person who edited the book. But in my defence, isn't what I wrote on the back cover my hook?"

"*That* hook serves to get the reader to open the book and read the first paragraph or two. It's that first paragraph where I honestly believe the writer has to catch the potential buyer's interest enough that he or she won't put the book back on the shelf."

"Did you ever read Jonathan Franzen's *The Corrections*? It was shortlisted for a Pulitzer."

"No, but of course I have heard of him. He's an Amer—"

"Well," I said, "in the first fifteen pages of his book, he describes in tremendous detail a Midwestern home where a father and mother are planning one last Christmas dinner with their three grown-up children who have long since moved away. There was no hook whatsoever. One needed a tremendous amount of patience to get through that first part."

"I guess the difference is a Jonathan Franzen can get away with fifteen potentially boring pages, but—" she paused for a second and placed her lips by my ear. She whispered, "maybe your book might have been more interesting had you begun the novel in Paris rather than drawing it out through good ol' Lester B. Pearson Airport." Her warm breath disarmed her harsh words. And I was in no hurry to shake off her hand, lightly scratching the back of my neck.

"Natasha, I wonder what you'd be doing to my body if I wrote the *worst* book on earth." I opened my eyes to a grin that said, 'Your place or mine?'.

"Well, next time you can write a totally horrendous book and you'll see what I'll do for you."

"I think I had too many sons in the story anyway," I said, forcing myself to concentrate on her candid comments again.

"I don't think so. Maybe you could have created a situation early in the book where they unknowingly film a robbery. Then Carson and/or the boys are chased from the beginning. That would create some added suspense throughout the book. I love the suspense you created when Rory went missing, but I think it happens very late."

"That's a good idea."

"I'm great at critiquing other books, but I don't handle criticism well myself."

"What do mean?"

"Well I'm changing the subject a little bit. I haven't been totally honest about why I came to Paris."

You and me both! The irony bottled me up inside. "This is wonderful!" I said and then laughed uncontrollably. Natasha must have thought I was deranged, but it was the only way to uncork too many dark, pent-up feelings from *my* past without revealing a word. I didn't give her a chance to speak. "Natasha please change the subject all you want! Let's grab a late-night drink and talk about it."

"No. I'm sorry Vlad. I've already told you about my parents passing away and some other personal things, but it takes a long time before I totally open up to someone."

God, I was crazy about this woman, but she changed her mind in a heartbeat. "We can speed up the process if you like. I mean we've already sped up *one* process."

She wrapped her arms around me and squeezed me with surprising strength. I loved it.

"Vlad, I knew from the second we first spoke you could have my body. But you're going to have to be patient if you want my soul."

"In fifty years, a woman has never said that to me. Maybe a couple of men did."

She slapped me on the butt.

"Hey, you said some things about my book that didn't thrill me and I took it in stride, so I doubt if you said more about your past that it would turn me off."

She put a finger on my lips. "Another time, okay?"

"Sure." I held her tightly as we strolled toward a café. We found a table a book's throw from Shakespeare and Company. Natasha ordered a glass of white wine to go with my *Leffe*.

"Natasha, I have to ask, what did you think about the relationship in the book between Carson and Monique?"

"I loved it. Their quick repartee reminded me of the dialogue found in any romantic Cary Grant movie."

"I was going more for a combination Woody Allen–Elmore Leonard effect. But I'll take a witty Cary Grant and whoever played opposite him. My pre-sixties movie knowledge is negatory, except *The Wizard of Oz*, of course."

"Maybe we can borrow some old movies at the library and have a Cary Grant film festival one weekend. My local library has a good selection of English classics. And some great old French movies as well. Do you ever watch movies in French?"

"Of course. Have you forgotten the Carlton cinema?"

"It's been a long time. I remember going there at least once a month when I was a French immersion student at Glendon College."

"Oh you're a graduate of that *other* university in Toronto."

"Well I never did graduate."

Meanwhile, I was expelled from the University of Toronto. "You're a bright girl—what could possibly have happened?"

"Remember . . . another time." She leaned over and kissed me on the cheek. "I love your childhood stories. You must have more?"

"Well, if you insist. I've got some great tales about my high school days."

"Where'd you go?"

"Forest Hill."

"I had some friends who went there." We tossed out some names, but our age difference, ten years, meant that we only knew brothers or sisters of the people mentioned.

"I remember the high school dances on Friday nights. As usual, we would walk in pretty-wasted. The majority of teachers chaperoning the dance were not there by choice and tended to spend as much time as possible in the teacher's lounge."

"And?"

"Well we tended to roam the school."

"What did you steal this time?"

"A trophy."

"How could you possibly have done that?"

"The trophies in the case weren't exactly surrounded by sensors. My inebriated buddies didn't have to lower me from the ceiling à la Tom Cruise in *Mission Impossible*."

"So what was your fascination with this particular trophy?"

"In the five years I was a student, we only won the Toronto District

---

23

Basketball championship once. I was a starting forward in grade twelve that year. Our school received a trophy, and the boneheads in the phys. ed. department forgot to have my name engraved on it. And the thing was as big as the Stanley Cup. They retired the trophy and my school got to keep it. It was the pride and joy of the athletic department."

"I don't think your school won too many championships."

"True. Anyway, I stole the trophy and put it in my bedroom. I told my mother that the school was getting rid of it so they gave it to me."

"How did you take it from the school?"

"In the summer before I entered grade nine, they were building an addition to the school. On weekends while the construction workers were off, we removed the nails from a makeshift wooden entrance cover and walked into the new and old part of the school. One day, I found an open wooden box containing every key in the school. I took about ten of the most important keys, had them cut, and then returned them a week later. I wasn't sure what I was going to do with the keys in the future, but I thought it was important to be prepared. I'm sure you've noticed I'm a planner."

"Well, if you only stole the trophy that wasn't so bad."

I pretended to cough. "Did I mention the discount students got on school clothes?"

"I had to open my big mouth and say that I got a kick out of your stories, didn't I?"

"Had I known you and any friend of yours back then I could have gotten you a two-for-one special on Forest Hill track suits. I remember the school logo was beautifully embroidered on the front in blue and gold. To make a long story short, I was always tipped off when a new shipment of rugby shirts or school shorts or T-shirts came in. Luckily, the accounting teachers never did the books for the phys. ed. clowns, so it was easy to steal and sell."

"Did you ever go a day without stealing?"

"January 12th, 1976. It was a Monday and I had a bad cold. Other than that, my memory can't be trusted."

"I have a feeling your memory is close to photographic."

"Only the thefts are etched in my mind. Maybe I'll write a novel and call it, 'A Gentleman Thief.'"

"Tell me you haven't stolen anything since?" Natasha shook her head a couple of times as she asked the question, as though she was trying to answer it for me. Feeling a rare moment of guilt, I didn't mention how I obtained the *New York Times* book review. Then it hit me—I may have been given one of the first honest breaks of my life and I *still* stole something. I thought I stole to help out my family, but I had to admit I liked the thrill of getting away with it. Was I able to stop? Was this my destiny—a lifetime of thieving? Worst of all, I had more in common with my father than I cared to admit.

"Well, how about I save some stories for later?"

"You mean there's more?"

"A few."

"I assumed you did stop."

Please lie, Vlad. You don't want this woman to think that's all you've ever done. "Of course." A good time to change the subject. "Natasha, did you have any summer jobs during high school?"

"Yes. My dad was friends with Sam Sniderman of Sam the—"

"—Record Man."

"Yes. I had a part-time job there for years."

"And?"

Her expression turned serious. "Don't *you* have more crazy stories to tell?"

Obviously she wanted to change the subject. I was a talker anyway, so I let it go. "Natasha, I've got backup stories for any type of awkward moment."

"I'm sorry. My past is private."

"*Really?*"

She sensed my sarcasm and gave me a light slap on the wrist. "So, Vlad, what are your plans for tomorrow?"

"I'm not sure. I might try and find out more about this Simon de Nadeau guy. Who does he write for?"

"It's a well-respected literary review in Paris called *The Lutèce Review.*

"Lutèce? What does that mean?"

"Paris was originally called Lutèce in French or Lutelia when it was once a Roman city. The whole Latin thing. The review is published biweekly and I sell them in my bookshop."

"Impressive, a bookstore owner *and* historian."

We snaked along the Seine and headed toward her apartment, nearing her place when I spotted the café *Les Deux Magots*.

I walked her back to the apartment and we sweated up the sheets under a jealous full moon peeking through the window.

25

Six days earlier
Toronto

Tuesday, June 19th

My bartender gave me a dirty look. "Vlad, see the sign above my head?" It read:

We close at 1 a.m. Tabs not allowed.
We have ways of making you pay.

Last call had come and gone. I let out a small gush of air between my teeth to show my displeasure. A few seconds later, we both laughed. Yes, I was a regular. Our routine over, I searched for two pieces of paper in my pocket. They felt crumply, but opened nicely into two twenties. And the two bills had laid the groundwork for a $50,000 pay-off the night before.

My Toronto apartment, the bottom floor of a row house, was a few blocks from the bar. Along the way I would pass by Robarts and other stately buildings belonging to the University of Toronto's St. George campus. And at the age of fifty, I still wore a wry smile anytime I walked by the Sid Smith building, where I had been caught cheating more than once.

The row house was made of red brick and was separated into three apartments. I doubted even two of them were legal. Each day a piece of a brick dropped like a chestnut in the fall. Strong squirrels, maybe? I think not.

The lock on the front entrance of the row house was always broken, which explained the never-ending pile of flyers on the doorsteps. This time, however, the flyers were scattered more precariously than usual. My door was wide open. My apartment had been broken into before, so I remained calm. "Is anyone here?" I said. "Bob? Johnny? Kinda late in the evening if you're playing a practical joke?" (My acquaintances had occasionally broken in to take some of my dope, but they always paid me sooner or later, so I let it go.) No answer.

I turned on the light in my bachelor apartment. The foldout couch had been slashed, tiny feathers still floating about. Christ, were the thieves still here? A knife was sticking halfway into my second-hand CD player, the speakers hollowed and spilled out, giving new meaning to

---

"surround sound." Cushion seats on both kitchen chairs had been carved up, and the six dishes, two ceramics bowls and a collection of empty mustard jars that I drank out of were smashed beyond recognition. Mac 'n cheese boxes were ripped open, along with the packages of cheese. The cheese? Really? These guys wanted something badly. And they found it! All $50,000 of it. I had stored the money in three cornflakes boxes, and each one lay ripped open on the floor. I made a mental note to never store money in cereal boxes again. Next time I'd go with the coffee cans. They did that in the movies, right? I should've been more upset about the money, but it wasn't hard earned.

Along with everything else on the ground was my entire paperback collection, ripped and trampled on. Imagine *Fahrenheit 451* right before the fire. It had taken me more than twenty years to accumulate all 500 of them, each traded for or bought—my pride and joy. The money *and* my sacred collection! These vandals were fuckin' cold.

The night before had been the biggest payoff of my life. I recognized the tell of every guy at the table. Sammy scratched the back of his right ear just a little too long whenever he had the flush going. Izzy, a full house specialist, didn't realize how often he inhaled through his nose in a particular way when the cards were good. The noise he made was so subtle I think only I and a German shepherd could sense it. I believe only two nose hairs would move instead of his full brush when he had a killer hand. Bartman—yes, Bartman—wore sunglasses all the time, but he should have worn a mask as well because his upper lip curled ever so slightly on the right side only when the aces were aflowin'. And last but not least was Al. Al had taken a few months for me to crack. For a split second, he would go from rubbing his chin to putting his right thumbnail into a scar perpendicular to a cleft in his chin. It briefly formed a cross, which I found ironic because Al had never seen the inside of a church. Over the years, there had been others players, other games, but I'd been working on these four guys' tics for months. They were bright, quick talking, amiable, in their sixties, but years of smoking and drinking and ordering other men to do illegal things for them had turned them into octogenarians.

Everything in the apartment had either been torn, stabbed, chucked, smashed, broken or stomped on except for two identical boxes stacked in the corner by the broom closet. And it was at that moment I started to believe in God. The unmolested boxes contained fifty copies of my self-published novel *French Like Me*. Did the vandals not think my book was worth carving up or was it a sign from God—my new buddy—that it was time to leave Toronto? I would listen to my new friend.

Wading through my collection of wrecked books, I upturned a chair and sat down. And that's when I noticed something spray-painted on the wall. It read: YOU'RE A DEAD MAN. There was even a drawing of a man's head in a noose, its eyes Xed out. Extending from one of the shoulders was an arm, five cards in its hand. The other hand was missing. Okay, Vlad, be cool. I've had death threats before—disgruntled girlfriends, losers in the odd barroom brawl (alcohol induced), fellow card players (the pot never exceeding a few grand). That was all just good fun and kept me from living on the street. I looked at the drawing again. It scared the shit out of me. *Not* good fun. My wall belonged in a serial killer movie. And I couldn't go to the police because after five "stays" at the Toronto East Detention Centre, they would've thought I'd just threatened someone else or I had it coming.

I took one of my books out of the box and mouthed the title. A deep breath later, I thought to myself, well Carson, my brother, I wrote a book about you and Paris. Maybe it's time *I* visited the city of light. And I'd bring my books, the only possessions I wanted to connect me to my past.

Thursday, June 21st

Early in the morning, the sun's orange rays beamed into my Parisian hotel room (the same hotel Carson had stayed in). Exhausted the night before, I'd forgotten to close the curtains. With one eye half open, my books stacked in four uneven piles resembled smoldering logs in a campfire. Thoughts of the flight attendant, her breasts fighting her blouse for the seven-hour Toronto–Paris flight, deliciously occupied my head.

In the middle of the night, the lights off in first class (this is a dream, after all), my seat stretched out for sleep, I waved to a comely flight attendant.

"You look tired," I said. "How'd you like to get off your feet for a while and jump in the sack?" There was plenty of room. I had lucked out and got the only other double bed on the plane.

"That would be great. Everyone's asleep, so I could rest for a while."

I moved over and opened up my blanket, allowing her to slide her curvy frame up against me. A warm hand slowly maneuvered up my leg, eventually resting on my thigh. I was reminded of the airline's slogan: "We do whatever it takes to get you off."

Leaning on my left elbow, my body parallel to hers, I sent my right arm on an expedition. I heard a knock.

"*Bonjour, Monsieur*, I can clean your room if you want?"

Panicking I grabbed a lamp and yelled, "Get the hell out of here or I'll call the police." I studied the lamp. Fuck, this wasn't my apartment. "Sorry, um, yes, please come back in fifteen minutes."

"*D'accord.*"

I showered and ran downstairs, arriving seconds before the ladies stopped serving the continental breakfast. After ordering, I stared at a wall across from my table. I think the pictures hanging on the wall were of Paris, but all I could see was the head in a noose drawing in my apartment. Words were one thing, but a drawing?! That took time and demented care.

I decided to book and pay for ten days up front—that way I couldn't blow my money on a few card games. I had trust issues—even with myself. I looked around my room and then at my wallet. Two hundred and fifty euros and fifty books—a paltry accumulation for fifty years on this earth. Shit, I wanted to live Carson's life, but I didn't have his money. For such a planner, I hadn't thought this one out fully. But did I have a choice? And if I'd gone somewhere else in Canada, those card players and others I'd ripped off would've found me. Card players were a tighter group than the mafia. I had a long, successful minor-league career as a gentleman thief, but I'd gotten greedy and begun searching for card games, the higher the anti the better.

Sitting on the edge of my bed I ran my hand through my hair a few times. Christ, how was I going to survive? I looked at my books. They would do no goddamn good just sitting there gathering French dust, and if anything, they reminded me of what had just happened in Toronto. They were no longer a source of comfort, no longer a positive connection to my past. Then I smiled. I brought them here, and the book is about Paris, so I might as well take them to a few bookstores and try and sell them. I desperately needed some cash—any cash. And I would play a little game in my head and pretend that for every book I sold I would earn back one year on a new, honest life.

I stuffed fifteen copies of my novel (unseen by anyone other than an old friend and a university English major, who edited it) in my faded blue knapsack and walked toward a bookstore. The challenge lay, as always, not in my level of confidence, which as a grifter was through the roof and plateauing somewhere on the moon, but in a profound inability to handle rejection. That was the main reason I'd never tried to sell my book back home or look for a publisher. And it didn't help that I'd secretly written about my brother's experience in Paris.

I walked by a café and noticed four men playing cards. Instinctively I studied their facial expressions. And there was no money on the table! Did I need any more proof that going cold turkey would be impossible? What saved me from finding a game was that my French was too rusty (although I'm sure the players would have spoken some English once they saw my euros). That and I had an end-up-on-the-street-in-ten-days cash flow problem. I forced myself to look away from the cards, my thoughts turning to finding a way to legitimately outdistance my past.

Traffic was brisk and the air still cool. I crossed St-Michel, snaked through a couple of tourist trap streets and found myself in front of the petite English bookstore, the Albany Bookshop. I shimmied sideways through the entrance to avoid knocking over mountains of books. Books covered the four walls and were stacked so high they alone appeared to support the ceiling. And were books crawling across the floor, looking for somewhere to spawn—God forbid—more books? The path narrowed as I moved deeper into the heart of this Congo jungle of paper.

I was forced on tippy-toe to avoid elbowing a conga line of salesgirls in their twenties wearing smiles you could find on the cover of *Seventeen* magazine. Lost in this literature hellhole, I spotted the owner—Kurtz (of *Apocalypse Now* fame). Okay, his name was Byron something. My brother Carson had met him before, not me. Byron was perched on a wooden pulpit, although bamboo would have been more fitting. The balding, I assumed sixty-year-old, looking more Christopher Plummer than Marlon Brando, calmly ordered his clear-skinned beauties to perform the most mundane of activities.

"Suzanne, would you do me the honour of buying a flavoured icicle?"

"Shall I pay for it?"

"Don't be a silly goose. Take the money out of petty cash, but leave the shiny fifty-cent pieces. They complement the loose change box—don't you think?"

"Of course, Mr. Byron."

Byron looked at me. "Hello, may I be of assistance?" His tone lay somewhere between indifferent and uncaring.

I glanced at the open cash register, all those fifties, twenties and tens resting quietly. They needed to be disturbed. *Come on, Byron, look somewhere else for a few seconds so I can survey the store for security cameras. Vlad, what the hell are you thinking?!* "Are you the owner of the store?" Based on Carson's descriptions I was fairly sure it was him.

His face lit up. "Guilty as charged. I am one and the same and—I might add—the only."

"I noticed you have a Canadian flag waving outside. Are you Canadian?"

"Yes, I'm originally from Westmount. You know *that* part of Montreal?"

"I had a girlfriend who worked as a hairdresser in Westmount." I made that up on the spot—sounded convincing as well.

He looked up at the ceiling and rubbed his chin in thought. "Ah, those foolish, halcyon days. I remember throwing caution to the wind once and letting a *coiffeuse* in Westmount have her way with my curly locks. I was such an impetuous cad."

I let that comment go and took one brand new, relatively hot-off-the-plane copy of *French Like Me* out of my bag. Then I paused . . . and dwelled . . . and hesitated. What the hell was I supposed to say? I had never done this shit before. *Christ, Vlad, talk!* I noticed a poster of the famous British writer Morgan Davis above Byron's head.

"Um, I almost forgot to mention," I said, "I'm following in the footsteps of my hero, Morgan Davis." A total lie, but I remembered Carson talking about Davis.

Byron angled his head up and beamed at the poster. "I'm a great fan of Morgan's as well. I find his writing one part whimsical, one part outlandish." He paused for a few seconds. "Oh—and a third part devil-may-care."

"Yes, you're right—Davis is a mixture of all three. And dare I add—a dash of panache." I'd never read any of his books.

Byron took the book out my hand. "What's it about?"

"It's about a father spending a crazy week in Paris, managing himself and harnessing his three teenage sons."

"Okay." He flipped it over.

Come on, Carson, I'm dying here. What else did you say about Davis? I scratched my head. And then it came. "I believe Davis mentioned that he stopped by your very store and asked if you would sell his first book, self-published. But I forgot the title."

"*Merde Doesn't Stink in France*," he replied in a nanosecond. "I believe other bookstores in Paris took his book as well."

"As I said, I'm following in Davis's footsteps and hope to sell my self-published book in Parisian bookstores. I'm kind of Davis's smart-as—sorry, smart-alecky Canadian equivalent." I had to pause for a second to take in this wonderful-sounding fib. I continued my lie. "Having lived in *Savoie* for two years, I'm a keen observer of the French." Of course, Carson had lived in that south-eastern part of France. I couldn't point it out on a map.

He took a minute and read the description—the "hook"—written in seventy-five words or less, as they say.

He giggled. "I think your book has possibilities," he said and then slapped his thigh as if the action had just given him an idea. "I'm going to gamble." He paused and smiled. "Throw the dice if you will and liberate five of your volumes of prose from the wilderness of self-published literary anonymity right this minute, my good man, and pay with this paper I have before me. I believe it's backed by President Sarkozy himself and seconded by the French Treasury, or maybe it's the other way around." He entered my book title and ISBN in his computer and handed me three ten-euro bills.

"You're very kind." I smiled, thinking five books, five years toward a new life.

"And the price of your storybook tour de farce soon to wreak comedic havoc on my lively shelves shall be?"

"No idea. I dunno, how about ten euros . . . sure. Why not ten euros?"

"I concur. Ten euros—a firm but fair price for a droll *oeuvre* such as yours."

One foot out the door, I turned around and thanked him one last time, and then I noticed a security camera discretely hidden in a corner. Damn! That cash register would not be an easy job. *Old habits, Vlad. Old habits, remember!*

I found some shade in a small treed park at the corner of Boulevards St-Germain and St-Michel. At noon, the park was shared by a mixture of high school and university students carrying their McDonald's lunches in shopping-sized bags. Sitting contentedly on a wooden bench, I dug into my pocket and fished around for my thirty-euro prize, the equivalent of fifty Canadian dollars. And in what decade had I last earned an honest buck? Maybe I wouldn't rob Byron's store after all.

I nibbled on a chicken and tomato half-baguette on my way to Shakespeare and Company, a famous English bookstore (and non-lending library) near Notre Dame. Hemingway, Stein and Joyce often spent late nights in the store, drinking hooch and trading slurred adjectives. Entering the freshly painted dark-green storefront, the sign done in black on gold, I spotted a picture of Hemingway. Did he ever participate in the five-finger discount? I'll bet that codger's old apartment in Paris was full of the Bard's books.

And I had my own five-finger discount stories . . .

Delivering papers as a youth, and often waiting weeks for customers to pay their outstanding debt, I supplemented my pauper's income by other methods. Saturday afternoons, the candy and card shelf freshly chock-o-block, my brother Carson and I would enter a restaurant or convenience store in our beaten Toronto neighbourhood. To the left of the front door sat the cash register, and in behind, a cubbyhole lined with Lik-m-aids, candy necklaces, SweeTarts, Black Cat gum, Musketeers bars, Mars bars, and stacks of hockey or baseball cards, depending on what colour the leaves on the maple trees were that time of year.

After entering the store, I positioned myself, a seasoned criminal at twelve, by the cash register, eyeing the potential stash. My distracter, Carson, of ten innocent and therefore still unproductive years, would ask Lena, the sole staff, a question (always rehearsed before entering the store) about the menu. If the routine had become stale, they would strike up a conversation about whether the plain bag of chips contained more chips than the salt and vinegars.

"Lena," Carson would say (we were allowed to call her by her first name), "I see a package of plastic G.I. Joes on the back rack, but I was curious. Do you have any *First World War* G.I. Joes?"

Whether Carson talked about fictitious war toys or asked about an order of plastic hockey players sporting baseball helmets (that was my favourite concoction), the key to the operation was to make sure that Lena was busy inspecting the shelves at the other end of the restaurant with my brother. While they spoke about G.I. Joes or Barbie dolls sporting beards, I routinely slipped twenty or thirty packages of cards in pockets deeper than a Chilean mine shaft. Lena would glance from a distance toward the front counter, possibly wondering what my tiny thieving hands were touching, but her black-framed glasses, housing lenses thicker than glass bricks, made it impossible to pick me out of a police lineup that included Dracula and the creature from the Black Lagoon.

Every theft was ritualistically closed out with a couple of Mars bars. They comfortably lined the tops of my pockets like icing on a cake or cherries on a jubilee. My Saturday thighs always grew to linebacker proportions, but they were still well covered by my thick house league hockey winter jacket, which draped down to my knobby, but never shaky knees. Occasionally, Lena would say, "Vlad, why you wear heavy coat? It ninety-five degree."

The stolen hockey card packages were sold to friends at half price. The Howes, Hulls, and Orrs, all future hall-of-famers, were extracted with surgical precision, the packages resealed with a similar-smelling glue I had stolen from a hardware store. In the summer months, I switched to the less lucrative baseball card market.

Two years later, packages of cigarettes vanished every Saturday. It was worth the risk because the resale was more profitable than the card business. And someone in the family had to supplement my mother's meager income as a part-time cashier because my bastard father had left us.

Shocked by my first sale and not having had to steal anything (a bigger shock), I entered Shakespeare and Company with a beaming smile. My body felt different from the way it felt when I stole something. This time the tingles ran up and down, wrapping me in a warm glow as opposed to the usual thieves' adrenaline rush, the heart pounding. A few paces from the wooden sales desk, manned by a woman, or 'wo-manned,' I grabbed one of my books from my carrying bag, the whole time desperately trying to make eye contact with her. In her late twenties, she leaned against the antique mahogany desk and directed the lives of everyone working in the bookstore, ordering five people around simultaneously. Shoulders erect, chest out, chin up and my big teeth flashing like the Enterprise's holodeck, I stood less than a metre from the woman and waited for her to acknowledge my presence. Her brown eyes locking on my non-brown eyes, she somehow didn't find a job for me. "Hello. How may I help you?"

"Hi. I'm following in the footsteps of Morgan Davis. I'm sure you know who he is?" *What the hell—it worked in the last store!*

"Of course." She pointed toward a stack of books. "If you look in the front left corner of the store, we have several copies of all three of his books."

"He has a third book? What's it called?"

"It's a new murder mystery, titled, *Merde Most Foul.*"

"Great title," I said. The title wasn't that great. "Well, as I mentioned, I'm following in the footsteps of Davis. Years ago, he went from English bookstore to English bookstore in Paris to sell his first self-published book."

"I wasn't here when he first came to our bookstore, but I do remember his story. Quite remarkable."

"Well I'm attempting to do the same thing. I consider myself to be the Canadian smartass equivalent of Davis." After hearing myself say this a second time, I was starting to believe my own lies. The book firmly in her hands, she grinned when she read the title out loud. "The title is interesting and the artwork on the cover is cool. And the woman is very alluring, but I am curious why you've made the Eiffel Tower and Cathedral so feminine?"

"If you notice the person in the corner of the cover filming, he appears to be ignoring the Eiffel Tower. The tower looks angry because the guy is filming the attractive woman and the Cathedral, yet the tower is being ignored." I had her snickering each time I explained more details of the cover.

"I like your book," she said. "It looks funny and your cover is funky."

I preferred cool over funky, but I kept that thought to myself. "That's great. Byron at the Albany Bookshop already purchased five."

Her grin turned to a look of consternation. "Oh yes, Byron. How's that goofy shit anyway? Does he still have a harem full of harlots working for him?"

That's two bookstores in a row where the owner or manager suffered from lexicon envy. Who uses the word "harlot" in this century? Her alliteration was funny and intended, I'm sure, but nevertheless, there was a problem. Too many loaded questions. How would I handle them? Byron did purchase five of my books without reading a chapter. That "goofy shit" as she so unprofessionally labelled him did put some money in my pocket.

"I've only just met him, and you're right. He's a little strange and speaks *Gatsbyesque*, but I'm sure he was putting me on."

She rolled her eyes. "No, that's him 100%."

"Maybe he was an actor and has fun playing a role."

"He plays a role all right. He's after all those hot little babes."

"Really? I never noticed how attractive they were." A smile instantly grew on my face, much like Pinocchio's nose lengthening.

"You're kidding! You mean you didn't notice the young broads working in there?"

Broads?! I don't even use that word. This woman's a riot. "I guess I was so concerned about selling my book I didn't notice."

"Wow, you must be serious about promoting your book or maybe you're um . . .."

I cut her off in a tenth of a second. "No, I don't swing that way. I'm extremely serious about selling my books. It's the only source of income I have." That last comment was true but not intended.

"Well, in that case, I'll double what Byron took, but I'll only take them on consignment."

"Thanks. That's okay. I'm sure they'll sell fast."

"What price are you selling them for? By law, I'm not to change the price by more than 5%."

"Ten euros."

"Sounds reasonable." I opened up my bag and took out the remaining nine books. She had cleaned me out.

We filled out two identical consignment agreements, one for her, one for me, stating that I would receive 70% of the sales of each book. Our signatures above the famous blue and red Shakespeare and Company logo sealed the deal.

She looked at the front window. "A few of your books will go on the front corner shelf, and the rest will go up in storage. As you can see, we only have so much space for each book."

"Thanks. That would be great." I folded the consignment agreement, matching the corners, and placed it inside my passport.

Later that night, the sun yawning, I bought a vegetarian pizza and a three-euro bottle of red wine and walked along the Seine. I descended a set of stairs and sat near a busker entertaining a group with songs in English and his native Spanish. He paused every twenty minutes or so to douse his liver with more alcohol. And I was one to talk. An inebriated Italian took over during the breaks and sang a famous aria. His powerful voice skipped across the rippling Seine and bounced off the other wall, creating a haunting echo. Tourists stopped in their tracks on the bridge above. They clapped and then laughed, realizing that the Seine opera was

---

composed of only one repeated line.

The talented singer/guitarist, able to sing more than one line, patiently waited for the bystanders on the bridge to stop laughing. Soon he drifted into a Spanish version of John Lennon's *Imagine*, the opera singer dancing along with the music, one awkward step from falling into the river.

And then he made the awkward step. Screams of bystanders boomed over the water. A police powerboat appeared upstream, its motor drowning out all noise in its path as it bounced up and down on the black water. Despite having lungs full of Seine water (that alone should have killed him), the inebriated one defied all conventional laws of sinking and stayed afloat long enough for a French marine cop to jump in and save the bobbing slab of soused cannelloni.

The fallen opera singer's silver hair hung over the edge of the rubber craft. With grey pants and silver, pointed shoes fanned out and stretched over the other side of the boat, he resembled a tuna captured after an epic midnight struggle.

Extremely wobbly myself, and leaning too long on the bridge railing, I accidently bumped into a man. No words were spoken, but he looked familiar. Had I won more than a few hands of cards against this guy? Had he helped destroy my apartment? How could he possibly have found me in the middle of Paris? Did three-euro bottles of wine contain hallucinogens? I took another swig and watched him disappear into the crowd.

Friday, June 22nd

I decided to visit two English bookstores, both in the 6th *arrondissement*, a short walk from Jean-Paul Sartre's and Simone de Beauvoir's old hangout, Les Deux Magots. Carson had mentioned that Morgan Davis had sold his book in these stores as well. The Galleries Lafayette map in my hand, plus Parisian street maps dotting many corners, simplified my route. It rained lightly as I strode. I spotted some umbrellas for sale, but the price was more than the retail price of my book, so the rain continued to fall on my head.

I glanced up at a sign, Alcatraz Books, in the shape of a book (how original). A row of misshapen bells rattled on the front door as I entered.

A sales clerk sat, his face half-hidden in a dimly lit corner by the cash register, engrossed in a book. He managed a monocle-eyed glance in my direction. Was I just another uninteresting air mass passing through? As I approached the counter, either my happy face or my gait convinced him to stop reading. His chair screeched as he turned his seated body in my direction, offering a full face for analysis.

And where the hell do I start? A monocle for each eye, I suppose, was as good a place as any. Surrounding his matching monocles was pale, greyish-white skin, covered with faded, olive-green pock marks, thinned and bevelled over time by I could only guess what combination of drugs and a bark stripper set to high. Haphazardly placed in the middle of his face was a nose that had long ago lost its perpendicularity to a pencilled-in straight line for a mouth.

Given the Roquefort skin, a handful of nose hairs growing up the eastern and western borders of his nostrils, and approximately eight strands of hair spun in perfect elliptical paths around his shiny head, like the planets revolving around the sun, I guessed he had been spinning on this earth for sixty lonely years.

I grabbed a book out of my knapsack. "Hi! How are you?" I said.

He widened his eyes, allowing the monocles to fall freely, catching them, one in each hand, the whole time never taking his eyes off the hot-looking woman on the cover. He gently placed his monocles on the wooden counter and eagerly held my book, caressing it, maybe.

"She new?" he asked, his unbespectacled eyes studying every French curve "Monique" had to offer.

"Yes, *she* is," I said proudly. "And I wrote it."

"I think the cover is gorgeous, but weeze only buys and sells used books."

"You're kidding. There must be tons of new books in this store."

He nodded with his solar system for a head. "Lookie 'round."

I placed my hand on three new-looking books. I grabbed two of them, my eyes becoming a pair of magnifying glasses. He was right. I ran my hands over more volumes on a neighbouring shelf. The same.

"Yeah, you got me," I said. "The books are used, but they're in excellent shape. I'll come back when my books are nicely used."

"Thanks." He paused for a second and smiled. "Weeze normally only buys books that's in mint condition."

"Reminds me of a baseball card collection I used to own."

He set my book on the counter. "I had me once over a hundred rookie cards worth thousands of dollars."

"What happened?"

———

"My mother throwed them out. I could ov' killed the bitch."

Wow, where did that comment come from? "Um . . . how do you *really* feel about your mother?"

"Yeah, sorry about that. I guess that shouldn't have comes out the ways it did."

"Do you always talk about women that way?"

"I can't says I've been overly successful lately."

"Paris is supposed to be the city of love, but I can easily see a guy having a tough time here," I said, trying to make the old guy feel happy.

"Tells me about it. Some of the bitches over in Pigalle won't even service me no more. Crazy, ain't it?" He paused, hoping I would agree with him. I was lost for words. He pointed both index fingers to his face proudly displaying his prominent features. And they were prominent. Then he yelled, timing it with a heavy fist to the counter, narrowly missing my sacred book, "I mean, what the hell do I *don't* got that some frog got?"

"It's a tough town, even when the "ho's don't want ya." I smiled, realizing I had tapped into his vernacular.

"I hear ya, bro. The bitches in this here town don't want nuttin' to do with ya if you don't have lots of coin in your pocket and if you ain't got no pretty mug."

"I hear ya, man." I think the last time I called a man "man" was in the eighties.

I stretched out my hand to introduce myself. "By the way, my name is Vlad Moranski."

He slowly motioned a hand as hairy as a gorilla's with fingers so large his knuckles had to be World Series championship rings buried under the skin. We shook hands. The pain was excruciating.

"No shit, Sherlock," he said. He laughed again at his line. "I mean, it's here pretty obvious—I sees your name on the goddamn cover."

I winced. "Ya got me again. That's a funny one. Ha-ha!"

"Fuckin' A, fuckin' A." His face turned serious. "Hey, how's about you and me go huntin' for some punani tonight? I knows a great new skin place. She just opened up her slutty doors last week in Pigalle. They got somes ex-Romanian gymnasts that bends sixteen ways to Sundee."

I was abreast of names for a woman's privates, but "punani" had to be something from out-of-town. Mildly perplexed, I said, "Are you talking about finding some ladies?"

"No kiddin'! You're a writer." He picked up my book and flipped through it, and then dropped it on the counter. "Surely you have the word *punani* in your book?"

"Um . . . no. It's not a term we commonly use in Canada, but I think I've heard of it."

"It's a British term Ali G uses for a woman's snatch, her hairy private cave, her home for wayward dongs, knows what I mean?"

"Yes, I think I understand, but I'm not familiar with Ali G."

He burst out laughing. "You're too much, you knows that? We gotta get out real soon." He stuck out his knuckle sandwich, unfolding it into something more giant waffle with a thumb sticking out than a hand. "My name's Clem MacPherson."

We shook hands again. Not good. Pain. And worse, this clown was hipper than me in the hot comedian department. "Clem?! Really?" Suffering immense discomfort—twice—from his toothless Rottweiler grip, why the hell did I question his name?

"Hey, dem's fightin' words where I comes from." His eyes bulged, but a grin soon took over his face. "Just kiddin', Kemo-sahbee."

"Unfortunately, I gotta go. There's still a couple of new bookstores I haven't visited. But I'll pop in again soon."

"Come on back tomorrow around closing time. I'll bring a case of brewskis. We'll get shit-faced, fondle the stripper's fun bags whens the frog bouncers aren't looking, then we'll pay for some whores. I usually just do that by myself, but it would be a fuckin' hoot if you joined me. And you're not a bad looking guy, so I don't mind somes sloppy seconds."

This guy was becoming too creepy even for me. "I have to tell you, this is a bad week," I said, knowing I'd never see him again. "How about you get all of that out of your system and we'll get out for a coffee next week." God that sounded super bogus. *Come on, Vlad, lie!* "Oh, um, I'm writing a book about interesting people I meet in Paris, and I would be privileged to interview you."

"You gots a deal." He wanted to shake hands. Not a chance. "You gots a phone number or somin'?"

"Not yet. I'll just drop in early next week and we'll work something out."

Five blocks down the street, my book bag no lighter, I found the other store. Hanging above the entrance was a red-and-white metal sign in the shape of an open book (again!?) that read, "Berlin Books."

I studied the store before I entered. It was smaller than the other, with only one front window to the right of the entrance. Books bordered on either end by potted plants were arranged in the front window. But they had one thing in common: second-hand. A lost cause. My eyes instinctively shifted, looking down the street, when the front door opened. I lightly rubbed shoulders with a woman who stepped outside, a cigarette, lit, first puff been and gone before I even had a chance to say hello.

"Hello, *bonjour*," she said, inhaling for a second time as she leaned against the storefront window. Holding the door, I turned around and looked at her.

"Walk in." She motioned toward the store with her cigarette. "Browse. I trust you. They're used books. I'll be back inside in a second anyway." Her jet-black hair reflected in the sun each time she turned her head up to exhale. Watching her curls spring off a pair of swimmer's shoulders, ultimately resting on breasts round and frisky, I decided to shut the door and watch her smoke. Though a confirmed non-smoker, there were special cases when I had to let my strong convictions pass.

"I'll wait outside and count how many puffs you take."

"Great use of your time."

"Ah, sarcasm. I enjoy that in a woman who's taken *three* puffs . . . by the way."

She put her foot against the wall and bent her knee. I sensed she wasn't in a hurry to step back inside. "You're pretty good with numbers."

"Oh, I've been around a couple of them in my day. I know how they work. I've been burned by one or two, maybe even three, but I've always survived."

She took another drag. "Are we still talking about numbers?"

"Well . . . sort of. That's four puffs." She sucked up one more drag and flicked the cigarette clear across the street. She smiled again and said thank you as I opened the door for her.

"That was five puffs and I could tell you were a champion croquinole player."

She burst out laughing. "Croquinole! You mean that game where you flick a little round wooden thing closest to the hole in the middle? That's funny! I haven't played it in maybe twenty-five years. My parents owned a cottage on Kennisis Lake and we used to play all the time."

"I just played in my basement . . . in the dark . . . against the rats. Occasionally they let me win." I kept a straight face.

She touched my shoulder and tut-tutted, "Oh, you poor baby."

I smiled back. "I'm surprised you touched me." *Okay Vlad where are you going with this?*

She touched my shoulder again. "You mean like that?"

Our situation, in my over-sexed mind, was moving at lightning speed. Sales tingles were beaten down by hound-dog tingles. My attraction to her undeniable, our courtship rounding all the bases and picking up speed as we headed for home, I waited for the right moment to grab her voluptuous body and make mad, fiery bookstore love to her.

And waited. Her cellphone went off, its ring—a popular Abba or Hubba-bubba hit from the eighties—killed every ounce of lust in my body.

"I have to take this outside." She stepped out, lit another cigarette and talked.

I couldn't make out the words but she was unhappy. A boyfriend? Husband? Disappointed with the interruption, I took one quick scan of her books. She was right—they were all second-hand. I let myself out.

"Wait! Where are you going?" she said, somehow talking on the phone to whoever and me at the same time.

I stopped. "You look kind of busy and besides, I was here to sell a book that I wrote."

She ended her phone conversation and again put her hand on my shoulder, reviving the quivers. Nothing to lose, I took a book out of my bag.

"I love the cover of your book." This time she put her hand on my back.

It felt good whether she was sincere or not. My back was getting horny. Is there an erogenous zone on a man's back?

"Come on back in the store. I only deal with used books, but I'm well connected with some other stores that sell new English books."

"Sure, I'll stay for a couple of minutes. But I have to ask. Was your boyfriend mad that you cut the conversation short for another man?" The boyfriend comment was only a guess, but I had a sixth sense in that department.

"How could you tell it was my boyfriend? Never mind. Don't answer that. I told him I'd call back later. He's the jealous type, which turns me off . . . among other things."

"I can see why. You're very attractive and you're touchy-feely."

She laughed again. "Thanks for the compliment."

"Why did you laugh?"

"I hadn't heard the word *touchy-feely* in a while."

"Do the French have a word for that?"

"I think they do, but it's kind of dirty."

"Go ahead—I think I can handle it."

"I think it's *peloter quelqu'un.*"

There was no hesitation in her voice, and despite me not having a clue what she had just said, my mind turned randy. I pictured her lying on my bed naked in my hotel room, my book in her hand while she read the erotic poem. Her words causing sufficient arousal after only one take, we would perform the dream scenes . . . both of them.

"That sounds kind of dirty," I said, my face screwed up as if I had just bitten into a lemon.

She paused for a second and, although her arms were still at her shapely sides, I pretended they were wrapped around my neck. My mind lost in a slow dance, I wasn't in a hurry to reply. I was dreaming.

"Do you hear what I just said?" she whispered in my ear.

"Don't have a clue." We both laughed heartily that time. "So where was your boyfriend calling from?" She put an index finger on her lips and pouted them although I could tell she would have preferred to smile. Raising her eyelids up and slowly shaking her head from side to side, she took her time answering. A good sign.

Entranced by her eyes (a bluish-green mix reminiscent of the calm waters of the Mediterranean), I pictured us moored in one of its hidden inlets making love on a glass bottom boat, the pimples on my rear for all the fish to see. My brain flashed to the whereabouts of her boyfriend. Taking her sweet time, and me playing along with no hurry to speak, her beau had to be in another city. Thirty delightful seconds later, she still hadn't answered my question. Beautiful. He had to be far away.

"Canada," she answered. My heart pounded. Despite the July 1st fireworks exploding in my head, my ego (growing with a few book sales) forbade me from overreacting.

"You took so long to answer I was beginning to think he was on another planet."

She grinned as she tapped my shoulder. "I was just having a little bit of fun with you. Men always ask me that question and I purposely take my time to answer just to see how they'll react."

Desperately wanting to touch her, I settled for what I hoped was an amorous smile. "You've got the devil in you," I said, meaning it as a compliment.

43

"I think that makes two of us."

"Touché."

A man—old, back hunched, sporting a brown, washed-out trench coat—entered the store, both hands holding a bag of used books. Her hands stayed on her hips as he entered. Good. Her touchy-feelyness had boundaries.

"I can see that you're busy . . . um . . . I guess . . .um—"

"We close at seven. Why don't you come back then with your books? I'm sorry, what's your name again?"

"It's Vlad . . . Vlad Moranski. And yours?"

"Natasha Smith."

"*Enchanté*, Natasha. I'll be back later."

"*Enchanté*, Mr. Moranski."

After lunch and empty-handed (my bag of "bestsellers" needing their beauty sleep), I went for a promenade past St-Michel, along the Seine and on toward the Bastille, trading the roar of traffic from the 6th for the din in the 4th. I settled for the café least likely to be hit by an errant car. Sipping on an overpriced espresso, I leafed through *FUNAC* and found ads for four bookstores selling new English books. I half spread the *Galeries Lafayette* map on the table and marked a Métro station near each of the four stores:

1. BJ Williams: Champs Elysées
2. World Books: St-Germain-des-Prés
3. Giuliani and Sons: Hôtel de Ville
4. Chicago Books and Grill: Place Monge

I ripped out the ads for the English bookshops and placed the magazine on another table. Dreams of Natasha took over my thoughts as I lazed in the Parisian sun, the occasional cloud popping in to guard my unprotected skin.

Too comfortable in my chair, I fell asleep and soon found myself in bed with Natasha. A horn woke me up. Then an endless number of attractive woman paraded by. I got a few smiles. Like my father, I was considered a ladies' man, although my timing was more acceptable. At fifty, a full mop of greyish blonde hair, temples greying, with a face that should have been round given my Polish ancestry, but instead, I got sharp, chiselled angles from my mother's Norwegian side. And despite years of adolescent road and house league hockey goonery, I still had all my teeth and both sky-blue eyes.

The traffic around the monument, normally spinning like a massive metal pinwheel, able to stop on a dime, was at a standstill. A French four-wheeled vehicle, small, cute and cuddly, ran into another French vehicle, its equivalent in cuddliness. A chain reaction ensued. And, given the multitude of tiny vehicles involved, the accident was more bumper cars gone wild than a demolition derby.

The route back to the hotel included several meandering turns. On one such turn I was treated to a perfect reenactment of an event in *French Like Me*.

A gypsy woman stopped directly in front of me and picked up a ring on the ground that *she* had placed sneakily.

"This is good luck, *Monsieur*. Did you lose this ring?" To her credit, her movements were so quick (she reminded me of myself) and nearly unnoticeable that, if I had not remembered Carson's similar encounter, I might have believed that she did randomingly find a ring.

Briefly, I was tempted to grab the ring and walk away, but I assumed plenty of gypsy "back-up" lay waiting around a corner. This activity was widespread and tremendously irritating, but I hadn't done any research in *French Like Me* to determine if Parisian gypsies carried knives, guns or cursed garlic.

"No, it's not mine," I replied.

She stood silent, the man's wedding band resting comfortably on her outstretched sturdy and dirty palm. My skeptical look warped into irritability when she continued to stare at me. And if she looked at me long enough with those pleading and annoying puppy-dog, gypsy eyes, would I claim the ring was mine and give her a reward? And we'd all live happily ever after, right? But that wasn't going to happen because, lady, I was sure you had more money than me.

We simultaneously decided that words were no longer of use and locked into a bizarre gypsy-versus-Canadian staring contest. I counted six warts on her face, none of them forming any well-known constellations. In turn, did she wonder how I got the scar under my right eye? A schoolyard knife fight, honey, my neighbour paying a bigger price.

I amped my stare with an evil grin and for the next minute watched it bounce off her. Was she was made of some kind of tough woman's Romanian Teflon? Fifteen ticks of the clock later, I sensed a potential break in our stalemate when she placed the ring back in her pocket. But she never took her eyes off me! God, this woman was good. Back home, I would have recruited her as a fence.

In a split second, her hand was back, out and open. She had balls to stand there and silently demand money. On the other hand, I had balls too, and had no intention of leaving, because I wasn't trying to rip anyone off—for a change, thoroughly enjoying taking the moral high ground.

After a few irritating minutes, I blinked first. "Listen, lady, I'm going to forget about the scam you're trying to pull on me. But if I ever see you—or any of your accomplices, and I'm sure there are hundreds of them—I have no idea what I will do." I gave a Jack Nicholson in *The Shining* psychotic look to scare the bejesus out of her as I spoke, but this woman was unflinchable. She had ice in her veins and deception in her bones.

The gypsy walked away, her scarved head held high and looking, no doubt, for her next victim. I moved in the opposite direction, unable to resist thinking about how I might try and beat her at her own game if our Parisian paths crossed again. My roots solidly based in con-artistry, how could I resist the challenge? You can take Vlad out of the gutter, but can you take the gutter out of Vlad?

I showered for the second time that day, threw on some cologne, and rushed out of the hotel, leaving myself a quarter of an hour to walk to Berlin Books. Near seven o'clock, I turned the door handle of Natasha's store. It was locked. A heavy knock turned the heads of bystanders. Four or five useless attempts later, I shifted my 190 pounds of sexual frustration to the right side of the front door. I cupped my hands around my eyes to block out the sun's tormenting glare and peered through the glass. No life inside. Tossing a few choice swear words, I knocked again. No reply. An evening breeze shook the sign above my head. And despite the sun blinding my eyes, I looked up. The hanging bastard continued to squeak.

Staring at the sun too long made me hallucinate. I lunged at the giant metal book, hoping to slap it. No luck. Not only did the book resemble a basketball backboard, it was also regulation height: ten feet. Worn out from trying to rap the sign, I looked for a rock or a plastic bottle, anything to inflict some pain. The sign continued to bait me with its mocking creaks.

Defeated, thighs exhausted from several useless leaps, I sat on the curb for a few minutes, planning my next move. I spotted a crushed plastic Perrier bottle—kind of symbolic of my feelings at that moment. I picked it up and hurled it in a grenade motion at the sign. The green bottle moved in the shape of a parabola. On target, but owing to its dehydrated state, it caught in a wind pattern and floated over the sign. My confidence was rattled by an inability to inflict pain on this metal prick. My eyes burned and, thoughts of undressing Natasha long gone, I dropped my shoulders and turned my dizzy body around at a snail's pace. "Goddamn sign," I yelled, and with no particular direction in mind, I tottered.

A few steps from the store, someone tapped my shoulder from behind.

"Your aim is way off," Natasha said, her warm smile and soft voice indicating I was more silly than dangerous.

I turned around and hugged her spontaneously. The muscles in her back tightened at first, tiny knots abounding, soon relaxing as if she was being massaged on the street, which she was. I forgot that I had unabashedly lost control with an inanimate object and whispered in her ear, "Did you know I'm a *massage*-onist?"

She broke my hug, though her hands delightfully found their way to my waist. "That's a funny play on words. Did you just think of that?"

"Yes, as a matter of fact I just did."

Her eyes rapidly shifted, scanning my whole body. With a look of surprise she said, "Where's your book?"

"Damn, I was thinking about you before I left the hotel and completely forgot about it."

"That's okay," she said. "Maybe you could get it later."

"Of course."

"Well, *Mister Moranski*, are you going to take me out for a drink?"

Sounding sincere I replied. "I would love to take a gorgeous woman out for a drink, but wouldn't that bother your boyfriend?"

She grabbed my hand and whacked my hip with it. "Hey . . . what happens in Paris stays in Paris. And you're not too bad looking yourself."

"I have been compared to a fifty-year-old Mel Gibson."

"I hope that's without Mel's renowned alcohol and racial problems."

"None of the above." I paused for a second, thinking, *Nastasha, I do have other problems: no money, number one; a lifetime of lying a close second; a thief and card player coming third and a profound inability to handle rejection rounding out my "top" four.* And despite knowing I had to hide the "Vlad, my bad" side from her, would she find out sooner or later? And, more importantly, what would she do? *Vlad, you just met this woman. Give your brain a rest. Say something to her!*

"I couldn't agree more with your Paris line, but, Natasha, I have to ask, why weren't you in the store when I arrived? I was there before seven o'clock."

She let go of my hand. "I was bored, so I closed up shop early and wandered around for a while—basically to kill some time, smoke a cigarette, before you got here. When I noticed you were trying to slap the sign silly, I hid around the corner and spied on you. It wasn't easy NOT laughing out loud. You put on quite a spectacle."

"Natasha, hold that thought." I grabbed her hand and scurried across a busy intersection leading us into the Luxembourg Gardens. Panting a little, I replied, "Well, I'm glad you were able to laugh at my expense because it wasn't a shining moment. And one other thing—don't worry; I'm not a violent person. As you noticed, I only take my aggression out on signs and most of them I never hit anyway. I'm definitely a lover and not a fighter."

We stopped to admire a fountain in the gardens.

"I love the shape of the two naked bodies sculpted in marble," Natasha said. "Their muscly curves turn me on. And then you have Zeus or Poseidon peering over them and hoping for a threesome."

"You can use up one of your lifelines and phone a female friend to join us."

"Hilarious!"

We followed a tight path running alongside a long, narrow basin inhabited by ducks and fish. About five metres from the marble statue, I abruptly planted my feet on the cinders. Natasha was quite happy to bump into me.

"Natasha this is so cool. I recognize this sculpture, yet I've never been here. Hell, I've written about it. It's in my book."

"You mean the book you were supposed to bring." She pointed a scolding finger at me. A scolding finger that turned me on.

"Um, yes. The book I was supposed to bring." My eyes flashed in every direction, meshing my written words with the scenery. The statue, the chairs, the ducks, the leaves, everything was exactly as Carson had described it, though his prose couldn't reflect how he thought or felt. But my words were on another level. Admittedly, I'd been having a competition problem with my brother and seriously losing for years.

She lightly tapped my back. "Well, tell me what you wrote."

"The protagonist has an erotic dream. He was sitting on a chair right here." I dramatically placed my hand on a chair in front of us. Natasha sat down and I stood behind her, my hands gently rubbing her shoulders. She slowly nestled the back of her head on my crotch. I placed my hands around her neck, my thumbs gently rubbing her cheeks and planted an upside down kiss. Despite her closed eyes, she had no problem wrapping her arms around my neck. Her tongue was on a mission to count the number of fillings in my mouth, my hands determining her bra size. The phrase "her cup runneth over" came to mind.

Coming up for air like the two oversized koi swimming nearby, I said, "Would you be interested in checking out my hotel and taking a look at my…um…book?"

She took her sweet time standing up. Still not speaking—still no need to speak—she put her hands on my shoulders and gave me a bonus peck on the cheek. Her warm breath moving from my cheek to one perky, horny ear, she whispered, "Yes, I can do that."

I burst out laughing, which led to a stare so cold I thought she could have frozen the water.

"You're laughing hysterically at me accepting an invitation to your hotel. Gee, thanks!"

"Sorry, Natasha. I laughed uncontrollably because you used the exact same line as the protagonist in my book used when a woman, in his dreams, asked if he wanted to make love to her."

She grinned and grabbed me with both hands. "I'm sorry. I guess I overreacted. She broke our hug, and put her thumb and index finger on my chin. "I have to read your book. Are there any other erotic passages?"

"Yes, there's a dirty poem."

"That's a good start," she said. "How about I read it to you when we get to your hotel?"

"Are you a captivating reader?"

"I'll be able to keep your attention."

I negotiated the quickest route back to the hotel, eight blocks of holding hands, strolling, laughing, dancing, ambling and grabbing asses.

With Natasha wrapped around me as tightly as a Fajita on some choice slices of beef, I asked for my key at the front desk. The night clerk leered a little too long at Natasha before giving up the key. Although his facial expression said, "I can take her off your hands," he settled for a polite "good evening."

I ran up the stairs, my clacking sandals spinning at roadrunner speed. Natasha, my sexy coyote, followed, laughing. Dangling from my hand was the key chain. It weighed a kilo and warned anyone on our floor of the presence of a couple of horny toad varmints. While I was fumbling with the key, Natasha pinned me against the door and kissed me so hard I dropped the key chain on an exposed big toe. I wanted to scream, but thanks to an overpowering will to have sex with this voluptuous dark-haired woman, I mentally transferred the throbbing from my big blue toe to my big red Johnson.

I clicked the door open. We tumbled into the room and fell onto the bed. My arms slid free and tugged at her sweater. I removed it, exposing a purple lace bra caging two mangoes, bouncing and seeking day parole. By this time, every tiny tingle in my body had been ordered to support my enlarged tinkle.

"God, Natasha, your mang—I mean breasts—are beautiful." I shut the door and dived back into bed.

After she had successfully unbuttoned my shirt, a graying shag carpet revealed, she laughed, unable to concentrate on the task at hand—undoing my belt. Watching her breasts jiggle in time with her laughter temporarily helped me forget about her unfinished business.

"Were you going to say mangoes?" She placed an elbow on each side of me, eventually resting them on the sheet and lightly touching the sides of my chest. With her hands on my shoulders, she slowly rubbed her accoutrements against my chest. She was on all fours, her tanned broad shoulders low and back arched, permitting a full spectacular view of a set of buttocks ripe for a squeeze, a kiss or a spanking. Although enamored by the curvature of her McDonald's arches derriere in the near background, I focused my attention on undoing the technology holding her bra straps together. Kissing her wildly, I guided both hands around her ripe fruit garden, carefully arranged in matching cornucopias, and proceeded to feel my way around the back of her bra. Along the tactile journey, the bumps and grooves of the lace reminded me of the days I was trying to learn Braille to bed a blind woman.

My fingers continued their journey, studying the cleverly spaced ridges and hollows of the lace along the way. Soon it was obvious what the lace was saying. And if I remembered my Braille correctly, it was, "I want to get laid."

I touched something claspish. With space in this region severely limited, three fingers on each hand gave way to the thumbs and index fingers. The "four surgeons," as they were affectionately called, had won several prestigious dexterity awards back home. However, I struggled with this enigmatic clasp, unsuccessful seconds mounting. Unfamiliar with the tiny French mechanical arrangement or these "bells and

—

50

whistles" as we say before humping, I silently cursed myself for having forgotten my remote control universal bra opener.

I felt two hands lightly slap my fingers away. "Vlad, have you never undone a bra clasp before?"

"That's the cruelest thing a woman has ever said to me." Mock tears followed. She sat up and undid the clasp in a nanosecond and tossed her bra into the air. I imagined the two excessively large cups forming twin parachutes. The bra safely landed, I shifted my attention to two round, plump horns of plenty, candy cherry nibs for nipples. I hinged my grateful lips to one of her magnanimous mammaries.

While I was busy bonding, Natasha made a second attempt at unbuckling my belt and unzipping my pup tent. She needed two free hands to do the job properly, shifting her body backwards, creating a "pop" sound when her nipple popped out of my mouth. I wanted to wail.

"Natasha, where are you going?"

She ran her hands down my coiled chest, imaginary sparks flying, and said, "Don't worry. I think you'll figure it out soon enough."

I smiled. My hands propped my head up so I could see over my still-covered mannschaft. (And we're not talking the German national soccer team here.) She had pulled my pants off and was heading back, first kissing my thighs before reaching for my underwear, which by this time had morphed into a tent comfortably sleeping eight adults.

She slid my gotchies off and tossed them aside. However, the underwear went into Frisbee mode and sailed out the open window. Thinking it an inappropriate time, I chose not to scold her. I grinned, imagining some Frenchie on the sidewalk below wearing an underwear beret.

After nibbling on my McBulge, she guided her tongue toward my McNuggets. I had to flip her around rapidly or my Happy Meal would have been finished in unsatisfyingly record time. With little effort, I got on top, soon enjoying running my lips (surprisingly plump for a guy), beginning with her sumptuous mouth, on past her mountain range, and camped my Range Rover tongue in her San Andreas Fault. Her hands stroked my head in appreciation. It was time for McBulge to do some canyoning. Pumping in and out with the rhythm and speed of one of those oil-pumping machines on a Texas oil field, my manpump flooded her canyon with a giant white tsunami seldom before seen or felt. Natasha responded, calmly saying my name seconds after the tsunami busted through her V-shaped Hoover Dam.

—

Tired and satiated, I looked at the clock before customarily lying beside a woman who had become my orgasm friend. And thank God she was quick because only ten minutes had passed. Looking at the ceiling, sleep my only thought, I had to think of something intelligent to say to remove the sudden quiet awkwardness. I leaned over and lightly slapped her on the thigh.

"Natasha, You flung my underwear out the window!"

She laughed and ran her fingers through my chest hair. "You're kidding! Honestly, I didn't realize I did that."

I jumped out of bed.

Eyeing my limp noodle, she said, "What are you doing?"

"I think it was the one with Homer Simpson on the ass."

"Oh, so you're a Simpsons fan?"

"Homer is my hero."

"Wow, that's impressive."

I noted a slight lilt of sarcasm in her voice. My hands on the windowsill, my naked buttinski visible only in the room, I shifted my eyes lizard-like, looking for Homer's huge, round, bald head. "Natasha, come quick before it blows away." Excitedly, I pointed to a tree below. "My underwear fell on top of the shrub. It's now the star on top of a Christmas tree."

Natasha ran to the window, her breasts jiggling up and down. She placed one hand over my shoulder and the other around my waist, rubbing her endowments against my back. I don't recall Marge ever doing that to Homer.

"You're right. I noticed Homer's happy face on your underwear when I took them off."

"I think you got *him* horn-dogged as well." She gave me a slap on my arse. I took one last look outside and hurriedly put on my pants.

"What are you doing, Vlad?"

"This is crazy, but I only have five pairs of underwear to my name. I gotta go outside and rescue Homer."

Natasha leaned her perfect hot-cross buns on the windowsill, arms folded. "Don't bother going outside. I'll buy you some new underwear."

My hand was on the doorknob. "Hey, what can I say? Homer's underwear and I are inseparable." She stood speechless. I stood with speech. "I'll only be a second. Promise me you won't leave. And I'd love to have dinner with you tonight as long as it's not too expensive." *Five pairs of underwear to your name! Inexpensive dinner! Christ, Vlad, shut up about not having money. Let her figure it out if she wants to. Don't give it away!*

"Don't worry. I'll be here when you get back."

"You can watch from the window. Just put some clothes on, ya tart."

After pointing at the various prepared dishes behind the front glass counter of the Vietnamese restaurant, we both settled for curried rice, three egg rolls and spicy lemon chicken. While ordering, Natasha's eyes bounced between the waiter and my book, continually flipping from front cover to back and randomly choosing a line or a paragraph and scanning it, her grin her acceptance, and then fanning the pages looking for more witticisms or Vladicisms. My hand on her shoulder and about to slow down this paper-spinning whirl-a-gig, I said, "Natasha, I'm thrilled that you're interested in my book, but compared to a Henry Miller's novel where it makes little difference where you begin reading . . ." I paused and with my big mitts gently caressed her fingers, eventually convincing them to locate the first paragraph. "There we go," I said with playful sarcasm. "*My* book, on the other hand, is even *more* fulfilling if you start at the beginning."

"Gee, I'll have to remember that." She kissed me on the cheek, which turned me on as much as her sarcasm.

After we sat down, I poured two glasses of water and ran my finger over each drawing and photograph on the cover of the book, explaining the significance of each.

"It's quite a coincidence, Vlad, but the woman on your cover bares quite a resemblance to me."

"Gee you've got a high opinion of yourself," I said, armed with a smile to make sure she knew I was pulling her leg.

"Well, she has dark, shoulder-length hair. And she looks a little busty." She paused and made sure I was staring at her seductive eyes. She slowly arched her back, accentuating her chest.

"Are you sure you're not auditioning for a Russ Meyers movie?"

She quipped. "Who's Russ Meyers?"

"He made those big-breasted 'women who kill' movies in the sixties."

"Something tells me you had a little too much spare time when you were growing up."

"Growing up? Hell I watched one of them the day before I flew

---

53

over. A buddy of mine has the whole collection." A surprisingly quick lie, as I had no close friends and didn't own a DVD player. And of course nothing would be said about the state of my Toronto apartment. I was having so much fun with her that I'd momentarily forgotten my reason for being in Paris.

"Great—your friends are weird, too," replied Natasha.

Pretending I was mad, I screwed up my face and replied, "Say what you want about me, but I draw the line when you make fun of my friends." At this point, the food arrived, saving Natasha from needing to respond.

We dug in with our chopsticks; however, after two minutes of holding my sticks like a gorilla, I had to ask for a fork. The last piece jammed down my throat, I came up for air. "Don't ask me why, but I'm going to ruin this evening by asking about your boyfriend. Judging by the fact that we've already been intimate and we're having dinner together, I don't think you and your beau are joined at the hip as they say."

In no hurry to answer, she took her time balancing a dollop of rice on her multitalented chopsticks. The yellowy glob firmly glued on her "sticks," she turned her attention to me. Despite my limited insight toward the thought process of the opposite sex, Natasha was pretty easy to read. Gently shifting her head from side to side and occasionally raising her eyebrows, she was clearly forming her response: one that would please me. She impressed me with her ability to reply either with rapid-fire quips or carefully constructed sentences, unlike me, who jumped into a conversation, words ablazing. The war euphemism "friendly fire" had its origins in my big mouth.

"I'm just waiting for the right opportunity to end our relationship," she said.

Exploding on the inside, stoic on the outside, I gently put my fork down on my plate. "Interesting," Even though I had visions of round two with her in my hotel, I pretended I was in deep thought. "Tell me about it."

She swallowed the rice in one gulp, and searched for a piece of chicken. "My boyfriend's been promising for two months to visit me, but he keeps mentioning that he can't get away from work."

Well, is she going to dump him or not? And what about her unpleasant phone call with the guy? "What does he do?"

"He's a stockbroker."

"You're kidding. Making the big bucks?"

"Yes, but his money isn't important. My parents took care of me in their will, so I'm not dependent at all on my boyfriend's means. I'm more in *love* with Paris than with him. We did talk about getting married at one time, but he doesn't want to live in Paris and I don't want to move back to Toronto."

Natasha's tone had changed when she said the word *love*. She was nervous. I just met this woman, but I had the feeling she wasn't telling me everything about her boyfriend. And who talks about dumping someone one minute, then possibly getting married the next? She put her chopsticks down and took a sip of water. Not sure what to say, I just stared at her.

"Concerning my bookstore, it's taken me ten years to break through all the French bureaucratic red tape. I'm never going to be rich, but with my parent's inheritance and the proceeds from my bookstore, I should be able to eat in this restaurant whenever I want."

"Wow—at six euros a plate, you're livin' the high life."

She stabbed my wrist again. I'm glad she wasn't eating with a fork. "That's about all I want to reveal about my life story for now." She pinned her last eggroll between her chopsticks with ease and guided half of it into her mouth. My fork scoured through the rice, madly searching for the last deserted morsel of chicken.

We left a small tip and headed toward an Italian ice cream shop a few blocks from the Panthéon. We crossed Rue Soufflot, the sun still painting the buildings a brilliant orange, the Eiffel Tower appearing to poke its top through the trees in the Luxembourg Gardens. Both gifted with long legs, we zipped through the Parisian traffic. One foot on the curb, I gave Natasha a kiss reminiscent of the one in the famous Robert Doisneaux photo, a spontaneous looking smooch by a French couple in the forties. At the ice cream shop, the lineup outside and ten deep, I gave Natasha another peck, this time on the cheek, though she had grabbed a cigarette, her first since leaving the hotel.

"Vlad, do you mind if I smoke?"

"No, it's not a problem."

To her credit, she only took four puffs and did her usual "flick-job," arcing her half-smoked cigarette cleanly over a parked bus. We leaned against each other, hips swaying with the beat of the ice cream cooler, touching each other's flesh made warm by the sun, and generally looking and acting over-couple-ly if that was possible in Paris. We were oblivious to the slow-moving line. I wrapped one arm around Natasha's shoulder and pointed my free hand toward the gardens.

"Natasha, look at the Eiffel Tower. Do you see the top? It's just a big metal tree fort in the Luxembourg Gardens, no?" The other anglophones in the line, dreams of double chocolate ice cream dancing in their heads, glanced toward the tower and snickered.

She stared at the brown metal icon as if for the first time. Although I was anxious to hear her response and generally considered a good listener, my mind became distracted. Someone had just brushed by me who reminded me of one the losers in my last Toronto card game. Again?! Was it the same person in less than twenty-four hours? Christ, did they think I stole something else? They got all of their money back *and* trashed my place. Wasn't that enough? I told Natasha that I recognized someone and would be right back. Would she think I was giving her the brush-off?

Fifty metres down the street, I saw his face without him noticing me. It wasn't the card player, although he resembled an older version of someone I knew---me!. Whoever it was it still unnerved me.

My breath a little heavy after jogging back, I said to Natasha, "I remember some tree forts I built with my brother near our house."

Natasha stared at me. "Vlad! You just took off and didn't say where you were going. And now you're talking about tree forts?!"

"It wasn't a big deal. I just thought I recognized someone." I smiled, although I was picturing those Toronto card players on every Parisian street corner. And were their hired hands around to finish the job? I needed a stiff drink rather than a soft ice cream.

Natasha touched my arm, a mother's caress. "Are you okay?"

I kissed her on the cheek. "Of course. What was I saying?"

"You've forgotten? Are you sure you're okay?"

"I hate to admit it, but I do occasionally forget my train of thought." Another lie.

"You were talking about tree forts."

"Oh yes, tree forts. I remember my brother, Carson—"

Natasha interrupted. "Is that the same Carson as in the book?"

"Yes, I have kind of a *complicated* relationship with my brother. How about I just tell you some fun stuff he and I did when we were young and foolish?"

"Love the fun stuff. That's what I want to hear!"

"My brother and I would go to a local dump and auto wreckers and

---

steal anything not nailed down. Obviously the dump was fair game—they were happy that my brother and I and a million others were depleting their stock—but at the auto wreckers we had to be far more careful. My extravagant taste in car parts made each theft more delicate than the last. I suppose this was where I truly found my gift for planning. Occas—"

Natasha gave me a light jab to my stomach and said, "Great—I'm hanging out with a car-parts thief!"

My eyes fell on the ice cream display. "God, Natasha, these stacks of ice cream are piled high enough that a five-year-old could learn to ski on them. Well, little Natasha, fancy a ski on Chocolate Chip Mountain today or maybe snowboard down Brownie Alps?"

She spat some laughter, then kissed and sucked on my neck. I'd check later for a purple miniature croissant-sized hickey.

"Oh, Daddy," she said in a bubbly, child's voice. "I would love to ski on Peppermint Peak." She pointed to the untouched mound of vanilla sprinkled with cinnamon. "Oh no, Daddy, I want to ski the virgin vanilla powder." Rarely had a woman been as able to embarrass me in public and turn me on at the same time. Oblivious to the pedestrians, we nonchalantly strolled toward St-Michel, making goo-goo eyes as we licked our ice cream.

Waiting for a light to turn green, she spontaneously put her ice-cold fingers on my neck.

"Eyyyy," I yelled." What was that for?"

"That's what you get for stealing car parts. I can never trust you in my store again."

She was kidding, but selling used books, her cash register presumably often dry, she didn't have to worry about me stealing anything in her store. Worse, I was disappointed that I would even think about what was "available" in this amazing woman's store. *Change, Vlad. You have to change.*

The sun's rays followed us in a last desperate attempt to light our path toward the St-Michel fountain. After a kiss by the water, we grabbed each other's hands and held on for dear life, bravely dodging four lanes of buses, cars and motorcycles. Despite the symphony of French horns, we made it to the other side and found a crowd surrounding some dancers. There were eight in total, broad shoulders and torsos so rippled that the young women in the crowd must have imagined running their fingers across them while the blue-haired old ladies, might have dreamt of washing their clothes on their washboard stomachs. Forming four rows of two, each pair took turns doing variations of the worm, combined with spins balancing on two hands, one or none.

In front of Notre Dame, we sat on a brick ledge bordering a prickly field of shrubs. South of our spot sat a handful of North Africans frantically waving their golden-skinned hands as they spoke and occasionally spilling their bottled Heinekens. They had carefully nestled three or four boxes in the bushes.

Natasha shuffled through her purse. "Vlad, do you mind if I smoke?"

"Of course not."

She lit up her cigarette, took one mega-drag and blew away from me, then nuzzled her dark mane into my neck. "You have to tell me more about your car-part stealing days. I lived in the Annex and there were no auto wreckers in the area, so *I* wasn't prone to stealing bumpers."

"Once upon a time, a young adolescent had a typical interest in cars and larceny. Back then, *and* today, people marked their individuality with tattoos, but we were of course too young and too afraid to get one. Instead, we sought uniqueness through decorating our tree forts. We lived in an area where trees were as abundant as black flies, and it was pretty easy to claim a tree for your own. I was a trendsetter in my neck of the woods, and my tree house even had chrome wing-tips from an early sixties Chevy, I believe. They were placed on the ends of each step leading up to the tree house. And my place was carpeted with a deep-red shag ripped out of a special edition Mercedes coupe. I waited six months for that model to come in."

She took another drag from her cigarette. "How could you possibly know what they had in stock?"

"I remember walking into the auto wreckers and pretending I was doing a project for shop class. I was in grade seven at the time, and all we ever made were wooden candlestick holders. I asked for a tour of the yard. And living nearby, I had a good sense when they weren't busy. With a clipboard in hand and looking surprisingly studious, I kept detailed notes of where everything was. I went in the front door occasionally and in the back door weekly." A few police sirens on the street caught my attention.

"Those cop cars aren't after you, are they?"

"Funny stuff." I gave Natasha a kiss and continued. "Each time I strolled into the front office, I was amazed by the grease. Greasy car parts and greasy car manuals occupied every square inch of the floor. I think even the grease had grease on it. I always wanted to make a joke about a wrecked oil tanker washing up on the shores of this store and not a single employee would have noticed." Natasha laughed.

I told her that an old retired guy would proudly take me around the dump and show me the latest smashed-up luxury car they'd towed in, its precious pieces only good for parts transplants and decorating tree forts. I even took inventory of the parts I would eventually steal.

After a fourth pull, Natasha flicked her cigarette. It landed somewhere near Poland. She moved sideways, her thin waist and long legs stretched comfortably along the ledge, leaning her head and back on my chest.

With one arm comfortably around her chest, I continued my story. "When my friends wanted to enter my tree house they had to tell me the secret password."

"Which was?"

"Dildo!"

Her spontaneous chortling was drowned out by the Cathedral's late evening bells. "There's no way that was your secret password."

"That *was* the password. Scout's honour. Remember, I was twelve or thirteen and stealing everything in sight. Also, some of us had reached puberty, so it was natural to use names related to anything about sex."

"I have to ask—what were some of the others?"

"Tallywhacker, biggusdickus, pearl necklace, twat-did-you-say?, snatchmagoo, cumquat, her-vagina-is-myna, cu—"

"Okay I get it. You were all horny little wankers."

I leaned over and kissed her forehead. "And nothing's changed."

Her back and shoulders gently bounced off my chest as she laughed. She slapped my thigh. "Vlad, continue your car-part stealing stories, pah-leeze."

"Well, word spread pretty quickly around the neighbourhood about the décor in my tree house. Soon, other kids asked me to steal some parts for them. Because they had measly paper routes earning five dollars a week they could only afford hubcaps, licence plates, mirrors and the odd headlight. You know boring stuff. But I always made major coin the day after their birthdays."

"What do you mean?"

"What does one normally receive on one's birthday? I'll give you a hint. It's green in the U.S."

She pursed her lips and gushed out some air. "Money."

"In my first year of "the business," there was only one guard dog, but unfortunately the vicious bugger wasn't on a leash."

The lights in the square flickered out. The streetlights sparkling on the Seine kept the area reasonably lit. Natasha yawned as I continued.

"During my walks around the lot, I carefully noted how high cars or large metal bins for storing parts were stacked and how close they were to the wall. Often, I would push the stack of cars to check the sturdiness of the mass of metal. The old guy always thought it was hilarious that a young goofball was trying to push over tons of metal. Then, while he and the other employees weren't looking, I'd throw a green spray-painted rock over the four metre–high metal corrugated walls, hoping it wouldn't land too far away on the other side."

"Why would you do that?"

"The junkyard was the size of a park and I didn't want to be banging a ladder against a metal wall all night trying to decide the best place to climb. The rock gave me a rough idea of where to put the ladder on the other side. I always had three options of where to climb. A green rock meant easy going, a yellow rock represented a slightly unsteady pile to climb down from and a red rock, which I never had to do, even the Wallenda brothers would have had problems negotiating."

"Ah, yes, the traffic light system put to *great* use. And what about the dog?"

"Well, I threw a huge steak with a dash of sleeping tranquilizer sprinkled in. Got the idea from a movie believe-it-or-not."

She slapped her thigh. "How did you possibly get those kind of drugs?"

"That was easy. My buddy's dad was a vet, so he and I had access to some great drugs."

"Where were your parents when you were doing this stuff?"

"My dad left during the seventh inning of a baseball game, after I gave up a two-run homer that cost our team the championship. And I never saw him again. At thirteen I shouldn't have been throwing curve balls. It was all my fault." *Did that just come out of mouth?*

Natasha slapped my back (I assumed because she thought I was full of shit). "Come on. Were you that bad on the mound?"

"Ha-ha! Anyway, my dad did leave us when I was young, but my mom refused to ever talk about it. Maybe she thought he was going to come back, but he never did."

Having ruined the rom-com mood, I finished the dog and drugged-steak story to avoid talking about my father. Natasha, probably having had a mountain of family problems herself, decided not to press the issue. To keep the moment light, she did ask how I made money from this venture.

"I maintained a healthy parts inventory in an abandoned printing warehouse that still had old equipment lying around. I could have left my stolen goods out in the open because no one ever came in there, but just to be safe I hid them in a corner and covered it with a canvas tarpaulin that blended in with the décor."

"I have to give you credit. You were quite an enterprising young man."

"Thanks. To make the bucks, I would show all interested parties a list of my current stock and a list of what I was willing to steal. Occasionally, if someone wanted something unique, then I charged a lot more money. Hey, I bought my brother and mother amazing birthday and Christmas presents and food was plent—" I stopped myself, realizing that maybe my "other side of the tracks" upbringing was beginning to show. *Who even talks about food being plentiful? Well, in my home it was because I often bought it.*

"Vlad, you didn't finish your sentence. Something about food?"

"It was nothing. Anyway, I've got a great ending to this story."

"So how many times did you steal parts?"

"Twenty, thirty . . . I no longer remember."

"You're kidding! And you never got caught?"

"Never."

"What made you quit?"

"Parents of the boys that bought my parts."

"Wow, so one of them got you in trouble."

"Not quite. They wanted parts as well."

Natasha hooted and slapped my thigh at the same time. I'm not sure which reaction I enjoyed more. Grinning from ear to ear, she said, "You writers are all the same! Forever bullshitting!"

"I kid you not. *Bah-lieve me*, this story is only a warm-up." Then it hit me—did I want to continue telling her that I'd become nothing more than a high-stakes poker player and a gentlemen thief? And besides, gentleman thieves generally don't tell others, especially women they've just slept with, that they steal for a living. Vlad, you have to convince this woman that you're a writer and nothing else.

Natasha grabbed my hands and stood up, her diamond earrings

glimmering as they caught a streetlight's glare.

I smiled, thinking about the time I stole a similar pair for a client years ago. His wife got them among many other things in the divorce, and he wanted them back. "Natasha, I have to ask. Those diamond earrings of yours are gorgeous. They must be worth a fortune."

"You're not going to steal them, are you?" She smiled as she said it.

"Hey, I'm a writer, not a thief." I hoped I sounded convincing.

"They were my mothers, and yes, they're worth a lot."

Silently, but contentedly, hand in swaying hand, we watched the moon playing peek-a-boo with the buildings as we moved on the wide sidewalks toward her apartment. Soon, yawning as often as we passed by a green lamppost, we decided to save round two for another night. At her apartment, we passionately kissed, hugged, and reminded each other ten times that we would meet the next day at her closing time. And what were those diamond earrings worth?

Saturday, June 23rd

Up early, I washed my face and headed for the complementary continental breakfast. My half-baguette and buttery croissant reduced to crumbs and my morning off to a perfect start, I opened my *Galeries Lafayette* map of Paris and planned to visit BJ Williams bookstore near the Champs-Elysées and World Books in the 6th *arrondissement*.

As I crossed a wooden pedestrian bridge, a cool gust of air whipping along the Seine smacked my face with enough force to shift my body without my consent. Then it happened for the second time: a gypsy appeared, a different woman this time—yet they wore holes in their sweaters, scarves, skirts, nylons, and shoes like matching badges of pick-pocket honour—and a seasoned veteran at the ring con game.

"This is good luck, mister. I've found a ring that I think you dropped." And not a word in French—she'd had me sized up fourteen gales ago. She caught me off guard and, if I'd had any thoughts about trying to out-scam these sneaky thieves they blew away with the breeze. It was the second scam in two days, and I'd lost any sense of humour to diffuse the situation.

My eyes narrowed and my mouth readied for a tornado of obscenities. With little thought, I thrust my middle finger in her face. Her visage—its size, shape and surprising amount of facial hair made her look remarkably similar to a coconut—remained expressionless. Not even a blink.

"Do you see this finger? There's no wedding band on it because I've never been married." I paused for a second, realizing that I was showing her the wrong finger, but I had to be dramatic. "Also, that ring is so large I don't think it would even fit Wilt Chamberlain's finger, his knob maybe!"

After some tense seconds, she grumbled something I assumed was in Romani. I pointed a menacing index finger at her, the irregular bump on my knuckle looking particularly threatening, and replied with what I thought she had said to me, "Get lost."

She hobbled away. Unable to unclench my neck muscles, I went in search of a cop. I found one near my hotel and explained what had happened. His response was short and to the point. "They want money. Don't get involved."

I calmed down. Why? I was only a few wrong moves away from becoming her: an unsettling reminder of nothing good in my past.

The BJ Williams bookstore had two giant wooden and gold-plated doors. It was so heavy I had to think about things like "leverage" to move it.

A woman wearing a flowery dress was alone at one of the cash registers. I strolled up to her and drew my book from my bag.

The cashier widened her eyes as she peered at the cover. "Hello, can I help you with anything?"

"Yes. I have before you the funniest book you'll read this summer."

"Ohh-kay."

"I'm dead serious. After only three pages, I can guarantee you'll know exactly where your funny bone is." I raised my right foot, making sure it was in her line of sight. "And I can guarantee you your funny bone isn't here."

Her eyes shifted from side to side. The other customers and the cashier at the other till were chuckling.

I continued my routine. "I'm following in the literary path of Morgan Davis. I'm his Canadian apostle. I assume you're cognizant of his collection of calamitous clauses?" My rare attempt at alliteration aside, posing a question so early in my sales pitch was risky. *Remember, Vlad, always control the conversation.*

She paused for a second. "Morgan Davis is world famous. My god his volumes are to die for. People camp out all night each time one of his new books is released. He comes in occasionally to sign overstocked

---

63

books and chat with the customers. I even fetched him a Lipton green tea once."

"Wow, I never pictured Morgan Davis drinking *green* tea. That's crazy talk."

"I remember Morgan walking into the store seven or eight years ago to peddle his book. He was so charming and witty and *humble*. All of the ladies working in the store, including me, instantly fell in love with those mutton-chop sideburns of h—"

I cut her off. "I believe I'm Canada's answer to *your* Morgan Davis." She looked confused. "What I mean to say is that Morgan Davis is, if you'll pardon the expression, a "smartass." He has a sixth sense about understanding the good, the bad, and the ugly of the French." I was starting to remember more things Carson had said about Davis.

"Yes, he does have an inoffensive way of . . ." she trailed off for a second, deep in thought. And this wasn't the first time I had experienced this "pause in the action." I was sensing that *every* bookstore vendor in Paris was forever searching for the perfect word. Her mouth revved up again. "Yes, he does have an inoffensive way … of offending the French."

It was the right moment to hand her my book. I looked at her straight in the eyes and said, "Well, I think *you* have another Morgan Davis on your hands. (I even pointed to her and winked.) Wouldn't you love to say that you started not only Morgan Davis's career, but mine as well?"

I think she wanted to speak, but only sputtered air. She placed my book on her chest. "Oh, I wouldn't dare take all the responsibility for Mr. Davis's success." The woman had gone into putty-in-your-hands mode.

"Hey, put credit where credit is due. I'm sure you had a lot of influence over his career."

"Do you think so?"

"Oh I *know* so." I didn't have a clue.

She smiled as she studied the cover of my book. "The woman on your cover is attractive."

"Yes, eventually she plays an important role in the book. The last long chapter is devoted to a very humorous evening with her and the protagonist. He's married . . . to someone else!" I stopped for a second and looked at her with dreamy eyes. "And in all honesty, I see *you* in her. When you read the book, and I *know* that you will, you'll find that it is through this woman we see that the protagonist's true love is the city of

---

Paris."

"Cool!" She turned the book over and grinned as she read the back. "Sounds funny."

"Thank you. I've already sold five to the Albany Bookshop in the fifth, and Shakespeare and Company is taking ten books on conscription—sorry, I mean consignment."

"I'm definitely interested in your book, but I have to call Veronica, our distribution manager."

I felt a chill, my spidey-sense no longer sending out positive vibes. Veronica soon appeared at the top of the stairs. She walked down the steps, a cold North Sea wind accompanying her arrival. This woman hadn't smiled since the falling of the Berlin Wall. Bright-eyed and "Guy Smiley," I stuck out my hand, hers feeling like a willow branch coated in the season's first snowfall.

"Hi, I'm Vlad Moranski."

"Hello, my name is Veronica Weatherspoon." The cashier handed my book to Veronica, who perused its contents in a tenth of a second. No reaction. She turned the book to the first page, with the copyright and printing details.

"I'm not familiar with Willowbrook Press. Are they a new publisher in Canada?"

My first thought was to continue my charade and tell this woman that Willowbrook Press was an avant-garde publisher interested in promoting daring, new writers, though she could Google me to death to prove I was a liar.

"No, Willowbrook Press is a name that I created. My book was self-published." Christ, why not toss in that I was up for the Man Booker just for shits and giggles because there was no excitement in her eyes.

"We don't handle self-published authors that come in off the street. And just out of curiosity, do you have a TVA account?"

"A who's a what's it?" I said, sounding Jerry Lewisish in *The Nutty Professor*.

She spoke for two minutes about French law as it relates to paying an author for his book. I tuned out after she said, "I can't pay you for your book because . . . " To make a long story short, because I didn't have a publisher and/or some kind of tax account with the French government, she couldn't take my book even she wanted to.

"My book is on the shelf of two other bookstores in Paris. Since this is also an independent bookstore, couldn't you put a couple of them on

———

your shelves?" I was getting cocky. And desperate. And when I'm desperate I can't shut up. "Morgan Davis went to every English bookstore in Paris to sell his book. He even came here, and I can guarantee you he didn't have a TVA account or whatever it's called."

Veronica folded her arms. "That never happened. It wouldn't have been possible for him to come in off the street and sell his books."

The cashier, sensing that our conversation was heading nowhere, interrupted. "Morgan Davis was here seven or eight years ago. I was even here when he walked in off the street. I'll never forget those sideburns of his."

"Fine," Veronica harrumphed, "but we don't do that anymore. I guess the laws were a little more lax back then." She paused, and then in a surprising act of kindness, half-smiled and said, "Google 'Tax Value Added' accounts when you have the time. If you can find a distribution company in Paris willing to distribute your book, then *they* will create a TVA account for you and *then* your book may have possibilities. French book distribution companies act as a middleman between huge bookstores and unknown authors such as you. And even if we ever accepted your book, we would never pay you directly. The royalties, etcetera would go to the distribution company and then they would pay you. At least you have an ISBN. That's a start." She left before I had a chance to ask her the names of distribution companies.

I thanked the cashier for her time. Browsing around the store, I jostled through a group of Morgan Davis enthusiasts, finding myself face to face with a life-size photograph of the smirking author. Thin and sporting lamb-chop sideburns, he could have just as easily been promoting a volume on health food.

On a lark, I took four *French Like Me*s out of my bag and nonchalantly moseyed over to a nearby shelf, its height the same level as Davis's denim-covered derriere. I grabbed four copies of his first book, *Merde Doesn't Stink in France*, which happened to be white paperbacks as well, and turned around and pretended I was going to pay for them. Acting as if I was the latest book jockey hired in the store, I sauntered back and placed all eight books on the shelf, ensuring mine were on top of Davis's. The new math: four equals eight. I did this twice. The symbolism alone of placing my books by his covered buttocks was worth the price of admonition. The company with the largest number of bookstores in the world now had my book, even though it was a stowaway. (They would be just as easy to smuggle back.) And—big surprise—no one in the store cared.

Studying a 6th *arrondissement* map for fifteen minutes, I found the general location of World Books. Tucked away in a maze of bar-lined streets, it was hard to imagine a sober person ever walking in there.

The store was slightly larger than Byron's bookshop and contained a second floor, which I never inspected; it housed the dreaded "factual guys," those boring pushers of non-fiction. The inside walls were painted a soft blue and supported rows of cherry mahogany, book-filled shelves. And the shiny, white pine floor politely creaked. Tickling the wooden ivories of the floor as I walked toward the cash register, I was reminded of the time I had opened up a floor cleaning business. At the age of twelve, word had spread through the neighbourhood like carnauba wax buttering a herringbone floor that I was the best hardwood waxer on the east side.

The lineup at the register was too long and, being in no hurry, I walked around, more interested in the floor for a few rare positive sounds of my childhood than in checking the bestsellers.

My addiction to hardwood floors began as a toddler. Our living room and hallway were lined with white pine floors permanently aching for a waxin' and a buffin'. We loved that floor, and given that our furniture had Goodwill written all over it, the floor was the only thing worth taking care of.

At the tender age of six or seven, I took a shinin' to the waxing/buffing machine whirring about the floor. My mother would let me handle the machine, its twin bristly pads endlessly spinning in search of more wood. I loved how the handle vibrated in my tiny hands. (When I grew older, I understood why women in particular were fond of using this machine.) Soon I was on hands and knees, rhythmically spreading the wax in sensuous circles. And of the left-handed and right-brained variety, I created an interesting counter-spin with the wax—my uniquely angled application bringing out a luster unmatched by a righty—one day earning me copious awards at local and provincial floor-waxing competitions.

In between my card stealing days and nipping auto parts, I started the floor-cleaning business. "Vlad's floor waxing: What's the crime in a good shine?" was the catch phrase, handwritten in bold letters on a flyer. My mother made several copies at work and I had them distributed throughout the neighbourhood by my minions, each earning a penny per ad.

—

I loved the irony of my slogan; I made every effort to steal something while I was working, the biggest challenge always offering itself when the housewives were puttering about. If they were home, I'd ask for a glass of water in the kitchen. From there, I'd hunt for loose small bills and loose cigarettes stacked in small glass jars. If I wanted the gals out of the house to do a more thorough search—looking for quick resell items like Playboy (centrefold had to be included and not sticky), comic books, model cars if the price was right, and the odd hamster—I only had to read over the daily food store flyers earlier in the morning. "Milk's on for $1.32 at the A & P" or "Safeway has four loaves for a dollar," I would say. The dames would scoot in seven seconds to save four cents. And I was getting bonus bucks for babysitting as well. After stealing the fancy cutlery of one family, I hung up my floor polishing machine for good. Rumours were starting to circulate about a local thief who had even stolen a marinating steak. Everyone loves a challenge. No! It was time to quit before they noticed that all the victimized homes had the same wax finish on their hardwood floors.

Eventually, I sold the machine, eight jars of wax and the goodwill of the "company" for a hundred bucks. Suddenly, my mother had extra money to send Carson to camp for a month, and she bought a new green dress. I think it's still stored somewhere in her rattle-trap, still-mortgaged house.

"Can I help you, sir?" said a tall man, his British accent guarding every syllable. Still lost in my halcyon waxing days, I was unaware that I had moved directly in front of his till. I took the two *French Like Me*s out of my bag and handed him one. With a smile on his face reserved for a pretty woman, he studied the cover.

"She's quite a temptress. I see Gina Lollobrigida, Marilyn Monroe, Sophia Loren, Catherine Deneuve." He paused and looked at the stucco ceiling. His beady eyes refocusing on the book, he added, "and Margaret Thatcher." This guy was older than I thought.

"Margaret Thatcher?" I asked, my face screwing up.

"Yes, I see Thatcher's sturdiness in this woman."

"That's the first time someone has ever made *that* comment about the drawing. I assume you're kidding?"

Feeling no need to answer my question, he flipped the book over and read the back cover. There was no laughter at my blurbs, which meant that either he wasn't amused or he'd read so many testimonials, real and fake, that they had blended into one long blur of bullshit.

"So *you* are the new go-to guy when it comes to writing funny French things. By the way 'go to' needs a hyphen."

"I lost my hyphen a long time ago," I replied. No reaction from Mr. Stoic. "I'll try again. How about, I lost my hyphenity a long time ago."

Mr. Stoic paused for so long you could cut the tension with a spatula. His face still expressionless, he slowly read the name of the phony critic. A wide, stupid grin covered my face as if I had just pulled one over him. I had to look down at the floor to avoid exploding with laughter.

"The Chicago . . . hmm." He paused and rubbed his chin, and then continued straight-faced. "Herald . . . hmm . . . Times . . . hmm ... Bu . . . gle."

I, on the other hand, was not of the straight face, desperately trying to suppress the cloud of laughter, tickling and billowing uncontrollably in my belly. "I made the quotes up," I said, laughing.

His face was still expressionless. Despite having the gift of being able to read people, I was unable to decrypt this bookologist. "Not being familiar with the Chicago Herald-Times-*Bugle*, it wasn't a stretch that you or someone else had made up the testimonial. I noticed that you put *Bugle* at the end of each newspaper. Is this some kind of tribute to Peter Parker?"

"That's pretty funny. But I can't help asking—you never laugh."

With that "dry as the Sahara Desert" British wit, he replied, "What is this laughter that you speak of?"

"You are priceless. Do you mind if I use you as a character in my next book?"

"Feel free to malign and torture my words if that gives you literary sanctuary."

"Thanks, even though I think you went a little overboard on the sanctuary part. Anyway, I should explain why I'm here." He half-listened as he finished reading my hook on the back cover, laughing as often as he did when he read the first phony blurb.

I continued talking, hoping a chuckle was buried somewhere deep within his frame. "Being a fellow Brit, you must have heard of Morgan Davis."

"Yes, his books are spread around our shop. Um...makes me think of poison ivy."

"I can't tell if you're joking or not. You're not a fan?"

"I've read funnier and less funny."

69

"Well, I'm following in Davis's footsteps. Consider me one of his literary apostles." Still no smile. Undeterred, I added, "Eight years ago, Morgan Davis walked around Paris trying to sell his book to local book…"

"I'm well aware that he self-published and dragged his parchmented words into our sacred store."

"Is 'parchmented' even a word?"

"It is now."

I smiled for the both of us, and looked around. No one was in a hurry to purchase a book. "I'm doing the same thing as Davis. I've already sold five books to the Albany Bookshop, and Shakespeare and Company has taken ten on our mutual old friend—" I paused and raised two fingers on each hand over my head and moved them up and down like two rabbits eating a carrot saying, "—Mr. Consignment." No smile again. Were Seinfeld or Dave Chappelle capable of making a small fissure in Stoic's funny bone?

"Well," he said, "in that case, if Shakespeare and Company has taken ten of your books, then I will double their opening gambit and call."

I sensed either he played poker and/or chess or he had something against Shakespeare and Company. Mild panic ensued. A multitude of swear words went off in my head as I searched every pocket in my bag.

"Shoot I only have two books with me."

"Okay, make that two books."

"I could run back to my hotel and get eighteen more."

"And the world could end on your way back and *then* what would we do? Don't worry about it. I only wanted two anyway. If your books sell, I'm sure you'll have more up your sleeve."

"Do you play poker by any chance?" I asked.

"I've spent time in the company of the Jakes and the Bags, though lately I've been plagued with trays and deuces".

"I think you'd be a great poker player. Your expression never changes."

"People tell me I used to smirk back in the seventies."

"Those were great times." Still no smile, although we were starting to connect.

"The only problem is I don't have a contract," he said. "And France has more laws about selling books than there are people. You'll have to come back another day with a contract."

Though a neophyte in the book business, I surprised even myself with a quick solution. I pulled out the Shakespeare and Company contract, containing no words greater than three syllables, and asked if this type of document was acceptable.

"Yes, this preposterous piece of pithy paper will do." He drew it to his nose and sniffed, his face still a blank page.

"Great," I said. "I'll rewrite this consignment agreement and bring it back tomorrow. Shakespeare and Company has two agreements, one for their records and one for mine."

"Aren't records wonderful?" he replied.

I had no clue what to say. "Yes, records are great. Anyway, I'm sure you're busy. Thanks for everything and I'll be back tomorrow. Just out of curiosity what type of books do you read?"

"I read exclusively books of a humorous vain."

"That's perfect. My book is hilarious. You have to read it. It's written from a slightly Canadian angle, but Davis and I are very similar, were both smartasses. I understand the French extremely well." I had no clue about the French.

"Lucky you," was all I could get out of him. We shook hands and I moved toward the front door.

"Excuse me, writer of *French Like Me*, what are you charging for your prose?"

"How about ten euros?"

"Purrrr-fect." He scribbled something in my book, which I assumed was the price.

Although my wallet wasn't jammed with euros from the day's visits of bookstores, I was still able to get my book on two more independent shelves. I would celebrate with another evening dinner with my favourite bookseller.

Near seven, I pulled a "Natasha." I stood about twenty metres from her shop and hid behind another building, watching the comings-and-goings of her store. Her comely face appeared in the front window a few times, until she drew the blinds and locked up the shop.

Watching her lock the door from a distance I cupped my mouth and shouted, "Hey, how does it feel to have someone spying on you?"

She turned around and replied, "That's really mature. Who, pray tell, did you get *that* idea from?" I walked over and kissed her on the lips. Her arms around my neck, mine around her waist, our bodies a tight fleshy Möbius strip, she said, "Well, Vlad, it was nice to see you didn't toss any plastic bottles at my sign."

"Your sign is my shrine," I replied lamely.

Playing along, she replied, "That's so sweet . . . I think." We sashayed hand in hand in the general direction of the Luxembourg Gardens. Close to an entrance, Natasha stopped, her right hand on my buttocks, "Would you care to go for another romantic walk through the gardens?"

"Oh you mean the Forest of Foreplay?"

"No, the Garden of Groping," she replied, not missing a beat.

The air was hot and heavy, and a few sweaty joggers kicked up some dust as they laboured by us.

"I went to two bookstores today."

"Two? You're kidding! And you didn't consult me?"

"Well, you're busy at your store and I was anxious to get my day going."

"Where did you go first?"

"Maybe you should sit down for this story. I have a feeling you're not going to believe what I did."

"You didn't steal any books did you?"

I let go of her hand in a phony show of anger. "Natasha! That hurt."

"Vlad, no offense, but based on some of your stories last night, I think your middle name is Klepto."

I forced a laugh. "No it's Vladimir. My first name is John, but there was already an Uncle John, so to avoid confusion, I was called by my shortened middle name. As I grew older, I preferred Vlad. It made me sound mysterious. But I have to admit, I did get tired of my nickname."

"Let me guess—Boy Bandit? Lad Larceny? The Klepto Kid?"

"Okay I get it. I've been clean for years. (I was lying.) And by the way, my nickname was Vlad the Impaler."

"*Sooo* original! Are you sure it wasn't Punky the Pickpocket or Leif the Thief?"

"Enough!"

"Phil the Filcher?"

"Geez, that's the problem with all you bookstore types. You sit around for seven hours trying to come up the perfect word or perfect phrase each time someone walks into your store. You and these other vendors have to get outside a little more often and be with real people...me for example."

Natasha folded her arms and gave me a cold stare. And then she laughed. "Okay, I'll admit we bookstore owners do have a pretentious habit of searching for the perfect word before we speak, and we'd sleep with a Scrabble grandmaster rather than an in-the-sack grandmaster. But don't you th—"

"You mean you prefer guys that use big words rather than guys with big 'Johnsons'?"

"Well, truth be told, I prefer both."

"Maybe I could kill two birds with one stone and just wrap a dictionary around my bo diddley?" We both chortled. "Even though I'm enjoying the topic, I forgot what we were originally talking about."

She kissed me on the cheek. "We were originally taking about your innate ability to pilfer."

"I remember. No, I didn't steal any books today; however, I did *smuggle* my books *into* a store."

"What do you mean?"

"Let's save that enthralling story for dinner. My treat, by the way.

"Where are we going?"

"It's a surprise."

"Mickey-D's, Mister Big Spender?"

"It's a Savoyard cheese fondue restaurant not far from your apartment." Carson had eaten there several times.

At the restaurant, Natasha and I ordered Raclette, a type of cheese made in Savoie sliced, melted at one's leisure on a flat pan, and poured over steamed potatoes and an assortment of cold cuts. A bottle of rosé would complement the meal.

We enjoyed watching the waiters hustle the crowd as they walked up and down the narrow side street directly in front of us. Soon, our waiter placed the rosé, an off-white ceramic dish stacked with the Raclette, and a small wicker basket bursting with freshly chopped baguette on our table. He returned with matching his-and-hers metal cheese-melting contraptions, each containing two metal-enclosed mini-frying pans tucked underneath. The waiter lit the flammable liquid encased in the tiny pans that emitted a florescent greenish-purple flame.

A rubber-faced accordion player played in the street. His notes were accompanied by a woman's voice that made Parisians stop in their tracks and forget what type of red wine they were going to order with dinner. Natasha turned her head and lost herself in the woman's voice, which was so eerily similar to Edith Piaf's that one had to stare at her face to be

---

73

convinced she wasn't a clone.

"Natasha, something in that woman's voice made me wonder about your younger days."

"Boy, have you changed the mood." She took a deep breath. *Christ, what the hell was she going to say?* "It's something very hard to talk about."

"Please tell me."

Another deep breath. Her eyes on the verge of welling up. "Both of my parents were killed in a car accident twelve years ago."

I touched her hand as fast as possible. "I'm sorry. That must have been horrible."

Natasha forced a smile. "In time, I could deal with it, but my brother never did. In fact he hated me after they died."

"What a prick!"

"What can I say. I guess we all have our problems."

"Did you come to Paris because of him?"

"I think it was a combination of my parents passing away and him being unable to handle it. With no other close relatives, I needed to make a clean break from Toronto. And what the hell—I had always loved Paris. I have French citizenship, so I was able to stay here and work.

"What did you do when you first got here?"

"I went through jobs in a few French bookshops. I even worked at BJ Williams. That was an experience in itself, keeping the "other hired French hands" off my body. Eventually I started my own bookstore."

The waiter placed the plates of steamed potatoes and assorted cold cuts on our table. Natasha went quiet.

"French hands, eh."

"I'm starving, Vlad. Let's eat."

I thought she was avoiding the subject, but I let it go. I was hungry too. I slapped a slice of cheese on the now-heated flat piece of metal. With less conviction, Natasha placed a slice on hers. Simultaneously, we grabbed our knives and forks and cut the meat and potatoes and arranged the food in strategic spots about the plate, soon to be smothered by the hot yellow French magma. I picked up my glass of rosé and pointed it in Natasha's direction.

"Here's to a perfect evening."

"Every now and then you know exactly what to say." Our eyes stuck in a Bogart–Bergman stare, we tinkled glasses.

"Vlad, I haven't had Raclette in a while. How long does it take for

---

74

the cheese to melt?"

"Oh, usually about a minute per side."

"Ha-ha!"

I scraped the molten slice over an unsuspecting mound of prosciutto. Ten slices of cheese each later, our plates spotless, the breadbasket empty, and a few vague comments about Natasha's boyfriend (a whirlwind romance starting in Paris six years ago and dying a slow cross-Atlantic–relationship death), I asked for the bill.

Anxious to start the day early tomorrow, I walked Natasha home and went back to my hotel.

Sunday, June 24th

On my way to Giuliani and Sons bookstore on Rue de Rivoli, I became enamoured with the Eiffel Tower. And who comes to Paris and not check out that elegant mass of metal? Giuliani could wait.

Walking by the tower, I got this sudden urge to sell my book on the street. I took a book out of my knapsack and then looked around. There were hundreds of tourists and vendors moving in every direction, many of them passing by me, not giving me the time of day. I wanted to open my mouth, but unexpectedly became nervous. What would I say? Shit, I needed some liquid courage. I found a grocery store a few blocks from the tower and purchased a flask of cheap brandy.

I sat on a bench about fifty metres from the base of the tower. It jiggled pleasantly after my third manly gulp of hooch. Six healthy gulps later, I swore it was doing the limbo under a low passing cloud.

I practised my paperboy/carny calls on a busload of Japanese tourists disembarking a stone's throw away from the tower.

"Honourable Japanese," I said, not remembering if I bowed. I waved my book high above my head. "This is the funniest book you will ever read. If you do not like it, I'll give you your money back."

A man, in his sixties, his face wrinkled and stoic, approached me. "Excuse me, sir. What does your book cost?"

"Ten euros, but tell you what, I'll give you one for free if you don't mind having your picture taken with me in front of the tower."

"Of course." He signalled a couple of his friends to accompany us while I asked a bystander to take our picture. I convinced everyone in the picture to hold a copy of my book high in the air as if we were paperboys.

The Japanese entourage flashed their cameras in our direction. I signed one book for my new friend and collected the others. Should I have given him two books, hoping they would spawn in Japan?

I shook hands with everyone in the picture and bowed as I made my exit. Under the tower, I looked up and lost myself in the mass of metal and bolts the size of my head. Drifting along a capricious path, I found myself amongst a mass of people coiling endlessly in three elevator/staircase lineups. Snaking through the overly cheery and cheesy tourists, I kept my eyes open for some vacant real estate. I soon expected my bookselling chants to jovially compete with a neighbouring gang of colourfully robed North African vendors who recounted vivid tales about their lives in three or four languages, while they hovered over their leather goods, wooden elephants and plastic Eiffel Towers. Their trinkets rested comfortably on thin carpets—magic tribal carpets, if one believed their legend.

But that was a fond or oddly romantic image still stored in the recesses of my brain from the last time I had visited the tower—thirty years before. Shit, that was Carson's memory, not mine. I remembered that story because one summer he said he needed a break from his university studies and didn't want to work. He had lots of rich university friends who backpacked all over the world every summer. Well, Carson, we weren't rich. And guess who paid for your flight?

Carson and I both lived in Toronto, though ironically we hadn't spoken in months. And the problem wasn't a mutually desired woman or that we—or shall I say *I*—was ultra-competitive. It was more as Carson put it, "Vlad! You're wasting your friggin' life." Or he'd say to his sons, "If you don't have any goals in life, you're going to end up being another Uncle Vlad. Is that what you want?" Telling his sons that I was basically the anti-Christ or the anti-Carson did sting. And to think my years of semi-profitable and well-organized stealing helped put him through university. God, I'm underneath the coolest tower on earth and I'm bumming myself out. I looked at the vendors to get my mind off my brother.

The nomadic merchants and their wooden goods were long gone, replaced by Indian and Gabonese vendors, their trinkets fitted around a circular-shaped coat hanger, endlessly hooked and unhooked to sell cheap plastic Eiffel Towers. It took little effort for them to shake their tambourines to attract the tourists' attention, but this was only a by-product of the "tambourine's" efficiency or usefulness. While the former tenants of the trinkets would have taken a morning to carefully pack up their wares if the police told them to move, their modern contemporaries redefined portability. And it was needed; only houseflies remained in one place for less time than these younger and pushier hawkers.

I gravitated to the only stationary vendor in sight. He had laid out twenty or thirty florescent rubbery things, each the size of a hacky sack, on a tea towel. Spurred on by his colourful display, I, in turn, took five books out of my bag, each the size of a typically hot-selling paperback, and laid them on top of my knapsack. His toys contained tiny smiley faces that could be stretched into a duck or, with more imagination, Sarkozy's rubbery face. My books, on the other hand glowed, and had a gorgeous French woman on the cover. I kept one in my hand and fanned its contents, stopping at random pages, half-reading a line or two in my head, and laughing out loud—even if the words were unfunny. Within minutes, my neighbour had sold four of the rubbery specials at four euros apiece, while I stood, slack-jawed, a metre away, hoping to lure some of his overspill tourists.

I would have been happy to sell at least one. No luck.

Maybe I needed to open my mouth. And after insulting the Japanese tourists, I was a little gun-shy to resume my carny calls. I looked down and noticed my leather sandals were no longer absorbing my foot sweat, with my armpits and back jumping into the act as well.

"Hey," I said, hoping the vendor would look my way.

The university-aged Indian guy turned a face that read, "I'll talk to you, but not for long." He shifted his coal-black eyes, making only brief contact with me, and then moved his head in a half circle as if he was on some kind of surveillance mission. He looked at me again, "No, I don't mind if you stay here." His English was understandable, but he spoke in such a low voice one would think he was being followed.

And he was.

A muscle-bound French cop, a circus bear on a bicycle, wheeled by. The street trader gathered the four corners of his tea cloth and sped off toward the bridge, to be joined a fraction of a second later by a hundred peddlers sounding like a massive tambourine band. One hawker nearly knocked my bag over as he rushed by me. Three more cops attempted to round the gang into a fenceless corner by the northwest cement leg of the tower.

I was tempted to run as well, wanting to be a part of this gang of illegal vendors. The thousand-ton tower leg and I remained stationary, while the "tambourine gang" ran halfway across the bridge to elude the cyclists.

After five minutes of holding my book and laughing out loud, alcohol-induced phrases soon fell off my tongue. The booze was finally doing what it normally does: turn me into a friendly clown. "This is the funniest book you'll read this summer," I yelled. Then I hit the tourists with an all-out rapid-fire "comedy assault," mixing phrases like, "I'm the new go-to guy when it comes to writing funny French things"; "Morgan Davis sucks, if you ask me"; "Canadian smartass writes about French foibles"; "It's only six euros, but if you can name the capital of Canada or the U.S., I'll knock off a euro" and "It's a runaway bestseller back home." (After nine or ten shots of brandy, that line still made me cringe.) The tourists, those of whom were mildly interested in my lines, must have thought I was part of a hidden camera act.

Sounding foolish for who knows how long, I gave up and sat down. Worse, I had a thousand tourists all to myself and wasn't able to sell a single book. In the distance, musicians played their guitars and sold their CDs. They definitely had the advantage over us word jockeys, belting out their tunes and letting the public decide their fate.

A man gave me a cold stare as he brushed by me. Christ, was that the same person I'd seen the other day on the bridge? Was he following me or was the booze clouding my ability to distinguish faces?

The swarm of vendors diverted my attention. They cut a path back underneath the tower and, had they worn striped yellow T-shirts, they would have looked like giant bumblebees. For the next half-hour or so, I sold zero books while three different vendors sold forty friggin' plastic blobs. (I had time to count.) Sadly, it crossed my mind to buy a couple of the stretchy toys myself and toss one in with each book sold. Then my wholesaler career had hit rock bottom when I considered joining forces with the toy merchant and suggesting that one of my books be tossed in with every toy sold.

I followed the Seine back to the *Musée d'Orsay*, drinking two double espressos along the way. Slowly passing by a queue wrapped around the art museum, I made one last crack at selling a book on the street. I parked myself a few metres from a group who wore enough professional sport caps and T-shirts that they had to be American.

"Okay," I yelled, trying to turn some bored heads in the lineup, "who wants to buy the funniest book ever written?" Jacked up on the espressos, I waved the book in the air like a winning lottery ticket. I garnered ten bizarre-looking stares from the tourists waiting to go inside.

78

Their brief attention should have inspired me to come up with another line, something clever to convince at least one person to buy my book. I had nothing and packed it in in a record time of only sixty ticks of the clock.

Placing my books by my knapsack, I was approached by a woman.

"This is good luck, sir," she said as she picked up a ring that supposedly lay on the pavement in front of me.

"Fuck off, lady," I yelled. This was the third time I'd had a problem with these con artists. I slapped the ring out of her outstretched palm with an upper thrust of my hand, shocked that her arm didn't disengage and travel skyward with the ring. She screamed (though I was unsure if it was out of pain or anger) as the cheap gold metal arced into the Seine. With no interest in waiting for the "kerplunk," I tossed the books in my bag. She grabbed my hand while I was zipping it shut. An errant elbow—*my* elbow—flew out. My untamed bodyguard? The same reflex action I recalled from the times I'd skated corners with opposing beer league hockey players I hated. Sometimes there was no puck to be found.

But there was a gypsy. And she was lying on the ground, crumpled in a tangled heap of dirty scarves, mouldy sweaters, stockings with saucer-sized holes, men's basketball shoes (missing laces), and a stream of fresh, clean, crimson blood flowing from her nose.

"Hey, what the hell did y'all just do?" yelled a man four or five metres away, his accent placing him from the deep south. His drawl coincided with a loud whistle, and something yelled in French, and maybe in Romani as well, from a distance.

"It was an accident," I shouted, as I frantically zipped up my bag. The zipper was stuck. "She was trying to rob me," I added, as I stopped fiddling with the bag and picked it up. My back was turned the whole time I pleaded my defence. My third hassle with the Roma, I hit her out of frustration or maybe I was just frustrated with my life. Either way I didn't have time to think about my actions.

At no time did I twist my neck for a peek, but that sixth sense of mine told me that a couple of French cops, a gypsy husband and his five scam-artist children were chasing me.

I turned right on the first street leading away from the Seine, the capricious move opening up an infinite combination of alleys, small parks, side streets, not-so-side streets and major boulevards. Paris was an elbowing escapist's dream. I made so many confusing turns that not only had I lost the cops, I couldn't find myself either.

———

I stopped a half-hour later, I guessed. A rapidly beating heart plays tricks with one's sense of time. Convinced the cops and gypsies were long gone—and they were—I poked my sweaty head around a corner to recognize anything on the street. A street sign high on a corner building indicated that I was in the 6th arrondissement (Natasha's home turf) but still lost.

No longer wanting to move along a path that resembled a six-year-old's Etch-a-Sketch creation, I darted into a café to ask someone where the hell I was. And I ordered a beer to calm myself down.

Though I'd shaken the cops and gypsies a district ago, I still jumped when my front hotel door automatically buzzed as I entered.

"What brings you here so late in the afternoon?" asked the desk clerk in some kind of accented French. He was forcing a conversation because he was more interested in searching for his cigarettes and lighter than hanging on to anything I was about to say.

"I knocked over a gypsy in the afternoon, and was chased by the cops and a gypsy posse," I replied, looking for a reaction.

He grabbed my key and handed it to me. "Fantastic weather today, isn't it?" he said as he moved around the desk, the cigarette dangling from his mouth.

I grabbed the key off the desk and arranged for a wake-up call in a few hours.

The walk to Natasha's bookstore took less time than usual. Avoiding eye contact with other pedestrians, the sidewalk and the occasional dog had become my only friends. Paris had taken on a dark side. In a barely audible voice, I sang The Doors' *People Are Strange*. The meandering route forced me to look up occasionally at the street signs, my eyes inevitably meeting disapproval from the local Parisian street-corner types as I scurried by like a rodent. Paranoid that every cop and every gypsy was giving me the evil eye, I darted into a Monoprix and purchased a frozen lasagna, a bottle of wine, and a four-pack of chocolate ice cream cones. And I would convince Natasha that we should stay off the tough streets of Paris for one evening.

Natasha took the lasagna out of the microwave and poked it with a fork. "It's ready, Vlad." After she placed it on the table, she wiped her brow with an oven mitt in a dated housewife kind of way. A lovely black curl had fallen over one eye. She blew at it. "I hope you enjoy this, dear.

I've been sweating over a hot stove all day." We kissed over the piping hot lasagna, our nostrils sucking in the sweet smells.

Then my big mouth happened. Feelings gushed out in words behind my control. "Natasha, I love y—"

"I didn't hear the 'L-word', did I?" She had camouflaged her question with a blank look.

"Um . . . no . . . You didn't . . . um let me finish. I . . . um . . . wanted to say that I love your sarcasm." Embarrassed, I plugged my mouth with lasagna and stared at the floor.

A pair of legs covered in faded denim, tiny rhinestones glimmering on her pockets, shifted around the table. Natasha parked her lovely derriere on my lap.

Her lips met mine; soon, either her tongue or a piece of hot pasta (I was happy with either one) entered my mouth. Worried I was going to swallow whatever this "dish" had to offer, I came up for air.

She spoke first. "Vlad, that was such a nice thing to say."

She grabbed my hand and motioned me toward the couch. With the other hand on the pull-out latch, she said, "Vlad, you don't mind if we finish our dinner later?"

I flipped her sweater over her pair of ripe, beefeater tomatoes. "No, I have no problem having dessert before the main course." I managed to move the sweater northward but it stuck at her neck and completely enveloped her head.

"Natasha, you look like an onion before it's peeled."

"How romantic."

She gave up opening the couch and waited for me to untangle her headdress. I think I raised her off the ground when I removed the sweater. I tossed it to the floor while she took a second shot at pulling out the hidden bed. I, in turn, stripped and then checked my naked noodle to see that it was still *al dente*. Natasha bent over and smoothed out the wrinkles on the bed sheet while I rubbed my rigid rigatoni up against her backside. She giggled and jumped on the bed. I followed the giggle trail.

The apartment windows were steamy. Was it the hot sex or the hot lasagna?

Natasha played with the hairs on my chest. "Well, Hemingway, what did you do today?"

I put both hands behind my head. "Not much, just a little trouble at the *Musée d'Orsay*.

"What happened?"

"I hit a gypsy woman because I thought she was trying to rob me."

Her warm breath had drawn every honest syllable out of my mouth before I recognized what I was saying. Natasha put her hand over her mouth as if I had turned to vomit; then she stood up and put her pants back on. A sweater went over her beautiful, bare shoulders, surely cold due to Mr. Douchebag's sudden bout of honesty. She haphazardly placed her plate of cold lasagna in the microwave. Was it the wrong time to reminder her my dinner was cold too? I knew the answer to that question.

I jumped off the bed and grabbed her hip from behind, but she slipped my grip. I sensed she wasn't going to turn around, so I nestled my nose in the waves of her hair.

"Natasha, it was a reflex action. The woman said she had found a ring that supposedly had fallen directly in front of me. It was the third time in three days that a gypsy asked me if I'd lost a wedding band." The microwave buzzed. She grabbed her piping-hot food and sat down, ignoring me the whole time. I played with my cold pasta, wondering what I would say next. Too much dead air.

"Natasha, please look at me." She stabbed a piece of lasagna and placed it in her mouth, her eyes never leaving the plate. I paused for a second, feeling that fork in my heart; a tired cliché, but it fit my feelings. *Keep talking Vlad!*

"The woman grabbed me and I panicked." Natasha harpooned another piece and looked at me, a look suggesting we had never been intimate. That hurt.

"Why would you hit a poor defenceless woman?" A tear came down her face.

"You're overreacting." I surprised even myself by making that senseless comment. And yet, I was crazy about this woman. What the hell am I doing!? Maybe with my small, recent success as a writer I was becoming self-centred. My foot searched for her gams under the table. People don't generally console with their feet, but I drew a blank on what else to do.

"Is that your foot?" she asked, forcing a half-smile.

"Maybe," I replied, reverting to my big-eyed puppy-dog look.

She cut another piece of lasagna and gently picked it up with her fork.

"I'm sorry, Vlad, but you touched a nerve when you mentioned that you had hit a woman. I get upset even when I see any clip on the news about a woman—or anyone for that matter—getting beaten."

82

She had one hand resting on the table. I placed a warm hand over it. She let me touch her.

"Trust me, I didn't intentionally hit her. She grabbed me, and I panicked. I thought she was going to steal something." I walked over to the microwave, hoping she would drop the subject by the time I'd reheated my lasagna.

Her look followed me. "Why did she touch you?"

Damn. I thought this conversation was over. I had to avoid the "smacking the ring out of her hand" part or there would be a flood of tears and maybe the unforgiving showing of the door. I grabbed my food out of the microwave, wondering how I would lie to her.

"She asked me if the wedding band belonged to me, and I said no. Then she insisted that I give her money. I felt uncomfortable and packed my non-selling books back in my bag. It was then that she grabbed my hand. Her grip was so cold I panicked, and an elbow came flying out. It reminded me of my ice hockey days when I inadvertently shot an elbow out against opposing players."

"Was she at least wearing a mask?"

Good—sarcasm—she must have bought my story. I was in the clear, though I forced a laugh. "No, but maybe she was wearing a cup."

She smiled. Great, back to normal.

"Shit." I paused and looked at the ceiling, a smile the size of the microwave washing over my face. "Natasha, I just remembered a great story. I was chased by the police and some gypsies today, but I've got a much better adventure to tell you."

She raised her eyebrows. I took it as a hint that she wasn't thrilled about whatever I was going to say, but she would wait before passing judgment. "The police!" said Natasha excitedly. "Now it makes sense why you wanted to stay in for the night. You're dodging half of Paris."

"What can I say? I'm popular."

"Did it take long for you to shake the cops and the gypsies?" Natasha was calmer.

"No. Paris is full of non–right-angled streets. It was easy to lose them. Anyway, I have a story that's ten times more interesting than what happened to me today."

"What did you steal this time?"

I proceeded to describe in detail how a friend and I robbed a chip truck a few minutes before our night class started at the University of Toronto St. George campus.

83

Natasha cleared the table as I spoke. I would omit the part about my friend and I being cornered by two cops, but at twenty-one years of age, it was pretty easy to scale a fence. Soon, composites of my face were appearing in more than one downtown university library. I would look at those pictures and think, the lengths libraries had to go to get students to return overdue books. I was cocky and went through an angry-man-in-his-twenties period, always feeling that the world owed me because my father left when I was young. In my preteens and teens, I stole because I was good at it and I needed to help out my family. In high school, despite no studying, I had high marks, particularly in English and languages. I'd been encouraged by more than one high school teacher to pursue a career in journalism. They found my writing to be surprisingly mature and enjoyed my sense of humour. I forever wrote about the middle class. Why? Because that's all I wanted to be. And despite my trying to dress middle class and act middle class, my teachers and peers could tell I wasn't. Carson always did a better job at fooling them than I. There I go again, comparing myself with my brother. In the end, with the campus police closing in and final exams on the go, I was caught cheating more than once. The first time they believed that the code on my arm was a harmless un-academic tattoo. By the third exam at the end of second semester, I was shown the door and never allowed back. From the first day, I never fit in on campus, and a few years later, my brother thrived. And guess who paid his tuition? Again, Vlad? You have to let go the rivalry in your head.

After I finished my chip truck story, Natasha placed the dishes in the sink and raised her eyebrows, mouth open in stunned silence.

God, if she only knew everything else I was thinking. I was convinced that she was trying to find a polite way of saying that I was an asshole . . . or maybe a not-so-polite way. Our eye contact continued. Would the impassioned look on my face win over her uncomfortable stare?

My judge, jury and executioner, all wrapped into one smokin' bod, had me in prosecution limbo. Deep down, she enjoyed holding time hostage—and me as well.

Natasha broke the silence. The verdict was in on my story. In a scolding voice, she said, "You are truly insane. Please tell me right this minute that you have given up stealing."

This was one of those times when a hug meant more than a few carefully chosen words of reassurance. I walked over and squeezed the bejesus out of her and the bejesus out of her chair too. I think they both felt comforted. I whispered in her ear, "I promise, Natasha. That was the last time I did anything that involved breaking the law." I was a liar.

"You're starting to scare me a little with your wild stories."

I kissed her neck. "Don't worry. That was a long, long time ago. And besides, Natasha, I would never do anything to hurt you." The look on her face read, "I don't believe you," but what could I do? I spent a few minutes trying to convince her that I was no longer *that* person. Whether she was convinced or not, she asked me to help with the dishes.

Sated with lasagna, wine and chase stories, we fell asleep close to eleven o'clock.

Two days later

Tuesday, June 26th (The day after NiR and Helen discover Vlad's novel)

Yesterday, Helen had given me the break of a lifetime by taking me and my book seriously, but today I still planned to visit two or three other bookstores. Why? I desperately needed money.

After a shave back at my hotel, I threw on some clean clothes and filled my bag with ten *French Like Me*s. My first stop was Giuliani and Sons, the store I had intended to visit before I was fatefully diverted by the Eiffel Tower. The sign on the front window caught my attention before I opened the front door. "Giuliani and Sons is the oldest English bookstore in Europe" was written in bright gold letters on a plaque in the shape of a wooden scroll.

The dark brown walls of the store reminded me of a nineteenth-century museum. I approached an employee and asked him where the English section was and if a Madame Pellegrino was working there. (Natasha had given me some inside information about her.) The employee pointed me to Madame Pellegrino, her back turned and busy taking inventory.

About three metres to her right I noticed a small gold purse wedged between stacks of books. It was just too easy. My head instinctively looked for security cameras and other salespeople. The coast clear, my body went into autopilot. I put the purse behind a stack of books, allowing only myself to see it, I hoped. I opened up a book with my right hand and pretended to look at it the whole time my other hand cleaned the purse of its cash. I stuffed the wad in my pocket. Madame Pellegrino's back was still turned.

I placed my hand on my heart for a second. Good, no pounding; felt normal. I grabbed a book from my bag and made the hardwood floor creak (a fetish of mine) as I approached her cigarette-reeking body. My last creak sounded like I'd stepped on a giant bug. The splat sound caused her to jerk her head around, along with a silver mountain of hair propped up with a record number of hair clips. I had stepped on one of her goddamn hair clips.

"Sorry about that," I said.

"That was a hair clip given to me by Mamie Pellegrino!" she said with disgust in her voice.

Good—at least she had no clue what I had just stolen. I held my book out to her as if it was a peace offering and told her that my books were already on the shelves of major independent bookstores in Paris. I also mentioned that the famous critic Simon de Nadeau had bought my book at BJ Williams and would be critiquing it in a week or two for *The Lutèce Review*. My exaggerations grew with my confidence.

She opened her mouth slowly. I think a wisp of exhaust escaped.

"Mr.—" She paused and then stared at my book, "Moronski."

"That's MorANski."

"Whatever." Her head turned toward the front door. Another friggin' hair clip fell. "Giuliani and Sons DOESN'T do business with amateur writers walking in off the street."

I started to dance on the hair clips. My arms went up, my fingers snapping; a Flamenco dancer gone mad.

"What are you doing to my hair cl—"

I sang *La Cucaracha, la cucaracha* to drown her out. Then trilling my "r"s nicely, I yelled , "*Arriba! Arriba!*" A security guard "*arriba-ed*" in less than a minute to haul me and my hot-tempered *zapatos* out of the store.

As I was strong-armed away, I bellowed, "Don't worry—I'm going to become famous soon, and you're going to miss the boat. You're looking at the next Morgan Davis!"

"Yeah, right!" she yelled back and then laughed hysterically. A second later, she was bent over and coughing nonstop.

Near Notre Dame, I grabbed a coffee and counted my haul: 360 euros. And I was more upset about how I handled her rejection than emptying a purse. Then there was the whole matter of telling Natasha I would never steal again. I downed my coffee in under a minute. Still tense, I leaned back on my wicker chair, closed my eyes, and let the sun's rays inject a milligram of vitamin D and a litre of common sense into my veins. My face calmly turned to a smile as it toasted in the sun. My yin and yang (or my Yao and Ming) working as one, my thoughts turned to analyzing my last two acts of deviant behaviour. Prior to my trip to Paris, I had forgotten the last time I was unable to string a few choice words together to cleverly put someone down and avoid anything physical. (Although I still enjoyed a good scrap; it gets the blood flowing better than any energy drink on the market.) My mind tossed out convenient excuses, "This was the first time I was selling a book, and the public should be

—

87

more sympathetic," but that was bullshit. And the money I stole? Judging by the wad of credit cards in her wallet, this woman spent a lot of time on the Champs Elysées.

The noon heat was beginning to cook my face. In no hurry to leave, I found another table under an umbrella and ordered a *Leffe*. A waitress returned with two large jugs of beer on a tray. One frosty was for a street person sitting two tables over, fidgeting with a mountain of coins, and the other was for me. The beer cost six euros. And it was the hobo's lucky day; I put fifteen euros on the waitress's plate and told her I was paying for both and to keep the change. I had redistributed the wealth in Toronto more than once, why not Paris? Both the waitress and the bum nodded in appreciation. He took a sip and then picked at some sores on his arms. Kind of spoiled the moment.

I forgot about his pick-fest and concentrated on some kind of peaceful "defence" system—some combination of words and/or gestures to be cleverly employed the next time I was confronted by an unsupportive book vendor or sneaky gypsy. (And the stealing? Maybe that would never stop.)

My remedy for the jumpy attitude was straightforward: count backwards from ten—and no more goddamn dancing—before responding to criticism. I also reminded myself of my simple (and assumed stolen) definition of intelligence: "Don't make the same mistake twice." I made a mental note as well that Parisian bookstore vendors were like disc jockeys when it came to influencing the public about writers, their customers blindly dropping fifty euros for three or four books, capriciously recommended.

After a half-hour of soul searching (and no longer able to come up with anything else in my quest to overhaul more than one disorder), I ventured off to another bookstore in the Latin Quarter. I was anxious to test my ten-second rule.

Chicago Books and Grill was located on the famous cobblestones of Rue Mouffetard. I pointed my head in the general direction of the *Panthéon* and meandered my way to the well-known street. A jazz quartet, featuring an octogenarian singer (flugelhorn in hand), was playing on the corner of Mouffetard and rue Lacépède. He was singing *Georgia on my Mind* with the pipes of a thirty-year-old.

Standing a metre from the entrance, I checked out the front window. The sales-tingles revving up, my game happy-face on, I entered the store. A bell clanged over my head as I forced the door open—my first hint that this store had seen better days. A man jumped off his stool and detoured around the front desk to greet me.

"Hi. Welcome to Chicago Books and Grill. Looking for anything specific?"

"Why books and grill? I don't see any remnants of a restaurant here, unless one twists that wall lamp over there and the wall suddenly makes a 180-turn. James Bond movie stuff. Is there a row of single seats, fifties diner-style, on the other side?"

He laughed at my B-material. I learned that if I was going to sell a humorous book then I had better show a humorous side to my personality. I made people laugh with little effort, but it was generally heavy handed, its roots in a mixture of fatherly racism (while he was home), bad North-American comedy shows, and the fact that I'd read every book written by Martin Amis and Mordecai Richler.

"People ask all the time about 'the grill,'" he said. "The bookstore was part of a restaurant at one time. There are still lots of places in Paris where you can order a meal and grab a book off the wall."

"What happened to the restaurant part?"

"If you look on the north side of the store next door, it is the mirror image of our store. And, surprise surprise, it *is* a restaurant. Years ago, the owner of this store, believed to be Al Capone himself, decided that it wasn't profitable to maintain the restaurant and the book store, so he greased some Parisian palms and had the building split in two. The name "Chicago Books and Grill" was kept because it had an unusual ring to it." His black-rimmed glasses permanently rested on the tip of his proboscis. From this ancient point stemmed purply-blue veins that flowed in more directions than exits around the *Arc de Triomphe*. Further south hung a moustache partially covering lips long since drained of all colour. The birds' nests for eyebrows hung precariously low, leaving some guesswork of the shape and angle of his eyes.

I took out one of my books and handed it to "Al Capone Junior." With his other hand, he slid his glasses up his nose, the path briefly leaving a yellow streak. "This is an attractive looking woman on the cover. I'm instantly reminded of one of Al's molls that haunted the Books and Grill."

Specs of sarcasm filtered through my words. "I'm sure you—" I paused, thinking I should go easy on the disdain. "Sorry, I forgot to ask your name."

"The name's Al."

What a *surprise*—his name was Al. I kept my sarcasm to myself. "Hi, Al. My name's Vlad. I'm here to sell my book." We shook hands and I continued to talk, even though I could tell by the sudden intake of air he was anxious to speak. "I'm sure you've heard of Morgan Davis? The British writer? *Merde Doesn't Stink in Paris*?"

"Yes, of course. Capone would have loved his style of writing." I had two goals in mind: one, sell my book as quickly as possible, and two, try and get him to say a whole sentence without using the word *Capone*. I mentioned that my book was in different bookstores in Paris, but he was fixated on the cover.

"I can tell just by looking at the cover that Capone would have loved to read your book, but this store only sells used books."

"You're kidding! You mean you don't take *new* books?" I paused for a second and grinned. "Maybe I could scuff them up a little bit."

"Someone did that once in the store and Capone had him shot."

I rolled my eyes slowly, my "pleasant" act surely blown, and then let myself out.

Two blocks along the cobblestones, I stopped at a clothing store and purchased a dinner jacket for fifty euros. (Helen had asked me to wear one for the dinner she was hosting.) It matched the only pair of dress pants I owned. Stylish clothes never interested me, though I always made sure my mother looked good. And I never needed any fashionable work clothes because over the last thirty or so less-than-profitable years, my jobs varied from dead end to cul-de-sac. The longest legitimate employment on my "resumé" was a two-year stint as a security guard at a trucking company, a haven for fencing merchandise. And a brief stretch in Pearson Airport's baggage department was like working in a candy store of stolen goods.

I also drove and dispatched more taxis than I cared to remember. Selling life insurance, as well, was a lost cause. And I pumped enough gas to fill Lake Ontario. I had hoped to relive my childhood car-parts stealing days, but the gas stations didn't carry a lot of inventory and it was closely counted, though at least I had a chance to hone my late-night after-hours poker skills.

The gas station laughs came whenever the manager (all mass-produced: fat, alcoholic, cigar-smoking, and racist) walked in, usually unannounced, to check daily receipts. Rummaging through the cash register, he would habitually drop a nickel in the candy or peanut machine. Then he would shake the glass bubble, causing the ears of his beloved guard dog to perk up. Either a black lab or a German shepherd or a German lab or a black German would come running, lift the machine flap with its nose and stick its thirty-five-inch tongue up the slot to gobble the treats. Half an hour later, a customer would unknowingly drop a coin in the same machine. With straight faces, the other gas station flunkies (or "losers" was a better term, since we were in our thirties) and I would stand within eyesight of the customer and watch him happily munch the food. We'd try and make each other laugh. Occasionally one clown would laugh like a hyena, making us nearly piss our pants. Talk about immature!

And few would argue, including my mother, that I was the marrying type. She would say I was too fun and crazy to settle down—a nice way of saying that I was a younger version of the old man and could never be happy with just one woman. I made it to city hall --- once--- with a girlfriend, but an argument by the front steps ended our future together. I was a good-looking guy, though often pleasantly insolvent. And I seldom invited the ladies back to my apartment because it was sparse, always joking that I was a minimalist. But women can tell. The attractive guy part appeals to them, but don't find the penniless part cool once you've hit your mid-twenties. And it shed more light why I stole Carson's French experiences, because after I was kicked out of university, I drifted and grifted through a few decades. It was time to move to the other side of the tracks permanently.

Helen's apartment was five or six blocks from the métro stop. She lived in a posh neighbourhood, with row upon row of elegant, perfectly landscaped apartments. And the deeper I walked into this den of perfection the more I felt out of my league. I kept looking over my shoulder, waiting for someone to escort me out.

I turned a corner lined with bright red roses, pink carnations and white chrysanthemums. She'd mentioned that two oval-shaped bushes, each the girth of a fridge and reaching the height of a basketball hoop, would "greet" me by the entrance.

I tapped B128, Helen's apartment code. Without warning, a blue-sleeved arm draped with a blue-white-and-red scarf the size of a truck-stop flag yanked my hand. I found myself lying on a half-metre high Chinese elm bordered by orange tiger lilies, pink petunias, white carnations and baby's breath. I wanted to yell, "What the fuck?" but Pam had put one hand over my mouth and placed an elbow over my chest, making the intake of air and the outtake of words extremely difficult. Oh and I felt like a building had fallen on me.

"Hey, faggot who writes words. I call them 'faggords' by the way . . ."

"Hello . . . hello . . . is there someone outside?" I recognized Helen's panicked voice on the intercom. Pam, all too familiar with the voice, whispered, yet maintained a scowl capable of scaring Al Queda. "If you yell when I take my hand off your girly fuckin' mouth, I will personally grab your tiny balls and stuff them in your fuckin' yap. Are we fuckin' clear?" She took her padded anvil for a hand off my mouth.

"Why don't you call us 'fiords' instead of 'faggords'? At least it's a real word." She promptly jammed her anvil into my groin. I screamed.

"Hello! Hello! Is that you Vlad? If it's not, I'm phoning the police." Helen sounded less frantic after repeating the same lines in French.

Although my head was pinned to the bush, I managed to shift my eyes. No Frenchies were around to witness this embarrassing and painful shake-and-takedown.

"You thought you saw the last of me, didn't you?"

Having no clue what to do I just shook my head up and down, and then side-to-side.

Her breath smelled of blueberry schnapps and blue Smarties. I sensed a theme.

"Is someone there?" said Helen.

I let a few seconds pass and then spoke to Pam. "So, what brings you and your lovely blue coat and matching scarf to the 8th *arrondissement*? And by the way, I think your blue tongue looks divine."

"Don't try and 'swelk' me! And I know exactly why the fuck you're here!"

Kneeling beside the bush, her hulkish body making the laws of leverage a non-issue, she continued to pin me down with one elbow. I felt like a monarch butterfly mounted in a natural science museum exhibit.

"What do you mean?" I said. "I was *just* out for a walk." I avoided eye contact, an obvious sign that I was full of shit. She responded by leaning a linebacker-sized shoulder into me. I think my windpipe flattened. Is that normal? My life flashed before my eyes. Was this how I was going to leave this earth? I would have preferred getting hit in the middle of the street by a car while ogling a gorgeous woman. Deathly romantic, no?

"This is the last time . . . hello . . . hello. Okay, whoever is out there—I'm calling the police."

Pam lifted her elbow and then stood up. She undid the top few buttons of her blouse. I looked away. She put her foot on my face and easily turned it, forcing me to look at her. "You're either going to sleep with me or have me kick the shit out of you."

"Great choice!?"

"You're fuckin' lucky this time. The cops will show up in thirty goddamn seconds!"

"You've done this before?"

"Shut the fuck up and let me finish."

I shut the fuck up.

"If it was a call in the 18th *arrondissement*, the police would have an espresso first and then maybe move their fuckin' asses. Anyway, I gotta split. Oh and one more thing." She paused and weighed her arms down on my shoulders. I thought about kicking her in the groin. "If you tell Helen, I will fuckin' kill you." Godzilla meant business.

"Fine! How the hell did you figure out I was here?"

She let go of my shoulders. "I work in a fuckin' bookstore, asswipe! The whole world knows that you're Helen's new bitch author. I call them 'newbitors.' She hasn't stopped talking about you since you left the store."

I wanted to smile, but I'm sure she would have knocked out a couple of my teeth. A police car wailed in the distance.

"See ya later, ya fuckin' *litbas*," she said and chugged her massive body in the direction of a local park.

"What does litbas mean?" I yelled. No answer. I brushed the dirt and twigs off my clothes and pushed the button again.

"I've already called the police," replied the voice on the intercom.

"Don't worry, Helen. It's me, Vlad."

"Are you okay? I thought I heard a woman scream."

God—was my voice that high? The door clicked. "A hundred percent, as always. I'll be right up."

"We live in 810." I looked around and saw a cop car drive by.

The red and white hall carpet resembled Napoleon's coronation robe. Hanging from Helen's heavy mahogany door was a fierce-looking, gold lion's head the size of my fist, the loose ring in its mouth patiently waiting to summon its master. I lifted the ring and set it down. What a racket!

"Coming . . . coming," said an excited voice. Helen opened the

93

door. We instinctively kissed on both cheeks, and she squeezed me tightly.

"Thank you, Helen, for the warm reception."

"I'm thrilled you're here." She stared at me for a few seconds. "Vlad, your hair is ruffled and your dinner jacket is torn." I looked under both armpits. The left one was torn. Sticking my head in front of a mirror for a nanosecond, I matted down my hair. A blade of grass fell on to Helen's mega-thick carpet. I put my foot over it. *Goddamn NiR!*

"Geez, Helen, I'm going to have to take this coat back. I never noticed the rip." I was too embarrassed to tell her what had just happened.

"You can't trust people these days; they'll try and sell you anything."

Helen, you could only imagine what I've been sellin' my whole life.

The living room was decorated in nineteenth-century French art. Tapestries and oil paintings fought for space on every side. Helen's wall work appeared to be arranged in chronological French literary order, beginning with a painting of Rabelais's Gargantua, followed by a colourful tapestry of Jean-Jacques Rousseau. Next were four paintings (all in different light and season) of Chateaubriand sitting on a horse. Tributes to Baudelaire and Hugo alternated between still life corpses and paintings of Notre Dame.

Helen's husband entered the living room and sidled up to me. I hated sidlers.

"Hello. You must be Vlad." I turned around and he hugged me.

I said hello and then gave Helen a cringing look.

"Oh, don't mind my husband, Reggie. He's not a wanker."

We all found merriment in that line.

"Please, Vlad," said Reggie, "have a spot on the loveseat next to my chair."

His chair was worth killing for. Was it the wooden lion's paws for arms or the gorilla's feet for legs? Or the wooden back, its high corners chiselled into falcons waiting to swoop? Or was it just the authentic fart sounds the seat made every time Reggie moved?

"Reggie, where did you get that chair? It's the coolest thing I've ever seen." He straightened up to reply, but Helen interrupted. "There's only one other chair in the world similar to Reggie's, and it's in the *Musée d'Orsay.*"

"Vlad, I have to say, after Helen, my chair is the most unique and solid thing I have." Helen walked into the living room and gave Reggie a kiss. "That's so sweet, Reggie. But what about our daughter?"

"Kate as well, darling, but surely that goes without saying."

"I know, dear. My God, Vlad," said Helen, "I'm such a terrible hostess; I forgot to offer you a drink."

"Not a problem; I'll have what everyone else is having."

"Nonsense. Just wait while I roll out the alcohol trolley." Fancy-chair boy clasped his hands and frantically shifted his shoulders back and forth. "Yip-yip-yippy! The booze-on-wheels truck is coming."

"Oh, Reggie, don't be silly," said Helen. "We have company."

"I can't help it, dear, I just lose myself when you roll out 'Betty the booze trolley.'"

"I know, love, but you'll have to control yourself tonight. Remember, you have to think about more than just pleasing Betty. We have an aspiring writer as our guest of honour, and Katherine is coming over as well."

Helen snuck away to a corner of the living room and wheeled in the cart: an eclectic, glass mini-Manhattan skyline of liquid-filled hexagonal and rectangular prisms, each tinkling joyously. Damn—*I* wanted to yell "yippy!"

The intercom buzzed and within a few minutes, a voluptuous six-foot blond with a cheerful look entered the apartment.

Helen's daughter and I shook hands as we met halfway into the living room. She looked about forty.

"Hello, my name is Vlad."

"Mine's Kate," she said with a smile that revealed huge teeth, all present and accounted for. And in relatively good order, like an old, trusty double stacked, off-white set of Britannica's, the M-N volume torn at the bottom right corner and the S slightly receding.

"Such a lovely, perky name," I said and offered her a spot beside me on the love seat. Kate hugged her father before she sat down. "Hi, Reggie."

"Hello, love. How is life treating you tonight?"

"Much better since my divorce officially came through."

"That's wonderful. You're truly free as a bird." Reggie motioned his arms as if he was flying. The guy was a few pepperonis short of a full pizza. Helen had briefly exited the room and returned with an unopened bottle of Rémy Martin. She pulled her chair closer to the trolley.

"Vlad, what do you prefer?"

"Well you went to all that effort to get the Rémy Martin. I'll have a shot of it, please."

"Good choice, ol' chum," said Reggie.

"Dad, don't embarrass him!"

"Sorry, dear. Just got a little excited."

Helen asked us to raise our glasses.

The four toasts were as follows:

"Here's to the next famous writer discovered by yours truly."

"Here's to the next charming and witty famous writer discovered by my mother."

"Here's to the next famous writer ... me."

"Here's to the booze."

Halfway through my third shot of the "Remstar" Martin, the ladies removed themselves to the kitchen to put the finishing touches on dinner.

Reggie came wrapped in a red paisley dinner jacket with matching belt and white scarf neatly folded around his—I guessed—seventy-year-old loose-skinned neck. Resting on his head was a full mat of dyed black hair (his?), well-lubed, and cut short above the ear. He lifted his drink and pointed it toward me.

"Well, Vlad, have you always been a devilishly handsome writer?"

I paused for a second, not knowing what to say to another man about my appearance. "Handsome, um no; writer, yeah sure, why not."

"Dinner's ready," chimed a voice from the dining room.

"Coming," I responded, not giving Reggie a chance to continue our awkward conversation.

My nose, lost in a bouquet of Provençal spices perking up some kind of meat, guided me into the next room.

The dining room was also full of paintings. There may have been a Picasso on the wall, but a combination of my third Remstar and the steam emanating from a silver platter of duck à l'orange made it look more like Munsch's *The Scream*.

The meat was passed clockwise around the table. Helen set the duck à l'orange dish in motion, followed in close intervals by several small white porcelain bowls filled with diced carrots, asparagus, beans and a fancy boat filled with gravy.

My plate plastered, I lifted my head to see how Reggie the "semi-inebriate" was handling the food. Every platter, tray and bowl had congregated in front of him; however, he was sound asleep. Helen gently shook Reggie. She walked him to a bedroom (I assumed), propping him

———

up along the way with a strong arm and a lullaby sung heartily in German.

Kate sensed a look on my face that read, "What the hell just happened?" "Don't worry," she said with impeccable timing. "Reggie takes a lot of medication and occasionally, if he dips too heavily into the Rémy Martin, he'll pass out. Mom or I usually watch his intake before dinner, but we were too busy tonight. It's not a big deal. He'll sleep it off and have leftovers in the morning. And as usual, his hangover will wipe out any memory of the night before." Her fork full of duck, she paused and slowly allowed her lips to nudge the meat into her mouth.

She finished her thought. "Unfortunately, he will not even remember having met you. But! I'm hoping that will be all the more reason for you to see us again." *Is this what old money does to people? The Addams Family and The Munsters were more normal than these guys. And where did the German come from?*

"Oh, I'm sure we'll work something out." I said.

A lock of Kate's long blond hair fell over her cheekbone. She swept it behind her ear and smiled, her eyes glinting in a way that said, "Your place or mine?" I think her bosom also spoke an ample language of love. To get my mind off her gorgeous body I jammed my first forkful of duck into my mouth, and one by one, every capillary gave in to the sensuous fowl juices, while I pleasurably masticated.

I needed half a glass of wine to wash it down. "Kate, this duck is wonder—"

Helen entered the dining room and interrupted. "Well, that's over with." She even wiped her hands, indicating some kind of accomplishment.

Copious mouthfuls of duck later, Helen proposed a toast. "Here's to a fabulous evening. There isn't anything more I could ask for." She looked at me. "To a soon-to-be-very-successful author." Then she turned and pointed her glass toward Kate, "And to my lovely daughter, who officially got her divorce from that scum." Kate blushed as we toasted, Helen smiled from ear to ear, and I was too tipsy to take note of what expression I wore.

The main course finished, Helen refilled our glasses, refusing no for an answer, and then told Kate and me to make ourselves comfortable in the living room. We gravitated back to our humble beginnings—the love seat—,the wine making waves in our glasses as we giggled over nothing along the way.

———

97

Our hostess returned from the kitchen with a tray full of rich French pastries.

"Ta-da," said Helen in a cheery voice as she waved the tray under our noses, creating a tease filled with sweet-smelling decadence. We sampled a *morceau* of each and snickered over their respective frilly French names. I called the red syrupy one dripping over cream and chocolate "Crème de la Coronary."

"Helen, you sneak," I said, trying to sound extra hammy. "These desserts are incredible, but I've run out of notches in my belt."

"They are decadent, aren't they?"

"I have to be honest; you are making me a little nervous tonight. You haven't said a word about my book. Have you had a chance to read it yet?"

Helen looked around the room as if she was trying to build some excitement over what she was about to say. I had to admit she had presence and, though she was controlling, she was personable.

"Vlad, I loved your book." And she said it with no hint of sarcasm, dishonesty, flippancy or mockery.

I wanted to cry. My body inexplicably leapt in her direction for a hug. And I wasn't a hugger. "Thank you, Helen. That means a lot to me. And I'm impressed that you read it in only a day."

"I couldn't put it down. It just took part of last night and a long lunch break today to finish the book. I *am* a member of Mensa, by the way."

"That's funny 'cause I'm a member of Womensa."

I stared at Helen, hoping she would laugh. She had a narrow face, sprouting an acorn for a nose. Her Japanese comic book–sized blue eyes had surely caught the fancy of every man when she was a young temptress. Unlike Kate, she had perky lips and semi-protruding cheekbones, a vase from another era. Kate's eyes and nose matched her mothers' but her cheekbones were flat. Both of them wore loose curls resting on Joan Crawford–sized, high-society shoulders, padding not included.

Helen didn't laugh, but in an excited tone, Kate said, "Mom is giving me a copy tonight. I cannot wait to read it."

"I'm sure, Kate, if your mother loved it, you'll love it as well. The two of you have the same sense of humour." The ladies looked at each other, sharing radiant smiles. They let me have the floor.

"When I was selling my books in Canada (a lie, of course), I would

---

98

tell my potential readers, if you're looking for a 'Chucky' Dickens or an 'Ernie' Hemingway or even a Vic 'the pedantic romantic' Hugo, then my book isn't for your reading consumption." I stopped and stuck my nose in the air. "For I *don't* write literary fiction, my friend. No, no, no, instead, my *mots* have carefully fashioned a new genre in the world of literature. It's not literary *fiction*; it's literary *conniption*." I paused and soaked in my admirers' smiles.

"I think that's the second time you've used the *literary conniption* line, but it's still funny. Vlad, I have to admit you are a publisher's dream. You have what we call in the business 'chutzpah,'" Helen said in a sweet voice coated with a sprinkle of business acumen.

"An interesting choice of words," I said.

"You remind me of a funny John Irving."

"No, Mom. He's got Hugh Grant written all over him."

"But his skin is so tanned looking. He has that swarthy Mediterranean look. Vlad, hold still. I'm going to take a few pictures of you right now. We can use them for your promotion. Do you mind?"

"Of course not."

Helen took several pictures of me and then of Kate and me.

"Vlad, I'll put a few of these pictures in the front window when you do your first book signing."

I wanted to comment, but Helen continued talking. "Something tells me you've been waiting a long time for this moment. Oh, and one other thing before I forget, I assumed you had written some other novels and a list of short stories; however, I googled your name but was unable to find anything else you've penned." *Was my arrest record online?*

"Well, *French Like Me* is the first book I've ever written and, as you know, it was self-published."

"All the better. Our readers love an underdog, an unknown, a fresh face. We have far too many drab books about supposedly funny adventures that take place in Paris. I thought I'd read every joke or description about a baguette, but you've managed to come up with fresh material. Also, I've never read an adventure that takes place in a flea market, and the relationship between Carson and Moni—"

"Mother!" interrupted Kate. "Don't give the story away—I haven't read it yet!"

"Sorry, dear, I just wanted to tell Vlad my impressions of the book. Anyway, as I mentioned before, as long as Simon de Nadeau reviews your book in a positive manner you'll be an instant success. And then the

---

customers will come in droves. I'm also on the phone once a week with London, New York, Los Angeles, Frankfort, Tokyo, even Shanghai—believe it or not, just to name a few cities—to talk about the latest trends in English book sales."

"I'm impressed with your connections." Helen's face beamed. I decided to test her. "Helen, your smile is so big it looks like an upturned baguette."

"Was it five or six pages into Chapter two of *French Like Me* that you used that expression?"

"Ya got me. I don't even remember what page it was on."

Kate looked at me. "Vlad, when it comes to books, my mother has a photographic memory."

"I can tell."

"Vlad, in your book, it's pretty ob—"

Kate cut in with mock sternness, "MOTHER!"

"Dear, why don't you give me ten minutes alone with Vlad to discuss book business, and then you can come back and tell him all about yourself."

"I'll be back in ten, but don't embarrass me. I'm a grown woman."

I cut in and raised my glass. "Here's to grown women." There was no clinking, but the ladies did raise their glasses.

Kate grabbed her glass of wine and smiled at me as she walked out of the room.

"Vlad, as I was saying, it's obvious that your protagonist, Carson, is in love with Paris. I don't think a single conversation goes by without him alluding to something about the city that pleases him."

"You're right; that's what Carson, I mean *I* intended. Though I write comedy, I wanted the reader to understand that the underlying theme is a person in love with a city. I'm curious what the French, those that can read in English of course, would think of my book. I've heard that the French even buy Morgan Davis's books in English."

Helen offered a business smile, best described as wide and bright, her incisors bent on an angle and euro symbol-shaped. "You're talking to the right person. Our Morgan Davis sales are through the roof, but I see a lot of room for you on our shelves as well. I think your book has more of an edge to it. I'm friends with several agents, and I'm good friends with one in particular, and I'm always inviting the hottest writers to read their latest work. My store easily has more writers reading their work than all the other English bookstores in Paris combined. I can also get Alcatraz

Books, a Parisian book distribution company, to stop their presses anytime and print as many copies of your book as I want."

Even though I had been drinking, I had to listen to every word she had to say. And I would speak to someone else in the business to make sure she wasn't bullshitting me. After all, a bullshitter can't bullshit another bullshitter.

Helen continued. "Your TVA account has already been arranged. Because you're not French *and* unpublished, the French government is not handing out the TVAs as easily as they used to, so it took some major string pulling. But, obviously, to make this work, you'll need a publisher. And before you get a publisher you need an agent. Hey, you need to make some money on this venture, not just me." She forced a smile. God, for a second I thought she only cared about herself.

"Yes, Helen, I want to make money, too." For some reason I changed the subject. "I think Peter Mayle was the first British writer to make it big in France. I believe he made the French, at least in the south, look quaint, capricious and generally drunk all the time. Ironically, when I first read *A Year in Provence*, I thought the book was whimsical. But over the years, and spending more time in France, I reread the book and found it insulting. I have French friends who are not drunk all the time." Thank God I remembered endless stories my brother recounted about living in France. And my lies—my deceptive life —would sooner or later bury me, but why stop the bullshit shovel now?

"Interesting." Helen paused and put an inquisitive index finger to her bottom lip. "So you would first compare your work with Peter Mayle's?"

"Yes. Do you happen to know him?"

"Of course. Like Morgan Davis, he drops in from time to time to sign books. We've even had Peter and Morgan over for dinner."

"At the same time?"

She laughed. "No, though it would be a scream. It would be an impossible task for both of them to attend with their business schedules, and besides, they are both private people."

"Maybe one day you could invite the three of us together: the past, the present and the future."

"Interesting. maybe one day I'll try." Helen offered me a digestif. Remembering that my brother drank Chartreuse often when he lived in Savoie, I pointed at the bottle with green liquid.

"Yes, good old Chartreuse," she said. "If this doesn't burn out your insides, nothing will."

"So you English use the word 'burn' in that context as well?"

"Of course." She poured one for herself.

We chinned.

"Vlad, what are you looking at?"

"Sorry—I was mesmerized by your Picasso."

"Why not take a closer look." I stood up and moved toward the painting.

"Be still, Vlad." I stopped. "I'll bring *it* to *you*."

"Great, takeout"

The painting in her hand, Helen replied, "I don't understand. What do you mean *takeout*?"

"At McDonalds—when you order something, you can take it out. You know, leave the restaurant with the food."

Helen laughed. "Oh, we Brits say 'takeaway.'"

She handed me the painting.

I grabbed it firmly by the frame and held it into the light. "Why, thank you, Helen. Is this painting a takeaway for me?"

"Very funny." She lightly touched the bottom corner of the actual painting with an index finger, and showed her finger to me. "Vlad, have you ever touched a Picasso?"

"I touched a *Julie* Picasso once in grade seven. Does that count?"

She laughed and grabbed my index finger. "Now touch a real Picasso. Well, are you a changed man after touching it?" she said, her eyes anticipating some inspirational words from yours truly.

"Yeah, sure, I guess I'm inspired."

Helen smiled at my indifference.

"Helen, what is this painting worth?"

"thirty million . . . American!"

"This weird looking drawing of a young girl is worth that much dough-ray-me?"

"Yes. There are only a few paintings Picasso did of his daughter. And it's insured, though I prefer you don't drop it."

"Where did you get it?"

"Reggie's grandparents were serious art collectors. He was the only remaining relative, so he inherited the works."

"The lucky bugger."

"Yes, you're right—Reggie *is* a lucky—um—chap." She hung up the painting.

102

"Helen, you better not turn your back on me 'cause I might steal it."

Helen walked back but spoke before she sat down. "Don't worry, Vlad, the security system won't turn *its* back. Ha-ha! Anyway, back to business. I have to ask, what made you decide to write the book?"

I downed the shot and turned my thoughts to why my brother wanted to write a book. "Well, after living in France for two years, I wrote a memoir about my family living in southeast France." More lies.

"You have a family? That surprises me."

"No . . . um." Even after several glasses of booze, I panicked. I looked at a painting for a second before I spoke. "Um, sorry. I got lost in my book for a second. No, I don't have a wife or kids. And I've rarely ever flown, so, as far as travelling is concerned, I lived vicariously through my brother, Carson."

"Have you been to France?"

"Never, but I read a lot and love French movies." And now she was going to tell me I was nothing but an imposter and to hit the road.

"That's amazing! I can't believe you could write that much without living here."

"Well, I, too, have a phenomenal memory and a wild imagination."

Kate returned, her glass empty and her timing impeccable; I was done stealing anything more from my brother that evening.

Helen looked at Kate. "Vlad was in the middle of explaining how he came to write the book."

"Mother, you promised!" Kate looked at me. "Vlad, please, not another word about your book."

I nodded in agreement. Kate poured herself a snifter of brandy and sat beside me.

"So, Kate, please tell me all about yourself." She first looked at her mother as if seeking permission.

Her mother spoke. *Big surprise.* "Kate, tell our guest everything."

Kate sipped her brandy and smiled innocently. "Well, I'm not sure where to start. I—"

"Start at the 'I'm officially divorced' part."

"Mother!"

Not having grown up with sisters, I had to filter Helen and Kate's relationship through the books I had read. And the obvious conclusion: dominant mother/subordinate daughter wanting to break free.

"Well, as my mother has mentioned *more* than once this evening, I'm officially divorced."

I raised my glass. "Congratulations."

"Thank you. My divorce wasn't that difficult. I found out that my ex, Arnaud, was cheating on me, so I decided to end it pretty fa—"

"YOU ENDED IT FAST!? I DON'T THINK SO!" blurted Helen.

"So, Kate, what do you do for a living?" I said, sensing an oncoming argument.

"Well, I'm in the book business, too, but it's more behind the scenes."

Helen walked into the kitchen, giving Kate and me some space. Kate filled my glass with more Chartreuse and continued. "I work for Atticus Book Distributers. They provide books in several languages for bookstores in Paris."

My ears perked up. "So you're able to print more *French Like Me*s?"

"No, unfortunately, our company does not deal with fiction; we deal with ed—"

"Ed-u-ca-tion," yelled Helen. "I've heard it a hundred times."

"Well, it's true."

I looked at Kate. "Why don't we just go into the kitchen? I don't want you two waking up Reggie."

"That's impossible," they said simultaneously and laughed. *And I thought my family had problems!*

We walked into the kitchen and helped Helen clean up.

"Kate, do you have a business card? I want to find out more about the distribution business in general." I looked at Helen. "I assume that's okay."

"Of course," she replied.

Kate handed me her card.

"Well, ladies, I hate to be a party pooper, but it's getting a little late. I plan on doing some writing tomorrow." My lie sounded convincing.

"I understand," said Helen. "I'm going to hang on to my itinerary that I had planned for you because I have to make some more calls tomorrow, but in the meantime, I would appreciate it if you could give me whatever *French Like Me*s you have with you. Just out of curiosity, how many do you still have?"

"Twenty-five, I think. But I can order a lot more from the company that printed them in Canada."

"That's okay. I can get hundreds of books printed in Paris, but let's start with your last twenty-five and see what happens with de Nadeau. As

I've said several times, if he gives you a positive review, the agents and publishing companies will come to us—I mean you."

"That's great. What time are you open tomorrow?"

"Ten o'clock."

"I'll have them at your door by 9:50." My smiley face looking as solemn as humanly possible I added. "Helen, I have to ask. What you're doing for me is incredible, but I've come to Paris with basically just the shirt on my back, if you catch my drift."

"Say no more. Trust me—when you show up tomorrow there will be a cheque waiting for you."

"Certified?"

Helen laughed. "As long as BJ Williams is written on the top left corner of the cheque, you have your certification."

"Thanks for the reassurance."

"Remember, an author is paid by his or her publisher, unless you're involved with Amazon, and yesterday you said you weren't."

"I'm familiar with the river. Does that help?"

"Perfect."

I thanked them for a terrific evening and showed myself out.

After midnight, the air humid, the sky dark but friendly, I decided to walk back to my hotel. Along the Seine, I listened to its whispering black ripples for some guidance. And why? I was interested in Kate, despite her dominating mother. And Kate and I weren't exactly teenagers, so why would her mother care? I was sure that Helen liked me and wanted me to become successful, but she could sense my lower class background. And for the first time all night, I thought about Natasha. I had a lot on my plate.

Wednesday, June 27th

I arrived at BJ Williams a few minutes before ten o'clock and knocked a couple of times. Without warning, panic set in. What if Pam or NiR or whatever the hell she called herself answered the door?

The door opened. "Vlad! I'm soooo happy to see you," said Helen. We instinctively kissed on both cheeks, kind of funny since we were both anglophones, but that's what Paris does to you—it makes you French.

Helen stretched out her hands and demanded to take a bag. I gave her the lighter one and followed her into the store.

"People" said Helen gleefully, "this is our next superstar writer." A group of fifteen or so employees huddled in front of the cash registers, a few polite metres away from Helen and me. She turned and motioned her hand toward my face. I wasn't sure what I was supposed to do with her hand, so I grabbed it and spun around once.

"Oh, I would gladly dance with him," said a BJ Williams employee.

Someone else yelled, "He's just another asshole!"

"Pam Pam Pam. Do behave," said Helen.

"It's NiR! How many times do I have to tell you people that? It's NiR!"

How did I miss that nutbar when I walked in?

Helen continued, "Could the gang please say hello to Vlad Moranski." I heard a mish-mash of greetings.

Pam was two metres away and lurking toward me, tidying up some already perfectly arranged books. Thoughts of John Lennon, Martin Luther King, Anwar Sadat, JFK, Bobby FK—you get the theme—flashed through my mind.

Pam whispered in my ear. "If you don't give it to me, I will mess you up bad, you fuckin' *litbas*."

I whispered back, "You're insane" and then smiled to the small crowd.

Helen held up one of my books in one hand and the bag in the other. "Everyone, we have to make room by the Morgan Davis display for twenty-five of *Vlad's* books."

"I'll do it," shouted three people at once. Two more ran to the display.

"That's okay! Back to your posts; I'll handle the display myself."

She told two employees to move twenty of Davis's books to storage. And she suggested that I walk around and familiarize myself with the store. She'd find me later. I meandered for a quarter of an hour, my mind more on keeping a safe distance from NiR than learning the store's geography. Helen caught up to me in the magazine section.

"Vlad, the job is done. Come back and see the display."

My books were stacked in four piles, and the top book on each pile had a *French Like Me* propped on a stand with a florescent pink sticker attached that read, "Helen's book of the month." And the books were nudged against Morgan Davis's latest bestseller.

Helen's face was radiant. "Well, Vlad, what do you think?"

"I would have preferred that you put my books right on top of Davis's." I smiled as I said it.

"You are a cheeky one." She gently put a knuckle into my ribs.

"The pink sticker is a nice upgrade from Pam's green ones."

"And I seldom put a sticker on any book."

A woman stepped between us and picked up my book. She read the testimonials.

Helen looked at her. "The author is standing right beside me and would be thrilled to sign your book."

"You're kidding," she said, comparing the picture in the book with me.

"Yes, Miss, that picture you see and I are one and the same."

"I'd love it, Mr. Moranski, if you'd sign my book."

Helen had a pen handy. The woman's name was Alice and I signed it: Dear Alice, Enjoy a different slice of Paris —Vlad.

Short and sweet and a tad boring, but it would have to do. Natasha could help me with a better catch phrase.

"Vlad, you don't have to stay, though it would be nice if you'd stick around a while to sign a few books."

"It would be my pleasure, and then maybe we could talk about the cheque."

"Yes, the cheque. How about you sign ten or fifteen books and I'll get the cheque?"

I signed some books, but my mind was on my brother. How would he react if he saw my book about him on the stands in BJ Williams or Indigo in Toronto? I grinned, imagining him taking the first flight over to Paris or just diving into the Atlantic, each breaststroke fuelled by his rage. He'd dry himself off outside BJ Williams to avoid dripping on their carpet (big surprise!) and then wrap his hands around my neck during one of the many book signings I foresaw.

Helen returned, waving an envelope. "Here's to our next superstar." I took it, but kept it sealed.

"Thanks. I'll go ahead and get a bank account in Paris."

"Already done! I've opened one, in your name, of course. It's the BNP Paribas just down the street, but more importantly, are you not going to open it?"

I pulled out the cheque. One thousand euros would go a long way. And, more importantly, it was honest money.

I dropped in on Byron's Bookshop to see if any of my books had sold. He was sitting at his pulpit, directing the hotties, as usual.

———

"Byron, how's it goin'?"

"It be well, Vlad, my literary laugh apparatus. And what brings you into my most humble book abode, you journalist with jive?"

"I couldn't resist, Byron, oh . . . um . . . oh, noble one," I said, struggling to speak his lingo.

"Kindly imbibe some of my libations, *gratis* of course, offered or I should I say proffered by the travel section just ahead. I've got tea, coffee—it goes great with good ol' Canadian maple syrup—and of course fresh bubbly Perrier. And if those don't tickle your taste buds, just ask and I'll have one of the girls fetch whatever your heart craves."

"That's nice of you, but I had a coffee a while ago, so I'm okay."

"Please. *Mi casa es tu casa.*"

"Thanks, Byron. *Muy bien.* Byron was about my height, six foot one, but his sullen shoulders made him appear smaller. His permanent phony smile diminished his height as well, for some unknown reason.

He glanced at his computer and then at me. "Have you been partaking in any bourgeois carnivals?"

What the hell is a bourgeois carnival? "BJ Williams took a couple of my books, but not much has happened," I said in a blasé voice, Byron not having to know my every move.

"Ah, BJ Williams—*the* tome knights of the round table." Byron pretended he was brandishing a sword. "I will slay them once and for all one day with my business acumen and superior book pricing savvy. Plus, my bevy of bookstore fairies get the "word of Byron" out with Godspeed or what I always say, Byronspeed." He closed his eyes.

I smiled at the "Byronspeed" comment. Hell, we all have egos.

Byronspeed continued. "Have you seen my blitzkrieg of ads posted throughout the 5th and the 6th?

"No, I have not."

"One day, my droll *romancier,* I will personally take you on a voyage through this lovely Paris-dise." He motioned his right arm out as if introducing an orchestra to an affectionate audience. "And you shall see of what I speak."

"Good stuff, Byron. I get a kick out of your play on words." He smiled from ear to ear and would have spread peacock feathers if he'd had them.

"Stop it, you. You're too caring." He briefly placed a hand on my wrist.

"I am curious—have you read anything from my book yet?"

"Excuse me, Vlad. Alice—yoo-hoo, Alice."

"Yes, Mr. Byron," replied a voice hidden behind a pile of books.

"Remember, I want you to pick up the stack of advertisements exactly at noon, and then post them in the area I've carefully outlined on the map. Please do not forget to pick up the map on my desk before you leave."

"I promise I won't forget, Mr. Byron."

"Fine. And please be cognizant of the relationship between the little hand and the big hand above my head."

"Yes, Mr. Byron. I see the clock beside your poster of Morgan Davis."

A curvy woman with cheekbones to match walked into the store. She squeezed by me, her heavily made-up eyes focused on the fiction section. I lingered over her perfume.

"My sincerest apologies, Vlad. What were we pontificating about? Or should I say about *what* were we pontificating? Must be careful with those devilishly dangling prepositions. Without a doubt, they have become the scourge of the English language."

I motioned my head back-and-forth a couple of times between Byron and the woman to get him to notice her. He didn't bite.

"Yes," he said. "I've digested the first thirty pages. You have some outrageously funny lines. And the affable affiliation you've fashioned with Carson and his precocious lads is a hoot."

"Thank you, though I'm afraid there are some serious typos— fifteen, I think, in all."

"Tut-tut and never you mind, oh writer of extreme Parisian merriment and mayhem. Why . . . I shall knight you "Sir M&M." He paused again. Too many pauses—I had to get out of there, and BJ Williams was helping me more anyway.

Byron continued. "Well, as always, what do I say about typos?" He paused again, yes again, and looked at his hired help. "GIRLS! OH, GIRLS! WHAT DO I ALWAYS SAY ABOUT TYPOS!?""

From three or four different spots in the bookstore, I heard in unison, "That's what second editions are for!" I thought I was in a Lick's restaurant in Toronto, ordering a burger.

"Well, I'm glad you're happy with the book. Anyway, Byron, it was nice talking to you, but I have to visit a friend. Thanks again. I'll drop in soon to hear your impressions of *French Like Me* when you're finished. But, hey, take your time—you're extremely busy."

"I shall be done with your humorous masterpiece in a few cognac-induced evenings. Now be off with you and take a devil-may-care walk around Paris . . . on me."

"I shall do that," I said, trying not to roll my eyes.

The streets warm and bright, I made my way to Natasha's bookstore.

"Vlad, *enchanté, mon amour!*" She ran over and gave me a big sloppy kiss on the lips.

"*Hiroshima, mon amour.*" We kissed again and then hugged.

"Whoa, Vlad! Is that a pistol in your pocket or are you just happy to see me?"

"Ha-ha!." I kept a tight but loving grip on her arms. I enjoyed the feeling of her biceps and triceps contracting and expanding, her toned muscles reminding me that she wasn't a pushover.

We let go when a group of Sulley-hatted and ball-capped old-timers hobbled in.

"Uh, um . . . Mr. Moranski," said Natasha in a deep, unrehearsed voice—a voice suggesting we weren't an item—"Maybe you could grab a sub for me around the corner. It's called Subway. Are there very many in Canada?"

"Tons,, the place is crawlin' with 'em. What'll ya have, Sweet Onion Chicken Teriyaki? Meatball sub?"

"I'll just have the turkey sub with all the fixings except onions. Oh and extra chipotle sauce. And get what you want." She grabbed a twenty out of her wallet.

"That a no candu-reactor, my dear. Put it back."

"Vlad! One: take the money and two: what is a 'no candu-reactor'?"

"I just threw the *reactor* in. Maybe they were built before your time. Anyway, I'm paying because I got a big-ass cheque today from BJ Williams."

"How much?" said Natasha, who had focused her eyes (she nudged me to look as well) at a man in his seventies wearing a Red Sox baseball cap, its brim covering his eyes. We watched him take a book off the shelf and place it inside his Sulley Indefatigable coat. Natasha whispered in my ear, "That's the problem with those goddamn Sulley coats—they've got too many goddamn hidden pockets."

The man took another paperback as we continued to whisper. "Natasha, I thought you were okay with the Sulley stuff?"

"The hats are okay for the older generation—you can't hide a book in them."

The man was on his third paperback.

"Vlad, I usually stop these guys at three. I have to say something, but I do get tired of these old farts always claiming dementia, or amnesia—anything that ends in *ia*."

"How about milk of magnesia?"

"Hilarious! Once I caught a guy stealing Steven Hawking's *A Brief History of Time*, and he claimed he suffered from dementia. And he's reading Steven Hawking! Give me a break. Anyway, you better leave. I don't think you want to see a *different* side of me. Shoot—I almost forgot—how much did you get from BJ Williams?"

"I'll fill you in when I get back."

I walked by a phone booth and thought about Kate. I would call her later and talk—strictly business . . . maybe.

Natasha was at the cash register with someone buying a Morgan Davis book when I returned with the subs.

"It's nice to see someone actually paying for a book," I said. "By the way what happened with *Mr. Sulley von Red Sox*?"

Some pieces of lettuce fell out of Natasha's sub when she unwrapped it. "I'll tell you if you tell me the amount of the cheque. I'm assuming you got as much as you spent on the subs."

"One...thou...sand euros. Put that in your pipe and smoke it!"

"What?! Are you kidding me?" We were sitting on two fold-out chairs, our elbows leaning on the desk as we ate. She leaned over and kissed my ear—my reward for my accomplishment.

"Congratulations, Vlad," she said, her voice a combination of heartfelt and passionate. Even though we loved to kid each other, maybe a little too much, I always got the tingles inside when she was sincere. This woman clearly had more dimensions than I could ever find in myself.

"Thanks, thank you very muh-ch," I said, doing a shitty imitation of Elvis Presley.

Our subs finished, Natasha sat on my lap. "We have to celebrate. Where will you take me tonight? And you have to stay over. I haven't seen much of you lately. I miss you."

"I miss you too. So, what happened with the Red Sox guy?"

"Was he wearing red socks?"

"I take it you don't follow baseball?"

"I guess not." She paused and grinned, "By the way, did Carlton

Fisk play more games for the Red Sox or the Chi'Sox?'

"Wow that was amazing—you had me convinced that you were not a baseball aficionado."

"My dad loved Boston. Anytime they played against the Jays, he'd always buy tickets. My mother refused to go, and my brother was usually playing baseball or working part time, so I went along...the daddy's girl thing." A sad look took over her face, and it wasn't the first time this expression occurred when she spoke about her past. I wanted to know more about her pre-Vladaeozoic period, but only got brief snippets.

"Natasha, your facial expression just changed when you said 'the daddy thing.'"

"Later, Vlad, later."

"You'll tell me more tonight, right?" *God, was there more than her parents dying in a car accident and her brother becoming estranged? And her boyfriend? An a-hole? What had happened to this woman?* "I'm going to tour the neighbourhood and spend some of my hard-earned cash. See ya at seven-thirty."

"You promise?"

"Of course."

"There's a cover band playing The Who at the other end of St-Germain tonight. Wanna go?"

"I love the Who, but I'd rather spend a quiet evening finding out *who* you are. Get it? Who?"

Natasha pointed at the door. "I get it. There's the door, my friend."

"Let's talk when I get back."

"I need time," she said and then kissed me.

I walked toward the Luxembourg Gardens, my rapid pace outdone only by two wind-assisted chocolate bar wrappers. Coloured blue and green and illuminated by the sun, the wrappers effortlessly bounced off each other and the narrow buildings, laughing at the wind and enjoying themselves like toothless rival roller derby players endlessly exchanging elbows. Spotting a phone booth on a busy street bordering the Gardens, I made a left.

The booth was unoccupied but covered with stickers and posters advertising everything from safe sex to choral performances to choral sex. Kate answered on the second ring.

"Education is our mission. Hello, this is Kate. How may I help you?"

"You must get tired of saying that."

"Vlad, is that you?"

"Yep. Do you have a couple of minutes?"

"Of course."

We spoke about the printing business, her job, and her mother arranging a meeting with an agent any time I wanted. Basically nothing new from last night except one thing that caught me completely off guard.

"You mean your mother said that you're not to go out with me?"

"Yes. I was kind of shocked when she said it." Great, my brother had always said I would amount to nothing and Helen had something against me. She'd appeared to be on my side, or was she a better actor than I? And she did give me a grand for my books; however, with a painting worth thirty mil, that "thou" was loose change. Was I was taking the "Kate is out of bounds" thing too personally? I'd had trust issues since the day my father walked out on us. Nice guy! That's what I got for putting him on a pedestal in my youth. Thinking about my father always either pissed me off or depressed me or both. And worse, my mother knew I was very similar to the old man. I needed to change my lifestyle, change my bad habits and earn an honest living which is all I ever wanted, but that goal had slipped away over time. I had to come clean, as they say, but I needed more people than Natasha to believe in me. Kate was on my side. Helen too?

"Vlad, are you there? Vlad? Hello."

"Sorry, I was just thinking about something. Where were we?"

"The *me* being out of bounds thing."

I collected my thoughts. "One, you're a grown woman and two, I do have a girlfriend, so it wasn't my intention to ask you out, and three, why would she say that?" Kate paused.

"Kate, are you still there?" Did she want to go out with me and now felt awkward? Her mother must have done a number on her once I left the dinner. And Helen mentioning a hundred times that I was going to become famous was just bullshit. Was she just stroking her own ego the whole time? I needed Kate to talk to shut down all these bad thoughts swirling in my head. "Kate are you there?" I said, sounding uncool.

"Yes, sorry, someone just handed me an invoice. I had to look at it."

"Obviously you're busy, so I better hang up."

"Maybe I can answer all three questions with one response: my mother is a control freak."

113

"Yes, I even figured that one out on my own. And?"

"My mother doesn't have to know my every move. You mentioned something about a girlfriend?"

"Yes, her name's Natasha."

"Vlad, um, do you think she would mind if you and I went out for a drink one day? Just something to do. Have a chat. We already have something in common."

"What's that?"

"Books! And we both know my mother is a pain in the ass." I chuckled. Kate was more open in one phone call than Natasha had been since I met her.

"You're right—we do have some things in common. It would be fun to go out for a drink."

"I'm glad you think so, but you still haven't answered my question. Would your girlfriend mind?"

"Nah, of course not," I lied.

"Well, I'm free for a drink tomorrow night."

"Perfect. We could even go out for dinner if you want, as long as your mother doesn't try and hunt us down?"

"Don't worry about that. Mom's the word. Ha-ha!"

"It's none of my business, but I think you need to have a let-me-live-my-own-life talk with your mother."

"Believe me, I've tried."

"How about we finish this conversation tomorrow? Could you meet me in front of Shakespeare and Company at seven? Then we can plan the evening."

"Sure, see you tomorrow night." I hung up the phone, wondering what I was getting myself into. Was I doing this because I resented Helen controlling me and wanted to get back at her through Kate or did I appreciate how Kate opened up immediately? And yet I thought I was in love with Natasha.

My room looked empty now that my remaining twenty-five "children," each conversant in approximately 73,000 words, had left me. They were in a better home. I fell asleep to a boring, dubbed American soap opera on TV.

Natasha buzzed me into her building a few fashionable minutes late, a bottle of *Chateauneuf-du-Pape* in hand and forty fewer euros in my pocket. At her door, we kissed, a passionate kiss suggesting she had forgotten about my recent quick exit from her store.

In the living room, I handed her the bottle.

"Wow! Vlad I haven't had a glass of *Chateauneuf-du-Pape* in ages." She walked into the kitchen to grab the opener.

I followed her into the kitchen, snuck up behind her and wrapped my arms around her slender waist. My chin gently leaned on her shoulder as she opened the bottle.

"Twenty years ago, my brother Carson used to visit *Marché aux Vins* in Beaune. He and his wife would pay fifteen francs and sample several bottles of wine in a cave. By the end of the tour, it was no surprise that the foreigners and Frenchies alike were pouring each other the *Chateauneuf-du-Pape*, one of the most expensive bottles offered for sampling. My brother got a kick out of how generous everyone was at pouring someone else's free wine."

Natasha's expression after the first sip matched the one after her first orgasm with yours truly (or so I hoped).

"What were you saying, Vlad?" She put the glass down, grabbed a serving tray and placed several pieces of cheese on it.

"Were you even listening?"

"No. I can't help it—it's the wine."

"Phew! That stuff on the tray reeks."

She slapped me on the ass and told me to sit down, shut-up and enjoy our pre-dinner snack. Sitting on the couch, making sure I was cozied up to my woman, I grabbed a piece of cheese and gently put it in her mouth.

Natasha nodded a thank you and then spoke after she finished the cheese. "Any ideas what you just placed in my mouth?"

"Not a clue."

"It's Roquefort. That's the creamy one with the blue-green mould."

"Mould!?"

"Yeah!"

"You're kidding. People can eat this?"

She laughed. "It's a good mould. Yogurt is made with bacteria. "

I grabbed a different cheese that was soft and yellow on the inside and white and hard on the outside. I put the whole thing in my mouth. Natasha laughed.

"Vlad most people scrape the white crust off the cheese."

"Thanks for the tip."

She recorked the bottle.

"We'll finish that wonderful wine another time." She was about to place the bottle on the counter when her cellphone rang.

"I TOLD YOU!" yelled Natasha into the phone, "NEVER CALL ME AGAIN." She dropped the bottle and it shattered on the floor.

"THAT FUCKIN' ASSHOLE!?" I hollered.

We instinctively stepped back, though the bottoms of our pant legs still absorbed some wine. I grabbed Natasha's phone. "THAT'S ENOUGH, YOU GODDAMN BASTARD! IF YOU CALL HER AGAIN I'LL COME AFTER YOU, YOU FUCKIN' ASSHOLE!" I added a variety of expletives, but by then he had hung up.

Natasha was kneeling on the floor, cleaning the mess. I straightened her up, wiped the tears from her eyes and gave her a hug.

"Natasha, this isn't good. You're trembling. Tell me, what's going on?" I squeezed her harder and *I* continued talking. "I remember when I first showed up at your store. You were talking on the phone, but you were hiding something. Believe it or not, I'm pretty good at reading people. You mentioned before that it was your boyfriend and some stuff about him not visiting you, ecetera. You also said something about wanting to dump him. The guy who called you that day AND today—is it the same person and is he truly your boyfriend?"

Natasha continued cleaning, more as a diversion, I thought. I grabbed her shoulders to make her stop wiping the floor. At least she had stopped trembling.

"Please, Natasha, take a break for a second."

"I know you're trying to help, but if I don't clean this soon there will be permanent stains on the floor and on the cupboards." She forced a smile.

"Can we at least talk about this at dinner?" I said while I picked up the largest piece of glass containing the label, which read *Chat*.

"Yes! Vlad!"

"I'm worried for you." The glass brushed to one corner, Natasha left the kitchen in silence.

"Where are you going," I said, my voice carrying throughout the apartment. No reply.

"Are you going outside? I'll come with you." Still no response. I peered around the kitchen wall.

Natasha walked back into the kitchen with a broom and pail. She smiled. "I'm sorry, but I have to sweep up the glass, and then I have to mop the floor." I touched her shoulder as she swept the glass. She jumped.

"You're trembling again."

"Fine, but at this split second there's nothing I can do but clean up."

After a few minutes of silent cleaning she said, "Well, *deeear*, that's all done."

"Him or the floor?"

"The floor. Him? Who knows! It's not the first time."

I touched her chin. Good, no jumping. "Can we talk about it?"

"The floor?"

"Good—you've got some of your sarcasm back. You must be feeling a little better."

"Not much, but at least you're here."

We hugged, and Natasha asked me to drop the subject. I agreed temporarily, though I wondered what the hell her boyfriend had done to her. And he still had a hold on her. On the surface, Natasha was a gorgeous, sexy, caring, bright, funny, sarcastic woman, but deep down, I had no idea who she was.

At a restaurant on Rue Mouffetard (as usual I picked a place that Carson frequented), Natasha dined on spring lamb and potatoes, and I went with the *coq au vin*. And despite endless attempts to start a conversation about "the caller," Natasha wouldn't open up. I quit when she threatened to withhold a pleasurable evening in the sack.

Thursday, June 28th

The bright colours of Natasha's studio apartment in full morning view, I turned over onto my shoulder and bumped into 130 pounds of well-proportioned nakedness, her five-foot-nine frame dead to the world. I threw on my dry, surprisingly unsmelly jeans and walked up St-Germain to buy some fresh croissants. A bottle of *Chateauneuf-du-Pape* in a store window caught my eye. Great taste, bad memories, never to be bought again. My woman was still asleep when I returned. I made a pot of coffee and wafted the Pyrex container by her sexy nostrils. Her aquiline nose twitched several times. Then, her mouth got into the act, starting with a grin and stretching its way into a smile that revealed every perfectly straight tooth she had to offer. After a nose and mouth warm-up, the morning pinkish hue returning to her cheeks, it was only a matter of time before she'd master the weight of her lids, producing the necessary

117

muscle to open her eyes. And she did.

"Vlad, why don't you put the coffee back. I can think of something else to warm me up."

I closed the curtains.

We finished the croissants and coffee and discussed our plans for the day. I asked again about her boyfriend and got the cold shoulder.

Walking toward Natasha's store, I asked for her cell. She handed it to me and with a perplexed look on her face said, "And you're calling who?"

A garbage truck had been moving slowly up St-Germain, emptying the multitude of green garbage pails in its path. Seconds later, it caught up to us, its hydraulically controlled metal mouth open and waiting for more food. I fed it with Natasha's phone.

She stood stunned and then yelled my name, followed by a solid right to my shoulder. I winced. "Are you insane? Why the hell did you do that?"

I gently grabbed her hand and moved her away from the truck. "You need a new phone. I don't want that asshole calling you again."

"God, you're so dramatic! Have you not heard of just changing the number!? Shit I had all of my pictures, business contacts, personal phone numbers, music, videos. My *life* is on that fuckin' phone!"

"Maybe you could have shown me that *life* on your phone. Apart from your parents passing away and your brother being a dick I don't know anything about you, your past, your friends. And *nothing* about your boyfriend. You work in a bookstore. What books do you read? What movies do you like? And the whole mystery asshole boyfriend thing is driving me crazy. Hey, I'm frustrated about this situation too. You won't talk about it and there's nothing I can do. Why don't you close your shop at lunch and we'll get another phone together and then we'll talk."

"Fine, but please don't throw *it* away as well. I'll just tell you flat out if you do that again we are through."

Worried about her threat, I would never do that again even if her new phone was radioactive. "I never owned a cellphone, but I assume it's possible to back up the works."

"I did, but that's not the point."

"Fine! Okay! I overreacted. I'm sorry." I kissed her to try and change the mood. I told her I would get cleaned up at my hotel and then meet her back at her store to go pick out a cellphone.

———

A message from Helen was waiting for me at the hotel.

I showered and shaved. Wearing my last relatively clean pair of underwear, I made a mental note to bring my dirty laundry over to Natasha's apartment. It was also time to buy another pair of pants.

Natasha picked out an iPhone 4. I paid for it and even offered to have the phone in my name so I could pay the monthly bills. She agreed that I should buy the phone, but laughed out loud at the "phone in my name" part.

"Natasha, why were you laughing?"

"It's been done before and it didn't work."

"What do you mean by that?"

"Someday, Vlad, but not today."

"Dear, you're becoming a mystery, wrapped in a panzerotti, heated in cryptic tin foil and sprinkled with twigs of curiosity."

"Good! Please let me stay that way." On our way back to her store, she bought two panzerotti. Given her sarcastic and teasing sense of humour, I figured she'd picked them because I had just compared her to one. Did she know it was symbolic of her? (Unless you knew what you were ordering you had no idea what was on the inside.) Or maybe she just liked panzerotti. We hugged as she unlocked the door. I grabbed her keys and my red Monoprix bag full of dirty laundry and headed for her apartment, looking for a phone booth along the way.

My pants stained red and my dress shirt wrinkled beyond repair, I set my bag by a phone booth.

"*Bonjour*, hello, this is Helen. How may I help you?"

I was dying to ask her why I was on the no-fly list with her daughter, but I had to learn not to mix business with pleasure. "Helen! How may I help *you*?" I said, trying to sound cavalier.

"Vlad, I've got some great news. I have a connection at *The Lutèce Review* where de Nadeau works."

"My girlfriend Natasha told me about that review."

"Well, you're not going to time for her once you make it big."

"Helen, you have an awful way of ruining what I thought would be a nice phone call. I draw the line at you being concerned about my love life. I'm getting the impression that you're a control—"

"Everything depends on me."

"—freak. I thought everything depended on de Nadeau."

"As I just mentioned, I have a connection—or shall I say a *spy*—in de Nadeau's office."

My emotions toward this woman were shifting rapidly between admiration, distain and jealousy; Helen was a schemer, able to play in the big show, where my antics were always B-league. And even if she thought I wasn't worthy of her daughter, I had to trust her and her connections.

"I have a spy," Helen continued, her voice barely audible. I had the impression she was hiding in a closet. "I mean a friend, who works near de Nadeau. She tells me that he has three books on his desk, each containing several sticky paper notes, and *French Like Me* is one of them. And she claims that it has the most sticky notes."

"That's amazing! But if there's more sticky notes in mine does that mean there's more negative comments?"

"Let's look at it in a positive way. He's spending more time with your book than the others. Listen, Vlad, I would love to talk about this all day, but I have to go. Got a store to run."

"By the way, how's Kate?" I should have left it alone but I can't handle someone controlling me.

"She's fine. Why would you ask?"

"Just being friendly. She's a wonderful person."

"She is, but she's newly divorced *and* vulnerable. She doesn't need another guy to break her heart."

And yet Kate and I were meeting later. "Of course," I said wisely, deciding to let Kate handle her mother.

Helen hung up.

At Natasha's apartment, I put my clean but damp clothes in a bag and decided to spread them out at my hotel. Her store was on the way back.

"Natasha! Think fast!" I said as I tossed her studio keys over an unsuspecting customer's head and in her general direction.

"Vlad!" she said in mock anger. "I have a customer here." I kissed her on the cheek and whispered, "Bonus, he's not wearing a Sulley coat."

"*Je suis d'accord,*" she replied in a normal voice, assuming the customer didn't speak French.

"*Oui, je doute que le mec va voler quelque chose.*"

The customer paid for David Sedaris's *Naked*. He turned around and looked at us just as he was about to leave, "*Que son idiotas.*"

I smiled at Natasha as he shut the door.

"Damn—that guy caught us at our own game."

Natasha shrugged. "It's no big deal. We were just having some fun."

"Careful, *dear*; you're not going to the dark side, or shall I say the *Vlad* side, are you?"

"Um . . . no . . . don't worry. I'll always be your Princess Loya. You do remember the actress who played her in those space mov—"

"Yes—Caroline Farmer *was* a hot actress back then, but I prefer the image of her in the past. She's gone weirdsville."

Natasha slapped my hand. "Vlad, that's not nice. Growing up in Hollywood with two famous parents, it's pretty normal that she's a bit screwed up."

"A bit!?" Another slap, which also went undeterred. "How many books does Farmer have?"

"Two. And besides she's funny. She's a fighter and rather outspoken."

"So she's your hero and not me!?"

"We're a little presumptive, aren't we, today?"

My look turned serious. "So, you see yourself in her?"

"She has recovered from some serious problems."

"Good—we're starting to get somewhere with you."

Natasha walked away from the cash register and stacked some books.

Damn—I should have just let her talk. Her back turned, I said, "So should I be reading any particular book by—hint hint—Caroline Farmer?"

She handed me a book and kissed me on the lips. "Here—read this," she said. It was Farmer's first tell-all, self-help book, *Jagged Postcards*."

"Do I have to pay for it?" I asked with a big grin.

"Just stick it in your Sulley coat."

"Funny."

"Please read it." She put her arms around my neck. "Vlad, I've got some work to do. So I'll see you tonight?"

I held the bag of wet clothes up. "I can't. I have to spread these out in my hotel." Two people entered the store. Natasha broke the embrace. She said hello to them, looked back at me and spoke in a business tone, which I loved. "So, Mr. Moranski, that job you spoke of will only take five minutes. And then what?"

Vlad, come up with a believable lie, fast! "I'm sorry, Ms. Smith, but I have an engagement tonight with the senior manager at BJ Williams."

Natasha frowned but continued her business tone. "Oh, so we won't be going over the contracts tonight?"

I liked that word—contracts—and planned to make that our pet word for jumping in the sack. "Sorry, I'm too busy. Could we discuss the matter in more detail tomorrow, say at noon?" I put my thumb up to encourage a yes.

Kate waved in the distance as I approached Shakespeare and Company. She wore a white dress that curved over a pair of ripe cantaloupes and then fell over a flat stomach and its counterpart, a tuchus that swayed from side to side in a way that said, "grab me." And how long did it take her to pull that tight piece of fashion over her body—a body that didn't drip sex; it was a waterfall.

I motioned her toward a bar around the corner that looked private. We found a love seat in the back, a Katy Perry video playing above our heads.

A waitress came over. "*Bonsoir, Madame, Monsieur. Vous allez boire quelque chose?*

"It's my treat, Kate. Order what you want."

"*Je vais prendre une Guinness.*"

"Large or small?" the waitress asked, switching to English.

"Large," said Kate.

"And you, *Monsieur?*"

"I'll have a *Leffe* pression . . . large."

"*Merci.* I'll be back in a second."

We chinned our beers.

"Kate, I was surprised how quickly the waitress switched to English."

"I'm fluent, but I don't have my mother's fancy French accent."

"Do I detect a note of bitterness?"

"Maybe a little. I hope you've already noticed that my mother and I are very different, which is good and bad. Charm *oozes* out of every pore in her body." Kate half-smiled. "Don't get me wrong. I love my mum. She even wheeled and dealed to get me my job in Paris. BUT underneath that smile is a well-organized, manipulative woman."

"I noticed at dinner the other night she was telling you what to do. Does that happen a lot?"

Kate took a sip of her Guinness and then looked in my direction. "Since 1973, the year I was born."

Amazing, this woman was incapable of lying. I had met my true opposite, though Carson was a close second. "So that makes you thirty-eight, if my math serves me well," I said. I mentioned that I was fifty and then changed the subject. "Have you read my book yet?"

Glowingly she said, "I loved it. Maybe it started out slowly, but once Carson got involved with the Parisians, and the boys ripping everyone off at ping-pong, That was funny. Then I couldn't put the last third of the book down once Rory was chased out of the flea market after winning at three-card monte." She took a sip. I was in no hurry to speak, sensing she had more to say. "Oh, and then you created the scene where Carson and Monique spend the evening together. You made me feel like I was there. The sexual tension you created between the two was obvious. He's married, yet dare I say it, in love with Monique—"

"But," I interrupted her and readied myself for my soon-to-be-patented line. "If you scratch a centimetre below the surface of my comedic novel, you'll notice that my book is indeed about a man's love for a city."

"Of course, there were several fond references about Paris."

"And the title?" I said, my eyes aglow. "What did you think about it?"

"Well, I assume the title is about someone who wants to be French."

"You get it," I said, a little too triumphantly.

"I guess the title, related to my feelings about the French, is kind of ironic for me because I don't see much good in anything they do." Her smile was long gone.

"Something to do with your "ex" French husband?"

"Bingo!" While drinking our beers, Kate told me some unpleasant things about her ex. I mentioned that I had never married and was happy being single. Our glasses empty, I placed fifteen euros on the table. The sun blinded us as we walked into the street.

"Vlad, I live in a nice neighbourhood in the 13th. There's a smashing Italian restaurant right around the corner from my loft."

"Smashing it is!"

A table opened up as we walked in. Kate and the maître d' kissed on both cheeks. She then proceeded to be kissed by any waiter carrying a main course ending in a vowel.

"*Voudriez-vous boire quelque chose avant le repas?*" asked the waiter as he handed us the menus.

I looked at Kate first. She shook her head. "*Non, merci,*" I replied.

"*Nous avons besoin de quelques minutes avant de commander. Mais nous voudrions un pichet d'eau.*"

"*Bien sûr,*" he said and then smiled at Kate.

"Well, Kate, the French love YOU here."

"Yes, I am a regular, but they feel sorry for me because they know my ex is a jerk."

I looked over Kate's shoulder.

"Do you think your mother is spying on us as we speak?"

She grinned. "No."

"I hope not."

"Let's make a deal that we don't talk about my mother this evening."

"Deal."

Kate ordered fettuccini alfredo and I picked the lasagna and a bottle of *Côtes du Rhone*.

The wine finished, all remnants of my lasagna sopped up by a few lonely pieces of baguette, we oohed and awed over our plates of tiramisu.

Without warning, thoughts of Natasha crept into my head. I briefly felt guilty, realizing this was the first time I'd thought about her all night. I made a mental note to start reading the Farmer book she'd given me.

"Vlad, you seem distracted. Penny for your thoughts?"

"Sorry about that—where were we?"

"Did I mention I live nearby?"

"More than once, I believe, this evening," I said with a grin.

"Would you like to take a look at my flat?"

"Sure, let's go."

The blue sky, one Titanic-looking cloud slowly sinking, and a few stars making cameo appearances accompanied us as we strolled to her apartment.

"Well, here we are," Kate said as she buzzed in her code. The sound reminded me of Helen's apartment. The image of NiR pinning me down was stuck in my head. I forced myself to think of Natasha—naked, even—but NiR remained front and centre. Was the image of NiR punishment for accepting an invitation to another woman's apartment?

"Kate, I'm sorry, but can we take a rain check on me coming up? Because I've had way too much to drink, and I can't be held responsible for anything I might do. Ha-ha!"

"Are you sure? I could make some coffee."

"That's very kind of you, but after pigging out and all that wine, I need to walk it off."

"Will you call me tomorrow?"

"Of course." I walked a few steps and then turned around and waved. "Thanks for the wonderful evening."

"Thanks, Vlad. I had a lot of fun."

I tiredly walked along the main roads. At the hotel, I asked the night clerk in a less-than-invigorating voice for my key; all I wanted to do was take a pee and dive into bed.

My body comfortably horizontal, my brain lost in a dream, I thought I heard a light tapping on the door. I opened one eye and checked the clock. It read 1:07 a.m. I cursed myself for having woken. I did a quick touch of my crotch, closed my eyes and went searching for that dream. The knocking became louder.

"Who is it," I said assuming someone had the wrong room.

"It's Kate," said a voice in a loud whisper.

"Kate! No?"

"Yes, please let me in."

"Just a second." I checked my manhood before I threw off the cover. Content with the bulge (her too, I hoped?), I stumbled to the door. I swiped the wall, feeling for the light switch but missed every time. Pitch dark, I fidgeted with the lock and opened the door, the whole time preparing a big smile.

Blinded by the hall light, I said, "Good evening."

"Good evening to you, or I normally say, 'Godeve.'"

"Fuck," I yelled. "There's only one person who talks like that." I tried to shut the door, but a foot attached to a leg the size of a rolled up carpet forced the door open. Pam had pushed my weak Western front back in seconds. She shut the door. Only the red numbers on the clock were visible. It was one fifteen. Petrified and limp, I think I was standing in the middle of the room.

The floor began to shake and pound. NiR screamed as she charged toward me.

I instinctively ducked. The gush of wind and the mountain of largesse came tromping by. How the hell did she miss me? The room was four by four metres; she'd have to turn around soon. Desperate for protection, I grabbed my mattress. I looked at the clock—my only friend in the room and willed it to talk to me, keep me calm. "You're doing fine, hang in there," I think it said, "and, by the way, it's 1:18." The clock was

---

125

cool. And NiR? Not so much.

NiR brushed a curtain with her body as she circled by the front window. The outline of an elephant became visible. She roared back toward me, her body lower to the ground and charging like a row of NFL linebackers with a vendetta.

"How the fuck did you get into this hotel?!" I yelled and braced myself for a tsunami the colour of raw liver. The impact caused my neck to snap back. And once again, this behemoth bitch had me pinned to the ground.

Her *Hellboy*-sized arm flailed at my exposed head. I took one whack to the nose, and then managed to turtle my head under the mattress. NiR rolled on top of the mattress and began moaning.

"You freak," I yelled. "What the hell are you doing?"

"Quiet, I'm trying to pleasure myself."

"You're goddamn sick."

"I know you are, but what am I?"

"Hey! That's my line!"

"I fuckin' *really* care, LITBAS!"

Struggling to breathe, I managed to sneak my head out the other side of the mattress and look at the clock for inspiration. It said, "Sorry, buddy I got nuttin' for ya. And it's 1:31."

I heard a knocking on the door. Good—a neighbour must have complained.

"*Y-a-t'il un problème, Monsieur?*" whispered someone in the corridor.

"HELL, YA, THERE'S A PROBLEM. OPEN MY GODDAMN DOOR!"

The hallway light swept the dark out of my room as he opened the door. I managed to poke my head out from under the mattress and greet a night clerk. His legs froze, mouth open wide as if he was going to say "O," his eyes the size of platinum CDs and a pair of bushy eyebrows angled up in a manner that said, "I can't believe what I'm seeing." And there it was, a full view of a woman the size of a mastodon masturbating on top of a mattress that was on top of me.

"Ahh, ahh," said NiR. Judging by the sound, I assumed she had just finished her business. She rolled off the end of the mattress and fell asleep. Was it NiRcolepsy? A severe case of BeatoffonVladitis maybe?

I stood up and walked around a sound asleep NiR. The night clerk helped me slide the mattress back. One spring had sprung through the mattress and wished it hadn't. "Well," I said, looking at the clerk. "I'm glad you got your ass here. This woman was trying to kill me."

The man replied, "I no think she want kill you. She want make love, *Monsieur*."

"MAKE LOVE!" I yelled. NiR was snoring. Rolled over in the far corner of the room, she looked like a dead moose lying on the transcontinental highway, waiting for the ravens to pick at her carcass.

"No scream, *Monsieur*. Is late."

I madly waved my hands. "Do you really think WE were trying to make love? This room is a mess." I grabbed a lamp and angrily waved it at the night clerk. "Do people break LAMPS when they make love?"

"*Monsieur*, I have story, much story about what happen in hotel. I no surprise anymore. Please, *Monsieur,* you phone taxi for prostitute and I no tell. *D'accord*?"

"PROSTITUTE!? ARE YOU OUT OF YOUR GODDAMN MIND?"

"Please, *Monsieur*. You scream more and I ask you leave."

"Why would you think I would want a prostitute? And her? This woman is insane!"

No response. NiR continued to snore. He began fluffing my pillow.

The muscles in my neck loosened. My voice surprisingly calm, surmising the situation more absurd than deadly, I said, "I'll ask again. Why would you think I would want a prostitute? And especially her?"

He stopped fluffing my pillow and pointed at NiR. "Woman come to hotel. Say she prostitute. We no have prostitute in hotel but she give me and Jean fifty euro, *mais* we say no words do you understand?"

"Great—you and Jean will fucking do anything for an extra buck." I looked around for a second. "Well, I guess I can't expect anything else—this ain't no four-star hotel."

He smiled proudly. "Hotel is one star."

"Yeah, well, Michelin removes a star if a restaurant isn't up to scratch. And this dump should lose its star."

The conversation going nowhere, I took a deep breath and looked at NiR. And she did something more vile, more heinous than the two attacks combined—she winked at me.

I walked up to her and lamely kicked her foot. "You've been awake the whole time. You goddamn weird, conniving bitch!"

"I call us godconbits," she said, her voice nonchalant. She rolled over onto her ass, sat up and leaned against the wall; the only thing missing was an after-masturbation cigarette.

"Excuse me, sir," I said, pointing at the night clerk and then at NiR. "I want you to call the police and arrest this woman for attacking me."

NiR cackled. "Vlad, honey, give it a rest. I listened to the whole conversation." She looked at the night clerk. "By the way, what's your name?"

"My name is Tahar." He put a hand out and bent over as he spoke, as if greeting an appreciative audience after a one-man show. He sat on the only chair in the room. After having introduced himself, he must have felt he had the run of the place.

I sat on my bed, not wanting to be the only one standing. I pointed at NiR. "Well, while we're still on the introductions, are you going to introduce yourself, PAM?"

"It's NiR, you fuckin' litbas."

"And I'm Vlad. *Sooo* pleased to meet everyone."

Tahar nodded in my direction and took out a cigarette, about to light it. "Not here!" I said.

He kept it unlit, but rested it in his fingers. "*Excusez-moi, Monsieur.*"

"*Excusez-moi* accepted," I replied. "Anyway, *Tahar*, as I was saying, I want this woman arrested."

"*Mais, Monsieur,* I no see fight. I only see love."

NiR chortled at Tahar's remark. "Yes, Vlad, he only see luuve."

"Maybe he saw you making love to yourself, but that was it." I pointed to my nose. "Do you see this bruise, Tahar?" He walked over and touched my nose with his index and middle finger, the cigarette resting comfortably between the two digits. And I let him touch me, so desperate was I for proof of bodily harm.

He felt around. "I no see *bleu ou noir nez, mais* you *nez est brisé.*"

I jumped up. "Yes, everyone heard that? Tahar said my nose was cracked."

"It was cracked, *fuck nuts*, even before I fingered myself."

Her last two words gave me the hibby jibbies. Tahar had a blank look on his face, her slang drifting over his head. Lucky bastard. Tahar sat down again.

"God!" I said, "I'm trapped in this, this *Huit Clos!*" NiR forced a laugh. Tahar waved his hand around, desperately wanting to light his cigarette.

"Vlad, you're such a drama queen. And you're sooo cool to say *Huit*

Clos instead of *No Exit*. There were *two* women and *one* man in that play, by the way. Oh and let me guess your next line. You're going to say 'Hell is other people.'"

"Damn straight!"

Tahar cut in, "*Excusez-moi, évidemment c'est un problème domestique.* I must have to go."

I opened my mouth to speak, but NiR jumped in and imitated Tahar. "Yes, *c'est un problème domestique.* Tahar must have to go."

"And Pam or NiR, whatever, get the fuck out of here, too, or I WILL call the police and lay charges myself."

NiR stood up and straightened her dress.

I pointed to something about the size of a man's shirt lying on the carpet. "And put your underwear back on, too, for Christ's sake!"

Tahar held the door open cordially for NiR and winked at her as she passed by.

"NiR!" I said. She turned around. "I will be telling Helen what you did tonight."

She gushed out a laugh. "You mean you're going to tell her I masturbated on top of you?"

I cringed. "Don't say that word. Just get the hell out of here."

"You know fuckin' well that it was me that discovered you and not Helen. And I only want what's coming to me. What I deserve! She put her hand over her crotch and jerked her pelvis à la Michael Jackson."

"Do you always attack men that won't sleep with you?"

"Sometimes."

"Forget the cops. I'll just call the psych ward."

"Been there, done that."

"You're insane!"

"Hey, babe, I'm just NiR."

Tahar closed the door. NiR repeated the "M-word" all the way down the hall. I think Tahar said it as well.

Four weeks later

Sunday, July 29th

My door was unlocked at exactly 8 a.m. A tray with a coffee and something roughly in the shape of a croissant was handed to me. It wasn't the time to ask the cop for an extra sugar.

A few minutes later, I was escorted by the same cop past six other police holding cells the same size as mine, their walls reverberating in morning grunting in equal amounts of French and Arabic. We passed through a hallway, rows of police gun lockers on either side. Beyond the hallway were a fingerprinting room and a medical office, where my fingers and forehead, respectively, had been taken care of about eight hours before. There were lines of desks supporting dirty, archaic computers. My sarcasm forever ready to get the best of me, I was tempted to ask a cop if they were still using Minatel. They wouldn't have heard me anyway because the low claustrophobic ceiling coughed out cold air. The air-duct noise died out by the time I entered a corner office of the police station. The cop grabbed a metal chair, pushed it in front of a grey metal desk and told me to sit down. His badge said his name was Alain Foucault. Alain and I did not speak. Forever the good guard dog, Alain waited by the door.

My metal chair creaked every time I twisted my body to look around. The room was painted an off-white. No chips on the walls; no pictures either. I assumed it was an interrogation room. Ironically, it was as nondescript as the ones I had spent time in in Toronto. Do all interrogation rooms came in a standard, no pictures, off white? A plainclothes man entered the room—my height, dark hair, and a massive forehead, matched by a jaw that opened like a garbage truck.

"*Bonjour, Monsieur Morunski.* Please have a seat. My name is Jean Clément. I am the lead detective on your case. I suppose you know why you are here?" He sat down and opened a red folder. It had my name on it.

"Yes and no," I said.

"What do you mean?"

"I was fingerprinted and then spent the night in a cell for hitting a policeman, which I did, but at no time was I drunk." I pointed at my forehead. I was then attacked by both cops."

"I read police report. They say you fall. Yes."

130

"Bullshit. I want a lawyer. NOW!"

"*Monsieur*, we wait to decide the charge *contre* you. By law, we can keep you here for twenty-four hour and maybe more. The *problème, Monsieur*, is *le Picasso.*" He opened up the folder and took out a piece of paper that had some numbers and fingerprints on it. He slid it along the table to me to be dramatic.

"*Monsieur* Morunski, we have proof your fingerprint on Picasso, on wood and on diamond earring."

I looked at the paper. My name was there beside two sets of fingerprints. "I want a lawyer."

"He will be coming soon."

Bunch of pricks! They were going to give me a lawyer all along but wanted to see the sweat on my forehead. And it was there for all to see. "I wanna phone the Canadian Embassy right fuckin' now!"

He narrowed his eyes. "You must be calm, *Monsieur*. We need more time, but I say it no look good for you. We find Picasso in your apartment. The painting is more than twenty million euro."

"I can explain the fingerprints."

"Please tell me."

"That painting belongs to Helen Northingham, the owner of BJ Williams bookstore in Paris, right?" I let out a gush of air as I said it. It felt good to admit it, regardless of how they would react.

"Yes, is her painting."

"One night, I was invited to her apartment and she let me hold it. I held the frame, but then Helen put my finger on the oil part of the painting itself."

"You no expect me to believe that?"

"Ask her."

"I spoke to her. She say you touch frame, but I will ask her today if she make you touch painting."

"Whatever. I want a lawyer." I pounded the desk.

"A lawyer will be here soon, *Monsieur*," said the detective.

"This lawyer better be goddamn good because I'm going to sue your ass."

"You make the situation more bad, *Monsieur*. I think you no speak until lawyer visit."

I leaned on the table with my elbows and briefly rubbed my forehead and scalp with my hands. "Ow," I yelled to myself. "That fuckin' hurts." I had completely forgotten about the stitches in my

---

forehead.

A man wearing a black suit that looked Teflon-y, but cost a few grand, walked into the room.

"Hello, my name is Luc Simpson. I'm your lawyer. Don't say another word." He shook hands with the detective and then me. The detective stepped out of the office. Same routine in Toronto police stations—lawyer arrives; detective gives them their space.

"I just want to say one thing—I did not steal anything. All that shit that they think I stole was planted in my apartment."

"The police still have another sixteen hours to keep you here, and maybe more, before they figure out what to do with you. You then could be sent to a judge for what we call a *mise en examen*."

"What the hell is that?"

"The judge is allowed to bring in any witness he wants, to either corroborate your story or use what they say against you. After that meeting, he can either throw out the case or formally charge you. Then, of course, there would be a trial."

"I'll say it again—I didn't do anything. But if he decides to charge me, do I go immediately to jail and wait there until the trial?"

"The judge would not put you in jail because you are not suspected of committing a violent crime. And even though you were allegedly caught with a Picasso worth millions, you would have to submit your passport and possibly wear an electronic bracelet."

"And bail?"

"None. Any more questions before we begin?"

"Are you French? Because you don't have a French accent when you speak English."

"Born and raised in Paris. My mother is Parisian, but my father is from New York. Shall we start? From the beginning, please give me your version of what happened."

The word "your" threw me off, but my story soon flowed.

Later, the detective returned. I then repeated my story to both of them, mentioning endlessly that I was framed. The detective informed us that Helen was going to press charges against me for theft, and she told the detective that at no time did she put my finger on the painting. She had balls to lie to a detective. The lawyer and the detective spoke French rapidly. I heard the word "judge" more than once.

My lawyer turned in my direction. "Mr. Moranski, because the

———

132

owner of the painting is pressing charges against you and the painting was found in your apartment, you will have to go before a judge. That will take place tomorrow morning."

"You're kidding me." *Shit, they don't waste any time here.*

"No, I'm not, but I'm sure when you tell the judge that the police were brought to your apartment under false pretences, he will throw out the case."

"Thanks. That at least sounds more comforting."

"Just one more thing and I'll ask again."

"What's that?"

"Just to double-check, you don't have a criminal record? Right?"

"Of course not." I had started a new honest life in Paris and no longer wanted to bring up my past. *Christ, was I taking a chance!*

"That's good, because if you did have a criminal record I couldn't guarantee anything."

My stomach churned—a sign from my youth that when I told one too many lies, something had to give.

The cop escorted me toward my cell, though my steps had become noticeably slower. A tornado whipping up in my stomach had taken all the energy out of my body. I could barely walk by the time I reached my cell. And then it happened. Exhausted, I stood beside my cell door, my side leaning against the wall and vomited on the floor. There was only a small puddle, but what scared me more was that I didn't feel better after I did it. God, I was in trouble.

"Are you okay, *Monsieur*?" said Alain the cop. *Great, now the douchebag talks!*

"I'm fine. I just need to lie down. And no one hurried to clean it up. I was in hell!

A pattern was developing in my head before I fell asleep: the painting belonged to Helen, the earrings surely Natasha's and the wood carving resembled the one in a restaurant I had been frequenting. Okay, a few people hated me and wanted revenge, but I believed that only Helen was vindictive enough to frame me.

Twenty-seven days earlier

Friday, June 29th

The morning sun blazing in my hotel room highlighted a dent in my luggage, sad proof that the fiasco the night before with NiR and her wandering va-jay-jay hadn't just been a nightmare manufactured in my head.

I slept in and missed breakfast, happy having had enough hotel attention.

Helen had left a message for me to drop in at BJ Williams. NiR occupied my mind the whole time I walked along Rue de Rivoli. Would I mention the attack if I saw her? Would she throw the word "masturbation" in my face and in front of the customers? Would I involve the law? Unlikely; I imagined her lawyer asking me too many questions about her mattress pleasure tour. I was in a no-win situation, which meant I would have to take care of it myself.

Moving toward my book display, my eyes twisted and turned, maintaining open sightlines for NiR. Someone behind me touched my shoulder. I jumped.

Helen turned me around to face her. "Hello Vlad. You weren't counting your books, were you?"

"No," I said smiling to hide my nervousness. My mind was so focused on NiR, I'd forgotten to check how many of my books were sold.

Helen grabbed my hand. "Come upstairs to my office—I have great news."

I sat on the other side of her desk but first slid a number of books to each end. Her office reminded me of Byron's bookstore—a mess. I made a mental note to visit Byron to see if he had finished my book. And I was sure if I didn't contact Natasha soon, she would wonder what was going on.

"Helen, it's nice to see someone more dramatic than me. So what's the big news? Does it have something to do with de Na—"

"De Nadeau!!" she said, ensuring that *she* told the news. I sat back and let her ramble.

"My source at his office has noticed that he's put the other two books away, and yours is the only one on his desk. He could have a review ready for the next biweekly publication in one week."

I jumped out of my chair. "You're kiddin' me!"

A woman knocked on the door. "Helen, you're needed at cash. There's a problem."

"Fine, I'm coming. Vlad, excuse me for a second, just make yourself comfortable."

My eyes caught hold of a book that Natasha had given me. Good omen? Bad omen? I wondered.

I stopped wondering after reading ten pages. Was Natasha as screwed up as the famous actress Caroline Farmer? I guessed that was the whole not-so-cryptic point, that Natasha had some problems. But which ones?

The door opened again. "I'm baaaack." I set the book on the desk. Helen picked it up.

"Interesting choice," she said in a tone that suggested a question.

"Yes, that same book was given to me by my girlfr—"

Helen cut me off. "It's plain and simple. Soon you will only have time for people in the literary business and your fans. Anyway, Vlad, unfortunately I have unfinished business downstairs so I have to go."

As I walked out, she told me to get a cellphone because she would be calling me regularly.

Looking for more good news, preferably from someone less manipulative, I walked over to Byron's Albany Bookshop. Byron was sitting at his pulpit and ordering his bevy of beauties around.

"Hello, Byron," I said. We shook hands.

"Hello, Vlad." He paused for a second and sent more commands into the airwaves. His harem of book stackers was hidden from my periphery, but I still heard the "Yes, Mr. Byron, no, Mr. Byron," loaded in thick British and French accents.

"I'm sorry about that interruption, but the 'greatest book show on earth' must go on. And of course, *mi amigo*," (Oh no—is he doing the Spanish thing again?) "do remember the coffee and good ol' Canadian maple syrup is by the travel section. Fill your cup till it runneth over."

"Thanks, Byron."

"Vlad, is Paris treating you well this fine morn'?"

"Great. Anyway, it's been a week—have you been able to finish reading my book?"

"Yes, I finished it."

"And?"

"It was vulgar."

I forced a smile. And what shocked me more? His negative

goddamn reply? Answering in a nanosecond? Was the bugger's mind made up long ago and was in automatic response mode?

Byron avoided making eye contact as he spoke. He then priced a few books at his pulpit and instructed one of his girls to file them in the I-don't-give-a-shit aisle. Byron didn't express himself in those words, but that's how I interpreted them, my brain confusing words and mood. I reminded myself that the new Vlad would count backwards from ten before speaking. The goal: keep the temper under control.

Outwardly calm, I replied, "Interesting comment, Byron, but I'm not sure what you mean, exactly." I felt a burning sensation in my heart, a stream of hot blood forcing its way through a microscopic tear in the artery that controlled the flow of literary criticism. And that tear was rapidly expanding. I grabbed a handful of bookmarks off his desk and moved toward the "Ms" in the fiction section. Waiting for his response, I silently counted backwards: ten . . . nine . . . I stopped at seven, when I spied Henry Miller's *Under the Roofs of Clichy*. I gently removed it from the shelf and slid in a bookmark on a specific page.

Byron priced more books, though I had a feeling the price was already there. "Well, the boys use profanity," he said, unable to look at me.

And though the tear in my artery had widened, I chose not to comment. I walked to the "J" section and grabbed Erica Jong's *Fear of Flying*. "six . . . five . . . four," I said, my voice hushed. I leafed through Jong's book, found a paragraph I had read several times, and placed bookmark number two. With two books in hand, would Byron sense a theme? Or would I tell him about Richard Ford shooting a critic's book after she gave him a bad review?

"But they're teenagers," I replied, my tone shifting from cool and collected to lukewarm and mildly hateful. "Do you happen to have kids yourself?" Like I *really* had to ask that question. Byron's *unique* (a generous use of the adjective) personality aside, he never left the store, so the act of copulation was a non-starter. And there was no room for a foldout chair, let alone a foldout bed. I moved to the "R" section and found a badly torn version of Richler's little known *Cocksure*. Bookmark number three accompanied a certain yellowed page. "three . . . two . . ." I said silently.

"No children," he replied. Slowly and proudly, he looked at the absurdly stacked four walls, one at a time. Was he telling me that he had 32,000 "children," and that was enough? His look turned serious. "I was appalled by those young cads gratuitously proffering words that I don't think even a bar of soap would suffice to wash out their cretin mouths."

I wanted to say, *Yeah, let's wash their mouths out with borax. Or how about some Anthrax?!* but settled for, "The father, Carson, spends a week in Paris with three teenaged boys who have their own minds. And they're prone to saying they don't want to do something or that they're unhappy, BUT in typical teenage fashion, they don't always use the most eloquent words to express their feelings." My words only sugar-coated a vein I felt mounting in my forehead.

"But the children are—" he said.

One . . . zero . . . "Adolescents!" Still under the "R" section, I found Philip Roth's *Portnoy's Complaint*. I flipped through it and strategically popped in bookmark number four. Four books in my possession.

Byron, sensing my abrupt tone, continued to price some books and pass them to one "Barbie" or another. And though my beleaguered artery was burning blood, I enjoyed that he was uncomfortable—in his own store. I walked over to the "D" section and paused. Shit, should I give this guy one more chance to change his mind about my book?

"Byron, in my book, at any time did the sons swear at their father?"

"No, but—"

"Byron!" I said, my voice getting louder. Do you have any idea how adolescents act in high school these days?" I didn't give him a chance to answer. "They swear all day! You think high school is still stuck in some sort of Byron sixties time warp, where students were polite with the teacher and with each other." Carson had forever updated me on the changing behaviour of high school students.

"Well . . . um . . . I have to confess I've been away from the high school milieu for a while."

"A while!?"

"Your tone is not appreciated here Mr. Moranski. I shall ask you to vacate the premises."

The vein in my forehead ready to explode, the artery punctured in several places, I laughed—a laugh belonging more to a mad scientist than a hip author. "Vacate the premises!? Byron, who talks like that? Man, you're not Canadian, nor are you French. You're just a weirdo."

I grabbed his hero Morgan Davis's book, *Merde Doesn't Stink in Paris*. Byron looked upset. You'd think I had just removed the Holy Grail off his shelf. Grail or no grail, my theme was complete. The five books resting comfortably in my hands, I opened up Henry Miller's *Under the*

Roofs of Clichy at the bookmark. "WELL, BUDDY?! DO YOU REALLY WANT TO HEAR SOMETHING TRULY VULGAR? Ladies please cover your ears. (And they did.) Here goes, Byron:

> *I have a list that could go on for several minutes, but I never could talk as fast as I could fuck. I hammer my dick into the bitch's fig until it's ready to split completely. But she's too unresisting now ... I give her ass a pinch to put some salt under her tail.*

How was that, Byron? Vulgar enough?" Less than three metres away, I tossed the book at his head.

He raised his hands just in time to deflect the literary Frisbee over his head. "You scoundrel! How dare you mistreat my books! I shall ask you to cease and desist this instant. *Au secours*! Help!" Even the employees were grinning. Byron jumped out of his pulpit and hid behind a stack of books, kicking over a mountain of them along the way. I countered and blocked the only exit.

"Byron, you're sooo fuckin' lame." I opened Jong's *Fear of Flying* at page whatever and read.

> *We drove to the hotel and said goodbye. How hypocritical to go upstairs with a man you don't want to fuck, leave the one you do sitting there alone, and then, in a state of great excitement, fuck the one you don't want to fuck while pretending he's the one you do. That's called fidelity. That's called monogamy. That's called civilization and it's discontents.*

There, pal. Was *that* vulgar enough for you?" I motioned to the left and then to the right, in an effort to get Byron to move from his hiding spot. He shifted to his right, allowing me to nick his head with my second flying volume.

"You! You! Creature of malevolence!" yelled Byron in a voice befitting a woman. I opened up Richler's *Cocksure*. My chosen words had a calming effect: the vein safely back in my head and flat as a crêpe, the artery, too, mending with TGV speed.

"Do you not see the irony here?"

"You leave me no alternative. You . . . you . . . mad gadabout."

"Give it a rest, bonehead. Are you ready for more vulgarity? Asswipe. Douchebag."

"That's enough—there are women present!"

"That's another thing! You say the book is vulgar, yet you only hire twenty-one-year-old hotties. Kind of vulgar, too, don't ya think, the way you use women?" I paused and stretched my neck out to see where the ladies were in the store. One was kneeling beside Byron and the others were at the back, sorting out books.

"I'm sorry, ladies," I said loudly. "I don't mean to be rude to you."

The one closest to Byron said, "That's okay, Mr. Vlad."

I smiled. "Just say Vlad; we don't need the "Mr." part." Although Byron was hidden from view, I directed my words toward him.

"You see what you've created here, Byron, you jackass? The women talk like slaves. Anyway, dickweed, have a listen to Mordecai Richler. Here goes:

Mortimer craved more information about the powered plastic dildo. Was it circumcized? Or black maybe? Conversely, were there attachments and coloring kits, such as went with a Mixmaster or a Black & Decker home drill? Could a female study subject unscrew the circumcized knob from the dildo and replace it with a goyishe knob? Or could she spray the dildo black or even Chinese yellow, if she fancied? Finally, if all these permutations were possible, which knob and color combo was the biggest hit?"

I snapped the book shut and then looked in Byron's general direction. "I wanted to read the scene where an elementary school teacher gives blow jobs to the top four students in the class, but I couldn't find the page. And, ladies, I apologize again for what I'm reading, but I'm trying to prove a point to moron over here." I threw the book in Byron's direction. Being old and yellow—the book, not Byron —it splattered on the wall behind him.

"That's enough, Vlad! I get the message. And you owe me twenty-two euros for those three books you've heaved at me."

"Heaved!? Try thrown or tossed or gunned—even launched."

Byron raised a white book.

I put my hand to my forehead and chuckled. "You can't be serious. Is that your white flag of surrender? What century do you live in?" Half of his head was in view, the opportunity to throw a book irresistible. I decided not to read from *Portnoy's Complaint* and tossed it instead. Its papers flapped like a distressed bird and crash landed on the bridge of

Byron's nose.

"Ow . . . ow that smarts." Byron put his head down and shifted to his right. I could see him in the corner mirror.

"Byron! You chicken shit! You're hiding behind *girls*? I thought only Bin Laden did that shit."

"Of course not. I'm just trying to protect her from your assault." The salesgirl whispered, but her voice carried throughout the store. "That's okay, Mr. Byron. I will protect you."

He yelled help and *au secours* a couple of more times, but no one had entered the store.

"Tell you what, asswipe. I'm going to give you a break and read an excerpt from one last book. I opened up *Merde Doesn't Stink in Paris* and read aloud:

> *"Luckily I had NBA-length arms, which made it easy to work my way under the table and up her soft-as-frog's-legs thighs. She quivered as my velvet fingers approached the opening of her moist—"*

"Lascaux cave," said Byron, finishing the sentence.

"Christ, Byron! Do you know the book by heart?"

"Of course. It's written by Morgan Davis, my—"

"Hero!" I said, finishing his sentence.

"Well, *hero* is not on the tip of my tongue. I would prefer 'favourite author'."

"Give me a break. I bet you have ten posters of him hanging up in your bedroom."

"Only one, I . . . I . . . mean none. Yes . . . um . . . I don't have any."

I closed the book. "So, *bonehead*, you think it's okay when Davis writes something vulgar, but if I do it, it's not okay. Aren't you a hypocrite?"

"Well, maybe a little."

"*A little*!?" I tossed Davis's book at him but missed my target.

"Please, I beg of you, not the Davis books!"

"Whatever," I replied. I put thirty euros by his cash register and calmly walked out the door.

Byron's voice followed me. "You'll pay for this, you scoundrel!" Then in a somewhat pleasant tone he added, "Oh, and please don't write about any of this in your next book."

A brisk wind whipped my hair as I made my way to Natasha's bookstore. She greeted me with a huge smile and a kiss.

"Well, stranger, how goes it?"

"Shit, Natasha, where do I even start?"

"How about you begin from when you saw me last." She turned around for a second and picked up a stack of books. "Vlad, sit down by the cash register. I have to file these, but keep talking."

I grabbed Patricia Highsmith's *The Talented Mr. Ripley* and read the testimonials on the back cover. Should I give this book to her as *my* unofficial biography (excluding the murder parts, although I did want to kill NiR)?

"Last night was kind of boring." I rolled my eyes a few times to accent my lie. Natasha wasn't looking.

"Yes, business meetings are a waste of an evening in Paris." Good, she believed my lie. A cigarette in hand, she walked toward the door.

"Natasha, has you-know-who been calling?"

She unconvincingly said no and lit the cigarette by the open front door, her exhaled smoke working a path back to me. She took two more puffs and flicked the butt across the Atlantic. "It's my first one in a couple of days and—read my lips—*that person* has not called me. I guess he hasn't figured out my new number."

"You see? It helps to throw out a cellphone. It clears the airways."

Natasha raised an eyebrow. "Anyway, I'm starving. I've got a craving for a slice of pizza. There's a place around the corner. Would you mind getting one for me and one for yourself if you want and then you can fill me in on everything else you've been doing?"

I was glad to go on an errand because I had not yet decided what lie I was going to tell about last night. Obviously I wouldn't tell Natasha about being with Kate. And I was too embarrassed to mention that I was attacked by a female nutbar.

Natasha groaned as she ate the pizza, though I winced for a second, thinking about the sounds NiR had made in my hotel room.

"Vlad is there something wrong with the pizza?"

"No . . . no, I was just thinking about something."

Two people walked into the store. "Hello, can I help you?" said Natasha. They shook their heads and walked toward the mystery section. I whispered to Natasha, "Bonus, they're not wearing Sulley 'hide a stolen book' coats." She rolled her eyes in response.

Natasha moved to rearrange some books. I found a second copy of the Caroline Farmer "tell-all" and opened it. I caught her looking at me as I read. (*Okay Vlad, that look meant that this book was a window into my Natasha's soul. Take its contents seriously.*) She smiled at me and walked toward the customers, asking them again if they needed help. The couple finished their silent search and settled on two books, one a copy of Jonathan Lethem's *Chronic City*, the cover with the tiger's mouth open with Manhattan skyscrapers for fangs, a brilliant piece of graphic art. I made a mental note to check who the artist was and use him or her for my next *oeuvre*. The other book was *Eat, Pray, Love* or *Pray While You Eat and Make Love* or maybe it was *Don't Pray and Talk With Your Mouth Full*.

After Natasha waved good-bye to the customers, she snuggled on my lap again, her arm around my neck. I had read a few pages, starting where I'd left off at Helen's.

"Are you finding out more about me through her book?"

"Am I supposed to guess what past you and Farmer shared?"

"Yes."

I would have preferred questioning Natasha straight up about her murky past, but the Socratic method was powerless against this woman. "Tell you what, Natasha. How about I go to a café immediately and read as much as I can and then we can discuss *it* or *you* or *it and you* or *me* or *somebody*?"

She kissed me on the forehead. "That would be wonderful."

While nursing a large draught of *Leffe*, I was surprised at the number of times I found myself raising my eyebrows. And after reading only twenty or so pages, I superimposed Caroline's name with Natasha's.

I marked my place with the *Leffe* coaster and bought a rose for my woman, a small gesture for someone who I think had gone through more than the loss of her parents.

I convinced Natasha to eat at the same Vietnamese restaurant as before. We were greeted by an Asian man behind the food counter, his hands gently folded, shoulders leaning politely forward, and his massive head shaking on a tiny stick body. He reminded me of a major league bobblehead doll.

"How you today?" he said with a smile containing a set of teeth so misshapen and coloured by every shade of brown imaginable they must have been donated by thirty-two different street people.

"Excellent," I said. We both ordered the curried chicken with vegetable rice and three egg rolls.

I got Natasha's attention and then framed the wall opposite the cash register with my hands. I was preparing my masterpiece. "Natasha, when I make it big, which will be soon I might add, and I'll tell you why when we sit down, I'm going to convince this guy that his restaurant could— no, WILL—be the next *Les Deux Magots*. Imagine me, the next Vlad-Paul Sartre and you, milady, the next Natasha de Beauvoir."

"This restaurant!" she said in a sarcastic tone. "Were you *smoking* something this afternoon, by any chance?"

"That's hilarious. Tell you what. Why don't you grab that table in the corner, which I will soon call *the Vlad Sanctuary* or maybe just *the Vladuary*."

"How about the Vlad Sanatorium or Vladtorium or Vladuct or maybe just Viaduct, since writers . . . " She paused for a second and rolled her eyes. " . . . will be flowing in and out all the time?"

"Funny stuff. Get that down. Write a book. I did. And that table in the corner is available, by the way. And there's a cool looking wooden carving near the table. Anyway, go on . . . shoo." I kissed her on the cheek and playfully pushed her toward the table.

I smiled at the man as he took our food out of the microwave. "I believe I don't know your name."

"My name Mi-Kong, but everyone call me Kong." He beat his chest. This guy was perfect. I had found my new hangout.

"Hello. My name's Vlad." We shook hands, and for a person I could fold up and fit in my back pocket, he put the vice in vice-grip. "Pleased to meet you, Kong." I brought over one tray and he carried the other.

Kong bowed his head and said, "*Bon appetit*."

While we ate, I scanned the walls for ideas of how I could make this place more literary. After dinner, I asked Kong to bring over two more *Leffes*. He beat his chest and nodded.

"Natasha, you have to admit this Kong guy is a riot."

"Yes, he is funny, but I have a feeling that you're laughing at him and not with him."

"A little from column A and a little from column B. That's what makes the world go 'round."

"Maybe your world."

"Uww. Was that a shot?"

"No, but just be careful. *Kong* might not be too thrilled with whatever you think you're going do."

Not sure if we were having our first ever argument, I let her comment go. Why? I was crazy about her.

Later at her apartment, she asked about Farmer's book.

"I finished the first two chapters."

"And?"

"Well, she was a product of a famous Hollywood couple, so I imagine she was doomed from the start. Which leads me to ask, were *you* born to a famous Hollywood couple?"

Natasha smiled. "Vlad, would you mind pouring me a glass of wine?"

I poured two glasses of *Merlot*—the choice of amateur psychologists.

We cuddled on the foldout and sipped our wine. "Well, *chérie*, lay it on me," I said. "Where did it all begin?"

She took a deep breath. "I was born in Toronto, which I may have mentioned already, to an overbearing father and a shrew for a mother."

I narrowed my eyes, trying to show contempt for her parents. "The story sounds great already."

"Vlad, you have to PROMISE you will never write about this. You writers are all the same—you take your life or other people's life experiences and then twist and turn them for your own folly."

"Folly!? Can I at least use *that* word?"

"My father worked as a chartered accountant for a big firm on Bay Street. My mother *doted* on him and raised me and my brother, who was three years older than me."

"Did your mother play favourites between you and your brother?"

"No, she basically just put in time with us and waited for the *king* to come home. I kind of felt sorry for my mother, even though I resented her for not showing more interest in us. She was caught under some weird overbearing spell my father had cast on her. He wouldn't let her think for herself. And he made a number of bad decisions for all of us."

"Fire away!"

"Bad investments! Inviting obnoxious friends of his on family vacations! Chosing wrong schools! ...the usual."

"We didn't do much travelling because money was always kind of tight in my household." *Money! Tight! That was an understatement! I had never gone on a vacation!*

Natasha continued to talk about her family but said nothing worse than what I had gone through. She was hiding something dark, but gave me nothing to work with. I changed the subject.

"My dear you work in a bookstore, yet I never see you read other than some French newspapers. I assume you're a voracious reader."

"I love to read, but since you've come on the scene I haven't been interested in starting a new book."

"I'll take that as a compliment."

"I hope so." She took a sip of her wine and continued. "Reading, okay, where do I start? I love science fiction, fantasy—*Game of Thrones*, *Lord of the Rings* kind of stuff. I'm a sucker for mystical powers. Historical fiction interests me as well. Ken Follett is amazing."

"The *Lord of the Rings* movies were cool, but I wasn't a fan of the books— never-ending fighting. And getting the characters' names straight or the races was impossible. Were they Orcs or Morks or what?"

"Orcs, you dork."

"Not bad." I looked at her four walls and commented that there wasn't a single book on any ledge. Ironic? She said she was happy to decorate her studio with something other than books. She loved her store but didn't want to be reminded of it when she was home. The conversation turned to what I read. And it came as no surprise to her when I mentioned that I preferred literary fiction that contained some humour.

"That's it? Just humour?" she said, suggesting I was one-dimensional. I was.

"No, for a change of pace, I dig Raymond Chandler and Patricia Highsmith."

"Ah, there's some killin' going on in those novels."

"But Chandler makes me laugh. Philip Marlowe is one of the most interesting fictional characters ever created. Tough on the outside, mush on the inside, and his self-deprecating humour? He has it all. Surely you read Chandler?"

"I hate it when you call me Shirley." We both laughed at that lame joke. I convinced her to read Chandler's *The Big Sleep* in exchange for me reading one of her favourites: *The Girl With the Dragon Tattoo*.

I refilled our glasses and took some cheese out of the fridge.

Natasha grabbed a piece of cheese. "Okay—humour, Chandler, Highsmith . . . what else?"

"You'll find out soon enough?"

"What does that even mean?"

"It's a secret."

Natasha barked out a laugh. I wouldn't tell her that I would be buying a number of books from her store. And it wasn't to replenish my five hundred paperbacks ripped up in Toronto.

We discussed movies as well. Our favourite happened to be the same: *Blade Runner*. God, I loved this woman.

Saturday, June 30th

A garbage truck woke me up early. Natasha purred away the weekend hours. A true Parisian—dead asleep while the machine's pistons mercilessly compressed and munched yesterday's debris.

Finishing Chapter two of Farmer's book, I glanced at Natasha each time I turned a page and wondered what she was dreaming about. The sun projected a spiral pattern through the curtain and onto her cheekbone. She must have sensed the sun's rays; she harrumphed in her sleep and turned over onto her naked side, muscles relaxed, a few freckles dotting the shapely landscape.

I shook her buttocks to remind her that she wasn't alone. More growling, which for some unexplained reason reminded me of Kate. After a shower, I reminded myself to call her; it had been a few days.

Towelling myself off, my junk ready for action, I wondered what the hell I would do with my package if Kate made a few moves.

I walked Natasha to her store and went back to my hotel, where I was handed two messages from the clerk. Helen had more news about de Nadeau (one exclamation mark) and Kate had sent a message ending in a question mark.

In my room, I lay down on my still made-up bed, channel changer in hand, and wondered what Helen had to say. I had a feeling it was good news, that de Nadeau would write a review of my book. But what if he carved it up with his literary switchblade? Would he say that having three sons in the book was too confusing? And how would I handle a potentially negative review? My antics in Byron's store proved that I was not exactly a fish capable of navigating a sea of bad comments. I flipped on the television to give my imagination a rest and soon fell asleep.

The sun threw everything but the kitchen sink at me to wake me up. Close to three o'clock, I called Kate from the hotel.

"Vlad!! I'm so happy you called. I hadn't heard from you since the other night. I was beginning to wonder what was going on."

"Not much. Been talking to your mother."

"*Great*. What's she done this time?"

"Every day she has news about if and when de Nadeau is going to review my book."

"Sounds promising."

"But at the same time, she tells me that I shouldn't be going out with anyone because I will be too busy with my book. I like your mother, but I resent being under her thumb."

"Are you really that surprised?"

"Probably not."

"I have a feeling that you're a handful yourself."

"That's what she said."

"What, my mother?"

"No, sorry, Kate, that's just a joke from an American TV show, called *The Office*."

"American? You mean there's an American version? Does is it star Ricky Gervais as well?"

"No, thank God."

"You're not a Ricky Gervais fan!?"

"Not really."

"Have you ever watched the English version?"

"The American one is in English."

"You know what I mean. Vlad, tell you what. How about tonight you come to my place and watch some episodes of the original *The Office*? You can decide which version is funnier."

"Fine, but I'll have to bring a lot of booze to get through this."

"I'll see you at seven."

Shit, I had to invent a plausible excuse to not spend the evening with Natasha, and then there was Kate's indomitable mother.

Helen answered the phone, her voice identical to her daughter's, while their personalities were completely different.

"Hi, Helen, it's your favourite author," I said, my voice coming out more cheery than my brain had planned.

"And who is that?" We both chuckled.

"What's your message about this time?"

She amped up her voice. "You're going to love this. My spy tells me that de Nadeau will be reviewing *French Like Me* for Friday's *The Lutèce Review*. Isn't that fantastic news? We're all thrilled in the bookstore."

"Great," I replied half-heartedly.

The life of the party was still in her voice. "I'm surprised you're not excited."

"You've been updating me daily, so I'm not as surprised as I am concerned about what he'll write. I'm not prepared for some intellectual, negative bullshit. Remember what I said before—if people want the heavy brooding stuff, they should read Dickens or Hugo. My job is to make people laugh."

"Vlad, don't worry about it. I loved your book and so did Kate! He'll write something positive."

"I hope so."

"Listen I have an important meeting to go to. Don't leave the city." She hung up.

"Don't leave the city?" I said to the dead line. Where did she think I was going? Back to Toronto? I pictured the superintendent painting over the death threat in my apartment. And then there was the question of the back rent. No, Helen, I wasn't going anywhere.

Excitedly, I stuck my head into Natasha's bookstore and mentioned de Nadeau's next review would be my book. After a congratulatory hug and kiss from her, I slipped in a comment about going to bed early in my hotel because I hadn't slept well the night before at her place. It was a reasonable lie to hide that I was going to Kate's for the evening. Natasha bought it. (I guessed.) We agreed to spend the next evening together to celebrate our native country's birthday. She recommended that we go to a Canadian bar for dinner . . . and in Paris! Oy-vey was all I could reply.

A few blocks from Kate's, I found one of those tiny, impossibly super-stocked variety stores and purchased two overpriced bottles of Chinon, accompanied by a bag of pistachios and a package of some kind of crunchy-looking surprise.

I greeted Kate at her apartment door with a kiss on both cheeks. She followed with an unexpected kiss on the lips. Was she trying to speed up the evening in one particular department? Kate's front window caught my attention. Shit—all I could think about was goddamn NiR. Oblivious to Kate, I walked to the front curtain and looked out. Had NiR followed me again? Another late evening attack?

"Vlad, is everything okay?" Kate walked over to me after she spoke and put her hand on my shoulder. I jumped. "Geez, I haven't dated much lately, but I don't usually make men jump."

"Sorry about that. I just had something on my mind, but now she—I mean it's—gone. How about we try some of the wine I brought over with the pistachios and the whatchamacallit thingies."

"They look weird, but what the hell let's try them first." She dumped the package in one bowl and the pistachios in another and let the wine breathe and sat as close as possible to me on the couch without sitting on my lap. And, yes, I felt some action in my Jackson.

I grabbed the bowl full of weird things and inspected one before I put it in my mouth.

"Kate, what the hell are these things? Fused Rice Frispies with corn niblets? And, more importantly, will I die if I eat one?"

"Maybe," she said jokingly. She walked toward the kitchen and returned with two full glasses of wine and a smile.

The couch was blue and soft—leather maybe? There were clear plastic stands on either end with red lamps in the shape of a goddess. In front of the couch was a low, cherry table. The floor looked to be a type of dark imitation wood covered by a huge off-white rug. Beside the entrance to the kitchen and in the corner, lay an army of entertainment equipment. A DVD player rested on top of a dusty videotape player. Stacked beside it were a CD player, a radio and a turntable. The paper-thin TV hung above and was probably the latest model. Along one wall were rows and rows of DVDs, CDs and record albums. I fingered through her collection of CDs, arranged by genre and in alphabetical order, and randomly picked one, the musical *Le Cathédrale de Notre Dame.*

"Kate, I noticed you enjoy musicals."

She jumped off the couch, eyes beaming. "Yes, I adore musicals." She leaned on me as I placed the CD back and continued leafing through, unable to find anything I'd listen to.

"Impressive collection," I forced myself to say. "You didn't by any chance make your husband watch these movies and then he became your ex-husband?"

She grinned and slid her hand around my neck. "That's funny and, no, he wasn't interested in my movies. His English wasn't very good and he had this thing against subtitles. This sounds corny, but my movie collection helped me get through a rough time. I love to read, of course, but it's nice to take a break from the books and relax and let a movie drift me away."

"You're a romantic, no?"

"Why, thank you for saying that. It's been a long time since a man has said the "R" word." She kissed me on the cheek, her lips hanging on for an extra second. Was that a message?

"Kate, I have to ask—does your mother know if you've been out with me?"

"No. And *I* have to ask—does your girlfriend know you've been out with *me*?"

"No, and how about we make a deal we don't talk about either one."

"Deal."

I grabbed a rom-com movie and clinked Kate's glass with mine, causing the wine to splash about the rims. "Here's to chick flicks that help women forget about their exes."

"Cheers," said Kate, a tear suddenly dripping down her cheek. I caught it before it reached her mouth. Kate put her glass down and kissed me. My eyes closed, I pleasantly imagined Angelina Jolie's bubble lips locked on mine.

The kiss finished, the embarrassment on our cheeks the colour of our wine, I moved over to her album section to put some distance between our wandering lips and picked out an album.

"God, Kate," I said with genuine excitement. "I love the song *Downtown* by *Petunia* Clark. Will you play it for me, please?"

"Petulia, and yes I will play it, but only if you dance with me."

I led awkwardly, though wrapping my arms around her back helped me forget about my feet. Kate wore a black silk blouse, making it easy to feel her lacy black bra underneath. My height minus a few inches, Kate rested her head on my shoulder. She looked at me for a brief second and then closed her eyes.

My imagination wandered to that moment when I had difficulty undoing Natasha's bra the first time we made love. Soon, pangs of guilt ran through me. Panting, Kate wrapped a leg around mine, a straddling action made easier by a convenient slit in her skirt. And though I wanted to grab this woman, toss her on her bed (although I wasn't sure where it was) and rock her world, I still had Natasha in my head. I gently pushed Kate away.

"Kate. I have to admit something."

"What!?"

"I'm uninhibitedly gay. In fact, every appendage on my body craves men."

She laughed loudly. "I think I already felt *one* thing that wasn't gay."

150

"That will never *stand up* in a court of law."

"I get the feeling sometimes that everyone and everything is just fodder for your jokes."

I raised my glass to her. "You've read my book. I'm a comedic novelist. No?"

"Of course, but I have to be honest—with your next book, you could consider cutting back on the one-liners."

"Point taken. I remember reading an interview with Gary Shteyngart. His latest book is *Super Sad True Love Story*, and he also wrote *Absurdistan* and *The Russian Debutante's Handbook.*"

"I think it's safe to say that you're fond of this writer."

"Yes, I love anything the guy writes. Even he admits that he hates getting rid of some of the humorous lines in his novels. And I guess it's true—if you eliminate some of the funny lines it makes the other jokes appear even funnier."

Kate took another sip of her wine and pressed her ample breasts against me on the couch, signalling round two. How many rounds would this go?

"I haven't read any of his work," she said, "but your obvious passion for this writer has caught my interest. Which would you recomm—"

"*Super Sad True Love Story* is one of the funniest books I've ever read."

"I'll pick one up at my mother's store."

"Ah ah—you broke our *deal.*"

"Bullocks, you're right."

We ordered takeout curried chicken at an Indian place around the corner. A bottle of red accompanied our meal, although a rosé or a six-pack of *Leffe* would have made more sense. Later we watched five or six episodes of the original *The Office.* I laughed more with each episode, a second bottle of wine helping.

Kate's silk blouse long since unbuttoned. She or I the culprit? (Who cared?) A few rounds of groping later, I abruptly stood up.

"Kate I think you're hot, fun to be with and incredibly open, but maybe we better slow this thing down a bit." It was cool to be involved with two voluptuous women, yet at the same time I felt ashamed. And I missed Natasha.

Kate looked at me briefly and then shifted her eyes away. I think I had embarrassed her. "You're right. One step at a time."

We agreed to see each other again, but I would call her.

I walked outside and paused for a second to take in some fresh air. Out of sight, I also tucked my shirt in and thought of making love to myself. Paranoid of NiR lurking about the neighbourhood, I reconsidered. I waved a taxi down and was back at the hotel in twenty minutes. And I warned the night clerk that if anyone comes up to my room, I would call the police immediately and sue the hotel. Okay, the second threat was lame.

Sunday, July 1st

Near eleven o'clock, my clothes still on from the night before, I heard a knock on the door and the voice of a cleaning lady.

I think I replied, "*Oui*."

Feeling no need to check out more English bookstores, I walked around the city for the day and read more of Farmer's book, which I renamed *The Natasha Diary*.

A Canadian flag waved in front of Natasha's store. "Happy Canada Day," I said as I entered—the first time I had ever said that.

After seven, the store empty, she gave me a kiss.

Natasha and I drank a Pastis (anise-flavoured alcohol mixed with water and ice that was popular in Marseille) at her apartment to soften us up for whatever Canadian thing we were going to eat or drink at the Great Canuck Bar.

The evening air was warm but not stifling as we found our way there. The handle of the front door was an old Sherbrooke hockey stick. I held the door open for Natasha and gave her a light body check.

"Vlad, what the hell!"

"You're in *my* sin bin *baby*!"

She laughed. "Sin bin!? It's the penalty box, right?"

The walls were plastered with Canadian flags and sports memorabilia. Beside a life-size plastic Mountie, a signed Montreal Canadiens jersey hung on a wall. Autographed pictures of players, from Stan Makita to Guy Lafleur to Jonathan Toews, occupied the other walls. To our right was the mother of all screens, and down the left side of the bar were a series of small TVs and a few tables to lean on. The bar looked similar to any Canadian bar except it was in Paris so it was a quarter the size, and half the people spoke French. The attraction—I guessed—were the wings and the burgers that were the exact size and shape of a hockey puck.

We ordered two beers and wings, hers honey garlic, mine Canadian hot and spicy.

I looked at Natasha. "Do you come here often?"

"Are you trying to pick me up?"

"Cute." The waitress placed our Sleeman Cream Ales on the table.

"I pop in here four or five times a year. Rare moments when I miss Canada. I hung out with a guy who worked here. He was originally from Vancouver, a Canucks fan—bleeeeck—but I think the mountains were calling and he went back home."

I raised my bottle of Sleeman. "Here's to relationships of yours that didn't last long—but not ours, of course." I had assumed she was ending her relationship with her boyfriend.

Natasha sipped her beer, listen to whatever came out of my mouth, and at the same time lend an ear to neighbouring conversations. The whole bar was chatting except her. *Shit—I just showed my hand. Come on, Natasha, your turn to play a card. Say something about our relationship.*

"Natasha, did you hear what I just said?" *Damn, I sounded like I was pleading.*

"You mean the part about the 'but not ours, of course'?" she replied with a grin.

"Yes, um, that part," I said embarrassingly.

She placed her moist, beer-holding hand on my dry, coaster-holding hand. "I'd like you to stay for a long, long time." The look on my face somewhere between overjoyed and ecstatic, I kissed her as rapidly as the muscles in my body would allow me to move. Spontaneous reactions of love were not my strong point. Was I becoming sappy? God forbid, romantic?

Later in the evening, the bar was full mostly of boisterous Canadians (that's not an oxymoron), the space between us and the big screen dominated by a team of female rugby players.

A waitress walked around with shots of Canadian Club mixed with maple syrup, a drink they called the Hoser.

By midnight, the singing of *O Canada* reaching a deafening tone, we bumped hips to Notre Dame. That time of night, the fire twirlers were always the main attraction. Their flames, one in each hand, spun around and looked like two bicycle tires alight, their smoky black plumes rising to the stars. Natasha and I found a ledge to sit on. She rested her head on my shoulder and yawned a few times. "Vlad, you haven't updated me much on what you've been doing lately."

"Oh, just a book signing here, book signing there, a few interviews with France 2 and Canal+. Other than that, not much."

She gave me a punch in the ribs. No pain.

"I can tell you're exhausted. Let's go home—your place or mine? I'm just around the corner."

"No, not your hotel. I don't have any clean clothes and there are no toiletries."

"Ah, the eternal problem: women and their toiletries."

"If we walk back to my apartment, you'll have to carry me."

"You're too heavy."

"That's not nice."

I hailed a cab by Shakespeare and Company. After I tucked Natasha in, I walked back to my hotel.

The air warm, the sky full of stars, place Saint-Michel—its marble fountain cascading water— provided the background for the filming of a movie or TV show. I watched for a few boring minutes before darting around the corner to a waiting bed.

Monday, July 2nd

After breakfast, I sat in a park and read Chapter three of *The Natasha Diary*.

A morning breeze tickled my neck as I walked to Natasha's store, her book forever in my hand. And was my exaggerated smile telling every Parisian passerby that I was in love with this woman? I watched Natasha through her store window. Her back was turned, her arms up and animated. I was dying to hug her. Approaching the front door, I felt a tearing, of my arm.

"NiR! What are you doing!?" I screamed, grabbing her pumpkin-shaped head with my desperately waving free hand. Where was this cavewoman dragging me? I anchored my heels into the sidewalk, but she effortlessly pulled me along. The more I struggled for my freedom—or maybe for my life—the easier it was for her to yank my 190-pound petrified body into a cul-de-sac.

"I think you can fuckin' figure it out, *litbas*."

Though in terrible pain, my shoulder surely dislocated, I replied, "I still don't know what *litbas* means."

"You'll find out sooner or later—that's *if* you're still alive." She growled, a safe indication that she was beyond professional help. It was time to lock her inside a mountain and throw away the key.

I held on to a pipe bolted to a wall, but she shook my frame like I was a wet shirt ready for the clothesline. My screams leaving me unaided, I found a crumpled pop can, its edges flattened and jagged. Cutting my palm as I gripped it firmly, I swung my arm madly backwards over my head. The edge stuck into something fleshy.

"Ai-ai-ai! Fuck! Fuck! Fuck!" yelled NiR, her blood dripping down my arm, face, and chest. She let go of my arm. I jumped up and watched her pull a spiky-edged can out of her cheek as if it was an errant nose hair. I nearly fainted.

NiR was on her knees and groaning, her white dress, the size of a parachute, covered in blood. I think she had forgotten about me. I brushed myself off, the matador staring at the defeated bull. "NiR, try that again and either I'll call the police or I'll kill you myself."

She slowly rose to her feet. "I shall never surrender," she said, raising her head, her cheeks and bull neck covered in blood.

"Where do you get these lines? You're fuckin' insane."

She belted out the laughter of a mad scientist in a B-horror movie, the echo scaring me more than the blood dripping down her neck. "It's Winston Churchill, asswipe! I've always wanted to say that."

I think Churchill used the pronoun "we," but it was the wrong time to correct my deranged assailant. I heard some footsteps around the corner. A street person turned into our "hood" and nonchalantly urinated against the wall, at no time acknowledging our presence. Words pointless and NiR more concerned about stopping the blood gushing out of her cheek, I made my exit.

"Chicken shit," she yelled. One could say our relationship had gone beyond complicated.

Natasha's store was thirty metres away, a clean bathroom awaiting me, but she'd be shocked if I walked in covered in blood. Luckily, there was a fountain three blocks up the street. I jumped in like a dog chasing a tennis ball and scrubbed NiR's blood off my clothes. The water turned red. A few kids stared and wondered what I was doing. Their mothers hurried them away.

"*Monsieur, qu'est-ce que vous faites là?*" said a cop. He snuck up on me. The fountain had flushed itself vigorously enough that the water turned clear. I smiled at him. He approached me with his arm out, immediately reminding me of NiR's actions.

"*Dégagez-vous, Monsieur, tout de suite!*" he said.

"I'm dégaging! I'm leaving!" I replied. He grabbed my arm. I panicked and spilled the beans. I told him I had been attacked by a crazy woman the size of a house. He laughed. I showed him the cut on my hand and mentioned that there was fresh blood around a corner. He stopped laughing. NiR was gone by the time we checked the dead end, which was littered with garbage and blood. He took my statement and radioed it in. I also told him where she worked and where I was staying. He gave me his name and number and asked if I was going to have her charged. I said no, thinking I would deal with her in my own way.

The sun dried me off as I walked up the street, leaving wet footprints for a couple of blocks.

Natasha was alone when I arrived. She looked worried the second she saw the mark on my face. She lightly touched it with her fingers. I winced.

"Shit, Vlad, what happened to you?"

I took her hand off my face and kissed her. That's what tough guys do in the movies. "Nothing much; I was sleep walking last night and clipped a door."

"I'm not stupid! I can tell it's a fresh wound. Obviously something just happened." I moved over and sat in the spare chair by the cash register. "And your shoes, Vlad. Why are they wet? It's not raining."

"Well, um, fountains are wet."

"And?" she said, her hands on her hips.

"*Chérie*, you should sit down for this." I took her hand and gently pulled her toward me. She sat on the corner of her desk.

"Remember when you talked about having a lasting relationship?" she said.

I put my hand on her knee. "Yes, I was even a little nervous when I said it. I was kind of worried about how you would respond."

"I hope you've noticed I'm desperately trying to open up to you," she said, close to tears. "But if this relationship is going to work, you have to be honest with me." She took my hand off her knee and cupped it with both hands.

"Well, Natasha, here goes . . . I've been attacked—twice—by NiR." Technically she had attacked me three times but the first one at Helen's apartment was blasé compared to the latest two.

"Is that a man?"

"No, a woman. And she attacked me both times."

"What did you call her? Nor or something?"

"NiR, but her name is really Pam."

"You mean you know this person by her nickname?"

"I wish I didn't, but yes, I'm familiar with her nickname. A couple of nights ago, NiR followed me home from a bar and attacked me in my hotel."

"Were you trying to pick her up?"

"Wow! What a question! Of course I wasn't trying to pick her up." *And yet what was I doing with Kate? Shit—was I going to be a liar for the rest of my life?*

She leaned over and kissed me. I prayed my forehead wasn't sweating. "O course, I was kidding, Vlad, but you still get me worried."

I forced a laugh. "God, if you ever saw this woman. She's huge with powerful shirt-splitting shoulders. But worse than that, she's insane."

Natasha put her hand over her mouth. "Why would she attack you?"

"When I *smuggled* my books into BJ Williams, someone eventually put a "book of the week" sticker on them."

"Yeah, you told me that, and then you mentioned that Simon de Nadeau picked up your book and blah blah blah." She became impatient and counted the cash in the till.

"Are you okay? Natasha? Did your boyfriend call?"

"No! It's close to six. The day's done. I'm going to close early. How about we go out for a beer and you can finish this crazy story?"

I let her mood change go.

Natasha and a toasted our beers in a café a few blocks from her bookstore.

"So, mister not-so-macho, what happened with this woman? Why would she attack you?"

"Well, Natasha, here goes, and I'm not making this up."

Natasha put her glass down, elbows on the table, her hands cupping her chin.

"The woman who attacked me is the person that placed the sticker on my book." I paused and sucked in some air and then breathed out heavily.

"Vlad, you're stalling. Spit it out."

"She said if I didn't sleep with her then she would expose me."

Natasha looked surprisingly calm, I guess because I had already mentioned I'd been attacked, so maybe the novelty had worn off.

"So let's recap the story." Natasha spoke in a tone that suggested I was creating some interesting fiction. "You're telling me that a huge, crazy woman is extorting you for sex?" She snickered, which didn't bother me. I grinned, thinking I would have reacted the same way.

"It's not bullshit. This insane woman told me at a Starbucks—"

Natasha laughed out loud and, for the first time, attracted negative looks from neighbouring tables.

"Starbucks! No way?"

God, I wanted to stop smiling, but my facial muscles refused the commands from my brain.

"Yes! Starbucks! When I snuck into BJ Williams to check my books, she confronted me. She had seen me put the books on the shelf right beside Morgan Davis's books in the first place. She told me to my face that if I didn't have sex with her, she would turn me in to Helen. I told her that we could discuss the situation outside. She suggested we go to a nearby Starbucks during her break. I said fine. I think even for a brief moment I agreed to do it."

Natasha raised her eyebrows in disbelief. "What?"

"Good, at least you believe me."

"I'm starting to believe that even you couldn't make up this bull."

"To make a long story short, we talked for an hour at Starbucks and got nowhere. I was embarrassed as hell just sitting near her because she was making lewd comments. The problem isn't how big she is, it's more that she's unbelievably obnoxious. I told her to go ahead and tell the senior manager, who turned out to be Helen. When the woman, NiR, as she insists on being called—"

"What does that even mean?"

"It stands for 'night reader.' This woman loves to contract two words into one."

"I'm sorry I brought it up."

I ordered another round. "When NiR returned to work, I decided to follow her. She spilled the beans to Helen, but unbeknownst to me, three of my books had just sold in the store, including one to Simon de Nadeau."

"So there was no need to sell your soul, I mean your body once you found out that you were on your way and didn't need her help." I nodded in agreement. Natasha wasn't finished. "And she attacked you in your hotel?"

"Yes, and she attacked me around the corner of your bookstore as well."

The waitress returned with two *Leffes* and a tray of peanuts. Lost in our conversation, the beers went untouched.

"That's awful that she would hunt you down. But, Vlad, I have to ask—if she's huge, wouldn't you kind of notice at least *a little bit* that a gigantic woman was stalking you?"

"It's embarrassing how she moves about undetected."

"So what happened by my bookstore?"

After explaining the bookstore attack as quickly as possible, I knew Natasha was upset.

"I need a cigarette," she said nervously

"I'm sorry, Natasha. My stories are usually a laugh-and-a-half."

"How badly was she hurt?"

"No clue."

"This woman is scary. Do the police know?"

"Yes, and don't worry, *chérie*, you're in good hands."

"That's what I'm afraid of." We finished our beers in silence and walked hand in tight hand to her apartment.

Tuesday, July 3rd

Natasha kissed me on the cheek as I lay half-asleep on the foldout. A hard-boiled egg, a croissant, and a glass of orange juice were waiting for me on the table.

"Vlad, yesterday's stories were so shocking, I forgot to ask if you'd read the next few chapters of Farmer's book."

I buttered and slapped a spoonful of jam on my croissant. "Yes, I have."

"You usually carry it around with you, but I haven't seen it lately."

"You're right, the last time I remember seeing it was in the cul-de-sac when NiR went after me. I'll just pick up another copy at your store."

"Shoot—I just sold the only other copy I had." Natasha mentioned another used bookstore that may have Farmer's book, but she cautioned me that the owner was eccentric.

"Not exactly the first strange bookstore operator I'll come across in Paris."

"That's not nice. What about me?"

I wanted to mention the irony of having to find out about her life through someone else's autobiography but decided to avoid that remark. "You're the only normal one, *chérie*, and an added bonus—you're hot."

"Why, thank you."

The heat rose off the Parisian streets and lingered waist high. I entered Brooklyn Books and browsed the shelves. "Hello, may I help you?" said a monotone voice with no immediate face attached to it. A man stuck his head out from the right front corner of the store. He'd been sitting in front of a computer and was surrounded by books to the point I think he was wearing some of them. And he was.

He walked in front of the desk and asked me if I was looking for a particular book. My eyes were glued to the white lab coat he was wearing, which was lined with twenty or so pockets, each holding a paperback.

"You don't wear that book-jackety thing all day, do you?"

"Usually just in the morning—it gets me psyched for the day." He turned around and arched his back as if he was putting it on display. *The Getaway* by Jim Thompson, *Star Hunter* by Andre Norton and *Vulcan's Hammer* by Philip K. Dick caught my attention.

"Thanks for the presentation, um, paperback jacket guy."

"The name's Bartholomew, but people just call me Stan."

"Stan! I don't get it."

"Either do I."

Fearing I was going to be part of a Laurel and Hardy routine, I rapidly asked if he had Farmer's book.

His eyes lit up. "I think so." I was out in two minutes with the book.

Wednesday, July 4th, Thursday, July 5th

I personally contacted ten literary agents in Paris. I told them that de Nadeau was reviewing my book for Friday's *The Lutèce Review*. Half of them mentioned they would contact me if he wrote a positive piece. Helen had done a lot for me, but I had to cover all my bases and discuss options with other agents. And she wasn't stupid—she had to know that I was no longer a country bumpkin in the book business. I also called Kate and Natasha each day, making sure not to mix up their names.

Twenty-four days later

Sunday, July 29th

It was late afternoon. I heard what sounded like a mop banging and swishing outside my cell. Was someone in the police station cleaning up my vomit? It was about fuckin' time!

No sooner had the mopping stopped then I began knocking my head against my cell wall. Achieving a new low in my life, I was unable to control myself. And it was only luck that the "caterpillar" on my forehead missed the concrete. A cop banged something against my door and barked a few words in French. I lay down and forced my eyes shut. I had handled prison stays (averaging a month) back home, but this police station was making me nervous and—I hated to admit—scared.

Hours later, my stomach normal and having reached my limit of staring at four blank walls, my thoughts turned to the "stolen" goods found in my apartment. The Picasso belonged to Helen, the wooden carving was Kong's, no doubt, and I could only assume the diamond earrings were Natasha's. Shit, did Helen want me in jail that badly to keep me away from her daughter? Was she that determined? Or was I that unhinged to even come up with the idea? I still believed that Helen was behind the set-up, but there remained one puzzle—an article of clothing found next to the earrings in my apartment. It was carefully wrapped in plastic and included a label of authenticity, yet it had no connection to anyone trying to have me put away.

Twenty-three days ago

Friday, July 6th

I woke up in time to have breakfast with the other tourists. The day clerk handed me a message as I exited my hotel. Helen mentioned that de Nadeau's review of my book was in today's *The Lutèce Review*. And not a word about the critique! God, was it that bad?

Clouds had swarmed the sky, forcing the sun to hide in a corner and wait for the coast to clear. I entered BJ Williams. No NiR. Helen greeted me at the cash registers, a piece of paper in hand, and a smile so big her face had to be in some kind of pain. She hugged me, my eyes the whole time on the *Lutèce Review* in her hand.

"Vlad, we did it! We did it! De Nadeau's article is terrific!"

"Shit! You're kidding! Fuckin' A!" Too excited, I let the "we" go without comment.

"The customers can hear you, Vlad. How about we go upstairs?"

"Sure."

"A cappuccino?"

"Do you have some rum in your office to celebrate?"

"No, unfortunately."

I snatched the paper out of her hand and read walking up the stairs. My jubilation getting the best of me I nearly tripped on the top step.

The following was de Nadeau's review of *French Like Me*:

French Like Me, Vlad Moranski (238 pages, Willowbrook Publishing [self-published])

You wouldn't think a book about a father trying to entertain three teenaged sons could be this captivating, this illuminating, this side-splittingly funny. But not everyone has Moranski's literary flair.

The story centres on a father, Carson Moranski (we assume the author's alter ego), a married, semi-retired teacher and amateur comedian who trucks his teenaged sons off to Paris for a week to film his antics on the unsuspecting French for a potentially lucrative cable show, but his celluloid and life are blown up by ping-pong corruption, flea market hucksters, a banker babe, organ traders and an iconic cathedral. Okay, that's above the surface. Below, there is simply no writer—not Thoreau, nor Bryson, nor Twain, nor Kerouac, nor Steinbeck—who better delivers a story about a man's love for a city. The author sheds so many new angles on Paris and its people that I would have seriously retitled the book "Parisonification."

Yes, Carson is front and centre in the novel, but the true protagonist is the city. (Need we be reminded of when the English dreadfully renamed "Notre Dame de Paris" to "The Hunchback of Notre-Dame"?)

And who would read this book? Its true power is that it transcends generations à la rocker, Johnny Hallyday.

Carson's sons—Rory, Lew, and Nik—each reflect a different characteristic of their father's personality. Then we have Monique, the female interest he happens to meet in a park. The scenes with her are worth a movie alone. (And who could create sexual tension better than Spain's own tinderbox Penelope Cruz?) While we're casting, my advice to Jon Hamm is, give Mad Men a rest—it's B-material compared to taking on Carson, a charming, compassionate mec who, depending on the bigger laugh, switches from wiseass to klutz.   And   the   three sons? Give Justin Bieber a try and a few taller Bieb-clones.

Moranski's details about life in Paris are well woven into the narrative and often entertaining in their fresh descriptions: "Guided by the Seine, which at night looked like shiny black anacondas slithering in unison." Carson and his sons attend a flea market where (spoiler alert—the quotation provides enough foreshadowing): "The district was so dangerous even the mannequins in the store windows had busted noses."

And the locals the family meets along the way: "Six dirty green benches circled the fountain, one of them already occupied by two worn asphalt faces sprouting patches of grey weeds and sipping on their morning cans of Heineken. Years of inebriation and missing teeth had created a French dialect only recognizable on their bench."

Carson's conversation with the lovely Monique about Notre Dame is worth the price of the book: "I'm still fascinated by Notre Dame. I was happy when the city cleaners removed the last piece of scaffolding from her a couple of years ago. It made me so jealous that they were allowed to scrub her body and not me. Who knows what they were touching behind those plastic sheets."

Monique: "Carson, I think you have an unhealthy relationship with the church."

"I must admit the workers did a good job. Her skin has that creamy white glow. The buzz on the street is that she looks five hundred years younger!"

And one more oddly romantic quotation (Carson has just left Monique's apartment.): "Only a frontal lobotomy would allow him to forget her. He hoped visiting an old flame would help.

Ten minutes later he stood by her. He couldn't turn away. Notre Dame was radiant that night. The pale, yellow lamps, alternating with the glowing green, amber and red traffic lights, reflected on the Seine's swirling black water. They had drawn a real-life Starry Night."

Moranski's writing has created a fifth literary French expat Republic. Ernest Hemingway's A Moveable Feast inaugurated the exile wave (although John Glassco's Mémoires de Montparnasse never received its due). Samuel Beckett's second republic moved the expat experience into a desolate, tragicomic outlook on human nature. Peter Mayle's A Year in Provence pushed the third wave by toning down the "tragi" and amping up the "comic," a bottle of wine never too far from his carefree Frenchies. Morgan Davis's work took the French and their culture into a hipper twenty-first century, though in a more sober direction. And, voila, Moranski leads us into the latest upsurge. How best to describe his voice? Imagine Chabon, Sedaris, and Shteyngart sitting down in a Parisian café, dictating a story to Albert Camus.

What can I say? I'm a born and bred Parisian, and even Moranski has me looking at my city in a different light. Let's hope there's a sequel.

Simon de Nadeau

Helen entered the room singing a song while carrying our hot drinks.

"Helen, this is unfuckin' real!"

"I can't wait to make some money. With that incredible review, the customers are going to pour in here."

She glanced at the article again and smiled. "We won't bother with a distributer, obviously. I'm pencilling you in for a meeting with my literary agent friend for later today. Then he'll get you a publisher, but this all has to happen fast. We have to take advantage of this great review. Pronto."

"I appreciate what you've done, but I told you already that I would be contacting some agents myself. Five agents have agreed to call back if I get a positive review. I have to return to the hotel right now because I'm sure they and others are trying to knock my door down."

Helen banged her fist on the desk.

"You ungrateful bastard! One, you never told me you would talk to other agents, and two, what door? You don't *have* a goddamn door, Vlad! You're still a nobody."

I held the review up high in my hand. "Not now!"

The argument over "who I am" lasted a few minutes, and then I walked out.

I burst into Natasha's store, waving the review. And although four or five people were standing in line to purchase a book, I walked behind the counter and hugged her.

She whispered in my ear. "I can think of a more fun way to celebrate later."

I put my hands around her waist. "That sounds good." I half-heartedly apologized to her customers and sat on another chair and read the review, most of it out loud.

Natasha motioned to me to grab two coffees down the street. It was her polite way of getting my obnoxious self out of the store for a few minutes while she tended to business.

When I returned, the store was empty. Natasha had read the review in my absence and congratulated me with a kiss. Several times she mentioned that I was on my way to becoming famous and that she was my biggest fan. After the mutual enthusiasm for my review had died down, I told her that I had to go back to BJ Williams later in the day to talk business. A lie. I was having dinner with Kate. And though Kate and I had done nothing more than speak over the last few days, I'd grown fond of her. I was being deceitful, but I enjoyed juggling two women at the same time.

Kate picked a restaurant near her apartment that specialized in southwest French cuisine. We both ordered *confit de canard* along with a bottle of red. My review in her hand, she set an indoor record for the number of congratulations. Our plates arrived with a leg of duck accompanied by butter garlic potatoes and string beans.

"So, Vlad, what would you like to do after we eat?"

Her comment caught me off guard because I was still lost in my meal, proving that men only think of two things (and one at a time). I lifted my head from my trough. "Any ideas?" I replied in a less alluring tone.

"Well, after the meal we could go up to my place," she said nervously.

165

"Waiter! Cheque please!"

We sat on Kate's couch, sipping a glass of brandy. She leaned on me, the amorous pulses passing effortlessly through our bodies. Kate downed her glass and rubbed her leg against mine. We kissed. Soon she had my pants halfway down my ankles, my jaguar ready to pounce out of its cotton cage. I threw off my shirt and helped her remove her blouse and bra, her voluptuous breasts wildly escaping after a year or two of good behaviour. I assumed she hadn't had sex in a while. Bonus! Half-naked, she guided her breasts, nipples rock solid and pointing the way down my chest, resting on my manhood. Then I lost control of myself, *guilt* just another word in the dictionary. I stood up and lifted Kate by her firm buttocks. She threw her legs around me, her breasts springing up and down as I carried her to her bedroom...

Saturday, July 7th

I gently positioned Kate's arm back on the pillow and put my clothes on, fully aware I was about to participate in the time-honoured screw-and-dash. I left a note.

> *Hi Kate,*
> *I have to go to BJ Williams to discuss something about my future.*
> *Last night was fun. I'll call you.*
> *Vlad*

Back at the hotel, I pocketed my messages and grabbed a coffee and a *pain au chocolat* along the way to BJ Williams.

I opened the front door and slid into the back of the store. Helen followed me to my books, a number of which were missing. The total was precisely in my head, but I wanted to hear it from her.

"Helen, how many books did you or I or we sell yesterday?" I sounded casual considering the blow-up that had happened the last time we spoke.

"Counting ten this morning, that's twenty-one." She straightened out my books. "Only three left. I think someone may have just bought one." She even smiled as she spoke.

A heavy finger tapped me on the shoulder. I jumped, my first thought that NiR had "escaped" from hell to finish me off.

166

"Excuse me, Mr. Moranski, could you please sign this copy of *French Like Me*," said a woman with an English accent. She was petite and charming and possessed a warm smile: the anti-NiR.

"And what is your name, Miss?" I said, trying to sound author-y.

"Beatrice."

"A beautiful name and it happens to be my mother's as well," I said with a straight face. The woman turned red.

"That's a wonderful coincidence," she said. "I must tell my friends."

"It would be an honour for me and my mother if you would spread the word. Please tell all your friends that the Canadian version of Morgan Davis has arrived in France and will one day conquer all of England." *Did that just come out of mouth?*

Helen rolled her eyes. Beatrice looked like she was ready to have my children.

She thanked me four times and floated away. I looked at Helen, her arms folded.

"Vlad, women can't see through you, but I sure can."

"Just having some fun."

Another woman tapped me on my arm. "Mr. Moranski, would you mind signing my book?"

"Of course. Where are you from?"

"Vancouver."

"My MOTHER'S from Vancouver—what a coincidence."

"What part?"

"The island part," I replied. "By the way, what's your name?"

"Sally."

"SALLY! Are you kidding me? That's my SISTER'S name." I signed the book.

Helen grabbed my arm and pulled me aside. "You don't want to constantly make fun of your fans. I'm assuming there will be a second book one day?"

"You've told me more than once to be sarcastic."

"That's true, but I'm just warning you—watch your ego."

"Whatever."

"Have you been talking to other agents?"

I took the messages out of my pocket and quickly waved them in front of her face. "I have five agents in my hand, Helen. I'll contact them later today and set something up. There's no hurry to make a decision. And I will see your agent friend soon as well."

"That's *sooo* nice of you."

"Sarcasm doesn't become you, Helen."

Our conversation becoming less pleasant, I suggested we go upstairs, but Helen, ever the businesswoman, told me to stay and sign more books.

No sooner had the display emptied than a man followed Helen and me to her office—Helen had pulled a fast one on me. He was a foot shorter than me, with less hair than a cue ball, and he wore a scowl even when he introduced himself. My first impression was *great*—Helen hired Napoleon to sell my books. Napoleon stuck out his hand.

"*Enchantez*, Monsieur Morunski. My name is *Gérard Deschamps*."

I said happy to meet you and call me Vlad. He shook hands with Helen, threw some books off a chair, and moved it beside me.

"Well, Gérard," said Helen, "let's get to business. I believe as Vlad's new agent you have the contracts."

"Helen," I said, "this is not a done deal."

"Yes, I bring the contract," said Gérard as if he either hadn't understood what I'd just said or didn't care. Was I with *two* people who didn't take no for an answer?

He pulled five bundles of paper from his briefcase and placed them on Helen's desk. Each bundle had a different-coloured paper clip. He took the blue paper clip off and handed a sheet to me. Thank God the document was in English.

"Please take a minute, Vlad. Read the paper." He handed one to Helen as well. She glanced at it and then stared at me. "Remember, I'm the one that got your career off the ground. It would be nice if you could do *me* a favour and forget the other agents. Just ask some quick questions, sign, and be off."

"I'm going to be honest with you. You've been unbelievably helpful in getting my writing career off the ground, but I'm fed up with you controlling me."

Helen's tone turned aggressive. "Just so you understand, it's one thing to get an agent and even get published, but you need me to spread the word about you. And as I've told you more than once, I'm in constant contact with BJ Williams all over the world. And do I need to remind you, *again*, that BJ Williams is the largest bookstore chain in the world?"

My tone unpleasant, I said, "I've heard it before."

Gérard cut in, probably sensing that Helen and I were on our way to a yelling match. "Vlad, please read the contract."

I read the first line or two of each paragraph. "Guys, I don't see any big dollar signs on these pages."

"Is a standard contract for a new writer."

He removed the black paper clip from the next bundle and handed Helen and me a copy.

"I see lots of percentages, but no advance."

"That is correct, Vlad," said Helen. Gérard repeated Helen's words.

"Helen, are you familiar with Andrew Davidson's *The Gargoyle*?" Carson never stopped talking about this Canadian writer. I think he was Carson's muse.

"Of course. We sold hundreds of his books."

"He was a first-time writer and got an advance of 1.5 *million*."

Helen looked at Gérard. "Tell him Gérard."

"Vlad, is only one day. I leave a message with four publisher. One call back *tout de suite*. I wait more message."

"Well I th—"

Helen cut me off. "Vlad, what Gérard means is he's got an advance from one offer and is waiting for the other three. Your review was only in the paper yesterday, but if you sign with Gérard, he and I can get your book published and promoted more quickly than normal. It's early July, and hundreds of anglophone tourists are looking for a new Paris read." Helen looked at Gérard. "Well, should you tell him or should I?" God, she was so dramatic.

"I will tell," said Gérard. "Vlad, we only hear one publisher, *mais* publisher offer advance of 50,000 euros. More offer will happen."

It wasn't 1.5 million, but I was desperate. "Who's the publisher?"

"Randonnée House."

"It sounds good," I said, "but I need time." *Don't give in, Vlad.* I smiled, remembering how Stallone held off on selling "Rocky" to the first bidder. And yes my ego was growing. The conversation about me signing went around in circles, though Helen did mention that fifty to a hundred other BJ Williams around the world would have a minimum of 200 copies of my book as soon as possible. I would also be flown around the world to promote my book, though she said I would have the most influence in Paris.

She gave me a list of questions typically asked of authors and told me to get a cellphone and be prepared for multiple book signings the second the first batch of books arrived, which, of course, would only happen if I signed. She gave me three days to decide; otherwise, she had other "fish to fry." She refused to elaborate.

I phoned the five agents, making arrangements to see two of them on Sunday and the rest on Monday. And I told Kate what was happening. She wanted to take me out for dinner, but I said I had some things to do, which included looking for a new place to live.

And, most importantly, honest money soon to come my way, I felt I had outdistanced my past. I was proud of myself and wanted to tell the world how my life had changed, but I wanted my past kept a secret (save a few youthful "stories" I had admitted to Natasha). And the death threats: the sum of all the thefts and scams I had pulled for a good forty years, would go silently to my grave. I needed an "ism" to characterize my life's work up until now. Sinnergism! Meh! Too lame.

My advance only a matter of time, I studied some three-room apartment advertisements in *agence immobilière* windows, the price starting at 1500 euros.

Natasha was standing in front of her store when I approached.

"*Chérie*," I said from a distance, "why are you smoking?" Was she somehow aware that I had slept with Kate last night? Shit! She flicked the butt over my head, bouncing off a church in Lyon, and threw a piece of gum in her mouth before we kissed. As I approached her lips, I thought for sure that I would feel nervous or distant or cold, but it was none of the above. Our kiss felt comfortable, unforced, normal.

"Natasha, did dickweed call?"

"No. I just wanted a cigarette." She sounded sincere.

"Are you sure? I've got some friends back home that can do something about those kind of people."

"Ah, you writers—you're always bullshitting."

"Well, *I* would love to meet him and kick the living shit out of him."

"You don't strike me as a fighter."

"Haven't had a fight since I was an adolescent, but it was a good one." A lie.

"I haven't heard any Vlad youth stories in a while. Do tell."

I told Natasha that the last time I was in a fight I beat up an older, bigger guy because he had called my mother a slut.

We walked back in the store, intentionally bumping hips.

"Natasha, I can't believe I forgot to tell you something amazing that happened to me today. I spoke to an agent and soon will be signing a big contract for at least 50,000 euros."

"Fifty thousand euros—that's amazing!" she said, her hands raised in triumph as if she had just won Wimbledon. She grabbed me and planted a kiss on my cheek.

"Yeah, I was happy when I heard the numbers."

"You don't sound too happy."

She tried to kiss me on the lips, but I turned my head. Shit, did I do that intentionally? Maybe I had a conscience.

"Vlad, is everything okay? You're distant all of a sudden."

Before I'd seen Natasha smoking outside, I had convinced myself that sleeping with another woman was okay. We weren't married or even engaged. Hell, maybe Kate and I did it because we just got caught up in my glowing review and wanted to celebrate. Or, maybe we just enjoyed being together and this was the next step in the relationship. Whatever the excuse I had worked out in my head, the guilt came after Natasha attempted kiss number two.

"It's rare, but I have a headache," I said.

She grabbed me again. "My poor baby. Tell you what: I'm going to close the store in a few minutes."

"You'll do that for me?"

"It hasn't been busy for the last hour. I'll take *you* out for an early dinner."

My head hurt less. "Thanks, that's nice of you. Can we go to the Vietnamese restaurant?"

I waved to Kong as Natasha and I entered the restaurant. He smiled and proceeded to beat the hell out of his chest. Natasha rolled her eyes and said, "Oh, no." Kong walked out from behind the glass counter.

"Who knew I could have that kind of effect on a restaurateur," I said under my breath. We shook hands with the Kongmeister and then he ran back behind the counter. I think he'd forgotten about the couple in front of us wanting to order. I leaned on the counter, studying the food and tapping the glass, the noise suggesting the service was a little slow. Kong must have read my mind.

"No worry, writerman" said Kong. "I be with you and lovely black-hair woman in second."

"That's okay, Kong," I said. My finger raised, I added, "but just this once, right? Next time I'm here, I'm going to create a business class line. I shall call it Vladclass—" Someone's knee in the back of my thigh interrupted my monologue. "Ow! Natasha, that friggin' hurt."

"You told me you wouldn't embarrass me in the restaurant."

171

"Who gives a shit! I was just having some fun."

"*Nice language, nice attitude,*" she replied, her sarcasm loud and clear. And it wasn't turning me on.

"Lighten up!"

"You NEVER talk to me like that. What's happening?" My tapping grew louder. "Please quit that." She nudged my elbow. "The people sitting at the tables are giving us dirty looks."

"Don't they know I'm going to sign a contract for at least fifty thou?"

"No, I *don't* think they are aware of that. Why don't you just announce it to the world and get it over with?"

I looked around the restaurant (not a chopstick stirring) and raised my hands as if I was about to address the masses. "Natasha, we have everyone's attention."

"*Well isn't that wonderful!*" She crossed her arms and gave me a look that said I'm out of here in a second if you don't smarten up.

Maybe I still felt guilty for the night before, but it just wasn't coming out the right way. And the right way was being honest, but there was no confession in my soul. Her sarcasm touched a nerve rather than make me laugh. My arms back at my sides, I directed my attention to Natasha. "Oh, and by the way, all of my books have sold out in less than two days and Helen said my book will become an instant success."

"Writerman, I take your order and I take wife order as well."

Natasha burst out laughing. "That'll be the day," she replied. She paused and nodded in my direction. "This guy's ego is bigger than this restaurant. How does he even fit his head in the door!?" A few patrons sitting near us gaffawed. Natasha glared at me. "Is this want you want? Are you happy with our conversation?"

"Who fuckin' cares?! Let's just eat."

"I'm out of here. Call me when you're ready to apologize."

"I doubt it! Oh one more thing, I'm getting just a *little* tired of the mysterious boyfriend, mysterious life thing. Can't you just talk about your past like a goddamn normal person?"

"YOU'RE A PRICK!" She moved past the lineup and out the door. I apologized several times, but my feet remained frozen. Was I hungry? Was I a jerk? The answer to both was yes. I looked back at the people, chopsticks back in hand and no longer interested in my spontaneity. I ordered. Kong personally guided me to a table that had just opened underneath the wooden carving of two dancing, semi-naked women.

———

I put my hand on Kong's shoulder. "You believe in me, right?"

"Yes, writerman who have mouth maybe a little too big."

"What?" I said, my tone hostile.

Kong laughed out loud, exposing brown, outdated teeth that only an archaeologist could love. "I make joke! Why you not laugh?"

"You got me on that one, Kong." He beat his chest and told me he'd bring my dinner over in a few minutes. I asked for a second beer as well.

Five beers later, the restaurant empty, Kong sat across from me with a glass of yellow liquid in his hand.

"Hey, buddy," I said, lightly slapping his back, "it's nice that you've come to join me for a drink, although I gotta tell ya, that stuff you're drinking looks weird."

"What you mean *weird*?"

I laughed the laugh of someone happily on his way to becoming drunk.

"PISS, yellow juice, lemonade, pee." I stood up and pointed to my crotch.

"That no funny, I no drink my urine."

"Sorry, Kong, just messing with ya."

We chinned our drinks.

"Here's to whatever the fuck is in that glass of yours."

"And here to you beer, which look funny, too."

"You got me, Kong. That was a good one." I put my hand on my throat. "I'm laughing right here. There's a shitload of throbbing going on there. Real funny stuff. By the way, Kong, what *are* you drinkin'?"

"It Vietnamese alcohol. Super strong. Clean bad things in stomach."

I looked at the wall to my right. It was surprisingly under-decorated, only a few Asian landscapes and symbols hanging about. There were two wooden carvings of wild horses, each the size of a shoebox and separated by a metre. Red tassels hung around the horses' necks. They looked like equestrian medals.

"Kong, I've got some great ideas for your restaurant." He was anxious to hear what I had to say. I pointed to the far wall. "Over there, you should put up some posters of famous writers, you know, Shakespeare, Hemingway, Joyce, Stein, Moranski."

"Who Moranski?"

"Me!" I had a bottle in my hand and was tempted to stamp it on the table to show my disapproval, but it had become obvious that I had very few friends and no male friends in particular. I set the bottle down gently.

"Would you be my friend, Kong?" I asked sincerely.

"Yes, we friend." He raised his glass. "I make toaster to friend."

"Here's to a new toaster, friend," I said. And it was pointless to correct him because more would come.

"Kong, my name is Vlad Moranski and I'm going to be a famous writer very soon."

Kong's eyes brightened. "What you write, writerman Vlad?"

"VLAD! Kong, just call me Vlad."

"Vlad."

"That's good."

"You write sexy book, Vladman?"

"Kong, just say *Vlad*. Okay? Repeat after me 'just Vlad.'"

"Just Vlad."

"No, just say *Vlad*," I repeated.

"No, just say Vlad," he said.

"Kong, are you putting me on? Are you being a funny guy right now?"

He beat his chest and smiled. "Yes, is obvious your name Vlad. I just pull your cock."

My eyes widened. "Careful with your slang there, my man. I'm assuming you're a little mixed up. In English we say "pull a fast one" or "pull your chain" or maybe "pull your leg." If you say "pull your cock," well, that puts us in new territory. A place, frankly, I'm not too keen on visiting. Know what I mean, jelly-bean?" I turned serious for a second. "Kong, are you gay?"

"Maybe a little."

"I've never heard anyone say 'a little.'"

He burst out laughing. "I make joke. I no gay. I love women. I want marry ten women."

"Is that allowed in Vietnam?"

"No. It just nice thinking."

"Well, I gotta tell you, Kong, I'm having a problem with three women. One is trying to control my career; I slept with her daughter last night. That's two, and the woman I was with tonight—my girlfriend, Natasha—doesn't know about it. I guess the guilt is coming out."

Kong rubbed his crotch.

"Kong, what the hell are you doing?"

He stopped rubbing. "I sorry. I get happy."

I finished my beer and asked Kong for another one. He went over to the bar and poured himself another yellow drink and opened a sixth beer for me.

"I your friend. You talk more about women."

"Let's backtrack a little because I think we were talking about some other things as well. Kong, I want to see posters of famous authors on your wall. And we can put rows of books on the walls as well. It won't cost you anything because I'm fuckin' rich."

"How you fuckin' rich?"

I sensed Kong's rate of inebriation was rapidly surpassing mine. That stuff he was drinking must have been eighty proof, but the bugger never winced once when he gulped it down. The guy was as tough as nails. I stared into his brown eyes.

"Kong, I'll be signing a book contract for 50,000 fuckin' euros, man!"

He smiled from ear to ear. "Fifty thousand fuckin' euro, man—that incredible. You buy strong water buffalo with that."

"Water buffalo!? Why the fuck would I buy water buffalo with the money?"

"Water buffalo useful animal in Vietnam."

I slowly waved a half circle with my arm, putting the restaurant on display.

"Kong, we're in Paris, not Vietnam."

"I think of homeland sometime."

I felt sorry for the guy. "So you miss Vietnamski?"

"Yes." He slowly put his head down.

"Are your wife and kids there?" I paused for a second. "Or maybe your mistress, ha-ha!" I said, trying to cheer him up.

"No, no woman nowhere. I too busy. I live your life. . ." I think he was searching for the word vicariously.

"That's kind of sad, Kong. Are there not some possibilities here in Paris?"

"I no try. Too late for me." He couldn't have been more than forty, with a full head of black hair, temples greying a smidge.

I wanted to tell him that if he would fix those goddamn chips of bark for teeth, he'd have a chance, but I just mentioned something about using the Internet and avoid a smiling photo. He said the Internet was full of women who lied about their age and used photos of themselves at a younger age or of someone else. Not a bad idea in Kong's case.

"That's nonsense, Kong." I put my hand on his shoulder. "One

175

night, you and I are going to go to one of those fancy dinners in Paris where singles pay a hundred euros and then later on in the evening get together and ask each other questions. You'll have five minutes to talk to a lady, then five minutes to talk to the next, and the next. We're talkin' the city of love, man."

Kong jumped up and thrust his pelvis back and forth, his hands up in the air, fingers snapping.

"Kong, buddy, save those cool moves for the ladies."

I pointed my empty bottle toward him. "I wanna try a shot of your stuff."

He brought over two glasses of yellow "nitroglycerine." I downed mine in one mouthful. "SON OF AN INCINERATOR!" I yelled, my head shaking uncontrollably. "Christ, Kong, I don't think even a fireman could put the blaze out in my mouth."

Kong downed his and smiled politely. You'd think he was drinking lemonade.

"What is that? Embalming fluid? Doesn't that stuff burn your throat?"

"I use it to clean bathtub, too."

"Funny shit." I studied his face for a few seconds. It was blurry. Christ, the yellow liquid had kicked into my system.

"Vlad, tell me more about night with women."

"Before I say anything else, we gotta do something about your teeth." I was getting heavily into the sauce because I don't usually talk to men about their teeth.

"What you mean?"

"If you want to impress the lay-days you've gots to have money and clean teeth." He stood up and checked his teeth in a nearby mirror.

"You right. I no care before. What I do?"

"Well, the first thing you do is give me another one of those drinks."

Kong shook his head, but I wasn't sure how many times or in what direction. "I no think you can stand up."

"Nonsense," I said. I stood up to prove him wrong, and quickly lost my balance. He grabbed my arm and helped me back in the chair.

"You finish for night."

"Fine, anyway what were we talking about?"

"You talk about my teeth." Kong blocked my fingers as I attempted to put them on his mouth. Yeah, I was drunk. "You no dentist."

I leaned back in my chair or maybe Kong pushed me back. "I just wanted to see your teeth, man. Anyway, just go to a fuckin' dentist or just grab something sharp and start chipping away at the shit in there."

Kong looked offended. "I no shit in my mouth!"

"Kong, it's just an express . . . shun. I'll tell you what. If you get me one more of those yellow drinks I'll get you a real dentist to clean your teeth and I'll pay for it."

"Thank you, Vlad, but I tell you, you girlfriend no happy tonight."

"It's the first argument we've ever had." I think I waved an index finger in the air to embellish my response.

"The women crazy, no?"

And though I was drunk, my thoughts turned to NiR. "I can think of one, but not my girlfriend. It was my fault. I was excited about my future contract and wanted to tell the world, but she is unbelievably private. And you've noticed I'm crazy."

"That true. You bring flower to her tomorrow, say sorry?"

I nodded in agreement. We were alone in the restaurant. I may have waved to the last waitress when she left, before I became intoxicated. Kong blabbed something about the restaurant being normally full at lunch with university students and busy at night with mostly local Vietnamese. Desperately trying not to slur my words, I told him that would all change once he turned the restaurant into a cool writers' haunt. Famous writers, actors, and musicians would hang out, attracting the paparazzi night and day. I guaranteed that his restaurant would become the "it" place in Paris.

He agreed to put some posters on the wall if I picked them out, and he would buy some book-racks as long as I bought the books. Or I think he said that. I smiled the smile of a happy drunk; I had one last lucid thought for the evening—I would buy the paperbacks at Natasha's, of course. (My plan before I had one drop of alcohol.) A way of getting back into her good books, no? My head spinning, I still envisioned filling the whole wall with books, although the books seemed to be floating.

At midnight, I gave Kong a one hundred-euro bill and told him to keep the change. The rain falling, my body shifting like a giant weeble (which wobble but don't fall down), Kong suggested that I take a cab, but I needed to be woken up by the fresh drops of rain. I staggered back to the hotel, listening to car tires swishing through the puddles.

Sunday, July 8th

During breakfast at the hotel, I read Chapters three, four and five of

-----

177

Farmer's book. Call it guilt reading, though I didn't substitute Natasha's name for Caroline's as I read. Was I thinking less about Natasha? Or was I more able to separate the two? Either way, I made some mental notes to prove to Natasha that I understood Farmer's plight. At the front desk, Helen had left a message.

Late morning, the sun burning everything in its path, I held up Farmer's book and walked back and forth in front of Natasha's store, waving my white flag. Oh, no—did I get that idea from lame-ass Byron?

"I come in peace," I repeated. Natasha yelled to open the door myself.

Sitting at the computer, she ignored me as I walked in.

"No kiss?"

She tapped loudly as she spoke. "Last night, Vlad, you went way over the top. How does your head even fit in the door? And thanks to you the whole restaurant thinks I'm a repressed weirdo."

"I got pretty sloshed last night, so I'm lean on the details." She had one hand on the keyboard and the other on the desk. I touched her free hand. She moved it away. Not good.

"Natasha, please look at me." She turned around, her look stern.

"I'm very,very sorry. My head did get a little big there. I was just a little too excited about the money I'm going to get." Was it the right moment to bring up that it was the first time I had ever earned that kind of money legitimately? She would have felt sorry for me, but I didn't want her to think that I'd been living hand to mouth for over thirty years.

"You scare me, Vlad. I thought we had something great going. And you normally never pressure me to talk about my past. You brought it up last night, but you just have to be patient with me." I wanted to speak but she put a finger up. "I'm not going to lie—you've changed."

And where do I start? Yes, Natasha I have changed. I'm earning an honest living. Yes, I'm becoming cocky. I'm a published writer. I love the adulation. I've earned it. And yes, I'm getting tired of having to learn about your life through someone else's autobiography. Not normal! And yes, I've slept with another woman. I've got it all.

I touched her hand again. She kept it still. "I'll back off about the whole mysterious previous life of yours thing. You bring it up when you want. And just warn me if I'm getting too high on myself."

"You're damn lucky you brought *that* book rather than *another* one that has gone to your head."

She was testing me, but given my performance the night before, I put my tail between my legs and accepted my fate. I placed my hands on Natasha's shoulders, taking a firm but loving grip. "I apologize with all my heart, Natasha, for being a total dick yesterday. You were right; I was wrong. I'm becoming a little too in love with myself."

"That's one rather polite way of wording it."

"Okay, okay. I apologized—don't push it."

"Fine." We kissed and hugged, but it felt forced on both our parts. I moved toward the extra chair by the cash register while Natasha filed some books. She spoke loudly from the other side of the store.

"So, Vlad, it's been a little while since we talked about Farmer's book."

I opened it up to Chapter three. "Is it Farmer's book or Natasha's book?" I said.

She half-smiled. "A little of both."

"Actually, I call it *The Natasha Diary*."

"Not bad. So, where are you so far?"

"She writes about *her* trauma, or shall I say traumas, about grade school, but more importantly, how were *your* elementary school days?"

"Well, I told you before, my father was rather dominant."

"And?"

"Even in grade school it was impossible to live up to his expectations. If I brought home a test that was a B+, he'd look at it and say why not an A."

"Aw, *pauvre chérie*," I said.

"Hey, don't make fun of me. I had a shitty childhood, which only got worse. My dad was unbelievable picky to the point he was phobic about cleanliness. If my brother or I left a cup or plate downstairs in the rec room and he found out, he would whack our asses. He even did it in front of my friends. I was so embarrassed I wanted to kill him. And of course, my mother sat there and blamed me even further, rather than suggesting to my dad that he back off."

I wanted to ask how abusive her father was, but I was afraid of her reply. And had he abused her sexually? Not the most mature guy in a sensitive situation, I went silent.

Come on, Vlad, speak. "Tell you what. Each time you leave an empty wine glass overnight on the table, I'll give you a remindful kiss that you forgot to wash it. How's that?"

"That's sweet." She walked back to the cash register, gave me a hug and filed some books.

179

"We're making a major breakthrough today," I said. "Do you want to try another chapter?"

"That will do."

"Are you sure? It's about Farmer's adolescent years? Some bizarre stuff happened. Drugs! Men! Drugs and men! Men and drugs! Books and drugs!"

"Books and drugs!"

A few customers entered the store. I grabbed a couple of take-out espressos around the corner to kill some time.

Natasha sipped on her espresso. "Well, Vlad, you haven't mentioned how the rest of the evening went *without* me." She purposely paused for a second. "Oh and *thanks*, by the way, for *chasing* me after I left."

"Guilty as charged," I replied. I grabbed her hips and pulled her onto my lap, no resistance given.

"The store's been dead for a while. How about I lock up for an hour and we grab some slices around the corner."

"My treat."

Sitting in the restaurant, I mentioned what I drank with my new and only male friend, Kong. Natasha laughed until I told her about the "decorating the restaurant" idea. After finishing her slice, she gave in to selling me a hundred books; otherwise, I threatened to take my business to the book-wearing guy. After lunch, I checked several *agence immobilières* near my hotel and noted any apartment in my price range. And wouldn't be fun if Natasha helped me decorate a future pad? Women are into that, no? The apartment also got me thinking about Kate. I decided to call her.

"Hello," said Kate.

"Guess who this is?"

"Morgan Davis?"

I laughed. "Morgan Davis! Kate, that's cruel."

"I knew you would laugh. Anyway, you-know-who told me about the contract you *didn't* sign, but was confident you would. Once again, congratulations." Kate's voice turned romantic. "So when are we going to celebrate?"

Thoughts of Natasha popping into my head, I ignored her question. "Kate I've got more great news. Tomorrow I'm going to look for an apartment in Paris. I will have enough money, and I'm tired of my hotel."

"That's fantastic news."

She offered to co-sign for the apartment, because I was a foreigner, but I told her I would find a way of getting it on my own.

I spoke about Helen's agent friend and changed the subject.

"I have to tell you about my new project in Paris."

"I'm listening."

My voice excited and a little higher than usual, I said, "I'm going to convert an Asian restaurant into an author's hangout." There was silence on the other end. I continued, "a super cool book salon."

Kate laughed out loud. "You are mad!"

"Trust me—I'll get the joint jumping! It'll be *the* place to hang out in Paris." There was laughter on the other end of the line. "Kate are you there?"

"Of course. Listen, I'm not busy, how about you come over and celebrate your future apartment, your future agent, and you have to tell me more about this crazy book salon idea of yours."

I spent a few hours at Kate's apartment.

Later in the day, I spoke to two agents. One promised an advance of 75,000 euros from the French publisher Folioatio. And the other had the publisher *Mardgalli* offering 100,000. I told both of them that I had three more agents to talk to the next day and would make my decision a day or two after that.

On the way to Natasha's store, I grabbed a double espresso to perk me up. I was burning the candle at both ends but enjoyed being the centre of everyone's attention. What's wrong with a healthy ego? At Natasha's bookstore, I picked out the first forty books that I would bring over to Kong's restaurant. It was pretentious, but I envisioned myself at one of my literary evenings appearing to randomly pick a book and discuss it. After about the thirtieth book, a theme had developed. The first batch included a collection from my favourites, Woody Allen, Dave Barry, Martin Amis among them. The tomes of Sedaris, Steve Toltz, Eggers, Shteyngart, Haddon, Twain, Henry "no plot" Miller, Adiga, Gopnik, Dahl, Chandler, Colin Bateman, Hiaasen, Leonard, Will Self, Chabon, Franzen, crazy-ass Brautigan, Vonnegut, Arthur Nersesian, Greene, Howard Jacobson (though it would have been funnier if he'd called his Man Booker prize–winning book *The Henry Winkler Question*), Evanovich and Lutz and Egan (if I could entice some ladies to attend), early Douglas Coupland, middle Christopher Moore, late Letham, dead John Kennedy Toole, King—yes, Steve King, but only his book *On*

Writing—Diaz, and no humorous collection would be complete without Roth's *Portnoy's Complaint*.

To build the Canadian content, I added Richler, Leacock, Will Ferguson, Paul Quarrington, John Glassco and Moranski.

Natasha, never having sold a hundred books at one time, was overwhelmed at my rapid picking pace. After a while, the books on the shelf moved like baseball cards I'd collected as a kid. Soon, I was saying "need 'em" or "got 'em" each time I touched a book. I tossed the "need 'ems" aimlessly over my shoulder, assuming she would catch them. I stopped doing that after she blindsided my head with a copy of William Boyd's *The New Confessions*, all 500 pages' worth.

The hundredth book (and Natasha was keeping count) was the first humorous novel I ever read as a teenager. *Ball Four* was a diary kept in the late sixties by journeyman, major league pitcher and all-around nut, Jim Bouton. Though a light read and the furthest thing from a self-help book, it had encouraged me to begin writing in my teens. The total for a hundred dog-eared books came to 700 euros. I told her I had only 300 left in my account. She said if I couldn't pay the balance she knew where I lived. Funny girl.

Natasha and I made fajitas at her place. During dinner, we found out that we both studied French literature at university. She looked stunned when I gave a ten-minute monologue about Emile Zola, my favourite French author. I surprised myself briefly describing fifteen of his twenty novels involving various members of the fictional Rougon-Macquart family. Natasha had vaguely remembered writing an essay on *Germinal*, but her favourite French writer was Alain-Fournier, an early twentieth-century guy. She loved reading *Les Grands Meaulnes* because it had helped her "escape" the life she was living with her parents.

Natasha asked when I graduated. I lied and said I dropped out because I was bored. Why bring up that I was expelled for cheating? That was the old, old me. And talking about university diverted my thoughts about my tryst with Kate.

For the first time since I'd meet Natasha, I turned down her advances when she jumped into bed. And yes, my "too tired" excuse was lame. My eyes wide open, I lay in her bed for an hour before falling asleep. It's called guilt.

Monday, July 9th

We packed the books into five sturdy shopping bags at Natasha's before she opened at eleven.

I spent the rest of the day talking to agents, finally signing late in the evening at Senderen's, a two-star Michelin restaurant in the 8th. The restaurant was so posh that only the waiter was allowed to refill your glass of wine, the bottle strategically placed far enough away that I had no hope of reaching it.

I received a 100,000-euro advance from the publisher *Mardgalli*. My new agent, Jean-Jacques de something, mentioned the money would be deposited directly in my account the next day. We discussed the availability of apartments. He said that I needed a guarantor and that most banks offered this service; however, I would have to freeze one year's rent in an account just in case the monthly rent wasn't paid.

Tuesday, July 10th

After breakfast, I went to my bank. They agreed to be my guarantor once I had a lease. The advance was in my account. I then went to a Western Union and wired 50,000 euros ($75,000 Canadian) to my mother's bank account. It was the same account I'd been filling since I was twelve. And she would be mortgage-free. Sadly, I also FedExed a copy of my advance, to prove to my mother that I had earned the money legitimately.

After an hour of window-shopping for apartments, I entered an *agence immobilière* near the corner of Rue Saint-Jacques and Rue Claude Bernard. A woman sitting behind a computer, her hair in a ponytail, said *bonjour*.

I couldn't make out her features. "*Bonjour, Madame*," I said, my eyes scouting her and the office.

"Are you interested in buying or renting?" She switched to English.

"Renting."

"One in particular?" she asked, her head still down and organizing. Her English was perfect. No accent.

"The apartment on Rue Monge," I said. "It has three rooms and costs 2000 a month."

She pulled a green file, 119 Rue Monge written on a label. Her pink fingernails matched her pink pearl earrings. She looked up, greeting me with an aquiline nose crafted no doubt by Paris's renowned *Noses-are-us* rhinoplasty clinic. Her turquoise eyes tilted on an angle just enough to create a mystery, cheekbones high and—I assumed—fragile skin, alabaster, but waiting for the right guy before she had it tanned on a remote tropical island. She began speaking. Her lips were full, moist, the colour of fresh strawberries. I began not listening; I was on that isolated island putting suntan lotion where it was and wasn't needed.

"*Monsieur*! Hello!"

"Sorry about that—I was daydreaming."

"You mentioned the apartment on 119 Rue Monge."

"Is it still available?"

"Yes, though I assume you're not a French citizen."

"That would be correct, but I just got my first book published with *Mardgalli*. I have an advance of 100,000 euros."

"That's good but I need to see the contract. Also, unfortunately, being a writer AND a foreigner does not guarantee an apartment in France."

"What do you mean?"

"Most writers don't have a regular income, and not being French doesn't help either. I'm sure it's not easy for a foreigner to rent an apartment in the United States?"

"I'm Canadian and—" She cut me off.

"Assuming that you will have a contract, I will speak to the owner of the apartment, but I can guarantee you that you will need what we call a *garant*. Someone who will pay your rent if you default on a payment. Do you know a French person? We also make exceptions if you know a *non-francais* of high standing in Paris."

"My bank will be my *garant*."

"Fine. Could you please write a check for 1500 euros in case anything is damaged in the apartment and a cheque for 2000 euros, our fee for finding you the apartment. Obviously if you're not accepted by the owner, we will cancel the cheques."

"That's a lot of money up front."

"I know, but it will prove to the owner that you are serious."

"If I can see the apartment right now, then I'll consider writing the cheques after. I'm sure you understand."

"Of course."

I was praying that *she* would show me the place. A man in his twenties popped out of a backroom door with a mass of keys in one hand and a motorcycle helmet in the other. He must have heard the whole conversation. My helmet not fitting properly on my head, I sat on the back of a cherry-red Vespa and toured the 5th *arrondissement* of Paris. The ride was a lot of fun, though he told me five times that I was leaning the wrong way when we negotiated a sharp turn.

The apartment was located at the bottom of Rue Monge, about six blocks east of the *Arènes de Lutèce*—a well-preserved and well-hidden coliseum in the middle of the city.

Laurent, my chauffeur and apartment opener guy, and I stepped into the elevator and proceeded slowly up three flights. Metal fencing surrounding us, I was in a batting cage stood on its end. The building also had a wide set of stairs that would come in handy because anything larger than a dresser would not fit in the elevator.

Inside the apartment, we entered a hallway. A step to the right, we walked into a small kitchen, the cupboards new. Laurent then opened a set of bevelled French doors leading into a living room the size of a squash court. The sun's rays bursting through two large windows made the hardwood floors shine. And having a lifelong love affair with hardwood floors, I fell in love with the place. The kitchen and living room both faced the vibrant Rue Monge. Further down the hallway was the washroom/shower and two bedrooms, both the size of a Parisian newspaper stand, the windows facing the side street. The floors were covered in linoleum. And no shine. Damn!

Not knowing what else to do, I flushed the toilet and turned on the taps to check the colour of the water. It wasn't yellow. After Laurent locked up the apartment, I offered him twenty euros to take me by the Eiffel Tower, and then a dangerous and exciting spin around the *Arc de Triomphe,*and the *Place de la Concorde.*

He looked at his afternoon schedule and smiled, proving of course, that everyone was for sale. Then the guy demanded fifty euros. I worked him down to forty.

Laurent revved the Vespa (that's close to an oxymoron). Just as I was about to straddle the seat behind him, the free spirit part of my brain clicked on. What the hell, I thought; you only live once. A few minutes of haggling and 200 euros later (my passport in Laurent's hands as insurance), I was travelling solo on the motor scooter.

My ill-fitting helmet made me look like I was supporting a white ten-pin bowling ball on top of my head. The drivers around the *Arc de Triomphe* laughed and pointed at me. (I briefly took the helmet off.) I smiled and flipped them the bird when I was comfortable enough to steer

---

one handed. And there were catcalls, but the Vespa's muffler drowned out the French verbal din.

Then it happened. Zipping along Rue de Medicis beside the *Jardin du Luxembourg*, I noticed a gorgeous woman crossing an intersection—against a red light. Despite gripping the brakes as firmly as possible, the bike skidded for an eternity. Worse, the woman froze. I veered off to the right at the last second and ran into an ice cream vendor's fridge on wheels, directly in front of the main gate at the *Jardin*. Luckily, I beeped enough times that the lineup had moved behind the stand. When the Vespa smacked the fridge, hundreds of keys from different apartments flew out of the back carrying case, causing the bystanders to shield their faces with their hands, the keys sailing like nails shot from a nail gun. A few people rushed to help me. Others picked up the keys, now indistinguishable, and dropped them into one pink Carrefour bag. Miraculously, there were few noticeable scratches on the Vespa and even fewer on me. I quietly rode the bike up a few blocks to Laurent, thanked him with a wry smile, and returned to the *agence immobilière*.

"Wow, *Monsieur*, you were gone for a long time," she said, feigning surprise.

"Yes, I went through the apartment thoroughly, checking every moving part, as they say."

"Are you sure you aren't talking about a car?"

"Cars, apartments—they're just objects to me," I said, trying to sound cool. "And I have to say, I'm impressed that you don't have an accent when you speak English."

"My mother is English. Anyway, do you want the apartment?" Her smile made it impossible for me to say no.

"Yes I do."

"I assume then that you will write out the cheques. As mentioned I will contact the owner, and then I'll get back to you by the end of the day. Do you have any more questions?"

"Yes, just one. Do you come with the apartment?"

She forced a smile. "I hear that five times a day, *Monsieur*."

In Don Adams' *Maxwell Smart* voice, I said, "Sorry about that, chief."

The look on her face suggested I was a jerk. Oh well. The "jerk" wrote out the checks. "Any *more* questions?"

"Yes. If I get the apartment, how soon could I move in?"

"The apartment's been empty for a while and the owner is anxious to get someone in, so I would say just three days. I would strongly suggest as well that you go immediately to the bank and get the *garant* organized."

I called Helen and told her the "bad" news—that I had signed with another agent. She was unhappy rather than upset because my agent had already informed her. I'm sure he earned his 15% on that nasty conversation. Helen had lost control over me, but she was still in business to make a shitload of money. More importantly, because Helen owned the most prestigious English bookstore in Paris, she finagled an advance run of 200 copies in only one week from my publisher. I would then do my first reading (ever) the next day. My agent would fill me in on when the other bookstores would be getting my book.

I spent the afternoon walking near my hotel and jotting down the addresses of furniture stores, appliance stores and so on. A message from the hot *agence immobi*-heiress waited for me at the hotel. The apartment was mine.

I jogged over to Natasha's store and made a grand entrance. A customer stood in a corner, lost in a book.

"Natasha, I have fantastic news."

She walked over and gave me a kiss. "What is it?"

"Do you remember when I told you I was going to rent an apartment?"

"No," she said, curtly. She walked over to the cash register.

"Are you sure?"

"You haven't said a single word to me about getting an apartment." Her back was turned. Shit, she was right; only Kate knew.

The customer, sensing an eruption, placed a handful of change by the cash register and fled. Damn, we were alone.

"Vlad!" yelled Natasha. I jumped.

"Shit, Natasha! What is your problem?"

"And what about last night? That's never happened since we've first met that you didn't want to make love. Something's wrong!?" I wanted to speak but I sensed she had more to say. "You better look straight into my eyes." I did. The air in the store was suffocating. "Is there another woman?"

Looking away and answering no was not an option. *Come on, Vlad. You've seen too many movies where the cheating "vermin" looks into his woman's eyes and lies through his teeth. Don't change the script! For the love of God, don't look away when you answer.*

I looked away for about the time it takes a hummingbird to flap its wings or maybe one beat of its tiny heart and said, "No." Eyes back, I added, "*chérie.*"

Natasha burst out laughing and then kissed me. *Christ, this woman is crazy.* "I was just putting you on. Had you going, didn't I?"

"Why would you do that?"

"I was just kind of bored."

"Well, if that's bored, I'd hate to see what excited is."

She put one arm around my neck and, with her other hand, waved a mock accusatory finger in front of my nose. "You better not have another woman, there, mister."

I looked at her dead on. Even refusing to blink, I said, "Of course not." We kissed. "Tell you what, Natasha. How about you close the store early and we look for furniture."

"You couldn't have read my mind any better."

"What's that line, Natasha? 'Let's shop—'"

"Till we drop."

And I was happy to kill two birds with one stone. Joking or not, Natasha was off the scent, and I had someone to pick out furniture for me. (Win–win, as they say.) And Kate? I think I'd promised her something as well.

In less than two hours, Natasha—I mean *I*—spent 15,000 euros on an L-shaped leather couch; two matching ottomans; a coffee table; a dining table made out of a type of wood I'd never heard of (its price equally unheard of); a funky, bright area rug that would fill half the living room and another matching leather chair. Two cylindrical glass lamps would sit on two wooden stands, and a fifty-centimetre HDTV would grace a wall. The other side of the living room would have wood and brass bookshelves reminiscent of Parisian cafés in the late twenties. I picked up a MacBook Air laptop and a printer around the corner. Kate could choose some sculptures, etcetera, but they had to be tasteful—no souvenir Queen Elizabeth teapots or plates prominently featuring Prince Charles and Camilla.

At a bed store, Natasha picked out overpriced beds and matching overpriced dressers, the bedding costing more than I'd given her for the books.

And she beat a path to an appliance store as well where a small oven, a fridge, a microwave, plates, glasses and cutlery were picked out with a woman's precision. I just sat on a chair that I may or may not have purchased and nodded side to side or up and down, depending on what she was holding up or pointing to. The cheques written, the deliveries promised for Friday, we celebrated with dinner at a restaurant just off Carson's—I mean my—beloved rue Mouffetard. The street was narrow but full of restaurants on either side. At our outdoor table, I ordered the *coq au vin*, Natasha, the steak and fries. And after dropping twenty-five grand, why not order the most expensive red in the restaurant.

She took a sip, smacked her lips and, with a straight face, said, "It sucks." She was kidding.

I grabbed a piece of baguette and ripped it into a few pieces. "For seventy-five euros that Mâcon better not suck. But, more importantly, when the *coq au vin* arrives, there must be absolute silence so I can savour every bite."

"Men are all the same—they're only after food and pussy."

"God, I love the newfound bawdy language, but where has that come from? Are you reading *50 Shades of Grey*?"

"A big no on that one, but that reminds me—have you been reading more of Farmer's memoir?"

"Yes," I said and popped a piece of bread into my mouth.

"And?"

I pointed to either cheek with my fingers and rolled my eyes a little, to show my mouth was full. I did read the chapters, but with all the excitement in my life recently, I'd forgotten some of the details.

"Okay, Vlad, I'll update you on my life. I'll tell you the two biggies." Shocked at her abruptness, I nearly choked on the bread. She paused and looked around before she continued speaking. *What the hell was she going to say?* "This isn't easy, but here goes. I had a child in grade twelve. My parents, being staunch Catholics, refused to let me have an abortion."

"Are you fuckin' kidding me?" I said, my voice inappropriately loud. The couples on both sides of our table stared at me. Sensing too many ears, we leaned in and whispered. A jazz duo warmed up their instruments in front of us. The timing was perfect; our table neighbours lost interest in Natasha's confession. The band played Brubeck's *Take Five*. And *Natasha and I* took five because it was pointless speaking above the music, the saxophonist on key, the trumpeter missing the odd note, but who cared. I loved that song. I listened, but wondered where

189

was her kid? Was he the waiter serving our salad? The backpacker walking behind the musicians? Was he one of the musicians? Wrong time for humour, but that's how my brain worked. Must deflect if I didn't know what to say or think. For the record, the musicians were Romas, so cancel them from the where-is-he-now sweepstakes. And who was the father? (Good, concentrating properly again.) Was it her boyfriend? No, she met him much later.

After the band left, Natasha continued her story. In the same breath, she told me to eat my salad and that her father made her go to some catholic convent out west to have the child. I lost count of how many times I put my fork down to listen. She wanted to keep the child, despite the unknown father, conceived during a wild night of multiple sex partners and drugs. She threw in some yaddah-yaddah-yaddahs as well, and I could only imagine what those were.

"Natasha, this might be kind of painful, but after about twenty years, I guess—"

"Twenty-two years."

"I'm assuming by that quick answer you haven't forgotten about him or her."

"Him." A few tears rolled down her face. She dried them with her serviette. I felt deeply sorry for her and wanted to give her a hug but I was too sandwiched into my table to move—damn Parisian restaurants.

"Have you attempted to find him?"

The waiter placed our main courses on the table and said, "*Bon appétit.*" We thanked him and picked at our food.

"I phoned the convent in Calgary once a long time ago, but they told me the records were sealed. The laws have changed since in Canada, but I don't have the nerve to try again." Natasha grabbed her knife and eyed her steak. "How about we try and enjoy our meal and forget about what I just said."

"I don't think it's the kind of subject to just drop. Are you sure you don't want to talk about it?"

"Yes! Eat!"

After dessert and espressos, we walked hand in hand to her apartment. The whole time, I wondered what the second "biggie" was that she'd planned to divulge about her past. Could it have been any worse than having to give up a child?

Wednesday, July 11th

———

I carried three shopping bags of books to Kong's restaurant. Near eleven o'clock, the morning sky grey, the roads still slick from a late-night storm, I witnessed a woman wipe out on her scooter. She looked like she'd slid into second base wheels high instead of cleats high. Traffic stopped on both sides immediately, four or five people jumping out of their cars or off their motorcycles to help. She and her scooter limped to the side of the street, braving a smile when the ambulance arrived minutes later.

Kong was busy cleaning and setting the tables for the lunchtime crowd. He beamed when I showed him what I had in my bags. "Books! That great. Look in corner—I have bookshelves."

They were white, the top corners chipped, and narrower than I had imagined, but it was a valiant start. And that poor bastard had no clue about the extent of *my* restaurant transformation—I planned to continue bringing books over until the whole north wall was covered with shelves of books and posters. Then the couches—no book salon would be complete without couches.

"Kong, do you remember that I said I would pay for a free teeth cleaning?"

He placed the last full *pichet* of water on a table. "Yes, but you think I need?"

"Do birds fly? Do fish swim?"

"I understand. And you eat bird and fish in restaurant."

"That's damn funny, but save some of those hot lines for the hot ladies when we go to the singles night."

"When we sleep with ladies?"

"We have to meet them first, you horny bastard! And I'm not sure when we're going, but either way, I'm not taking you until those teeth are clean, ya hear me? We must look good if we want good-looking women. Understand?"

"Yes, but you no look so good. You no shave, hair mess."

"Don't worry Kong; I'll fix myself up. Anyway, here's the deal, I have to sign the lease for my apartment. Along the way, I'll look for a dentist and book a cleaning for you, and I'll pay them up front. Do you have a business card? Something they can use to contact you?"

"No card, dentist near in corner."

I immediately looked in the corners of the restaurant. The restaurant was empty. "Kong, what the fuck you are you talking about?"

"I no talk fuck with you!"

"Sorry, man, we're having a Led Zeppelin *communication breakdown . . . it's always the same*." I paused and did a solo on my air guitar. Something about this place releases a lot of pent-up energy in me—and not alcohol-induced for a change.

"You crazy!"

"Damn right! Wanna see me bite the head off a bat?"

"We no have bats here, but I do have cats we use if no more chicken . . . taste same."

I put down my imaginary guitar. "Are you fuckin' kiddin' me, man? So the myth is true? You guys do cook up stray cats?"

Kong laughed out loud and beat his chest. "I make joke. I pull your cock again."

"LEG, Kong! LEG for Christ's sake! You can't say *pull your cock*. Straight guys don't say that shit and, I doubt if gays use that phrase, either."

"Sorry I pull your leg—yes, pull leg. I understand." Kong smiled in self-congratulation.

"We got off topic, Kong. You said something about a dentist."

He walked to the front door and pointed down the street. "Dentist hundred metre in corner."

I put my hand on his shoulder as I was about to leave. "How come you never go see him?"

"He communist."

"What!? Who gives a shit if he's a commie dentist or not?"

"I pull your co—I mean leg, again. I make joke."

"Kong you're a crazy motherfu—I mean crazy mother." Kong's misfiring of the English language bordered on the salty, even without my help.

"That cool. I crazy mother."

"So do you want to see this dentist or not?"

"Yes, I go! You pay!"

"Fine. Remember, in a few days I'm going to bring over a lot more books, but I want you to get more bookshelves. I'm looking at our book salon opening in less than two weeks."

Mid-afternoon, I signed the apartment papers and made all the banking arrangements. The knock-out at the *agence immobilière* wore a purple cotton dress above the knee. God, even her knees were hot. I was dying to make the same joke as the other day about her coming with the apartment, but the look in her eyes said, "Don't even go there."

The clouds had cleared by the time I called Kate. She was thrilled about the apartment and offered to decorate. I hesitated for a second when she asked about the address; it dawned on me that this was going to make it harder to separate the two women.

When I returned to my hotel, there was a message from my agent. The competing French bookstores Albert Ado and Albert Josephine wanted me in for a book signing. Word had spread fast about my book. They had ordered 200 advance copies each and wanted me to be available the next week for a book signing.

After showering, I looked at my clean and lean volume of clothes. Since I'd be attending book signings all over the city and abroad, it was time to buy some new clothes and even a suit. Not wanting to pick out clothes on my own, I called Kate back. She recommended a place where her ex used to shop. She got off work early and we met at a Hugo Boss on Boulevard St-Germain. I picked up five dress shirts, two casual pairs of pants (the price not so casual), black dress shoes, brown dress shoes, a pair of casual shoes, lots of too-expensive matching socks, four ties (each one came with a free lesson on how to tie), ten boxers, and—the coup-de-grace—a charcoal grey, Hugo Boss something-or-other suit for 2000 euros, a sum greater than all the clothing I had bought in twenty or maybe thirty years. An hour later and 5000 euros lighter, Kate and I walked out with hands so full of bags I think even the bags were carrying bags. Looking at myself in a front window, Hugo Boss bags in hand, I had become the person I'd forever mocked—the metrosexual.

Kate wore a woman's business suit. She spent more money on clothes than Natasha, I'm assuming, because she routinely had business meetings. Natasha was prettier, but Kate was more voluptuous, if that was possible. (I was a typical guy, forever lost in a woman's appearance and/or body. Though I prided myself on my own appearance, I no longer lifted weights but still did push-ups and sit-ups daily to stay relatively muscular.) Both women laughed a lot, though Natasha's humour was sarcastic. (Mine too!). And Kate? Anti-sarcastic. They were both spontaneous; however, lately, Natasha got a perverse thrill out of pretending she was mad at me for something or other. Most uncool, but being a liar my whole life, it shouldn't have bothered me.

Kate and I grabbed a couple of pizzas and a six-pack of *Leffe*. We tiptoed around the partiers spread out on the quay facing Notre Dame.

"Vlad, how about we sit here?" I stared at the spot for a second. Bizarre, it was the same bench where Natasha and I had sat. I grabbed Kate's arm. "No, I see a cooler bench a few metres over." Even when Natasha wasn't there she was still there. A premonition?

We sat down and silently ate a few bites.

"How's your pizza, Kate?"

"It's wonderful. I don't usually get the vegetarian, but I already ate some meat today." I threw a few pieces of the spicy chorizo on her pizza. "Hey. What's that for?"

"That's for helping me." She gave me a kiss.

I stared at her. God—was it lust or was I falling in love with this woman? Did that make two? Or was I not in love with Natasha? Or was I not in love with either one of them and just being selfish?

"Vlad, you seem to be drifting, yet you have this romantic look on your face. I hope you were thinking about me?"

"Of course," I said, as I stared into her eyes. And was I lying to a second woman? I wasn't even sure.

Our slices finished, we walked by my apartment building, a light wind whistling down Rue Monge. The Censier–Daubenton métro stop was nearby. Kate wanted to drop in on Friday, but I told her to wait till a few days later, claiming I had to buy a million little things for the kitchen, wait for the deliveries in the afternoon, and think of answers to the questions I would have to answer at my first book reading/signing. Helen had faxed me the exact questions and reminded me that the reading was in one week. And my goal—try not to appear like it was the first ever book reading/signing, my other-side-of-the-tracks roots hopefully disappearing forever.

Kate and I kissed at the top of the steps and then she slipped into the metro.

Thursday, July 12th

I spent the whole day running around Paris, organizing the electricity and water bill with EDF, the cable, land phone, and Internet with Bouygues, and the direct deposit with my bank Paribas. And I dropped in at Orange to buy my first cellphone ever. My number was 07 88 04 04 88. Loved the semi-symmetry.

Tomorrow was the big day to move in to my expensive Paris apartment—proof I was at last controlling my destiny.

———

Eighteen days later

Monday, July 30th, 10 a.m.

The morning sun blinds me as I step outside the police station for the first time in two days, the smell of the foliage infinitely more pleasing than the lingering reek of my cleaned-up vomit. Two cops are to escort me to the courthouse, where I will be interrogated by a judge. It's called *mise en examen* and is the second step (after the police station *garde à vue*) toward possibly going to trial. My lawyer will be present. He thinks that I will not be charged with the theft of the Picasso or the other articles found in my apartment because someone is trying to set me up or play a practical joke on me. As well, he believes that charges are doubtful because when I first spoke to him and the detective at the police station I said that I'd never been involved in criminal activity. I lied about my past to the lawyer and detective, thinking, one, I have a new life and two, my jailing and criminal business happened in Canada and they will never know.

I hear a voice yelling at me as I'm about to step into the police car.

"Hey, Vlad, over here," says the voice. Shielding my eyes, I move toward the outline of a person roughly my size—it's Carson. I'm in shock seeing my brother. I motion my arms toward him. A hug is something I want and badly need.

A cop grabs my hand. "Do not move, *Monsieur*."

Another cop pulls out his gun.

"Listen, it's my brother. Surely you're not going to shot him or me!"

The cop with the gun tells Carson to stop. Carson stops two metres away from us.

"Hey, I know my rights," I say. "I was allowed to call a relative, but I didn't bother because they all live in Canada. Can I at least speak with my brother? I haven't seen him in months!"

"*Oui, Monsieur*. You have five minute. Then we must go to the courthouse. We must first check him for any weapon. And you must stay beside us." They frisk Carson. *Big surprise—no weapon!*

Carson and I hug in silence for an eternity. No words are spoken. We separate, and then he punches me in the face, knocking me down instantly. I stand up wearily and check my nose. Not broken, but the blood is trickling down my face. I try to stop it with my shirt. The cops do nothing. No one is helping me. Christ, I'm not even safe in the streets of

Paris from my own brother.

"WHAT THE FUCK DID YOU DO THAT FOR!? YOU FUCKIN' ASSHOLE!" I yell.

"YOU GODDAMN WROTE ABOUT MY LIFE IN PARIS AND DID IT ALL BEHIND MY GODDAMN BACK!"

I wipe the blood from my nose with my sleeve and step out of Carson's wingspan, putting me closer to the police. How ironic.

Carson has the look of a Rottweiler ready to pounce. I never remembered us putting on the gloves, always settling our arguments with a series of "go fuck yourselfs."

I look toward the police station. "Do you have any idea where I've just been?"

"I don't give a shit. Stealing my life story has to be the worst thing you've ever done to me, and believe me I can come up with some other *doozy* examples. You CANNOT expect me to forget about what you've done just because of where you were or are or whatever."

"Well, then, why the hell did you come?" I say, feeling sorry for myself. "No, I have a better question. This bullshit that I'm in only happened recently. You must have already been in Paris. And how the hell did you know I was in this goddamn place? Or even in Paris, for that matter? Or fuckin' France?"

"Well, it's not the first time I've found you in a cop shop."

I put my hands up looking like I've just been arrested. "Ya got me, Carz, but I've changed." I see him rolling his eyes. I force myself to let it go. "Don't get me wrong—I'm thrilled you're here, but we haven't seen each other in a long time and not on purpose, right?"

Carson feigns a smile. "We've kind of drifted. Anyway, I've been in Paris for a few days."

"Well, I have to ask again, how the hell did you know to come here?"

Carson's hands unclench. He takes a piece of paper out of his pocket and is about to pass it to me. A cop snatches it.

"*Monsieur*," says the cop, "you can not give anything to the suspect!" He gives it back to Carson. Carson apologizes to the cop.

"What were you going to give me?"

"It's a brief news clipping in the local paper, *Le Parisien*, about the alleged theft of a Picasso, among other things, by a Canadian writer."

"Is my name in it?"

"No, they aren't allowed to do that."

"And you knew it was me, how?"

"*Messieurs Morunski*, you have two minute," says one of the cops.

"I'll look at it another time. Whatever was written is bullshit anyway."

"Do you know who owns the painting?"

I turn my shoulder to shield my conversation from the police. "Yes," I say, lowering my voice. "Her name is Helen Northingham. Carz I'm thrilled that you're here, but I don't want to talk about my case in front of the police. I'm going to the courthouse *tout de suite*. My lawyer thinks I'm in the clear and won't have to go to a trial."

"Is he aware of your past?"

"No."

"You're taking a huge chance by not saying anything."

"It's the new me, Carz," I say, forcing a smile.

"They may find out anyway."

"I'm not worried." I am worried. "Anyway, Carz, just come to my apartment late in the afternoon. I hope to be there." I tell him the address, front door code, my cellphone number, and to bring his suitcase—he's moving in. "Carz, you're good with numbers; can you remember all that?"

"I got it; don't worry. I'll be at your apartment, but I'm not bringing my suitcase."

"*Allez, Morunski*. We leave *maintainent*," says one of the cops.

"No confidence in me, eh? Anyway, Carz, just try and find out anything you can on a Helen Northingham. She's the owner of BJ Williams bookstore in Paris." The cop pushes my head down as he guides me into the back seat.

Seventeen days ago

Friday, July 13th

After checking out of the hotel, I picked up the keys at the *agence immobilière*. The same woman, her face movie-star perfect, greeted me while remaining in her chair. We exchanged pleasantries. She handed me the keys, we exchanged more pleasantries, and I was off and nearly running.

Some old habits never die. I bought wax and rags and shined up the living-room floor, though it didn't need it. And buffers belonged in wax museums. (That's a pun!) The previous occupant had left cleaners for every surface, along with a pail. I scrubbed the bedroom, kitchen and bathroom floors; the sinks followed. And why the sudden attack of cleanliness? It was my apartment, and I would be entertaining, plus I had thousands of euros' worth of furniture, etcetera coming. And the name of my apartment? The Vlad-pad.

I made one more run to a Monoprix that specialized in cheap clothes and household items and picked out as many things as I could think of to fill the kitchen drawers, including towels for the bathroom and kitchen, a few pots and pans, and a giant fig-shaped vacuum cleaner.

By late afternoon, the last delivery had arrived. The sectional L-shaped couch came individually wrapped only in cellophane, a godsend, given that one corner of the apartment resembled a cardboard factory.

Preferring to spend the evening by myself, I walked to a traditional French restaurant a few blocks from my apartment and ordered a peppercorn steak and a bottle of *Cahors*. After dinner, I took a long walk to get rid of the spins and came home and fell asleep on my brand new leather couch.

Saturday, July 14th

A buzzer woke me up at eleven o'clock; the sound scared the shit out of me. My eyes scanned the four walls. Nothing. The buzzer rang again. I grabbed my keys, ran down three flights of stairs and opened the foyer door just before a man was about to leave.

"*Monsieur, vous êtes Vlad Morunski?*"

"*Oui. Je suis Vlad. Vous êtes qui?*" He handed me a package. It was from my agent.

"Please sign here."

Great, I was so hung over I had forgotten to simply push the button on my intercom to let the poor sap in.

My agent had given me a bottle of champagne as a house-warming gift. Pure class. I would save it for whichever woman I invited over first.

Included in the fifty-euro–monthly bill were three free months of Canal+, which showed *Les Guignols de l'info*, a daily, ten-minute satirical news show with puppets, modelled after the British program, *Spitting Image*. It had been Carson's favourite show when he lived in Savoie. He must have recounted fifty sketches over the years, but one was particularly clever. The sketch took place a few days after 9/11. The puppet presenter of the news, Patrick Poivre d'Arvor (a famous retired French newscaster), held up the front page of *L'Equipe*, the French daily sports newspaper, and its title read as a soccer score: Allah: 1–Jesus: 0.

I phoned Natasha, Kate, and Helen to give them my cellphone number. And I thanked my agent, as well, for the booze.

Then it hit me—how will I communicate with my adoring fans? Natch—a website.

I Googled "website specialist Paris." I phoned the first three on the screen, picked one, and arranged a meeting at their office near the corner of St-Germain and St-Michel. For a grand, they would create something fancy with lots of designs and colours. I would be able to blog and make announcements whenever I wanted. Perfect. I would tell my fans at the book signing to keep checking my website for updates. My book contained a domain name that I had bought but never used—Willowbookpress.com would connect me with the world.

After the meeting, I went over to Natasha's store.

"Well, hello stranger," she said. "And your name is what, by the way?"

"Mud," I replied with a smile as I leaned toward her. Preoccupied with the computer screen, she gave me a half-assed kiss on the cheek. Two people were in the mystery section, one, a woman reading a book intently, the other wearing the Sulley Indefatigable jacket, his eyes bouncing between me, Natasha, his *900* hidden, zippered pockets and the book in his hand.

I whispered to Natasha, "Sulley Indefatigable at nine o'clock." Quickly forgetting what I had said, my mind turned to the website. How many hits would I get? Was Morgan Davis's website cool or douchy?

Shit, how many hits did he get? What did he blog about? And what would be the subject of my first blog? A rags-to-reaches story minus the stealing-for-a-living part?

"It's okay. Today, it's two for one. If you're wearing a Sulley Indefatigable jacket, you're allowed to steal one book as long as you pay for another."

Someone was talking, but I was somewhere in my website, my new creation.

Natasha stood up. "Did you even hear me, Vlad? God, you're lost in your own little world."

"I wouldn't call it a 'little world.'"

She put her hand on my hand, maybe sensing an argument and wanting to defuse it in a hurry. "I was just having some fun, but it's pretty obvious you're changing."

"How?" I said, feigning a smile.

She put a finger up and gave a sigh, meaning she had something important to say to me but needed to tend to the customers. They purchased a few books and left.

I moved to the desk. "Do you think he stole anything?"

"No," she said as she walked back and sat on my lap. She put an arm around my neck. Was she preparing me for something? Was there another kid out there?

"Vlad, your ego is growing rather quickly."

"What do you mean?"

"Well, you're just becoming more arrogant in the way you speak, the way you treat people in general—even me."

I stood up, forcing Natasha to stand.

"You see? You overreact."

"You're just jealous that I've been published and I'm becoming popular and successful."

She looked at me straight in the eyes. I looked away more than once. "I can honestly tell you that I'm not jealous. Do you remember I used to tell people even in the bookstore that you would become famous?"

I paused. "Yes, I do," I said grudgingly.

"I'd say that's proof."

"Well, you haven't said it lately."

"True. One, because you're around here less and less and two, it's safe to say we're becoming more distant."

I put my arms around her waist, my actions feeling unnatural. (Not a good sign. Could she tell?) "It's just that I've been unbelievably busy, and I have this big book interview and reading soon. My first ever." I paused to be dramatic. "Helen sent me a pile of questions, but I'm worried about what I'm going to say." I offered semi-believable excuses to skirt her comments.

Natasha took my arms and wrapped them even tighter around her body and leaned her head on my shoulder.

"Vlad, I love you. I don't want to fight."

Damn the "I'm becoming distant" one second and then the old "I love you" in the next breath. I picked the wrong time to go silent.

She raised her head, her apricot-scented hair falling off her shoulders. "And?" she said waiting for my answer.

"*Je t'aime, chérie. Je t'aime*," I said, thinking if I said it in French it would sound romantic.

She squeezed me and gave me a kiss. "Will you spend the night?"

"I can't. I'm honestly worried about how I'm going to respond to Helen's questions, and I want to deliver more books to Kong's."

"I can help you with the questions if you want."

"Thanks for offering, but I'll give it a whirl by myself."

"I'll help with Kong as well, but I'm not going to your book salon thingy."

"No one is asking you to." I broke apart our embrace and placed the two bags of books by the door. "Did I mention that I'm going to buy another hundred books from your wonderful establishment?"

Natasha rolled her eyes.

Silence ensued.

"Obviously you're not happy with this venture of mine, but it's going to happen and will be a hoot."

"I'll sell you the books and even help carry them over, but, as I said, I'll pass on the *soirées*."

At Kong's front door, books in hand, I was blinded by a set of clean, ultra-white teeth. I put my hand over my eyes.

"Jesus, Kong, you gotta turn those thirty-two lights off in your mouth."

"What you mean light? I no light at mouth. I have teeth shine."

"Kong, it's a joke!"

He laughed, and then pointed at me. "Got you again. I pull your leg."

"Well, buddy, at least you're just pulling my *leg*." I filled the shelves with books, but there still wasn't enough room. I held a few books up and said to Kong, "We need more shelves and a couch for the corner." His eyes narrowed when I said couch, but he eventually nodded in agreement.

Before I went home—I liked that word, "home"—I bought a bag of pasta, a jar of bolognaise sauce, black olives, parmesan cheese, a bag of mache, a bottle of vinaigrette and a bottle of Bordeaux, and made my first home-cooked meal. The bottle empty, the kitchen a mess, I fell asleep again on my leather couch. My goal tomorrow—find my bedroom before my eyelids closed for the night.

Sunday, July 15th --- Tuesday, July 17th

The next three days were split among my agent, Natasha, Kate, answering Helen's questions, and a lame attempt at starting a sequel. *French Like Me* had been easy to write because I'd stolen Carson's life experiences in France. The new book would be more difficult. I had to imagine Carson's sons in their twenties, no longer dependent on their parents, and living in Paris, but I was unable to create a plausible reason. Studying in Paris? Studying women in Paris? Working as English/French tour guides? Boring! Robbing banks while working as tour guides? That had possibilities.

Tuesday evening, Kate came over for dinner. Though I overcooked the steaks, they still tasted great with some HP sauce and a bottle of Chinon. Kate took a late-night taxi home, and I pulled out the Jack Daniels—or Jacky D, as I affectionately called it. After refilling my glass more times than I could remember, I passed out on the couch.

Wednesday, July 18th

The phone rang by my head. "Vlad, where the hell are you?" Hung over and half-asleep, I took the phone away from my ear and studied it as if it was a foreign object. The voice continued screaming. Satisfied that it was a phone, I put it back to my ear.

"Vlad!? Are you there, for Christ sake? You better not be playing a game with me."

I grimaced. "Is this Helen, by any chance?"

"Who do you fuckin' think it is? Angelina Jolie?"

"Is she doing a book signing today as well?"

"Goddamn hilarious. You're already half an hour late." I looked around my apartment. Shit—no clock. I snickered.

"Are you laughing at me?"

"No, of course not, and I apologize a thousand times for my tardiness, but I'm just laughing because I spent a shit load of money on furniture and I didn't even buy a clock."

"You're an idiot!"

I let her comment go because I was an idiot. "What time is it, anyway?"

"It's twelve-thirty! And there's a hundred people waiting for you." Her voice became muffled. "Listen you smug, drunk, ungrateful bastard, I'm sending a taxi over to your apartment. Be ready in fifteen minutes." I apologized again and gave her my address.

I showered and put on the casual black pants and white dress shirt that Kate had helped me pick out. The suit wasn't ready. I threw on my fancy argyle socks and loafers. I glanced at the metrosexual in the mirror, forgetting my responses to Helen's questions on the living room table.

The cab whipped through the city in Indy 500 style. I felt like Mick Jagger being fashionably late for a concert. The cabbie dropped me off and I pulled a few twenties out of my pocket. He rolled his eyes.

"*Monsieur, BJ WILLIAMS a déjà payé.*"

"Right on." I stuffed the bills back in my pocket.

I jumped out of the cab and noticed my picture and name on the front window. Very cool. There were no lineups outside the door, but Helen had underestimated the crowd inside. I guessed 200, half of them sitting in chairs at the back of the store along stacks and stacks of my books, enough to build a tree fort. A few women touched me as Helen escorted me with a firm hand on my biceps to a table with two chairs. No amount of flexing could produce a smile or a word out of that kisser of hers. But when she sat down beside me and tapped her microphone, it was as if the bright lights of a Broadway stage had been lit; the woman was "on." Still hung over, I rolled my eyes and was unfortunately snapped by a couple of photographers: my first legitimate experience with the paparazzi.

"Well, ladies and gents," said Helen. She stopped for a second and grabbed my hand. "We have him here and in person—and he's not going anywhere because I have his hand."

I whispered, "Jesus, Helen, who writes your material?"

Everyone laughed.

"Vlad. I believe it's *you* who writes my material."

"Touché, my dear."

"Well, now that Mr. Moranski has figured out that the microphone picks up every little sound, he'll be a little more careful. Anyway, Vlad Moranski is from Toronto, Canada." A few people in the back row yelled, "Go Leafs!"

"They suck," I said with a grin.

Helen smiled, though a brief look in her eyes told me that I would somehow pay for showing up late.

The crowd spread its tentacles into the aisles.

"Vlad will first read from his book, *French Like Me*, and then I will ask him twelve questions."

Before I held up my book, Helen whispered in my ear, "Watch what you say or you'll be back in Canada writing about hockey or maple syrup or beavers or whatever the hell happens over there. Does that country even matter?"

Pretending I was looking for my first excerpt, I whispered back to Helen, "Lots matters, *dear*. Wood-chopping festivals are in every town. We play underwater hockey during the warm weather season. We also have the coolest competition on earth, called So You Think You Can Dance With a Polar Bear. In the winters, we have pissing in the snow impressionist art contests, and we also have annual writing competitions about who our favourite Mountie is." Helen shook her head from side to side. This woman was about to detonate.

Forgetting to whisper she replied, "That's enough—you're insane." The crowd laughed, thinking Helen and I had jokingly created a hate-each-other routine.

Under my breath and trying to piss Helen off even more, I whispered, "Oh, I almost forgot—my favourite literary contest in Canada is the monthly If you could be a Tim Horton's donut, which one would you be and why in a thousand words or less."

Helen nudged me and with a strained smile, said, "Please hold up your book."

I held it up. My voice strong and clear, I looked at the crowd. "This is my first reading ever and I'm proud to do this, considering all the work I put into this novel." The audience clapped. *Would I tell them how this book found its way to Paris?*

"My first excerpt is about the protagonist, Carson, and his sons, walking toward the French Open, or Roland-Garros as it's known in Paris. Here goes.

Carson pointed to a water fountain that looked like a series of interconnected metal thick-crust pizzas.

"Allez, les mecs. On peut s'asseoir et se relaxer près de la fontaine de Pizza Pizza."

Six dirty green benches circled the fountain, one of them already occupied by two worn asphalt faces sprouting patches of grey weeds and sipping on their morning cans of Heineken. Years of inebriation and missing teeth had created a French dialect only recognizable on their bench. At their green-and-brown bare feet, guarding their unopened brew, was a sleepy German shepherd. Even the dog had a tough time understanding his owner's commands.

Two locals, a well-dressed man and woman in their thirties, approached the drunks. Worried that their stash of Heinekens was being threatened, the dog leapt at the young man. Slipping on the green metal banana peels, the pooch punctured a couple of holes in the cans, sending a golden spray in unintended directions.

One of the spontaneous fountains was aimed directly at the dog owner's mug. With surprising quickness, he opened his mouth to catch the liquid; however, the fountain of gold faded quickly. He grabbed the deformed beer can and performed mouth-to-mouth on the hole. The other tin was unapproachable, wetting the two as it spun like a water-sprinkler. After sucking the tin dry, the dog's owner became enraged at the animal's incessant barking. He kicked it so violently in the ribs that it was surprising the animal didn't try to bite him. The pet subdued, both bums wiped their frothy faces with their less-than-clean sleeves, laughed like a couple of gravel-voiced baboons and grabbed another beer.

Carson turned to the boys. "Well, this park is pretty animated, wouldn't you say? I think these guys are cursing themselves for buying the tall cans." He paused for a second to build the moment. "Guys, I've got great news. We're going to Roland-Garros—you know, the French Open."

The crowd politely clapped.

"My second reading is about Carson organizing a poetry reading at Notre Dame. He had even posted signs around the district, advertising the reading. He had some poems to read and thought it would be funny if

Rory filmed it, but of course, unexpected things happen. Try and imagine yourself as a father of three hip adolescents. Lew, the joker, is fifteen; Rory, the smart-mouthed filmmaker, is sixteen; and Nik, the lover, is nineteen. Here goes.

The bells at Notre Dame chimed eleven times, signalling Lew to start his rap. Under a soft yellow light by the south door, his words began to flow.

"Yo, yo, yo, everyone. It's eleven o'clock and it's time to stop. Hey, word-up!
Gives your props to my Pops cuz his words got da hops.
He's killable with da syllable."

Four people walked over. Carson had Lew repeat it. He said it again with less enthusiasm and skipped the last line. One person quietly walked away. Carson got Lew to say it one last time.

Unhappy, Lew decided to improvise. "Hey, people, get your butts over here. The old man's got something to say."

Another person left. Carson noticed only two people remained who weren't related to him. He assumed they were a couple. They were attractive and looked touristy. He thought they were too attractive and too touristy to be seen at a poetry reading, especially given by him in Paris.

Carson read his first poem:

Ode to the Doberman

You were the pet of royalty, found in every castle.
Your once lofty position has now taken its toll,
For you've been replaced by the pit bull or Rottweiler,
Who can be found in the home of every asshole.

Everyone laughed at the punchline and the couple offered some constructive criticism. Carson read his second poem.

In Front of Every Man is a Good Woman

I was at Starbucks the other day, sipping coffee and writing a few lines,
while sitting at a table and looking in my direction was a gorgeous feline.
My hormones, swearing at me, in chorus no less, for ignoring her beauty,
obviously, not knowing that my wife was only ten feet behind

her behind.

The couple laughed again and offered even more constructive criticism. Carson just smiled, knowing he was playing the whole thing for laughs.

"I'd like to read my third poem. It's titled *Writing About Footb—*"

"Do you mind if I recite one of my poems?" the man interrupted.

"Not a problem," said Carson, caught off guard by the request. He didn't expect anyone else to be as silly as he was. His thoughts turned to Rory, and he hoped something funny would be caught on tape. He winked at Rory (a wink that meant, "Is the camera ready?"), filming at a distance and trying to look like he wasn't related, despite having the same mass-produced face as his brothers and father.

The man assumed a gangsta rapper yo-yo-yo pose with a contorted body, fingers open and pointed down. "Yo-yo-yo, everyone, I'm Charles Z."

I paused and contorted my fingers into what I call the rap "yo yo yo" pose. I looked at the BJ Williams crowd and said, "Imagine a lame white guy trying to imitate Ice-T as I read. Here goes:
"My poem is called The Kitchen."
He's one evil muhtha,
When he showd me dat grin.
I haveta keel dat fahkah.
Gots to plan ma sin.
Dares a blade in ma kitchin,
gunna put it in ma car,
cuz it's time to slit a throwt,
and say hardy-har-har.

The crowd burst out laughing. Some even clapped.

Completely stunned, Carson went into the nice-guy-with-compliments teacher mode. "That was really good, Charles Z."

Lew said under his breath to Carson, "Yeah, that was great, Charles M-for-Manson."

Excited, the woman smiled, clapped her hands, and gave her hubby a big kiss. She quickly regained her composure, and with the enthusiasm of a sixth grader presenting a project at the local science fair, she asked Carson, "Do you mind if I recite one of my poems?"

"That would be great," replied Carson, leaving his sarcasm in *his back pocket.*

She turned directly to her husband as if nobody else were there.

I paused and noticed some restless young children in the BJ Williams audience. "Okay, I have to warn you—the woman has a potty mouth. Here goes:

> <u>Love</u>
> *I love you in my pussy,*
> *all day long.*
> *I feel a schism with your jizzum . . .*
> *or I feel your jizzum in my chasm"*

She knitted her brow. "I'm sorry, stopping my poem like this, but I need some help. Which of those two lines makes more sense?"

Carson, who would have had a very different reaction if his sons hadn't been there, turned nineteen shades of red. The whole time she spoke, Carson glared at Rory and emphatically gestured a slash across his throat with his hand. He put his hand over his mouth a couple of times and said "Cut." Rory ignored him. There was no way he would turn off the camera! Lew enjoyed his father's reaction more than the woman's poem. Nik was going to ask for her phone number.

Carson replied to the woman. "Both are good. Keep going. Go, go, go."

Then Nik piped up as the expert on poetry and the female anatomy. "Personally, I prefer the second phrase. I didn't really like the use of schism. I think you were after a quivering effect, but to me it sounded more like a splitting in two, which feels kind of painful, don't you think?"

Carson's jaw dropped. Rory kept filming.

"Yes, you're right. The second sentence makes more sense. Thanks."

Her husband even thanked Nik.

"Yeah, thanks, Nik. You're so helpful," Carson whispered. Then, speaking French for the first time that night, he growled, "When we get back to the hotel, we'll discuss your reading list."

"I'll start again," said the woman enthusiastically.

Carson interrupted hastily. "No, no. Doing great . . . keep going . . . love your work." He looked up at the cathedral, hoping his lady friend had turned a blind tower to the salty language.

208

"Fine!" So she took it from the top.

Love
I love you in my pussy,
all day long.
I feel your jizzum in my chasm." She had a big smile for Nik.
"I need your dong.
You choose the position,
I think that's super.
For it doesn't matter to me,
I'll even take it up the pooper."

"Hey, that was terrific. Unfortunately, we gotta go. You two are the best; don't forget that now, and enjoy the rest of your holiday, ya hear." Carson set an outdoor record for sarcasm.
"Wait! I've got more," the woman blurted out.
"I've got more, too," said Charles Z.
Carson didn't hear them. He was long gone. Lew joined him. Nik, on the other hand, needed to be alone behind a statue for a couple of minutes, and Rory tried to film him."

The BJ Williams crowd roared.

I continued, "The third excerpt takes place at the Luxemburg Gardens, where Carson relaxes by his favourite fountain in Paris." Here goes:

Carson awoke at seven o'clock. Another night of limited drinking made it easy to jump out of bed and greet a sunny room. While washing his face, he decided to replace his run with a long walk and eventually peruse his French sports daily in his favourite chair in Paris. In truth, he knew it was a different chair by the pond each day, but he liked to pretend it was the same one.

Before opening the paper, he scanned his sacred retreat, checking that everything was in its place from the day before. The pond looked like two bowling alleys side by side, with ducks and geese for pins and balls. Trees with massive green leaves, hanging like shields, bordered the pond. Carson's Zen moments were occasionally disrupted when a shield fell into the water, causing some wing flapping. He was more annoyed by the noisy tourists who suddenly came running over to take pictures of the animated birds.

Carson always sat on the west side in the shade, halfway between the ends of the pond. At the north end, a running fountain was defended by Neptune, the size of a full-grown bronze Canadian Maple tree. The Crustacean Sensation, as Carson liked to call him, came equipped with a seriously large trident covering his privates. He overlooked a naked couple (sculpted in a position only legal in Paris), and appeared happy to do so. On Neptune's head and shoulders were several pigeons trained to chirp, in six different languages, "Paris is for lovers," while their cousins from Pigalle, who visited occasionally, cooed, "Make love to me, big boy."

More laughter from my rookie audience. I waited half a minute and then said, "I can't lie; I honestly believe that's the funniest line in my book." I paused for a few seconds. "Okay? Shall I continue?"
Several people replied, "Yes, please do."
"Here goes:

Everything was in order. Carson leaned back in his chair and closed his eyes, his thoughts wandering pleasantly.
   He felt the warmth of her breath on his forehead as she whispered, "Make love to me, big boy."
"Yes, I think that's something I could do," Carson replied.
   Her hand slowly moved down his torso, thrilled to discover that his manhood was as rigid as the trident. She swiftly slid her petite frame on top of him, their bodies rivalling the position of the marble couple. Carson moaned enough for two, his Eiffel Tower about to strike oil.
   Then the soft and alluring voice began to cackle and torment him. The sweet smell of her became something foul. He opened an eye. Two squawking pigeons, aiming through the leaves, had disrupted his dream. Carson frantically jumped out of his chair and tried to wipe the bird shit off his forehead before it dripped into his mouth.
   "Goddamn little bastards!" he yelled.

Helen interrupted the crowd's merriment. "Great stuff, Vlad. Before I ask my questions, I'd like you to tell the audience a bit about yourself."

"Thanks Helen. I thought you'd never ask. Let's see—where do I start? I grew up in Toronto, losing every elementary spelling bee I ever entered because I would only the spell the word backwards. And I was never asked to spell kayak. By the time I went to high school, I was writing other students' essays or poetry assignments for money or hockey cards. I also coined the phrase 'I know you are but what am I?'."

Helen looked at the crowd and then at me. "I don't think this guy has a serious bone in his body."

"I totally agree. And besides, how much more do we need to know about anybody anyway."

Helen was stunned after that line. "Oh-kay . . . anyway, are there any more jokes about what you have or haven't done in your life before I start my formal questions?"

"Well, if you must ask, I've had lots of meaningless jobs, including sitting in for the vacationing David Letterman and Dog the Bounty Hunter. And I wrote a weekly column analyzing your cat's dreams." A few people laughed, Helen not among them, plainly tired of my act.

"Oh-kay," she said. "First question. Vlad, what inspired you to write the book *French Like Me*?"

I had thought about that question for a couple of days because I didn't want to mention outright that I had stolen my brother's life in Paris and successfully written about it. I cleared my throat and looked at my adoring public, swelling in number.

"I had spent a lot of time with Carson—who is both my brother and the protagonist of my book—and his three sons over the years, always listening carefully about their adventures in France. He and his wife and sons had lived in southeast France for two years and they'd skied on holiday in the region several times. He always had some great stories, so I originally decided to write a family-in-France memoir and give it to his family as a Christmas gift. But a Norwegian buddy of mine by the name of Torvic Ekuf—" I stopped and addressed the crowd. "Okay, gang say the name *Tor-vic Eh-kuff*. It's tricky, *n'est pas?*" I had them repeat it three times amid their giggles and then continued my story. "Torvic Ekuf, who encouraged me to write, said, 'Vlad, your brother, his wife and their sons will have their own memories of France, so why not take their stories and twist the truth a little; in other words, create your own fiction. They'll get more of a kick out of your fiction than a potentially boring memoir.'" I paused again, this time for dramatic effect, and held up my book, the irony inescapable, as my brother and his family were unaware that I had even written a book.

Helen's eyes rolled and rolled, a pair of marbles caught in an endless loop. "That was a wonderful answer, Vlad. I *hope* you didn't stay up all night. . ." She paused for a second and made the "glug-glug" sign with her hand. Everyone laughed except me. She continued, ". . . to think of that response."

I whispered to Helen, "And your husband drinks like a fish."

Helen beaded her eyes at me for a second and then turned on her high-beam smile again. "Next question. Vlad, who, if anyone, inspired you to write *French Like Me?*"

"Hmm . . . (I rubbed my chin in fake deep thought.) I can't say anyone in particular. It was just a case of getting the laptop out and tapping the keys."

"Okay, number three. It appears that your book is really about a man's love affair with Paris. Is this true? And if so, was it intentional?" Helen looked at the crowd. "Don't worry, I'm not giving anything away in the book."

"Yes, it is true. I'm a writer of humour, but if the reader scratches about that much (I held my hand up and showed a centimetre between index and thumb) below the surface, he or she will understand that the book is truly about a man in love with a city." A few women in the front row sighed. I stopped for a second and winked at them. "Carson never has a bad word for the city or its people. I think it's rare to find a work of fiction never-endingly positive about Paris." More sighing.

"You're sure making *my* heart flutter." She was lying, but I think she sensed mid-interview that we'd better get along because the point was to sell my book and me.

"Question four. The title *French Like Me* suggests that someone is either French or wanting to be French. Was that intentional? What was the reason for the title?"

"Another great question, Helen. The meaning of the title is twofold in the sense that it is about someone that wants to be or even thinks he is French, but it's also meant to be a take-off on the lighter side, of course, of the racially charged book *Black Like Me*. Racism exists in Paris, Toronto, New York—wherever—but I made a point of staying away from those issues in my book. For a brief moment, I also thought of calling my book *The Franco-phoney.*"

"Are you fluent?"

"*Oui et non.*" The crowd laughed at that one.

"How much time have you spent in France or any French-speaking country?"

"Not as much time as Carson and his family, but when I was in Canada I would always watch TV5, the all-French TV station. Also, I've spent numerous weekends in Montreal and love that city as much as I love Paris." I smiled to myself, thinking that my answer was a complete fabrication.

"Next question. Are the personalities of the three sons in the book—Nik, Rory and Lew—just three different sides of Carson?"

"You or I or somebody is on a roll with these questions. Yes, the three sons are each a different characteristic of their father. I teased Carson's sons by telling them that I made them more interesting in the book than they are in real life." Another lie. I looked at the crowd and said, "Is this interview on a podcast or a YouTube kind of thing?" Someone from the crowd said it can be done easily. I bit my bottom lip, thinking, What if any of my relatives saw this?

"Next question. Who would you compare your writing style to?"

"Well, Helen, I don't write literary fiction; I write literary—"

"Conniption!" Helen jumped in and finished my catch phrase, a phrase mentioned maybe a little too often in her presence. Half the crowd laughed; the other half wore an admiringly look that said, "He's so clever."

"Ya got me Helen! And, because my style is very light-hearted, I put the *brie*—that's b-r-i-e—in *breezy*. I assume you get that? Right?"

I heard comments like "What wordplay!" and "How creative!" and "He's a cad—no, worse, a scoundrel—but I can't take my eyes off him."

Helen looked at the crowd. "Can you hang in for four more questions?" The majority of the group quickly nodded their heads.

"Vlad, do you feel you've been influenced by any writers? If so, who and why?"

"To be a great writer, one has to be a great reader. I'm always careful what I'm reading when I'm in the middle of my manuscript because inevitably the book creeps into my head and on to *my* pages. I don't share the same style, but I'd say I'm most influenced by Mordecai Richler, a good ol' Canadian. And though he's left us, his books are still here."

"But, we want the people to buy *your* book."

"Of course, Helen. I just couldn't help putting a plug in for another Canuck. Richler's work was so remarkable because he could write a sentence that evoked laughter from some and bitterness in others. He made no apologies for his prose and I admire him for having the bal—I mean the guts—to say it."

"Are you influenced by any others?"

"Another writer I admire and would love to imitate, though I'm afraid it's not in the genes, is Michael Chabon." People looked at their neighbours and nodded in agreement. "Chabon is a genius. Whether he wrote about comic books or a frustrated professor or a Yiddish detective, each novel won an award. He could write a novel about a phonebook and somehow win a Pulitzer."

"Is there another? And you can only pick one more."

I paused for a second and looked around the room. The audience was still swelling. "Raymond Chandler," I answered. "His descriptions of people, places and things are legendary. And as an added bonus, he regularly threw in fabulously funny lines that generally had to do with self-deprecating humour. Richler was a genius with that type of humour as well."

"Three questions left. You've just named a few of your favourite authors; now name a few of your favourite novels. Tell you what—I'm sure your fans are anxious to have you autograph your book, so how about we keep to four books.

"Wow, Helen, that's tough. That's like asking me who are the four most beautiful woman in the world."

Helen rolled her eyes.

"Okay, my four favourite books are—and in no particular order— *Portnoy's Complaint* by Philip Roth, Woody Allen's *Getting Even*, though it's a book of short stories of the absurd."

I heard some people whispering, "Yes, I have that one" and "great taste in humour" and "If he's read it then I must read it."

I briefly looked up at the ceiling and then back at Helen. "Two more books. Wow, Helen, you're backing me into a corner. I'll go with Dave Barry's *Big Trouble*, which in my mind is the funniest book I've ever read. I honestly believe he made up a couple hundred jokes and then wove them into a story. I believe his plot points were his jokes."

"And . . ."

"Martin Amis's *Money*," I said with no hesitation. "Amis is Michael Chabon's evil genius twin brother." A chorus of "ohs" and the word "interesting" were heard from the crowd.

"Vlad, we're near the end. Do you have a second novel on the way? If so, what's it about?"

"I'm working on a sequel, but I'm keeping the details in the vault if you know what I mean."

"Well, I'm sure your faithful readers," she stuck her hand out and swept it in a semicircle, "will be patiently waiting for a second book."

"As we're drawing to a close, Vlad, what advice would you give to the first-time novelist out there trying to get published?"

The crowd leaned in.

"Be prepared to write more than one novel. And those first 200,000 words . . ." I paused and pointed an authoritative finger at the throng. ". . . might have to be thrown in the *poubelle*."

I heard lots of "hmms" in the audience.

"I would also suggest writing schools, of which there are many. Try and pick one that offers one-to-one interaction with a mentor who is a professional writer. Let's see, what else? Choose one person only to critique your work. Too many critics spoil the book."

"I'm sure the audience is anxious for you to sign your book. How about we just take one question from the audience and that will be it."

"Sure."

A woman's hand shot up a few rows back.

"Yes, Madame," said Helen.

"First of all, Mr. Moranski, I have to say that I loved your book."

"Thank you," I replied.

"Could you give some more advice on the writing process for the aspiring writer?"

"Of course. And your name?"

"Margaret."

"Well, Margaret, I'll paraphrase two very important comments that I think about each day before I open up my laptop. When anyone, particularly a relative, is annoyed by a character or a scene or the plot, etcetera, I repeat Stephen King's line, 'Why would I write about the world as *you* see it?' I paused for a second to soak in the general agreement of the crowd.

Soon, above the mild din of accord, I added, "And lastly, I'll repeat Mordecai Richler's line about handling the naysayers. Here goes. 'If my writing makes you uncomfortable . . . I can't help it.'"

Sensing the end, the crowd clapped. Caught up in the euphoria, I blurted out, "My book salon will be opening next week in Paris. Please check my website in the book. Drinks the first night will be on me. The admission is free, but you must bring a copy of my book."

Helen had a shocked look on her face. "Please excuse us for a second. Vlad and I have to discuss some business and then he'll be right back to sign the books. Just form a line in front of the interview desk."

We moved to a corner away from the customers. My agent, Jean-Jacques, trailed Helen like a puppy dog. Another one of Helen's followers?

Her tone hostile, Helen said, "What's this about a website and a book salon?" I opened my mouth to speak, but she continued. "This isn't the twenties, and *you're* not Gertrude goddamn Stein."

"Shit, even she had a website!"

"That's *really* funny, Vlad."

"Listen, I'm new at this, but I'm pretty sure publishers want authors to have websites, and the site could have a link to your store."

"Fine. My other authors have websites as well, but you're using it to announce a book salon. Give me a break, Vlad." She paused for a second and smiled sarcastically. "Is it going to be just more bad jokes? More self-indulgent bullshit?"

"For sure. Shits and giggles, that's my scene, know what I mean?"

Helen let out a gush of air that I'm sure meant I wasn't funny. "Go ahead with the book salon, but I don't want you badmouthing me or my store. I still have to sell other books."

"Why would I badmouth your store? I need to make a living."

Helen stared at me for a few uncomfortable seconds. "There's something about you that I don't totally trust."

"Well, you're a control freak and that doesn't exactly thrill me. I can tell you're pissed at me because I didn't pick *your* agent. Also, I'm doing book readings at other stores in Paris, and soon in other major cities, so back the hell off."

"Watch your tone. And while we're getting things off our chests I've heard that you've been going out with my daughter."

"Yes."

"I thought you had a girlfriend."

"Kate is well aware of what's going on."

"She's been through enough. She doesn't need your kind!"

"Helen." I glared at her. "Let her live her own life."

The agent raised his hand to get our attention. And it wasn't the first time. "*S'il vous plaît*, I say something."

"No," Helen and I said simultaneously.

"Helen, I'm not going to go all *Charlie Sheen* on ya and blog some messed-up stuff." She went to speak, but I put up my hand. "Let me finish. I can open a book salon or even a brothel if I want. Hey, that just gave me a great idea. Why not hire some hot ladies at a book salon to read, and then the guests can go upstairs for a quickie?"

"That's already being done in the 4th, 5th and 6th *arrondissements*," said Helen.

"And the 10th," Jean-Jacques said excitedly. Both Helen and I stared him at him. He put his head down in shame.

Helen pointed a raging finger in my face. "If you defame me or my store in any way, you will be sued. Do you understand?"

"Fine, but you're missing the point. Am I not creating more publicity for your store by the sales of the book?"

"Just watch your step!" A clerk walked over to get Helen's attention. "What do you want?!" said Helen, her tone somewhere between miserable and wretched.

"The people waiting to have their books signed are getting restless."

"Vlad, get your ass out there," said Helen. "And you will stay till every single customer has a book signed! And longer if I need you!"

"You're *so* kind!"

Jean-Jacques piped-in. "I just remember. There's one in the 13 *arrondissement*, too."

"Fuck-off, Jean-Jacques!" said Helen.

I walked back to the table and, for two hours, signed about 150 books. The lineup gone, I bolted toward the front door. And I had completely forgotten to look out for NiR.

The afternoon sun at its zenith, I grabbed a sandwich along Rue du Rivoli and ate under a tree in the *Tuileries*. At my apartment, there were messages from Natasha, Kate, Helen, Jean-Jacques and Kong. I deleted all of them, took the phone off the hook and took a nap.

Later in the afternoon, I walked over to the *Carrefour* to stock my shelves with booze and buy a clock. Food would come later. I poured a glass three fingers thick of *pastis* and added a few ice cubes and water.

After dinner at a local Savoyard restaurant, I went nightcapping. I ordered a Jacky D at a bar playing sixties music half a block up from my apartment. My amber liquor raised, I nodded and toasted a woman who was peering in my direction. From a distance, she looked cute, thin, and a few years my junior. She nodded back with her glass of red wine. More nodding ensued.

I sat beside her. "*Vous parlez français ou anglais*?" I asked.

"English," she said timidly.

"You sounded embarrassed when you said English."

"Yes, Americans aren't generally known for speaking another language abroad; although some speak Spanish."

"Hey I'm from Toronto, and Canadians, at least anglophones, aren't much better. Anyway, where are you from?"

217

"San Francisco."

"Did you drove or did you flew?" I asked with a straight face.

"I flew," she said with a puzzled look.

"Don't worry, I was just putting you on. Did you ever watch SCTV?"

"Yes, I did, as a matter of fact. They were a comedy troop of Canadians and Americans."

"Yes, you're right. I thought they were all Canadians, but Joe Flaherty and Andrea Martin were American. Sorry, I haven't mentioned my name. It's Vlad. And yours?"

"Sara." We shook hands and exchanged please-to-meet-yous.

"So, Sara, what brings you to Paris?"

"Well, this is my last night in Paris. Then I fly to Rome tomorrow afternoon. I work for Cisco Systems in San Francisco. I'm rolling through Europe trying to drum up business for our company, but it's tough. There's so much red tape. But I don't want to talk about business on my last night."

She took a sip of wine and curled some hair behind her ear. A sign? She removed her black coat and hung it up, her blouse unbuttoned low enough and exposing enough flesh that the freckles on her breasts in my mind spelled "My place or yours?" We had a drink at my apartment.

Thursday, July19th --- Monday, July 23rd

Sara spent the night but disappeared before I woke up. She left her business card by my pillow. "Call me whenever you're in S.F." was written on the back. I placed the card on my bottom lip. My imagination had me sitting in a San Francisco bookstore signing books, Dave Eggers introducing me.

Over the next five days, I did book signings at three different bookstores in Paris. Helen was furious when I did an afternoon signing in London instead of appearing at her store. Caught up in the free trip to England, I had completely forgotten to tell her. I did apologize profusely when I returned to Paris. My agent also informed me about some book signing possibilities in the States and Canada, including Toronto. How ironic—I would have loved to do a signing in my hometown, but it was still unsafe to return.

I staggered visits from Kate and Natasha at my apartment, for obvious reasons.

Kong kept his head down when I entered his restaurant near eight o'clock in the evening. He covered the food counter with a long cloth and taped pictures of me on it, along with funny cartoon captions I had written for each picture. The captions included my catch phrase, "I don't write literary fiction; I write literary conniption" and from the book, "In the 18th arrondissement, the neighbourhood was so dangerous even the store mannequins had busted noses" and "He's killable with da syllable."

Kong was taping the last caption, which read "Vlad's writing is part com-edy and part whims-ical—call it com-ical." He raised his head and said, "Business go down like stone no can swim." I sensed he wanted to get something off his chest, so I let him ramble.

"Asian customer say I sell off at English man who think he Captain Kurtz in movie *Apocalypse Today*." I stayed silent, though I desperately wanted to correct his movie faux pas. I walked over to the north wall, which now contained 200 books, alphabetically arranged in a funky array of bookshelves. Between the shelves were large posters of me. I had a few pictures taken by a photographer and blown up.

"Fantastic job, Kong. It looks great. The couches in the corner look comfortable, and in time we'll get rid of these chairs (I pointed to them in front of the bookshelves) and put in more couches."

Kong slapped the counter. "No more couch!"

"I'll buy them, Kong. Don't worry my main mandingo."

"Business shit, Vlad. And more bad—no book in Vietnamese, no dinner customer want read English. And why I no sell food to customer tonight?"

"Kong, tonight is about me and the book salon. I promise, the next salon you can open up a buffet."

"Fine. And when you take me to party where I fuck woman?"

"Slow down, Kong. As promised, you and I will go to a singles' party, but you have to give me some time. Hopefully you understand I'm super busy."

He raised an index finger. "I give one week for sexy party or I close book salon."

I walked over to him and put a buddy arm around his shoulder. "Come on, you crazy bastard." I lightly tapped his chin with my fist. "Just give me two weeks and I promise there will be lots of ladies for you, and

---

219

your place will be crawling with patrons when they find out your restaurant is the coolest place in Paris. Then you can start preparing lobster and more expensive shit. I'll even do a comedy routine once a week for free." I put my other hand out to shake. "Just give me a little more time. I promise everything will work out. We got a deal, right?"

He thrust his pelvis back and forth. "We got deal, Vlad."

"One more thing. Don't do that pelvis shit when the people come. It's weird." He did it one more time. "Kong, I'm telling ya . . ."

"I pull your leg! And your cock, too! Ha-ha! I make joke." Kong beat his chest. I made a mental note to put him in my next book.

An hour later, the front right side of the restaurant was full of people waiting for me to baptise the book salon. The main couch, which I would occupy, was empty, the chairs full, a few individuals having to stand. I guessed about forty people were in attendance, most holding a plastic glass of cheap champagne. (I didn't want to pay extra for the bubbles.) Kong had his restaurant smile going as he strode around, making sure no glass was empty.

Kate arrived a few minutes later. And I wasn't worried about Natasha also showing up; she had said adamantly, more than once, that she would never attend the salon because she felt I was using Kong. I think it was her indirect way of saying I was a bastard. Meh.

My third glass of champagne in hand, I kissed Kate and asked her to sit on the Vladcouch. Kong handed Kate a glass of champagne and as she turned her back to him, he moved his pelvis again.

I yelled at Kong, "Hey, Kong, that's enough; she's mine."

From a distance I heard him say, "I pull your leg." Good—at least he got that one straight in public.

I asked everyone to stand and toast the wooden carving. There were a few awkward smiles as they focused on the wood carving of the two semi-nude dancers, each a foot-and-a-half tall. The toast added a nice touch to the proceedings and put the biggest smile possible on Kong's face.

A jolt went through my body as I was holding the carving. Did NiR just stick her head in the front window? I whispered to Kong to take a look outside for a large, psychotic woman.

"Okay, gang," I said. "Grab some plastic and sit down. I'm going to tell you a few little known facts about myself. I mentioned the spelling bee line and a few other repetitions from my first book reading at BJ Williams. Most people laughed, but I did hear someone say, "I heard those lines already." It wasn't NiR.

I then read parts of my book, with lots of pauses for laughs. Kong continued to fill glasses with champagne and pass out trays of mixed nuts. Kate remained mostly silent, happy to laugh along with the crowd.

"You may have noticed the collection of books I have set up are mostly in the humour vein; however, as you see here . . ." I walked over to the French writers translated into English. "Just to show you I'm not totally one-dimensional, I've added a section devoted to the French masters—their English translations, of course. And tonight, I'll pick out nine writers, a batting order if you will, and explain with a little bit of humour why I chose them. For those of you unfamiliar with baseball, a batting order consists of nine men who take turns trying to hit a ball thrown by a pitcher.

The nine French books were on a stand by the couch occupied by Kate and myself. I held up Chateaubriand's *Rene*.

"I picked Chateaubriand as my lead-off writer. Although not your ideal quick lead man, as his words tend not to be as light-syllabled, I thought, what the hell—the downhearted bastard got the whole romanticism shtick up and writing." The crowd laughed.

"Now for the fun, book-throwing part. Anyone in the audience want this copy?" A dozen or so raised their hands eagerly, as if they were competing to answer a question in grade school. I gently threw the book to a woman about four metres away. She caught it and then waved the book at me in thanks.

Kate handed me *True Confessions*. I held it up. "Well, my number two guy in the order is Jean-Jacques Rousseau, a writer well known for laying down some quick satirical wit." The crowd looked a little stunned. "Sorry about that—I'm sure we have some Brits here. Let me explain. In baseball, the second hitter should be able to lay down a bunt—a light movement of the bat to, in a sense, deaden the ball. It only moves a few feet. The joke is that Jean-Jacques lays down some quick wit or 'laying down a bunt.'"

"Why don't you make some jokes about football for Christ's sake?," yelled a Brit.

"Tough crowd," I replied, feeling like a comedian on amateur night at a Yuk Yuk's in Toronto. My nervy, sarcastic self back in record time, I added, "Tell you what—the next book salon I organize, I'll make a soccer joke, but only if someone in that sport *somewhere* actually scores a goal."

"Right on," said a burly, dark-haired man in the second row.

221

"You must be a hockey fan."

"Yessirree, Bob," he replied.

"And a tipsy one at that."

He held his glass up. "Not yet, but I'm working on it." He turned his head toward Kong. "Waiter, hit me."

"Listen, buddy. I'd be careful when you say, 'Waiter, hit me.'"

"What do you mean?"

"I'll let you find out."

I looked at Kong. "Kong, have you been filling their glasses?"

"Yes, masta."

A collective "ooooh" was heard from the crowd. I raised my eyebrows at Kong, hoping he would say something else to get the crowd back on my side.

Kong smiled. "It okay, Vlad. I pull your—"

"Leg, Kong! Leg!" I said, warding off potential embarrassment.

"Listen, everyone." I paused for a second, having to think of something to say to get the group in a humorous mood again. "Could you please give Kong a nice round of applause for working the booze and providing this wonderful restaurant."

Kong pounded his chest. Perfect timing—the crowd loved him. I tossed the book to a bald guy at the back of the room. I waited for the laughs to die down. My voluptuous assistant handed me *Germinal*.

"My number three is none other than Emile Zola. Simply put, the third writer has to be able to do it all, and Zola does it with aplomb; he can go deep with his words or spray his subject matter around." Half the crowd chuckled. "Let me guess—YOU guys are the baseball fans." They shook their heads in agreement. I tossed the book. A Canadian who said he was from Vancouver, caught it.

"And for you baseball fans, does anyone remember Mr. October?"

"Reggie Jackson," yelled someone with a New York accent.

"You got it, Pontiac," I replied. "You might wonder why I brought up Mr. October. Well, it's because"—I held up *The Hunchback of Notre Dame*—"our fourth writer is Victor Hugo. 'Mr. Melancholy,' as he is affectionately called by the French, is your prototypical clean-up guy, his prose and poetry a crowd favourite and able to sway the outcome with one stroke of his pen." The baseball aficionados ate that joke up, however I also had my first serious heckler.

"Your whole baseball as literature shtick is lame."

"Have you not read DeLillo's national bestseller, *Underworld*?

Christ, he wrote fifty pages about Bobby Thompson's famous homerun. His book is considered a masterpiece."

"Whatever," said the heckler.

You're not Morgan Davis, by any chance, are you?" I replied.

"Who the fuck is he?"

"I'd say he's my competition."

"One, I don't think writers compete against each other, and, two, why would he waste his time at this bogus event?"

I looked at Kong and smiled. "Kong, could you please remove this guy?" Kong moved toward him. I put my hand up. "Kidding, Kong. Just give the guy some more booze."

"I'm out of here," said the heckler. He walked toward the front door.

"I'll put you in my next book," I said.

"I'll sue."

The crowd laughed.

"Okay, where was I?"

"You were talking about my favourite book, *The Hunchbook of Notre Dame*," said an earnest fan.

"Perfect response. And what's your name?"

"My name's Kelly and I'm from Los Angeles."

"Nice to meet you, Kelly. Okay back to business. I agree—the *Hunchback of Notre Dame* is an incredible book. And what is the title in French? The winner gets the book."

"*Le Cathédrale de Notre Dame*," said a woman in the front row.

"You are correct, Madame, and that's a lovely little accent you have."

"But I am Fransch," she replied. I handed her the book.

"That's great—we don't discriminate around here. Okay, I'm sensing that some of you are not getting the baseball analogy, so I will quickly rhyme off the last four and throw the books as quickly as I speak. Number five, Jean-Paul Sartre's *Huit Clos*. Sartre's prose was hard-hitting and reflective, yet he wasn't afraid to drop a symbol down the line if the infielder/reader was looking for something too deep." Only a few laughed out loud. *Damn—I thought the baseball pun was hilarious. Okay, Vlad, you better wrap this up fast.*

"Number six in the order is *Flowers of Evil* by Charles Baudelaire, who was a living hell when he ran the phrases. Number seven was George Simenon, or the 'Mystery Man' as he was called. Damn—he slept with a lot of women, common practice for a number of baseball players, so he deserves to be in the lineup. I tossed *Flowers of Evil,* Simenon's *The Yellow Dog*, soon to follow.

"Almost finished—two more to go. Southern France's own Marcel Pagnol would hit eighth. He had a keen eye in the word zone and wrote great cicada noises." *My Mother and Her Castle* bounced off a woman's hands two rows back and landed in front of her dog, who quickly made a meal out of it.

"And hitting ninth and finishing the order?" I heard a few Bronx cheers. "I'd go with the light-writing Marcel Aymé, whose humour . . ." I didn't finish my sentence, having more fun just tossing *The Man Who Walked Through Walls* in the air and not even looking to see who caught it.

"Okay, how about we mingle for ten minutes and then I'll read from one of my favourite books, *Getting Even*, by Woody Allen. After that, I'll do the opposite and read from a book I hated."

Kong filled my and Kate's glass. Kate kissed me on the lips and made a toast. "Here's to a very successful opening of your book salon, Vlad."

"Why, thank you, my dear." I looked around the room for a second. "It's not quite Gertrude Stein's hangout, but it's a start."

"Do you have any other ideas for it?"

"More couches, for one thing, and eventually, when this place becomes the *it* hangout, Kong will start preparing lobster and other classy, expensive food."

A shapely woman, early thirties, wearing a flowery dress, nudged herself in between me and Kate. Unbothered, Kate walked over to mingle with a few Brits.

"Hi, Vlad, my name is Susan Whitehead and I write for *Paris Weekly*. I'm sure you're familiar with our anglophone magazine."

"A little."

"I was hoping to interview you, if you don't mind. We're always interested in anglophones who make it big in Paris."

"I'm honoured, but I am kind of busy."

"Here's my card. How about sometime next week?"

"Sure, but have you spoken to my agent? He usually handles that stuff."

"No. I'd rather work directly with you."

"Fine."

"Since I have you alone, are you strictly a French literature guy or do you have other favourites?"

Would I tell her the last time I read the French greats it was right before I was kicked out of university? "Come on over to the 'C' section," I said. I was tempted to ask her if she had ever had one, but I hadn't been drinking enough. I grabbed Chabon's *The Yiddish Policeman's Union* and placed it in her hand. "This is one of the most interesting and funny crime books I've ever read. And I don't even read crime novels except for Chandler."

"I've heard of Chabon, but I'm not familiar with his work."

"Well, you should be. The guy has won a Pulitzer for *The Amazing Adventures of Kavalier & Clay*. And there's a movie based on his book, *Wonder Boys*. The book you have in your hand is Chabon's tribute to Raymond Chandler. But if you ask me, it's much better than anything Chandler wrote, simply because Chabon tells a better story."

"Well, I am familiar with Raymond Chandler."

"Don't get me wrong. I love Chandler, too. The whole Philip Marlow, tough guy, warm heart, dark humour thing, but Chandler's work is all about character, the plot borderline non-existent or convoluted."

Kate returned and whispered in my ear. "I think the natives are getting restless."

I looked at Susan. "I'm sorry, Susan, but I have to get the show on the road as they say." She handed me back the book.

"No, no, just take it. I think I can afford another one."

"Thanks. Don't forget to call me."

Kate gave me a "who was that" look.

"I'll explain later," I said.

I called the salon to order. Again, we toasted the wooden carving. I was too lazy to walk over and pick it up.

"Okay, ladies and gents, and anyone caught in the middle, let's get this party started." I held up Woody Allen's *Getting Even*. "I have in my hand what I consider to be one of the funniest books ever written. I'll warn you right off the bat—um, don't worry, that's just an expression—I'm finished with the baseball stuff."

Another heckler in the back row yelled, "Good!"

I let it pass. "In case you haven't read Woody Allen, he is *the* king of absurdist humour. I'll start with an excerpt from the short story, *A Look at Organized Crime*. Here goes:

It is no secret that organized crime in America takes in over forty billion dollars a year. This is quite a profitable sum, especially when one considers that the Mafia spends very little for office supplies. Reliable sources indicate that the Cosa Nostra laid out no more than six thousand dollars last year for personalized stationary, and even less for staples. Furthermore, they have one secretary who does all the typing, and only three small rooms for headquarters, which they share with the Fred Persky Dance Studio."

The crowd laughed louder than they had all night. I was happy to entertain them but would have preferred more guffaws when I was doing *my* routine.

"I told you guys he was funny. Here's another, titled *If the Impressionists Had Been Dentists*. Vincent Van Gogh writes a letter to his brother:

Dear Theo,
I took some dental X-rays this week that I thought were good. Degas saw them and was critical. He said the composition was bad. All the cavities were bunched in the lower left corner. I explained to him that's how Mrs. Slotkin's mouth looks, but he wouldn't listen! He said he hated the frames and the mahogany was too heavy. When he left, I tore them to shreds! As if that was not enough, I attempted some root-canal work on Mrs. Wilma Zardis, but halfway through I became despondent. I realized suddenly that root-canal work is not what I want to do! I grew flushed and dizzy. I ran from the office into the air where I could breathe! I blacked out for several days and woke up at the seashore. When I returned, she was still in the chair. I completed her mouth out of obligation but I couldn't bring myself to sign it.
Vincent

The crowd laughed again. Someone put up his hand. I nodded for him to speak.

"Mr. Moranski, it's rather obvious that you admire Woody Allen's writing. As a fellow Allen enthusiast and scholar, do you mind if I put forth a question?"

My ears perked up when I heard the word scholar. "Put one forth or forth one put."

He cupped his chin, giving the appearance he was in deep thought. "Mr. Moranski, do you believe that Allen's absurdist humour is more a symbolic expression of the common man's struggle with a world he

226

cannot truly comprehend?"

I rolled my eyes. "Before I even try and answer whatever the hell you just asked—I assume there is a question in there somewhere—I'll give you ten euros if you can even repeat that friggin' question." And he did, word for goddamn word. I handed him a ten-euro bill.

"Ya got me, buddy. And in answer to your question, you gotta get out a little more often. You've gone a little too deep with the common man thing. Let me guess: that question has to do with some kind of cheesy thesis you're writing. And when you graduate, do you get a doctor of absurdity with a major in Allenguistics? That's the problem with you academic nerds—you sit around all day, smoke your drugs and play your video games. Then you spend the early hours of the morning trying to slap as many ten-syllable words together as you can, and only you and your geeky overpaid mentor will understand. Now be off with you or I'll have Kong rip out every ten-syllable word from your vocabulary."

Defeated, the man put his head down and ran out. I looked at the animated crowd and said, "The kid has to play a sport or something, or maybe get laid." *God, where did that comment come from? Maybe I was bitter after all about being kicked out of university.* I read a few more excerpts and we discussed Allen's latest movie, *Midnight in Paris*.

"Okay, people, it's the last segment of the evening, but first, again, let's toast the carving." By this time, only about twenty hard-core Vladites remained. Someone mentioned that we were out of champagne. I promised more bottles the next time. I held up Douglas Kennedy's book, *The Woman in the Fifth*, and shook it a few times for dramatic effect.

"And now to the book that belongs in the garbage pail. Ironically I enjoyed the first three-quarters of it. The male protagonist leaves a university teaching position in the States in disgrace and decides to run away to Paris, where he gets involved in the double-m's: mayhem and a mysterious woman. The humour is incidental and of the scatological variety. I generally never read mysteries unless there's some humour involved. And, believe it or not, I couldn't put the book down, when all of a sudden, on page whatever, we find out that the mystery woman the protagonist's been bangin' has been dead for years." I could use that kind of language by now; the people remaining appreciated my sense of humour or were drunk or both.

"So we're to fuckin' believe that she's some kind of weird-ass guardian angel who's dead yet satisfies his loins twice a week. *Right!* And worse, three or four times, the writer mentions that the Panthéon is

---

227

in the 6th. What the fuck? Did the writer even set foot in Paris to do his research or did he just rely on his kid's grade nine Paris Google Maps project? Okay, my friends, the Panthéon is in which *arrondissement*?"

"The 5th," they replied jointly, though someone said the 13th.

"Thank you," I replied. "Well, at least the author got the title correct. The mysterious woman did have a mysterious apartment in the fuckin' 5th. An apartment, by the way, that one minute the furniture is covered and appears unused for over twenty years and the next minute, when the protagonist arrives to get laid, is sumptuously lived in. I thought only Stephenie Meyer wrote that shit. I think Douglas Kennedy and Stephenie Meyer are co-writing a sequel where the mysterious woman ends up becoming a—." I stopped and let the drunks answer.

"A vampire," they said in unison.

"Fuckin' A," I replied. Five more people left. Was I swearing too much? No fuckin' way! The rest stood and cheered. They wanted more. I'm not sure why, but once my rant was finished, I stood up as well. I urged Kate to join me. I hugged her and then placed my wandering semi-inebriated tongue down her mouth.

Natasha slipped into the restaurant. My eyes met hers from a distance, my tongue-otomy cut short.

"YOU GODDAMN BASTARD!" she yelled, attracting everyone's attention. Her eyes bulged, lips gushing out air, head shaking violently, hair forming a tornado. Not a good look.

"Cat fight comin'," yelled someone. I unlocked my embrace with Kate and jerked my head around. "Kong, Kong, where the hell are you?" He had to get Natasha out of there and in record time.

I yelled his name again.

"I in kitchen," he yelled back. "I get water."

"Christ, get out here! We have a problem!"

"So that's *the* Natasha," said Kate as she moved a few feet behind me. There was no time to analyze her tone.

Natasha's arms picked up speed. She hurled the first things she could get her hands on (three or four glasses—thank God they were plastic) toward Kate and me. We ducked as the glasses tumbled end-over-end and hit the wall behind us.

"I TRUSTED YOU!" she yelled.

"Natasha, just be calm," I said, which of course made the situation worse.

"You goddamn fuckin' bastard!" I froze. Kate froze. Natasha didn't freeze.

A blitzkrieg of swear words continued, though her mounting anger jumbled her words. Her mind not her own, and desperate to throw something else, she grabbed the white counter cover, my face and captions attached, and threw it at us. It fish netted over the front row, causing a handful of drunks to tumble. Though the incident was unintentionally comic, I resisted laughing. I moved toward Natasha, my hand stretched out.

"Don't you EVER goddamn touch me again, you prick." She banged both hands on the food counter and turned toward the door.

"Natasha! Take it easy. Listen, I'm sorry. I can explain," I said, but it was too late. She had run out, an angry black panther loose into the night. I turned and looked at Kate, who by this time had her purse in her hand and was eyeing the front door. With a pleading look on my face, I mentioned her name several times. She silently brushed by me.

"Hey, who turned out the fuckin' lights," screamed one of the drunks squirming under the cover. I raised a leg to kick his ass (or was it his head?) to shut him up and release some frustration at the same time.

Someone grabbed me from behind and pulled me back. "No kick, Vlad. Make worse," said Kong.

"Man, you're strong."

I sat back on the couch, wondering what to do next. Only a few people remained in the restaurant, but I was too ashamed to look at their faces. One of them walked up to me. "Next time just stick to writing instead of dunking your donut all over Paris."

"Thanks, pal," I replied sarcastically.

"Keep it your pants next time. Do you read me?"

"I get it. And, by the way, go fuck yourself."

I held my head with my hands and stared at the floor. And that's when he caught me with a knee to the side of the head. "You fucking bastard," I yelled. Livid, I grabbed him by the waist and tackled him to the ground, knocking over a pile of chairs. We threw some punches, but the chairs kept getting in our way. Sliding around on a nut-covered, alcohol-soaked floor turned our bout into a wrestling match.

"I CALL POLICE," yelled Kong. I ignored him, my goal simple—just land one good punch. My combatant and I continued to roll around, knocking over several chairs, never once landing a blow.

A cop car siren whirred in the distance, but we continued rolling around. The siren grew louder.

"*C'est fini, messieurs*," yelled a cop. My wrestling buddy and I lifted our heads up and stopped. Two cops stood at the door, their muscles bulging everywhere. Both wore expressions that said, "Mess with me and you'll pay dearly."

The police looked at Kong, who was cleaning up behind us. The place was empty. One of the cops upturned a chair. It broke into two pieces. He took his time surveying the place, its perimeter strewn with chairs. Empty plastic glasses were lying everywhere, along with a handful of my books, all badly torn and stomped upon. The floor reeked of cheap champagne and wrestler's sweat. Kong had rolled the white cover into a wet and dirty snowball, a torn picture of a smirking me dangling from the snowball. I looked at it and grinned. You had to love the symbolism: I was down, but not out . . . still smiling, as they say.

I should have been thinking more about Kong and his café, which resembled the aftermath of a frat-house party, but I only felt sorry for myself. One could safely say, and with little argument from me, that I was an arrogant, self-centred asshole. Ironically, I'd been a nicer person when I was a poor gentlemen thief than as a successful, adored, earning-an-honest-living, soon-to-be-rich writer.

"*Monsieur, voudriez-vous porter plainte?*" said the cop, looking over at Kong. That potential lawsuit comment brought me out of my self-analysis.

"It was an accident," I said to the cop. Then I looked at Kong. "You wouldn't try and sue us, would you, big guy?"

The wrestler chimed in before Kong could speak. "Come on, pal, it was just a little skirmish. No harm, no foul. Even Hemingway had a boxing match with another writer."

"That was Callaghan, a Canadian," I said. "And by the way, he kicked Hemingway's as—"

"I no sue. Both you get fuck out of here!" said Kong.

"Thanks," I said. "I promise I'll make it up to you. Just tell me what you want me to do."

The cops took my name and the wrestler's name—Steve—and contacted their superior. They left after giving Steve and me a lecture about fighting in public.

Our demeanours calm, both smiling—two NHL players who fought against each other throughout a playoff series and shook hands after it was all over—Steve and I straightened out our greasy clothes. Peeling off a napkin stuck to my shirt, I looked at him and said, "That was fun. So,

---

Steve, how about we go out for a beer sometime?" He continued brushing off his clothes, too tired to talk. "Steve, Norman Mailer once said he always had to fight someone before they became friends."

"He was full of shit."

"A good fight-slash-wrestling match helps bring out the honesty in someone. And I have to admit, I'm kinda' low on friends."

"*No, really!*"

"You're actually more sarcastic than me. Listen, I don't care if you want to go out for a beer or not (I was lying), but did you like my book?"

"It was funny, but you have a long way to go before you become the next Steve Toltz."

"Are you talking about "*A Fraction of the Whole*?"

"What else?"

"That book was fuckin' funny. Toltz can stretch a plot to the point that it's absurd but you somehow want to believe it's plausible." We sat down, ready to engage in a conversation about books. It was a book salon after all. No?

Kong yelled at us again.

"Listen, Vlad," said Steve, "I have your email address. I think you should be helping this guy out. We'll continue this conversation some other time."

"Over a beer?"

"Sure." We shook hands. Before Steve left, he said thanks to Kong, but Kong told him to fuck off.

Kong's back was facing the front door, a mop in his hands. Just the two of us left in the restaurant. I had to help clean up and make amends, fast.

Two men walked in while I was rearranging some chairs.

Kong turned around. "I tell you get fuck out of here!"

I kept my mouth shut.

"Be cool, buddy. I just wanna talk to this here guy." It was Clem the pervert from the Alcatraz bookstore. And "Al Capone junior" from the Chicago Books and Grill was at his side. Clem must have thought that Kong was talking to them.

Kong shook his dirty mop at us. "All you get fuck out."

Unperturbed, Clem took his time checking the surroundings. Then he looked at Kong and then me. "Both of yous guys look a little uptight. I thinks you needs some punani. How's about you join me and Al here for some lovin' up in a massage parlour in Pigalle." He slapped Al on the shoulder. "Theys open all night."

"I have to tell you Clem, Capone would have loved that massage parlour," said Al. I rolled my eyes.

Kong turned his back and continued mopping. I think he gave up. I kicked a few empty plastic glasses and sat on a chair.

"Hey, guys I'm happy that you came even though the place has been trashed, but NO I'm not going out for some punani, as you call it."

Clem dropped a card on my lap. "This is where we'll be if ya changes your mind." It was a massage parlour in the 9th *arrondissement*.

"Well, Kong, old buddy, it's just you and me. Tell you what—just leave all this shit till tomorrow. Let's get hammered. It's my treat, by the way." Kong grabbed a book and threw it at me. It sailed over my head and out the door.

"You go fuck you. You make lots enemy."

"It's good to have some enemies. It means you're alive."

"You crazyman!"

I placed the massage parlour card on his glass counter. "Kong, I leave you a peace offering. Use that card sometime."

I strolled out the door as if I had just eaten there. On the sidewalk, I picked up a copy of *French Like Me*, its cover twisted, a few pebbles stuck in the pages. I straightened the cover as best I could and stared at the drawing of the vivacious woman. And with an innocent smile, I said, "At least you'll never leave me, right?"

Wednesday, July 25th

My phone rang at eleven-thirty in the morning, or maybe earlier, but that was the first time my brain signalled my legs to get out of bed. I picked up the phone and lay on the couch. My mouth wasn't ready to produce words, though the person on the other end went into rapid fire.

"Vlad!? Is this Vlad Moranski?" My eyes grew heavy. "Vlad!! Jesus Christ!! Are you there?" The receiver fell out of my hand, missing the carpet and clunking on the hardwood floor, hitting a section I'd been particularly proud of when I'd waxed it.

"Vlad!!! You bastard."

My eyes opened again. I picked up the phone. "Yes, this is 'Vlad the bastard.' How may this bastard help you?" I said, my imagination placing me at the book salon and doing a bit.

"It's Helen, and you're late again! Did you not remember you have a book signing here at BJ Williams every Wednesday for the rest of July and the first two weeks in August? And you skipped a signing at my store on the weekend. Thanks for being *sooo dependable*. I gave you and your agent an agenda listing all the book signings."

"Listen, Helen. I'm sorry, but I had a rough night last night." I heard the words asshole, prick and fucker yelled a few times. I hung up, thinking maybe it was better to call back in a few minutes, hoping she would have calmed down.

Then it hit me—last night I had jerked around the three people closest to me, all of whom would do anything for me. I looked around my apartment, studying every piece of furniture, and it didn't mean jack shit. How ironic—I had it all: new, legitimate successful career, girlfriend(s), a friend, an endless number of adoring fans, etcetera, but Helen was right—I had become an asshole. I hoped it wasn't too late to make amends. I should've called Helen back first, but I thought it was even more important to call Natasha and Kate.

I heard Natasha's recorded voice on her cell and on her landline and pleaded with it for a second chance. I left messages with Kate as well, but there was less desperation or wimpishness in my voice. Thinking too much about Natasha and Kate, I completely forgot to phone Helen. I checked my website and then emailed Natasha and Kate. The phone rang again. I picked it up as I sorted through my emails. There wasn't an immediate scream. Good, I thought. It must be either Natasha or Kate.

"Hello," I said as I zeroed in on an email that didn't resemble typical gushing fan mail.

"Vlad, don't hang up. This is Helen."

I had to give the old gal credit for calming down "What's up, doc?" I said.

"I hate having to do this again, because it pisses me off to no end how irresponsible you are, but—"

I tuned her out. The email read, "There's a plane ticket waiting for you at *Charles de Gaulle*. It's a round trip Paris–Los Angeles–Paris. I'm hoping you'll do a reading at my son's sixteenth birthday tomorrow (Thursday) at 3 p.m. sharp. When you pick up your executive class ticket, please go to a Western Union near the Air France ticket booth. There will be a 10,000-euro advance waiting for you as a sign of good faith. We keep our family life private, so you'll just have to trust me. You'll find out soon enough who I am, and don't worry—I'm one of the good guys. You will be picked up at LA International and driven to a five-star hotel, where you'll spend the night. Then we'd like you to read from your book the next day. Also, you'll be back in Paris by ten p.m. Saturday night, in case you have further readings/business on Sunday."

My mind wandered to those seven-figure salaries that Nelly Furtado and Mariah Carey earned for one-night performances in front of some dictator or other and his loved ones. Were there dictators in LA? And who has a birthday on a Thursday afternoon? Strange, but money was money.

Helen brought me back to earth. "Vlad, what is going on?"

My tone conciliatory I said, "Helen, I have a reading in Los Angeles tomorrow and I will be well paid. It's a good business decision. I have to catch a flight later this afternoon and I'll be back Saturday around ten p.m. I'll even come in for a book signing Sunday afternoon if you want."

"Vlad, I don't give a shit about this LA crap. I'm going away Thursday and I won't be back till late Saturday night myself, but I don't want it RUINED, thinking about how you fucked me around." I let her ramble, my mind trying to guess the mystery person. A movie star? A musician? A pro athlete? A drug cartel owner guy?

"I changed my mind about the taxi. I'm not going to get in the habit of having someone pick you up every time you fuck up. If you don't get here by noon for this book signing, YOU WILL HAVE NO IDEA WHAT I'M GOING TO DO!"

"And what's that?"

"Listen, you prick." She'd at least stopped yelling. "You're also screwing my daughter around. Kate called me last night. She was extremely upset. I TOLD you not to hurt her."

"First of all, it's none of your business, and secondly, I'm trying to call Kate to discuss the situation. Believe me, I don't want to hurt her, but the situation is a little complicated."

"Complicated! That's an understatement. And I heard you made a total ass out of yourself last night."

"Well, to be honest, I wasn't the one who freaked out. Listen, Helen, I have to catch a flight." There was an endless amount of swearing on the other line. I hung up and took a taxi—to the airport.

I left a message with Natasha, Kate, and my agent to explain I was in LA for the weekend for a reading and that I would call from the States.

I picked up my executive seat ticket at the Air France booth. The woman asked me to check inside the pouch for further instructions. As the emailer had promised, there was 10,000 euros waiting for me at the

Western Union kiosk in the form of a certified cheque. I immediately wired half of it to my mother. She needed new furniture. After the in-flight filet mignon dinner, I watched a movie and fell asleep.

I walked through the LA arrivals waiting area, reading the signs with different last names, held by a row of chauffeurs. It was nine p.m. LA time (six a.m. in Paris). Exhausted, I failed to notice the palm trees lining either side of the passageway. A stocky man of my height, bald and sporting a moustache containing a few specks of an evening snack held a sign that read "Moranski," and it was spelled correctly. Cool! The sign had revived me. I excitedly extended my hand as if I was meeting the governor. Hell, maybe I was going to meet him.

"Hi," I said, my smile ear to ear. "My name is Vlad Moranski. Nice to meet you." We shook hands.

"My name is Milos. My boss sent me to pick you up and take you to hotel. I will pick you up again tomorrow at 2 p.m. for the party. Dress good clothes."

"I'm dying to know who your boss is."

Maybe *dying* wasn't the best choice of words. He replied with a sly smile. "My boss tells me not to say who boss is. Ha-ha!"

I should have been more worried, though I couldn't recall anyone being murdered after reading some funny excerpts from a book.

He dropped me off at the Beverly Hilton, a five-star hotel steps away from the Los Angeles Country club.

Thursday, July 26th

In my Hugo Boss suit and shirt, I waited for Milos by the hotel pick-up area. It was close to two o'clock. The sun burning down between the palm trees, my imagination wandered. I looked at the label inside my suit. I was going to Hugo Boss's mansion? But was there even a Hugo Boss? Or maybe it was Hugo Bossinovich, Jr. Or maybe he didn't exist at all. I could tell I was nervous because my mind was on stupid things. And worse, I'd forgotten to call Natasha, Kate and my agent.

Milos drove along a road dotted with huge cedar trees and shrubs of every shape and type imaginable and laced with security gates, all making it difficult to see the mansions along the way. Despite the air con, I was sweating bullets by the time he dropped me off at a stone residence.

A butler greeted me at the door and introduced me to Bobby "The

Chosen One" Howzky.

With four garages, a stone façade entrance and oak panelling throughout, Howzky's mansion reflected the eight-year, $100 million National Hockey League contract he had signed four or five years ago.

And it was true—Howzky was one of the good guys. No arrests for drunk driving or vehicular manslaughter. He preferred a few "wobbly pops" after a game to decompress, and no articles or even rumours about drugs or mistresses or drugged mistresses. He loved his wife (who would become his agent and run his charities) and doted on his three sons. A Toronto boy himself, Howzky was your typical, low-key Canadian superstar hockey player, happy just to play in Hollywood but avoid the hyped lifestyle.

We shook hands; then, for a joke, I ducked. "You set all those scoring records, Mr. Howzky, but some other NHLers have complained about those infamous well-carved elbows of yours."

The thirty-five-year-old smiled (all teeth present). He was quiet, I sensed some time and space for more jokes. "Forget any hockey players," I said. "I don't believe even an LA cop would go near you in a dark corner."

He burst out laughing. "This guy's hilarious. Listen, just call me Bobby, eh."

"Hi, um, Bobby." The smile on my face was unwipeable.

"I picked up your book in Paris about a week ago. It had a florescent pink sticker on it. I immediately read the back cover. It seemed like a funny story about a father and three sons, so I decided to buy it. I have three sons as well, and we travel a lot, so I felt I had something in common with the protagonist." In my element I felt no need to talk. "And, Vlad—can I call you Vlad?"

"Of course."

"The main reason you're here is that my son, Neal, the birthday boy, really enjoyed your book. And he hates reading. I thought it would be fun if the actual author could read from his book."

"With pleasure."

"I have to ask—are you going to write a sequel?"

"Will you pay me?"

"That's funny." He put his huge hand on my shoulder. "Care for a drink before I introduce you?"

"Sure, Mr.—I mean—Bobby. I'll have a beer, eh."

"We have several brands from up north."

"Do you have Sleeman Cream ale?" I said, apologetically.

"Of course." He handed me the beer himself.

I made a point not to crack any jokes about the scars that had formed Highway 1 from his chin and up the left side of his face. After I thanked Howzky a thousand times for the opportunity to read and collect some dough-ray-mi (though I didn't ask about the second instalment), he got a word in edgewise and introduced me to two of his sons, his wife and his Canadian linemate, Johnny "McScorer" McSorley, who must have worn a visor (not to the birthday, of course) because there were no scars above his mouth.

Howzky pointed to a man nattily dressed and wearing a ponytail. He was the agent of Mitch Mays, the famous Canadian comedic actor. He mentioned that the agent was filling in for Mays, who was attending a *Saturday Night Live* reunion and normally never missed a Howzky birthday.

Quick hellos and how are yous were exchanged with a famous Canadian actress, a famous Canadian basketball player, a famous Canadian singer, a less-famous Canadian actor (Brandon something-or-other) and more famous Canadians. After schmoozing with the Canadians for a few minutes, Howzky grabbed my arm and told me it was time to meet the birthday boy.

"Hi, Neal, my name is Vlad Moranski. I'm happy to meet you. Oh and happy birthday."

"Thanks, and I'm happy to meet you as well, sir." We shook hands.

"You can call me Vlad."

"I thought your book was cool. I'm not that interested in reading, but once the middle son got lost, I had to keep reading to find out what happened."

"Well, I'm thrilled I can add another teenager to my list of readers. I don't have sons of my own, but I have three nephews as nice as you."

After looking at his watch, Howzky cut in. "Well, son, we have so much going on today that Vlad should start reading."

I had a feeling that Howzky liked me but wanted me in and out in a hurry. And why was he having a birthday at three o'clock in the afternoon on a Thursday? A Hollywood thing?

He tinkled his bottle of Labatt's Blue to get the group to assemble in the living room, which was surprisingly bereft of hockey memorabilia. I'm sure it was in another house and the hockey hall of fame, of which he would occupy a wing after he hung up his blades. The living room was at

237

the back of the house. Through a floor-to-ceiling window, I could see a backyard the size of a high school gym. And there were at least ten men setting up a stage, equipped with a tractor–trailer load of amps. Christ, who was going to play here? Maybe Howzky *was* Hollywood.

About forty people were in the room, some sitting on a leather couch the size of an NHL players bench, others on the softest leather chairs I had ever felt, but most were standing, a drink in hand. Two hostesses served hors d'oeuvres, their light steps creating a perfect pitch on the herringbone floor, the V-shaped design I believed was the Holy Grail of wood floors. I was hypnotized by its geometric perfection, each V perfectly fitting into the next V and the next one after that, the room so spacious I watched the Vs extend into infinity. I wanted to wax them. Someone nudged me. It was Howzky.

"Vlad you're staring at the floor."

"It's magnificent!" *Christ, did I just compliment his floor?*

"Yeah, sure, I guess." The hockey legend looked at the guests. "Well, everyone, I'm pleased that we have yet another Canadian, Vlad Moranski, here to read one of the funniest books Neal or I have ever read. The book reminded me of one trip in particular when I took the boys to Europe by myself." He paused and looked at his watch. "Well, I'm sure you'd prefer to hear Vlad speak than me." He looked at his watch again. Shit, was he just going to give me a sixty-second shift to read?

"Thanks, um, Bobby, for that wonderful introduction. I picked a few excerpts that your son Neal would enjoy. By any chance, is he a hockey player as well?"

"Yes," said Howzky proudly. "He can fly on the ice, but I'm most proud of his work in a few LA soup kitchens." The tall, thin birthday boy, who looked like a ladder with blond hair on top, was sitting with his mother and I guessed grandparents on the leather couch. And he looked embarrassed as hell after his dad's comment.

"Well, then, I shall call him 'Neals on wheels.'" The group burst out laughing, making the connection with *Meals on Wheels*.

"I'll quickly explain the plot. Carson, the protagonist, and his three sons, Nik, nineteen, Rory, sixteen, and Lew, fifteen, go to Paris to film Carson doing funny things for a potential YouTube–type show, but then one of the boys becomes lost. The lost son seems to grow up in a hurry."

I read the hobo story, where Carson and his sons sit and watch two drunks get angry over spilt beer, the poetry night, and Carson's wet dream to warm up the crowd. Hoping Howzky's son was a *South Park* fan, I read the following:

In his best Cartman voice, Rory said, "Listen, everyone! I've got a plan that will make all of us goddamn rich . . . aaah, screw you, gaahz. I'm going alone on this one if you don't mind, but hey—if you want to learn some business acumen, free of charge, from the master himself, then gather 'round. Also, for the slower ones—you know, the retards—take notes if you must. Here goes— listen up, assholes! The next time I'm on this butthole of a plane, I'm bringin' a thousand bags of Skittles and then working on an after-tax profit margin of 45%. I'm going to undercut Quickzoomfast's overinflated Skittle price, pocket a cool $150 in the process, and put those bastards out of business—sweeet!"

The adolescents laughed; the adults smiled to be polite.

"Vlad, I thought your sardine bit was funny," said Howzky. "Would you mind reading it?"

"Thanks, Bobby," I said. "Well, here goes. Carson is sitting in an open air park/coliseum. The boys have already eaten and run down below to explore.

Carson was starving. The pressure was on a small tin of spicy filet sardines, waiting silently all morning to satisfy their master when called upon. Their taste was to die for, but one's breath was to die after.

Carson was intoxicated after the first bite. He pictured himself with Kim Basinger redoing the famous erotic food-eating scene in 9-1/2 Weeks, although sardines were never on that menu. He washed down each bite and morsel of bread with a swig of lime Perrier. Ten minutes later, he finished the last of the shiny headless fruits of the Mediterranean.

Stomach full and well oiled, Carson was about to belch when he saw a small child wandering dangerously close. His sardine burps could put a kid in a coma, but this one detonated without harming fauna or flora.

The empty sardine tin safely buried in a plastic bag, Carson smelled perfume and turned. A gorgeous woman sat less than a metre away.

I put my book down for a second. "I'll skip ahead," I said. "It's the first brief conversation between Carson and the attractive woman that eventually provides the sexual tension in the book." I continued reading.

Carson speaks to her. *"Je suis désolé. J'étais occupé. Vous venez de tomber des ciels?"*

Her perfect smile could have been carved by Rodin. "No, I didn't just fall out of the sky. I've been here for a while. You looked so happy eating your sardines that I didn't want to bother you. I turned around when I heard a sound like a foghorn coming from your direction. I wondered if you were okay."

Carson was deeply embarrassed. He tried to look her straight in the eye while angling his mouth thirty degrees left to spare her any reeking breath molecules. "I burped," he mumbled.

She laughed. "I figured that."

He felt more comfortable, but changed the subject. "I've sat on enough benches over the years to develop some highly scientific theories about the likelihood of a man and a woman engaging in a conversation based on where they first sit."

"Sounds interesting. Please continue."

"Okay. If a woman arrives first and sits in the middle of the bench, it's pointless to try to sit there because, one, she didn't leave room, and, two, she most likely wanted to be by herself."

"Good. Okay. What if she sits about half a metre from the end of the bench?" She referred to her own position.

"Funny you should ask. Well, I believe that if a woman sits closer to the end of the bench, it's fairly obvious she's willing to engage in a conversation. If she sits at the extreme end of the bench and falls off, she isn't worth talking to at all."

She laughed without restraint, and Carson's calm veneer hid the party in his head. He'd made another French woman laugh. He didn't give her a chance to speak. "I was praying you wouldn't fall off the bench laughing because I didn't want to really test my theory." They smiled at each other.

The Howzky-clan laughed.

"I know it's none of my business," I said to the group, "but I don't see any presents."

Ms. Howzky said politely, "They're all in the backyard." I noticed Howzky looking at his watch. Christ!

"Okay, given the number of terrific athletes in this room, I have a sports bit. Lew ends up playing soccer in front of the Pantheon with some university students. They are actually running around on cobblestones using small pillars for goal posts. Here goes:

The ball found its way back to the pitch. It was the only one that bounced. Carson was tempted to tell the guys that if they took a little air out of it, it would be easier to control. The injured player told them to continue playing. He was fine as long as he could lie down and tilt his head back to stop the bleeding. Walking of his own volition, he found the crudely constructed player's bench hidden in the shade. There was only one problem. It was already occupied.

"Get the hell off the bench," yelled the pretend Arsenal attacker, holding his bloody nose up with his bloodstained fingers and in no mood to be bloody friendly.

A bum was stretched out on ten empty plastic containers once used to transport dairy products in the district. They were lined up in two rows of five, wrapped tightly by an aroma of expired crème and expelled urine. The bench was normally used for handling injuries, a rest, a sip of water, a sip of Heineken, a puff on a joint, or a meeting (when everyone had to bring his favourite salad). The street person was sound asleep and covered in a newspaper duvet. He moved after five minutes of being kicked in the ass by the player's good foot.

The hobo was as tough as a professional hockey player. His problem was that he liked to drink before the game instead of after. French hobos generally even look like NHL players during the playoffs: lots of facial hair, an assortment of cuts and no front teeth.

It was easy to count the NHL players in the group as they almost threw their backs out as they laughed.

"This scene takes place at an outdoor market in the 18th district, an area that's unsafe at night. In fact, I make a joke in the book that the neighbourhood is so dangerous that even the store mannequins have broken noses." The gang loved that line. "It's true—I have a picture of the mannequins with the busted noses and at one time was even thinking of using it as the cover of my book. I decided not to because it didn't appear to be French in any way, shape or form."

I briefly explained to the guests how three-card monte worked and how the shills worked together. I also asked the group how often they thought someone who wasn't part of the team would win. Replies ranged from 10 to 25%. I told them, in the hours I had watched and had taken notes (of course it was Carson who had done the research), I didn't see one single person win who wasn't part of the team. I continued out loud:

By this time, Carson realized that he'd drifted about three or four metres from the three-card monte game, his back turned to

Rory, who was race-walking toward him.

"Pops! J'ai gagné!" he crowed.

Carson turned and saw the Daltreys mobilizing mercurially toward Rory.

"Sorry, let me explain. 'The Daltreys' is the collective nickname I gave the team members because they acted as wooden as Roger Daltrey did in any movie he's appeared in. Okay, back to the book."

The men (Daltreys) didn't speak, not wanting to arouse any suspicion from the police.

"Rory, get the hell out of here!" Carson said in English, hoping they wouldn't understand.

Rory bolted in the opposite direction of Nik and Lew, toward the main entrance. Carson, pretending he didn't know the Daltreys, nonchalantly stared at the ground as if he'd dropped something and then moved into offensive lineman stance. As the three men whisked by, he managed to grab the foot of one of them. The result was like a Cincinnati Who concert without the deaths. All three capsized, along with several tourists (who were lucky to be knocked over because two minutes later they would have lost another 200 euros at the next three-card monte table). The tumbling of bodies disrupted a neighbouring game, snapping the table and dispersing the newspaper, discs, euros and various curses. Miraculously, within seconds, everyone picked themselves up and pretended that nothing had happened.

"I'll skip ahead and paraphrase. Both Lew and Nik sold facial tissue at the market (Carson's original idea to make some honest money). Carson was in an awkward position. He was reluctant to tell the police that one of his sons had disappeared while being chased by a group of hucksters over money he had bet at an illegal game, and his other two sons were missing because they were being chased by a couple of cops for illegally trying to sell facial tissue."

Trying to look serious, I said, "Try and put yourself in Carson's position. He's in a foreign country, in a potentially bad part of town, and his three sons are missing. Obviously, this is the part of the book where the tension begins."

For some reason I looked at Mays's agent; he was slowly moving his head up and down. Wow! Was he agreeing with me?

Howzky looked at his watch. "Well, let's all thank Vlad for that hilarious reading. I believe he has a plane to catch." *Shit, I had three hours to kill.*

Everyone clapped, but a few riffs of a guitar from the backyard drowned it out. I turned to Howzky. "Is that Lenny Kravitz?"

"Yes, and I only have him for an hour. Thank God he loves hockey. We don't normally have a birthday party on a Thursday afternoon, but this was the only time I could get Len."

No food offered and only one beer, I was just a last-second, thirty-minute warm-up act at a ridiculous sweet sixteen party. I was in Hollywood, after all. Howzky signalled Milos and nodded toward the front door. I looked for Neal to say happy birthday again, but he was already in the backyard.

Sitting in the limo, Milos about to shut the door, Mays's agent came running out. The music was already blaring. Shit, *I* wanted to listen to "Len."

"Mr. Moranski, I'm Mitch Mays's agent. Do you have a minute?"

I looked at Milos. "Milos, do you mind?"

"No problem."

The agent and I shook hands. "Hi, my name's Barney Salomon, but just call me Sal."

"Nice to meet you, Sal. Just call me Vlad. Are you Kravitz's agent as well?"

"I wish. Vlad, do you mind if we sit in the car? The music is incredibly loud."

I pointed to the seat. "I assume you want a signed copy of my book."

"I got a kick out of the Carson character. And that was just from a few excerpts you read. He's a funny shit—amiable, sympathetic. The potential love interest has possibilities as well. And the whole story takes place in Paris. Coolsville! Well, I guess what I'm trying to say is, I could see Mitch Mays playing Carson."

"Are you fuckin' kidding me? This isn't a joke, right?"

The agent smiled. "No, I don't have time to kid about stuff like this. Mitch needs to branch out and play a *relatively* mature adult with teenage children."

"I've seen all of his movies and loved them. He always plays the eternal adolescent, but I can't lie—there's an unusual amount of farting and penis jokes in all his movies."

"Exactly, and that's why Mitch has to attract an older audience. Ideally, I want that audience to transcend over a couple of generations.

We have to build his fan base because it's been shrinking. Mitch is an amazing talent and deserves to be on the A-list again."

"Well, you've come to the right book. Given that a father travels for a week with three teenagers, I think someone only farts once and no penis jokes."

"Knowing Mitch, he'd want to throw in a few penis jokes. How are you on poetic licence?"

"You could add a fourth kid for all I care."

"Listen, I'm in a hurry. I'll take that signed copy you were offering if you don't mind."

I took one out of my suitcase and gave it to him, along with my business card.

"Do you have an agent?"

"Of course." I gave him my agent's card as well.

"Thanks, Vlad. I'll pass your book on to Mitch ASAP and see what he thinks."

"Mitch and I are Toronto boys. Maybe he and I could get out for some road hockey and talk business. I believe that's how Canadians seal a deal."

"That's a good one, but I have to admit you Canadians are crazy about hockey." He wished me a safe trip back to Paris.

At the airport, my skin tingling, my feelings euphoric, I phoned Natasha and Kate. Talking about meeting Mays's agent might have helped them forget about the book salon debacle, but both calls went to voice mail. (It was early morning, Paris time.) I had come up empty on both calls but my joyful mood remained unchanged.

Saturday, July 28th

I arrived at *Charles de Gaulle* airport at nine o'clock in the evening, local time, collected the remainder of my fee, 20,000 euros, at the same Western Union. I wired 10,000 euros to my mother. She needed a new furnace, and the paltry backyard needed resodding. Howzky could have paid me in LA, but he had his ways. I hailed a cab. My cellphone back on, there were no messages from Natasha or Kate, but my mother did thank me for the cash and mentioned that she was thrilled that I met Mitch Mays's agent.

Opening my apartment door, I checked my cellphone again. I was stunned when I looked at the screen. Mays's agent had emailed that

Mitch thought that the first fifty pages were hilarious and asked that I be a good "hoser" and only deal with a fellow Canadian. I wanted Mays to "grow up" as well, so I was more than willing to deal with him exclusively, though I would still talk to my agent. I dropped my bags on the kitchen floor, poured a double Jacky D, tossed in some ice cubes and went into the spare bedroom to reread the message on my laptop. I toasted my reflection.

Sipping my third Jacky D, I was picturing myself hanging out at Mays's mansion in LA, working on a screenplay and tanning by his pool.

Someone knocked on my door, yet no one had buzzed from downstairs. My ears perking up, I looked in the peephole. It was the police. One of them knocked on the door again.

"Please open the door. Police. I have some question for you," he said.

My nerves shaking, I didn't notice that he spoke English. "Give me a second," I said. "I'm unlocking the door. You won't shoot me, right?" I wasn't kidding; I had heard too many stories about French cops shooting first and asking questions later. Maybe it had only happened in French movies; either way I wasn't thinking straight. I opened the door. Two cops walked in, badges in hand, no guns drawn. Good. The taller cop politely asked me to sit in the kitchen. I obliged. They declined a chair. The ice rattled in my drink as I set it on the kitchen table.

Arms crossed, feet comfortably apart, the taller cop said, "*Monsieur*, we have phone call someone say you have woman in apartment and she is screaming."

An impulsive laugh came out of my mouth. "I just got here about ten minutes ago from an overseas flight. The Air France sticker is still on my suitcase. Anyway, there's no one here but me." I pointed my finger toward the bedrooms and said loudly, "GO WALK AROUND THE APARTMENT!" They told me to stay in the kitchen. Both bedrooms and washroom were straight down the hall from the entrance. I could hear the opening and closing of closets. When they returned empty-handed, of course, I told them the living room was to the right and that I hadn't even been in it since I returned home. The drink was back in my hand, acting like a pacifier.

"*Le Picasso c'est là*," said one of the cops.

I immediately ran into the other room, spilling the drink all over my crotch. "What the hell are you talking about?"

"*Monsieur*, no touch." The cop took a picture as I looked at the painting. It was Helen's goddamn Picasso. And it was hanging up in the living room! Whoever had done this had balls.

"I'm being fuckin' framed," I yelled. "I've never seen that goddamn fuckin' painting before." In hindsight, I should have said I *had* seen it before but I didn't steal it; however, when someone is fuckin' with your life *and* you appear to have pissed your pants, words don't come out in Hallmark form.

No longer in control of my body, thousands of pin-pricks poked my veins. In deep pain, I yelled "fuck" several times, but neither the pain nor the cops went away.

"Be calm, *Monsieur!*" said the taller cop. The second cop carefully unhooked the Picasso and set it on the kitchen table. And there was more. Kong's wood carving, a pair of diamond earrings; dead ringers for Natasha's and a pair of underwear in a package, everything on display on the far table next to the couch. I laughed and even scanned the room with my eyes looking for a hidden camera. I pointed to the articles, though careful not to touch them.

"Listen it's obvious someone's playing a horribly bad joke on me. Do you see those things on the far table? They're not mine either and I didn't steal them. And there's no woman in my apartment. There never was! Obviously someone called the police and made up a fool-proof reason to get you to come up here." I paused for a second, my hands stretched out in opposite directions as if to say "this situation makes no sense."

"And, of course, once you got in here you would see all these things that appear to be stolen. AND, if the painting was stolen, why the hell would I hang it up for the whole world to see? That would be unbelievably stupid."

"*Monsieur*," said the taller cop, "we have phone call that someone steal the same Picasso that you have in apartment. You will have to come to the police station. We have important question to ask."

"Who phoned?"

"The caller give no name."

"That's a real fuckin' surprise!"

"*Du calme, Monsieur!*"

I forced a smile again, trying to convince myself that this was some kind of joke. Was Helen behind this somehow? Was she trying to get back at me because I blew off a few book signings and was late for a reading? Surely even she wasn't that vindictive. And why would she take a chance and leave a painting worth millions in my hands? Was she hoping I would hide it and then she would collect the insurance?

"Am I being arrested? I didn't do anything. It's obvious that someone or maybe a bunch of people are fucking me around." Big surprise I lost my cool again!

"*Monsieur, du calme*. Your language is bad," said the taller cop.

A look of rage on my face, I said to him, "THESE THINGS ARE NOT MINE!"

"*Monsieur*," he replied. "The painting, the diamond earring, and the wood carving are stolen, no?"

"I assume someone stole them, but it wasn't me. I keep telling you I'm being framed." He ignored me and studied a document attached to the underwear. "And you have *culotte* wear by Brigitte Bardot."

"Brigitte Bardot's fuckin' underwear!? You can't be serious!? Obviously this is some kind of weird joke," I said, my shoulders raised, my hands out, my body language trying to help out my defence. "Come on," I continued, "Just the fact that these items were even together suggests a set-up."

The taller cop took out a set of handcuffs. Was it a threat? And it didn't matter because I went berserk. I sent a right cross so fast and vicious it knocked him down, the cuffs sent flying through the air. My back turned, the smaller cop grabbed my left arm, twisted it behind my back and pushed me down, not caring that my head hit the floor with a thud. Add the colour red to my carpet. The felled cop stood up and grabbed a kitchen towel, but before he handed it to me for the gash in my forehead he gave me a kick to the ribs. I winced. It's true they wear steel toes. My head and side were throbbing. The cuffs went on. They felt tighter than the ones I'd worn in the Toronto precincts. The taller cop opened the door.

"*Monsieur*, we go to *garde à vue*, where you answer question."

And despite the pain I managed to calm myself down. "What's a *garde à vue*?" I said, awkwardly trying to keep the towel on my head while handcuffed.

"It is not prison, is police station. We ask more question. We make charge *immediatement* because you attack police."

"Do I get a lawyer?"

"We talk at station," said the taller cop.

The smaller cop sealed the "evidence" in clear bags. At the police station, someone doctor-ish stitched me up, a reddish-purple "caterpillar" lodged on my forehead. I was fingerprinted and then spent a few minutes in a holding cell with two drunks, an addict who stared at me as if I was a giant needle and a penis exposer who continued to flash his guilt.

Since I had attacked a cop (not a lie) and was drunk (a lie), they told me that I was to "dry out" first and then a detective would discuss my situation in the morning. And they dismissed how I got the caterpillar on my head, claiming I must have fallen down in a drunken stupor. I asked about a lawyer, but they told me that one wasn't needed at this stage. *Right!*

I yelled, "I WANT TO SPEAK TO THE CANADIAN EMBASSY" several times.

Close to one a.m., I was moved to a different part of the police station lined with cells on either side. It wasn't a prison, but felt like one, my cell the size of a one-car garage (room enough for a Mini Cooper), containing a wooden bench and a blanket that reeked of urine. The front door was padlocked and had a window the size of a shoebox lid. Doghouses were more inviting. Exhausted from a long flight, I fell asleep in seconds, the blanket staying on the floor.

Monday, July 30th, 11 a.m.

After my surprise morning visit with Carson on the street, the cops drive me to the courthouse. I'm still shocked that my brother is in Paris. My lawyer greets me in a room about half the size of a classroom, the walls painted taupe, with more than their share of chips and dents. The wall opposite the front door has three windows. Some trees are visible outside, their leaves making a scratching sound on the window. The noise is irritating. My lawyer and I sit at a rectangular table in the middle of the room. The table would comfortably seat ten for dinner.

A man about sixty enters, robe flowing. A woman trails behind him. I assume she is the stenographer. My lawyer and I stand up immediately. The judge (*juge d'instruction*) introduces himself. We exchange polite hellos. He asks me to remain standing. The judge sits across from us. Too close, in my opinion, and done on purpose to intimidate the suspect. The stenographer sits in a corner, fingers ready.

"*Nom, prenom, et date et lieu de naissance?* Your family name, first name and date and place where you were born?" asks the judge.

"Vlad Moranski, born in Toronto, Canada, June 30th, 1961.

"*Nom de votre mère?* Name of your mother?"

"Vivian Moranski.

"*Nom de votre père?* The name of your father?"

I pause and pause.

"*Monsieur Morunski*, is not a game here. *Votre père*, please?"

"Jack Moranski," I reply bitterly. Even in front of the judge I can't let go any bad feelings about the old man.

"Profession? Your job is?"

"Writer—um—*je suis écrivain*."

"*Address du domicile?* Where do you live?"

"119 Rue Monge, *5ème arrondissement*."

He speaks extremely good English with me and bounces between English and French with my lawyer. During the interrogation, the judge can summon any witness he wants—he's even allowed to throw us all in the same ring—cops, detectives included—to hash it out.

The judge mentions that he has in his possession the sworn statement of the police from the night they brought me into custody. He feels there is no need to bring them in to confront me. He reads the statement out loud, taking his time to loosely translate it into English for me. *How nice!*

The highlights of the translation are as follows: A Picasso, among other stolen articles, was found in the apartment of Vlad Moranski, a Canadian writer currently living in Paris. We had originally received an anonymous phone call that Mr. Moranski had brought a woman, against her will, to his apartment. After careful inspection, we did not find a woman in his apartment; however, that is when we discovered all of the stolen property in Mr. Moranski's living room. Previous to entering the apartment, we had been informed that a Picasso matching the one found in Mr. Moranski's apartment had been stolen from Helen Northingham's residence.

The judge puts the statement down after he read it and then looks at me. "Monsieur Moranski, do you agree or disagree with anything in the statement?"

It surprises me that nothing is mentioned about how I got the stitches in my head. I did sucker punch one of the cops and then the other one knocked me to the ground, followed by a violent kick to the ribs. I let it go, thinking we were "even Steven," as they say.

"I agree with the statement, but it's obvious that I was set up because there was never a woman in my apartment."

"I'm well aware of that, *Monsieur*."

My lawyer speaks French to the judge. I think he is reinforcing what I had just said.

The judge asks me a few more questions about the police entering my apartment, but nothing new is revealed. The whole time, my lawyer lets me speak freely. Both the judge and my lawyer are working together to get at the truth. No cat and mouse stuff that I was used to back home.

The questions finished, the judge picks up his cellphone, turns his back and calls someone. After the phone conversation, he tidies up his papers. He tells us to wait a few minutes. My usual smart-ass grin back on my face, the scratching noise on the window sounds like something sweet coming out of Miles Davis's trumpet. I imagine the judge just booked a table for lunch at his favourite restaurant and the inevitable dropping of my case. My lawyer is happy as well.

I stand up and stretch my legs, eyes on the door and then on the judge. He looks at me silently, but he has a grin. Shit, we both have a grin. My spidey sense tells me that something's wrong. Why is he grinning, too? I have no time to analyze his mug because the door opens.

250

It's goddamn Helen. I thought this dramatic shit only happens in movies.

She says hello to the judge and to the lawyer. We exchange glances that border somewhere between glacial and frosty. (NiR would call it "glasty." *NiR?! Why the hell am I thinking of her all of sudden?*) Helen finds a seat beside my lawyer. She's wearing a woman's black suit with grey stripes wide enough and the same colour as the bars that had enclosed me in a Toronto prison. And worse? Her earrings are similar to the stolen ones. Rubbing it in by any chance, Helen? Every ounce of swagger I built up in my body is zapped by this conniving bitch.

During the interrogation, Helen points out to the judge that there's something about me that she doesn't trust. She tries to discredit me with a plethora of adjectives among them—let's see, how about irresponsible (mentioned several times), womanizer, arrogant and sarcastic? But the judge is not interested in Helen's personal opinions about me. Chalk one up for Vlad. And when the discussion turns to the question, did Helen put my finger on the actual painting, Helen remembers that she did do that. *Way to go, Helen.* Now the judge has corroborated proof that I touched the painting right in front of her. I remind the judge again with a question—Who would be stupid enough to steal a painting worth twenty million euros and then hang it up in his apartment?

The mood still tense, the judge changes tack and asks me a few questions about my writing. And—big surprise—Helen interrupts more than once to mention how my success is due entirely to her. I cut her off to tell the judge that my book is in most major bookstores in Paris, London and New York City, to name a few major cities. I offer him a future signed copy, but he is not amused. I am trying.

"*Juge, le roman est formidable,*" says my lawyer.

I look at my lawyer, "Have you read it?"

"The first fifty or so pages. It's great."

"Thanks."

The judge excuses Helen, but just before she walks out the door, she pauses and looks at me with disgust. Predictable. My voice is pleasant, though I'm being phony. "So, how's Kate?" The judge grabs his phone again and ignores us. My lawyer is on the phone as well.

"You're kidding, right?" says Helen.

"Of course not."

"Don't you call her anymore! She wants nothing to do with you."

"I don't believe that."

Helen is laughing. "You're delusional."

"Let her decide."

"That you're delusional?"

"*Real* funny."

"Let me guess—you've been calling the ex-girlfriend, too?"

"I've been calling her only to try and convince her not to press charges against me. That situation with her is over, obviously." And yet I'm hoping it isn't. *Fuck, I am delusional and selfish. And I still want both Natasha and Kate. Vlad, give it up.*

"Vlad," says my lawyer. He puts his finger on his lips for me to shut up. I shut up.

In the middle of his call, the judge tells Helen to leave. Walking out, she gives me a look that says, "Fuck you."

Within seconds, Natasha walks in. And after Helen, what fun would it be facing only a single barrel shotgun? Why not have both of them go after me at the same time? Go double barrel or go home, I always say. My sarcastic thoughts try to pull me through an uncontrollable situation. Natasha looks at everyone but me as she moves toward Helen's vacant chair. She's wearing a tight, sky blue dress that accentuates her ample breasts and rounds her derriere nicely. The hem is mid-thigh, exposing some sinewy thigh muscles that speak their own language as she walks. And the message is clear: "You'll never touch these legs again." God, she's stunning. I want to make mad, fiery, interrogation room love to her.

She catches the leering attention of the judge and my lawyer as well. Bunch of bastards! After exchanging hellos, the judge, with a smile as wide as the Seine, asks Natasha the big question: Did I steal her earrings? She looks at the judge and then leans back and smiles. And it's the smile of the devil. She crosses her legs and flings her hair back with both hands, making her breasts stand up, gravity just something we were led to believe in elementary school. She undulated her body like this with me endless times in the past. (*And who's complaining?*) She's holding the room full of horny men hostage (even the stenographer looks amorously at Natasha), playing with us all. Imagine a dark-haired Sharon Stone being interrogated in *Basic Instinct* and you have Natasha. Sharon—I mean, Natasha—lets out a little teasing gush of air and speaks. Her body oozing sex, I don't think any man in the room could locate her mouth.

"Vlad Moranski," she begins (did she have to say my last name— that hurt), "has told me endless stories about stealing car parts, hockey cards and high school track suits and robbing a chip truck when he was young. I never believed him at first because he's a writer of fiction, so I figured he was just making everything up, but after my earrings went missing and other stolen things were found in his apartment, I would say, yes, definitely to your question. I think he stole them."

"There's no way I would do that. It's all bullshit." I yell. The judge tells me to be quiet and let her finish. My lawyer cannot wipe his "grade nine boy's crush" look off his face. Natasha tells the judge that I was overly interested in her earrings and even joked about stealing them.

The judge asks Natasha if she saw me steal the earrings. Natasha answers no.

My lawyer points out that thinking I stole them and seeing me steal them were two different things. The judge agrees and asks Natasha about my character. Adjectives like arrogant, untrustworthy, delusional, mean and manipulative easily slip out of her candy red lipstick, sensuous mouth. For a brief moment and despite the character assassination, I do have some rational thoughts about her. Her boyfriend's continuous harassment had made her vulnerable. And then along comes Vlad. All she wanted was someone to trust, and then I let her down. She wishes I was dead, but in my limited defence, I did get her to open up about her past (vicariously through a famous actress's autobiography).

And what was the final terrible thing that happened to her? First, she told me she was forced to give up a child, but what was the second thing? Was she beaten? Raped? What can I say—being in this situation is making me think dark thoughts.

After another round of questions, the judge lets her go. Natasha and I do not speak as she exits. My lawyer mentions that both testimonies are nothing but hearsay. Neither woman saw me steal anything and only assumed I did because of my personality. The judge writes something down after the lawyer's comment.

I remind the judge that, apart from the stolen goods discovered in my apartment, there is no proof that I actually stole them. He nods in agreement and then opens a file. I'm starting to feel comfortable, even eyeing the closed door, again. He holds a paper in his hand and then asks a question.

"Have you ever been convicted of a crime in Canada?"

Shit, I thought I was in the clear and now the bugger throws me a hand-grenade. I pause too long before responding, just the same as saying yes. Though an accomplished liar, I stop pretending that it isn't too difficult for the judge to check my criminal record.

"Yes," I say, my heart sinking down somewhere in purgatory and on its way to hell. "I was convicted of theft under 6000 euros."

"They use euros in Canada?" He smiles as he says it. *Fuckin' smartass!*

"No, I thought you wouldn't understand if I told you in Canadian dollars." And it sounds like less money.

"Is that about $10,000 in Canadian dollars?"

"Yes, how did you know?"

"I travel there a lot." Will talking about currency exchange get his mind off my criminal activities? I'm desperate.

My lawyer looks extremely unhappy. He asks the judge if he can confer with me. Trying to control his anger, he looks at me straight in the eye. "Why did you not tell me about your problems with the law in Canada?"

"It's a long story."

The judge looks at his watch and interrupts. "I want to finish this up soon. I only have one more question." My lawyer and I go silent. Even the leaves briefly stop scratching the windows. "*Monsieur* Morunski, have you ever spent time in jail in Canada, or anywhere, for that matter?"

A shot to the gut! "Yes," I answer quickly, more or less trying to end the charade about my chequered past. "I've been in jail in Canada five times, never longer than a month." *Yeah, Vlad, that really matters.* The judge does not react. He writes down a few things and then collects the papers in front of him.

My lawyer is speechless.

The judge is with speech. "Monsieur Morunski, based on my investigation at first, I believed that because there was no woman in your apartment when the police arrived and Ms. Northingham and Ms. Smith never saw you steal anything, it appeared to be a set-up. But, now that you have admitted spending time in prison and specifically for theft, and that the stolen goods were found in your possession with your fingerprints on everything but the package of underwear, I'm inclined to believe that you were capable of stealing the painting etcetera. As well, I have your criminal record in my file. You are being charged with the theft of the Picasso, the diamond earrings, the carving, and Bridgette Bardot's authentic underwear. The trial will take place in three months. In the meantime, you will give up your Canadian passport and you are not allowed to leave Paris."

"Fuck!" I say under my breath. My emotions move from quiet anger to melancholy. Why? Given my criminal record and past life, the judge's decision does not surprise me. Am I destined to never outrun my past?

The judge and my lawyer speak French, but it's too rapid for me to understand. The judge then looks at me and says, "And thank your lawyer because he just talked me out of ordering you to wear an electronic bracelet. You do have the right to get your own lawyer, for whom you will have to pay, but I would strongly suggest you keep your present council."

I tell him that I was happy with my present lawyer. I thank the judge for not making me wear the bracelet. There is no point freaking out at this stage. I have to hope in time my lawyer can prove that I am innocent. I also thank him for putting up with my lies. He even manages to smile when we speak. Working in criminal law, I'm sure he's used to dealing with liars.

My lawyer mentions that he is on vacation for a week. He gives me the number of another lawyer just in case I have any questions but says nothing is going to happen in his absence. He suggests I try and relax with my brother over the next few days. He gives me the name of a private investigator that his law firm occasionally uses, but I would have to pay.

At my apartment, I check my email. Word must have spread fast on the Internet. Mays's agent emailed and said Mitch doesn't work with convicts. The agent said he personally thought it would be a great idea that they make a movie based on a convict's book and that it's been done successfully several times in the past, but Mitch has his squeaky clean reputation. According to the agent, Mitch no longer trusts me. How the hell did they find out so fast? And what about innocent till proven guilty, at least, in Paris? I write back, the length a short story in itself, to explain that I'm being framed, that the matter will be settled soon, and that Mitch and I could collaborate on a screenplay. Wishful thinking, but I have to be positive. There is no reply from Mitch's agent when I check later in the day.

I buzz Carson up to my apartment. He asks immediately about the judge's ruling. I tell him to unpack his suitcase first and then we'll talk. For a brief moment, I want to pretend there are no problems. I even withhold comment about Carson telling me in the morning that he would not bring a suitcase to my apartment. No faith in his older brother! He and I exchange some funny stories from our adolescent days. I watch him place his clothes neatly in the closet and dresser. He is no different from the first eighteen or so years we shared a bedroom—organized to a fault. I walk him around the apartment and then pour us each a glass of Perrier. We sit on the couch.

"Hard to tell where to start, Carz."

"Start with the judge."

"*Go tell it to the judge!*" I say to make my brother laugh. As usual, I use humour to deflect the seriousness of the situation.

Carson laughs. Does he think I'm in the clear?

I briefly look around the room. "Well, Carz, guess who's going to court in three months?"

"Are you kidding me!?"

"Nope! At least I'm not in jail awaiting trial. I had to give up my passport and I'm not allowed to leave Paris."

"Let me guess—he found out about your criminal background."

"Based on all the interviews the judge had with different witnesses, it appeared that my case was going to be dismissed, but then he asked if I had a criminal record and if I had done time. I assume you remember from our brief surprise reunion this morning that I didn't tell my lawyer about my criminal past, so that's why he thought everything would be finished quickly. But I did tell the judge. I got thinking about what you had said to me outside the police station. Given my admitted criminal background, all of a sudden my fingerprints on the painting and earrings etcetera made for a stronger case against me."

"If you didn't tell the judge and then he found out, you probably *would* be in jail awaiting trial."

"He had my records all along, so I'm glad I told him. Made me appear less of a liar."

"You didn't do it, did you?"

"Of course not!" I put my glass on the table and look straight in Carz's eyes. "Three people are trying to frame me."

Carz calmly sips his Perrier. There is no reaction. The wheels are turning in his head. "In the morning, you mentioned something about a Helen, but you're telling me now there are three? That many people who hate you or want revenge or whatever?"

Despite his negative comment, I breathe a sigh of relief that he believes me. "I don't know for sure, but I'm trying to put the pieces together. There wasn't enough time this morning to explain everything to you."

"*Allons-y.*"

"I had just come back from doing a reading at Howzky's mansion in LA."

Carson's eyes widen. "You're not making this up, are you?"

"Yeah, sure, Carz, and I just spent thirty-six hours in a French police station for shits and giggles. Anyway, I digress. I also met Mitch Mays's agent. Mays is—I mean *was*—interested in my book."

"No way!"

"Way! When the police found the stolen Picasso in my apartment, I was reading an email from Mays's agent. He was into my book and hoped I would not promote it to any other agents. Word must travel fast because his agent sent me an email today saying that Mays is no longer interested in the project. I wrote a huge reply to explain that I'm being framed, but I haven't heard back."

"That's amazing."

"The Picasso that I supposedly stole is owned by Helen, the manager/owner of the BJ Williams bookstore. She's the one who believed in me more than anyone. Hell, she even arranged a meeting with an agent. To make a long story short, I'm following in Morgan Davis's footsteps. I met him once."

"Vlad, *I* met him—not *you*."

"Shit, that's right! I'm starting to believe my own lies."

Carz rolls his eyes. "Nice to see that this vicarious thing hasn't gone too far."

I ignore his sarcasm. "The painting was even hanging up in my apartment."

"I can't believe someone would go to all that trouble to frame you. And you said your fingerprints were on the painting?"

"Yes!"

"How the hell did that happen?"

"One night, I had dinner at Helen's in the 8th. Her swank apartment is full of big-name artists' paintings. And, yes, I held the Picasso by the frame and then Helen put my finger literally on the painting, so obviously my fingerprints were all over it."

Carz blows out a gush of air. I recognize that gush. It's his way of telling me I'm screwed. "Obviously, since you're in the system, they've matched up your prints. Are you going to stick with your appointed lawyer or will you find your own?"

"I think he's fine. He was just pissed that I lied to him about my past."

"Why did you do that?"

"As I already told you, apart from *this* bullshit, my life has completely changed, Carz. I'm earning a legitimate living. I pretended that my past didn't exist."

"Fair enough."

I walk into the kitchen to grab some cheese and crackers. Carson and I nibble while we speak.

"Where do the diamond earrings fit in?" he asks.

"They belong to my girlfriend, sorry, my ex-girlfriend, Natasha."

"Cool name."

"I thought it was at one time, too. I've handled her diamond earrings more than once, so obviously my fingerprints are on them as well. Sure enough, her earrings were sitting on one of my end tables along with the carving."

"Yeah, but you can easily claim that she forgot them one night."

"Sounds kind of lame."

"I'm just brainstorming. Anyway, Vlad, is she hot?"

"What kind of question is that!? I thought you cared about what's going to happen to me."

"Come on, you would've asked the exact same question."

"Ya got me. She's a knockout. Super pretty, hot body, raven-coloured hair, cheekbones as high as the clouds . . . a gorgeous ass and a smartass to boot."

"God, you had all that. How did you screw it up?"

"I slept with another woman or two."

"That'll do it every time. Damn, you can't compete with a woman's scorn. How did she find out?"

"Technically she didn't see me sleep with anyone else; she just happened to see me in a rather amorous embrace with the other woman I was spending time with."

"And?"

"She flipped out. And when we were in the interrogation room today with the judge, she pretended I wasn't even there, so it's pointless for me to talk to her. Maybe you can speak to her sometime."

"I'll try. And what about the other woman? What's her name?"

"Kate. She's British and as sweet as the day is long. And she's Helen's daughter."

"Are you able to speak to her?"

"No. I've left some messages with her, but she's never responded, and she wasn't at the hearing. I have to tell ya, Carz, only the mafia is tighter than the 'womanhood.'"

"I here ya, bro. I hear ya." And that's the first time Carson had ever used the word *bro*.

"Shit, Carz, I just remembered—did you bring the article in *Le Parisien?*"

"Yes." He takes out the perfectly folded article from his pocket and hands it to me.

Canadian writer suspected of stealing a Picasso valued at 20 million euros
(Le Parisien, 29 juillet)

A fifty-year-old Canadian writer of the novel French Like Me was placed in a holding cell in a local police station overnight for allegedly stealing a Picasso. La fille de l'artiste avec un jouet is currently valued at 20 million euros. Other alleged stolen articles found in the apartment were a pair of diamond earrings valued at 10,000 euros and a Vietnamese wooden carving.

The article is in French but easy to understand. I slap the paper on the table. "Total bullshit!" I reread it. "Carz, my name isn't here. How could you possibly have known this theft bullshit involved me?"

"I was dumbfounded by the title of the book. That was the title I was going to use for *my* book about *my* life, by the way. And how many fifty-year-old Canadian writers are out there that would use that title?"

"One."

Carson has a look on his face that says, "Brother, I'm going to take the high road and not argue about something I cannot change." He pauses for a second and eats some more cheese. A crumb drops on my 5000-euro couch. I pick it up and don't say anything. "Vlad, I decided to Google your name. An anonymous article turned up that linked your name to the theft."

"Christ! Word travels fast!"

"I think it's safe to say that someone's out to get you."

"No fuckin' kidding!"

"This isn't going to thrill you, but you *have* been in police stations before. And prison! How many times? Two? Three?" It was five, but he only knew about the first two.

"Okay, I get it—I've fucked up more than once. Oh, and thanks for pointing that out for the thousandth time in my life." Carson is right and he can haul his ass outta here any time he wants. I lighten up. "In case you're confused about the women, it was Natasha, the dark-haired one, who caught me in an amorous position with the other woman, Kate. And it happened at my book salon."

"You had a book salon? In Paris?"

"Fuckin' right! In a Vietnamese restaurant!"

"In a restaurant? Vietnamese?"

"I convinced Kong, the owner, and I'm not making up his name, to convert his restaurant into a late-evening book salon. I even asked him to remove anything Vietnamese-like from one wall and replace it with mostly humorous books and posters of me."

"And he went for it?"

"Yes. I paid to get his teeth cleaned. And I was planning to get him laid at a singles 'do', those speed-dial five-minute interview date things"

"Why did *this* guy frame you? And I can guess it had something to do with the Vietnamese woodcarving."

"I suppose because I turned his Vietnamese restaurant into an informal book salon, and I think he lost most of his business. People thought of him as a traitor. I'm going to apologize to him today or tomorrow. He's my only friend in this town."

"Well, Vlad, you have another friend."

"Thanks, Carz, even though you sound sappy as hell."

"Take it or leave it."

"I'll take it, thanks. Never look a gift-Moranski in the mouth."

I grabbed some cheese and continued speaking with my mouth full. "As I said, Kong lost most of his business."

"And let me guess: the woodcarving that was once in his restaurant, which, sure enough you grabbed at one time, was found in your apartment."

"Yes, but there's one more thing that was found in my apartment, yet wasn't mentioned in the newspaper."

"What's that?"

"A pair of Brigitte Bardot's underwear."

"Did you sleep with her as well? Christ, Vlad—she's old!"

"Yes, Carz, I slept with her and stole her underwear as a college prank to prove I did the deed."

"That's what I thought."

I crack a big smile.

"What's so funny?" asks Carz.

"Well you have to love the irony. Do you remember when we were teenagers, we went to that Bridgette Bardot film festival at the Carlton?"

"Yes, and?"

"Which movie was our favourite?"

"*La Méprise*, of course. Bardot was unbelievably hot in that movie."

"Well, guess which movie the underwear came from?"

"You're fuckin' kidding me. *La Méprise!*"

"That has to be a total coincidence. Whoever is screwing me could not have known that that is my favourite Bardot movie."

"That's unbelievably weird. Were your fingerprints on that as well?"

"No. It was in a package that had some kind of label of authenticity."

"How did it get there, then?"

"No idea. As I said, the painting, the wooden carving and the earrings all belonged to people who helped me a hell of a lot, yet I basically jerked them all around. So I could see them plotting against me. But the underwear doesn't fit in at all."

"Do you think all three of them would set you up? Really?"

"It's clearly Helen, the owner of the Picasso. She's by far the most vindictive person. Plus, she's devious enough to pull this off without getting caught."

"But if she owns a Picasso, I assume she's loaded, so why would she care?"

"She and her husband own several paintings by impressionists, post-impressionists, you name it. They're super rich, but I believe even with all her wealth she still has to get back at anyone who crosses her path." I walk to the front window. Carson joins me. We watch the Parisians milling about on the street.

"Vlad, I've always dreamed of having a place like this in Paris. Kind of ironic that you have it and not me."

"You can stay as long as you want."

"Thanks." We chin glasses. "I planned to be here for two weeks, but because of your situation, I'll stay longer. I going to take some day trips to Versailles, Reims, Chartres, Giverny—the usual tourist stuff. Maybe even go down to Savoie to see my friends, and, of course, we have to sit down and figure out how I could best help get you out of this mess."

I slap him on the shoulder. "That's the spirit."

———

"I'm going to head out for a coffee by myself and walk around a little. I need some time to take in your situation. You don't mind?"

"Of course not." I hand him my extra set of apartment keys. "Why don't you walk over to BJ Williams and buy a copy of my book while you're at it."

"I do want to read about *my life* and *my sons' lives* in Paris, *if* you don't mind."

"Don't mind at all. I'd give you a free copy, but, ironically, I don't have one."

"Fine. I'll come back by about seven. Then we'll go out for dinner and discuss your situation and the book."

I hug Carz at the door.

On the Internet, I Google any dirt I can find on Natasha and Helen. (Googling *Kong* is pointless.) The women are squeaky clean, which makes me wonder if it's worth hiring a private investigator. I will ask Carson later.

I decide to get some fresh air and visit Kong. The weather is balmy. And is he in a sunny mood? His back is turned when I enter the restaurant, which no longer has any remnants of a Vlad Moranski. That had to happen.

I give him a light, but animated, punch to the shoulder. "Hey, buddy," I say, sounding so over the top that even I'm ill at ease. I wait for him to turn around before I apologize. He looks right through me. "I'm sorry for everything that's happened." I put my hand out, willing him to shake it. "I hope we can still be friends. I'll make it up to you. I promise." He says nothing and begins wiping the glass counter.

"Hey, I can understand you being pissed off, but I've been through hell and I'm still going through hell."

Without warning, Kong's face turns angry. A vein and its tributaries bulge in his neck. He bangs the counter with his fist. "YOU THINK ONLY OF VLAD!"

"Kong," I say, "you have to calm down." He bangs the counter again, this time with both fists. How did the glass not shatter?

"Why you steal my wooden carving? It mean nothing to you. Nobody come to restaurant. Why you make big trouble for me?"

"Kong! Relax!" I say, trying to wash the panic out of my voice, but it's not easy. He says nothing, though the pumping veins in his neck deflate.

"Listen, pal, it will all be okay. I swear on a stack of bibles that I did not steal your sacred carving. I was set up."

Silence ensues. His eyes look cold and dark. "I no believe you. You die in jail one day. GET OUT! I see you here again I call police."

I sit on my couch, flipping TV stations, and Carson returns at seven o'clock sharp. Good ol' Carz—those anal math teachers are always on time. He happily shows me a bottle of red in one hand and *French Like Me* in the other. I grin, waiting for him to say "p-arrrrty."

"Well, Carz, what'd you think about the book? Not bad, eh?"

He sets the bottle on the living room table and sits on the couch. The book never leaves his hand. "Well, of course it's great. It's about me! I'm glad you didn't make me out to be a nerd. And I thought you made Rory, Lew and Nik look larger than life—frankly, more interesting in the book than they really are. Ha-ha! But you won't tell them that when you go back home, right?"

"I wouldn't worry too much about that. Assuming I beat this rap, and knowing that someone is out to get me, it would be far worse if I return to Toronto."

"What do you mean?"

I open Carz's wine and let it breathe in the kitchen. "I don't want to get into any detail, but my place in Toronto was trashed and there was even a death threat on my wall. I had no choice but to get out of the country." I vowed when I left Toronto that I wouldn't tell anyone the real reason why I left, but not only do I need to make an honest living, I also need to *be* honest. And as competitive as I was/am with my brother, I still love him. He's the easiest person to start being honest with. Then I'll work my way through the rest of the world.

"Are you fuckin' kidding me?" says Carz.

"Not at all." I pour us each a glass. "How about we quickly drink our wine? Then I'll tell you about my $50,000 card game in Toronto AND the woman in Paris who attacked me three times."

"Your life has always been a thousand times more interesting than mine."

"And let's keep it that way. You always were the stable one."

In an Italian restaurant, I order a pizza Regina (mozzarella, ham and mushrooms), Carz, the penne carbonara. A bottle of Bordeaux accompanies our dinner. Carson and I finish the basket of bread before the food arrives.

263

"Carz, you haven't mentioned anything about Ann. I'm sure she's still your loving wife."

His look turns sad. God, he wouldn't have lasted one second in that police station or any other. Once again, I am tougher than him. And *again* with the competition thing. *Vlad, you have to let it go.* I touch his shoulder in an attempt to console him. "Carz, has something happened between the two of you?"

Shit, is he going to shed a few tears? I love my brother, but he is weak. Or maybe I'm insensitive. I will go with the former.

"She left me for a writer."

"Published or self-published?"

"Does it MATTER!?"

The waiter arrives with our wine. Perfect timing. I ask Carz to do the taste test to get his mind off my insensitive joke, although I'm still laughing on the inside.

"Sorry, Carz. I'm not the best person to go to with personal problems. Hey, I never said I would be a psychiatrist."

"Vlad, you were born to be one thing and one thing only."

Carz having repeated the line a thousand times, I still ask. "And what's that?"

We say "a thief" at the same time.

"Just for the record, Carz, who put you through university?" My voice becomes louder. I cannot control it. "How did you get to take a few summers off during university to travel the world without working? You always wore the nicest clothes. How did that happen? Mom didn't have the money." The other restaurateurs are staring at me. I stand up and point a finger down at Carz. "Dad was long fuckin' gone." Carz looks at the customers and then taps my hand. I sit down.

Carz leans in. "Calm down, Vlad. Your voice is way too loud. Listen, I've always been grateful for what you did for me *and* for mom. I just wish you had gone about things more honestly."

More relaxed, I put my hand on his shoulder. "Dad bolted—what can I say? Mom had a part-time job. We needed food on the table, clothes, education. I *was* very good at stealing, and after a while, I couldn't stop. Something I'm sure I inherited from the old man."

My brother wants to comment, but he lets me unload. And I have to give him credit; he always let me speak my mind without him overreacting—except for that punch I took the other day. But I had that one coming. "And then to top it off, Carz, I've always had this competition problem with you."

"I always sensed that about you, but I guess we're lucky because I'm not the competitive type, except when it came to school."

Our salads arrive in half-moon-shaped bowls. Very cool.

"Listen, chief," I say, "let's make this the last time we talk about my tainted past. As I've said already, I've changed. I'm a successful writer. I'm making a legitimate living. I'm finally you! I've moved to the other side of the tracks, although, ironically, I could be on my way to a French prison." I pause. "Let's change the subject. Tell me more about what happened with you and Ann."

"She left me for some guy that writes Harlequin-type bullshit."

"I could never write that Harlequin crap."

"If you're on a second book, I would *love* to know what it's about. You've stolen *my* life. Whose life are you going after this time?" It surprises me that he stops speaking about Ann. I let it go.

"That's *hilarious*! Anyway, I think I will write a book about *this* adventure." I wave my hands in the air as if I'm still in the police station. *"This great fuckin' adventure that I'm experiencing right now!"*

"Good—at least it will be about you."

"Can I throw in your marital problems?" I couldn't resist a joke.

Carson smiles. I can still make him laugh. "Fuck off," he replies, but it's the "happy, brotherly, metaphorically tickling one's balls" fuck off and not the "I'm going to kill you" fuck off.

"It happened about a month ago," says Carz.

The main dishes arrive and we talk about what our mother knows about Carz's separation and my problems in Paris.

"Mom is aware that I'm here, but she assumes I'm in no trouble. Let's not say anything, right?"

Carz nods his head in agreement. We both order crème brûlée. Between bites, I open up about NiR.

"The woman who attacked me was the first person to discover me as a writer."

"I think this person has a love–hate relationship with you. What was that movie with Kathy Bates and James Caan?"

"Very funny. She's an extremely large woman and, believe it or not, I wasn't repulsed by her size—it was her personality. She's vicious, homophobic, crude, rude, crazy—"

"I get it. Where did you first meet her?"

"She works at BJ Williams. Did you happen to see her when you bought the book?"

"I think so. Does she have a big scar on her cheek?"

Will I tell Carz how she got it? "Yeah, that's her."

"So how did this person get involved with you?"

"I decided to smuggle my book *into* BJ Williams, more for a joke than anything."

"You're kidding! That's a great idea. Damn original!"

"Thanks. One day I checked back, and found a *green* "book of the week" sticker on them. And sure enough, it was the insane woman, NiR—her real name is Pam—who put on the stickers. She liked the book, but she knew all along that I'd put the books on the shelf—she'd seen me do it. She told me if I didn't have sex with her—"

Carz gushes out a laugh. "You're making this up."

"Not one word of a lie, my friend. I took her out for a coffee that day, to convince her to forget about the sex business or should I say *business* sex."

"And?"

"No luck. But by the time she walked back to the store to rat on me to Helen, her boss and the owner, three books had been sold, one of them to a famous French book critic. I got an excellent review from the critic and became the toast of the town."

"*Good for you.* Anyway, I will help you, but I'm also never going to let you forget that you stole the story I was going to write."

"Fine—I'll take the good with the bad."

The waiter clears our empty dessert bowls and asks if we want a digestif. I order a Jacky D and Carz asks for a Chartreuse. I dare him to say "shaken not stirred," but he won't. Meh. Out of the blue, Carz asks where the celebrity underwear came from.

"Of the four items *stolen*"—I put my hands up in the air and wave them to further emphasize my bewilderment—"the underwear is the only mystery."

"Are there shit stains?"

"Gross! Christ, Carz! You never talk like that!"

"Starting to!"

"I never checked! Okay?"

"Fine."

"To make matters worse, NiR attempted to kill me."

He gags on his drink. "You're kidding!? Did you call the police?"

I give him all the details of NiR's last attack, including my official

266

statement to the cop. He puts the cop's name and contact number in his cellphone.

Back in the apartment, he updates his cellphone with business addresses and phone numbers for Natasha, Kate, Helen, Kong and my agent. "Well, Vlad, given all this crazy information, I'll check the Internet and ask the police for any kind of pattern of robberies on the stolen goods. I'm kind of anxious to practice my French."

Ya gotta love the math guys—forever in search of a good pattern.

Tuesday, July 31st

I leave a message with Kate for the umpteenth time. And as hot as Natasha appeared in the interrogation room, that relationship is finished. My phone rings after I call Kate. I pick it up on the first ring, assuming it's her.

"Hi, Kate."

"Kate!!" says the voice. I hear a cackle on the phone.

"Who the hell is this?"

"You're in a shitload of trouble, aren't you?"

"Oh. And. How. Are. You. Do. Ing. To. Day. Hel. En?" I say, sarcastically accenting every syllable.

"Let's make this as short as possible. I'm calling because we have a business arrangement. You're supposed to be here tomorrow for a reading."

"I'll be there. It will give me an opportunity to clear my name with my fans."

"Good, that's all I wanted to hear. Pretty obvious that you'd say that, so I've decided to cancel your book signing."

"Is this going to be your life's work—trying to set me up every chance you get? First the Picasso, now this."

"Well Vlad, I th—"

I cut her off. My voice loses control. "YOU CAN'T DO THAT. WE HAVE A DEAL."

"Normally, having a con for a writer is great business, but I can't take a chance having you tarnish my name and the reputation of my store."

"Helen, you're screwin' me around, no doubt, but I promise I won't say one negative word about you or your store."

She laughs mockingly. "Your word is nothing but garbage. Even from the day I met you, there was something about you that was low class."

"Thanks—you're all heart."

"Please do not show up tomorrow or I will call the police."

"Even though I did not steal your painting, I fucked up with you and both Natasha and Kate. For the record, I've apologized every time I've been late or missed a book signing. As you can see, I'm in some serious trouble here. Can you please help me?"

"Too late. You didn't show up for two readings and you were late for another. You made a fool out of me!"

"So this is how you're going to make me pay?" I don't give her a chance to answer. I lose my cool. "How would the police even know to look in my apartment?"

"No idea. I did not mention your name when I reported it stolen. Although with your fingerprints on the painting, it's pretty obvious you stole it. And you stole other things as well. You are seriously fucked up!"

"My fingerprints were on the painting because you handed it to me."

"We went through that already with the judge."

"For the last time, I did not steal your painting! Christ, I was gone from Thursday till late Saturday. And besides, that's not my style."

"I was gone all weekend too."

A few seconds went by. "Helen!? Helen !? Are you there?"

"Yes. I just noticed my other messages." I hear a clicking on the line. Helen's voice turns eerily calm, as if she has a split personality. "Anyway, Vlad, was there anything else?"

"You called me."

"You reap what you sew." She hangs up.

I scream into the dead receiver, "YOU GODDAMN BITCH. YOU SET ME UP!"

My agent calls and mentions that enough other bookstores in Paris want book signings and not to worry about Helen and BJ Williams.

Carz is in and out of the apartment all day. I suggest a private investigator to look into Helen and Natasha's backgrounds, but he thinks it's a waste of time and money. He promises me that he will try and speak with Helen, Natasha and Kate. Thank God he's in my corner.

Wednesday, August 1st

I walk to Helen's store, the whole time thinking, *Screw you, lady. I'm*

---

going in to clear my name to anyone who will listen. BJ Williams is not exactly a court of law, but at least in my mind it's a court of public opinion. In the front store window there are no pictures of me or any mention of me doing a signing, although my book is still on display. I desperately want to open the door, but I change my mind when I see two cops walk by on the street. They aren't there to watch me—I don't think—but just seeing them gets me wondering: Do I need another confrontation with the Parisian police? No! And Helen wins another round against me. I hate that woman.

Late in the afternoon, Carz and I grab a beer in a café down the street. They're playing Motown. Carz mentions for the umpteenth time how he should be living in Paris and listening to this music and not me. He's not trying to be mean; the guy just happens to appreciate this city more than I do. (I made his feelings about Paris obvious in *French Like Me.*) And I will not rub it in that I want to spend the rest of my life here as long as it's not in a jail.

"So, Carz, have you been able to talk to any of the *usual suspects?*"

"Yes, I spoke to Keyser Söze today. He says you're fried."

"Ha-ha!. And great movie, by the way."

"Actually, I spoke to Kate. And Natasha."

"You're kidding!?"

"God, Natasha is hot!"

"Yes! And?"

"She hates your guts."

"Tell me something I don't know."

"And you're right about Kate. She's as sweet as the day is long."

I take a swig of my *Leffe* and then clear my throat. "Do you think there's any point in me calling her?"

"I'm far from an expert on women, but my advice to you is to give her some time."

"Sure."

Carz and I eat in a Vietnamese restaurant in the 13th, a few blocks from Avenue d'Italie. The restaurant is so petit that benches are built into all four walls to maximize seating capacity. A huge aquarium (able to sit two scuba divers, if necessary) is the centrepiece of the eatery. The restaurant reminds me of the old joke: the room was so small I had to step outside to change my mind.

Carz and I order their Michelin-recommended bowl of thin

marinated beef over cooked, cold vermicelli noodles and various greens. As always, I fumble with the chopsticks, my brother no better. Good. Big surprise—I'm still competitive. Neither one of us has anything to add about my trial. Is it too far away? Or no leads? Or both? Carz even jokes about me converting the restaurant into another book salon. I seriously look around and comment that there isn't enough space for books. Will I ever learn?

Thursday, August 2nd

Early in the afternoon, I receive a phone call from the courthouse. I'm to appear in front of the same judge at three o'clock; my lawyer need not be present. He's out of town anyway. The caller says it's good news but hangs up without elaborating. I'm dying to tell Carz, but he left the apartment before I woke up. Out detecting, I hope.

At the courthouse, the judge asks me to stand up. Again, I state my name, etcetera. The judge wastes no time telling me that they found new evidence that overwhelmingly suggests that I was set up. He will not say who is responsible. He hands me my passport and tells me I am free to go. My body feels electric for a few seconds; then I scream my head off. The judge asks me to leave the room as quickly as possible because someone else is coming in. The guilty person, I wonder? I ask the judge to confirm my thoughts. He will not answer.

In the hallway, I see Carz frantically waving at me. He has that same smile on his face he had when I bought him his first ten-speed. I forgot what theft I had pulled off to finance that red Simpson's special that he crashed more than once. And how many flat tires did I fix?

We hug and sit down on an empty bench in the hallway.

"Carz, I haven't seen that smile in a while. I assume you somehow knew I was free as bird, but I have a feeling you have more news. I'm thrilled that I'm free, but I have to know who the hell did it. Nobody will tell me. Is it Helen?"

"No!"

I look around for a second and take a deep breath. "Well who is it then? Sarkozy? The Pope?"

"NiR!?" he says excitedly.

"NiR!? Are you fuckin' kiddin' me!?" I yell, my voice echoing off the granite walls. The bust of some famous French law guy shakes when I speak. More than one passerby shushes me. I try to lower my voice, but it's impossible. "Christ, I don't believe it! I thought she was only interested in killing me, not trying to frame me. What made you decide to talk to her? And, more importantly, how could you possibly deduce that she set me up?"

"I was standing next to her in BJ Williams this morning and starting talking about books in general. I pretended I had no clue who she was. Obviously at no time did I mention that I was your brother. And she never asked for my name. She talked about her life story. She's from the Midwest."

"And?"

"She must have thought I was interested in her, because she got weirdly personal. She made one amazingly stupid comment. And it was embarrassing as hell, too." Carz pauses and looks around.

"Carz, spit it out. Nobody gives a shit around here."

Another deep breath. Then he leans toward me and speaks. "She mentioned that I should come up to her place sometime and see her collection of celebrity underwear. Who collects celebrity underwear!?"

"Yeah, so."

"What was found at the crime scene?"

"Underwear? But that could have been a coincidence."

"Sure, but that's when I decided to do a search on major thefts in France over the last five years, and, believe it or not, there have been five major thefts involving a Degas, Dali, Seurat and a David. Various carvings and jewellery have been stolen as well."

"Was it stolen from art galleries?"

"No, always private collections. Each time a major piece of art was stolen, a famous French actress's underwear was found at the crime scene. And if you recall, the article in *le Parisien* didn't mention anything about stolen underwear. The police must have decided not to tell the press about the underwear. They do that back home as well, just in case someone provides more information than what was given about the crime. It's a way of entrapping them. I think NiR must have felt comfortable talking about the underwear because nobody had a clue she was behind the whole operation."

"I've never heard of an *underwear* calling card. That's a hell of a fetish. And a woman? Shit, I could at least understand a man collecting lady's underwear. So were the cops able to trace the underwear directly to NiR?"

A gorgeous woman, in her late thirties, wearing black from head to toe, slowly walks by us. Her heels click so loudly that Carz and I stop talking. She smiles at Carz. I give him a soft elbow to the ribs and motion my head toward her. She turns the corner and is out of sight.

"Not bad, Carz. She gave you a look."

"You think so?"

"Go get her, man."

"Right! Anyway, brother, you asked a question before that amazing woman passed by. I lost my train of thought."

"That makes two of us." We both share a throaty laugh, something remotely good I inherited from my father. "I asked you if the cops were able to trace the underwear to NiR."

"No. When I spoke to a detective, he said that the underwear was bought anonymously at celebrity charity auctions before the string of thefts began."

My look turns serious. "How were you able to convince the detective to check her apartment?"

"Even after mentioning the underwear, he said he didn't have any real reason to look, so I told him about the time you reported to a cop that NiR had attempted to prematurely remove you from this earth. He did a cross search of your name and Pam's and found the report."

"I'm so glad the cop did a follow-up."

"Damn right! You should be thanking that cop because at least his report was filed in the police database."

"True." This isn't the time to tell Carson I hate all cops. My own doing, of course.

"The detective put two and two together and figured out that NiR had it in for you. He decided to investigate. When the cops searched her apartment, they first asked the super if the residents had any storage areas outside their apartments. Each resident had a private storage area and that's where they found all kinds of stolen stuff."

"Christ, how could NiR possibly be involved in that shit?"

"Maybe she's moonlighting. Who cares!?"

A man walks by pushing a trolley full of mail and documents. I point at him as he passes by. "Carz, that's my next job in Paris—something nice and calm, no possible way of getting in trouble."

"You'd find a way, bro."

"Anyway, do you think other people are involved with NiR and her thefts?"

"There has to be, because there's no way Pam could have stolen that stuff all by herself, but the detective said so far she's the only one who's been charged. I guess she won't rat on her accomplices."

"I have to give the psycho credit for not being a snitch." I pause for a few seconds and replay the crime scene. "NiR must have known through big-mouth Helen that I was in LA, so it was easy to plant the evidence. And Helen was out of town, so her place was fair game. Breaking into any apartment is easy-peasy. And NiR or an accomplice tipped the cops off that I had allegedly dragged a woman to my apartment. She had to call just in case Helen got home late and didn't call to report anything missing."

"So what does your lawyer have to say about all of this?" asks Carz.

"He's out of town."

Carz and I walk toward the front door. The sun is beaming through the hallway.

Someone enters the building, blocking all of the sunlight. We're only five metres away when the human eclipse starts screaming.

"You goddamn fuckin' *litbas*. If it's the last thing I fuckin' do, I will cut your balls off, then add a nice béarnaise sauce and eat them for lunch. I call it *bearballs*."

NiR, Carz and I are a few metres apart. Two cops are making sure that NiR walks by the wall to avoid a confrontation.

I stop and coldly stare at her. She stops as well. We are a metre apart. The cops at her side motion her to keep moving, but she won't, a stubborn, gigantic British bulldog.

"Pam . . . Pam . . . Pam," I say slowly.

She screams, "It's NiR!"

"Okay, *NiRRRR*, what does *lit*bas mean, anyway? You've said it to me a million times."

"You dumb shit—it means liter— ah, fuck it! I'm not tellin.'" She turns toward Carz, who looks as if he's ready to shit his pants. "And it was you who put me here! I'll get your ass, too. Christ, I should have known you two fags were related."

Carz is speechless.

I am with speech. "You're goddamn evil!"

Pam continues yelling down the hall.

I turn to my brother and slap his shoulder. "Carz, it's 'literary bastard'."

"What are you talking about?"

"Ah, it's nothing."

273

The sun back in our faces, Carz opens the front door and pauses. He has a serious look on his face. Why now, all of sudden? "Well, Vlad, I think one day NiR will be after three Moranskis."

"What do you mean? I'm sure she wants to get rid of you and me, but who's the third? Is Mom in Paris? Surely NiR wouldn't seek revenge on an old woman?"

"No. Keep guessing."

"One of your sons?"

"No"

"I don't have a clue."

"Dad's in Paris."

"You can't be serious!"

ACKNOWLEDGEMENTS

My thanks to Richard Scrimger for his concept editing, Sherry Hinman for her line editing, and a handful of Parisian law students for setting me straight on French criminal interrogation procedures.

Ken Samanski is a graduate of the Humber College School of Creative Writing and has degrees in Commerce, French, and Math.

Ken's first book *French Like Me* is available in three English bookstores in Paris including the vaunted Shakespeare and Company.

His second book *Banking on Paris* (*Comment Buhb a fait sauter la banque* (French translated version)) is currently being shopped around many publishers in Paris. As well *Banking on Paris* received terrific reviews from *Foreword Clarion, Kirkus, and IndieReader*.

Ken's shelf life as a high school Math teacher has expired. And he still has all of his *marbles*. He now lives and writes full-time in Paris.

www.ingramcontent.com/pod-product-compliance
Lightning Source LLC
Chambersburg PA
CBHW020247180626
46810CB00006B/2402